The D

Adrian Magson has written eighteen crime and spy thriller series built around Harry Tate, ex-soldier and MI5 office, and Gavin & Palmer (investigative reporter Riley Gavin & ex-Military Policeman Frank Palmer). He also has countless short stories and articles in national and international magazines to his name plus a non-fiction work: *Write On! – the Writer's Help Book.* Adrian lives in the Forest of Dean, and rumours that he is building a nuclear bunker are unfounded. It is in fact, a bird table.

Also by Adrian Magson

Smart Moves

Inspector Lucas Rocco

Death on the Marais
Death on the Rive Nord
Death on the Pont Noir
Death at the Clos du Lac
Rocco and the Nightingale
Rocco and the Price of Lies

The Gonzales & Vaslik Investigations

The Locker
The Drone

ADRIAN MAGSON

THE DRONE

CANELO

First published in the United States in 2017 by as *The Bid* by Midnight Ink

This edition published in the United Kingdom in 2023 by

Canelo
Unit 9, 5th Floor
Cargo Works, 1-2 Hatfields
London SE1 9PG
United Kingdom

A CIP catalogue record for this book is available from the British Library.

Print ISBN 978 1 80436 337 9
Ebook ISBN 978 1 80032 373 5

Printed and bound in Great Britain by Clays Ltd, Elcograf S.p.A.

1

FSC
www.fsc.org
MIX
Paper from responsible sources
FSC® C018072

1

The room was a box within a box. It was cramped, gloomy, short of air and heavy on heat, especially in daytime. It held two metal folding beds, an old wooden chair and a bucket in one corner that was already attracting flies.

The walls were bare, and of simple stud construction, scarred with the signs of transportation and handling. Gaps showed in the corners where the fit had focussed more on urgency than care. A small slit window on one side was the only natural light source, with a battery-powered storm lantern on the chair for emergency use. The window itself offered a limited view of a patch of coarse grass leading to a weed-dotted concrete surface running arrow-straight into the distance, and further over, a huge wood-and-concrete slab building that had seen its best days half a century ago. A door in the opposite side of the room had a small peep-hole showing the concrete strip going the other way. Beyond that was a long view of nothing; flat, dun-coloured ground interrupted by acres of scrub and a bunch of large rocks lying scattered to the horizon like toys on the floor of a child's playroom.

A driver travelling along the little-used road a quarter of a mile away would, if he were curious, see an abandoned airfield from the nineteen forties with an ancient hangar and a tired, clap-boarded workshop with a sagging roof and an air of decaying desolation. No planes, no people, no engineers or smart terminal buildings; nothing to draw anyone in closer save for idle curiosity and maybe the urgent call for a rest-stop.

If he had any degree of instinct the driver wouldn't bother; he'd keep this foot hard on the gas until he hit the next township thirty miles away.

Uncomfortable, perhaps, but at least that way he might get to live longer.

What he wouldn't see was the newly-constructed room inside the workshop, put together two weeks ago under cover of night by an imported construction crew. Neither would he have cause to wonder at the recent confusion of tire tracks and foot traffic left behind during the construction, which had been impossible to eradicate altogether – although the crew's final task had been to try as best they could, even if they hadn't fully understood the reasons why.

Most importantly of all, the passing driver wouldn't notice that, in a supposedly abandoned structure like this, there were supplies of canned food, fruit and a pallet of shrink-wrapped bottles of water. Or that one of the beds had been fitted with two sets of steel handcuffs; one at the head, another at the foot. Of law-enforcement grade, they were impossible to pick, break or cut through, and snug to the bone to avoid a desperate man attempting to slip them off.

Like the prisoner currently lying there, being watched over by a second man.

2

'I'm sorry – Ruth who?'

The woman standing in the doorway of the elegant Georgian townhouse in London's Chelsea was tall and slim, immaculately dressed and carefully composed. She sounded faintly American, but as Ruth Gonzales knew from the briefing file she'd read ten minutes ago, that was because she spent a lot of time jetting back and forth to the States. Right now, though, Elizabeth Chadwick was at her London home and appeared unware that she was the subject of a Code Red alert after her husband had dropped off the radar.

'I rang earlier,' Ruth reminded her. 'From Cruxys Solutions.'

'Oh, that. You'll have to remind me; you said something about my husband?' Chadwick held up a cell phone as if it were a living thing too vibrant to ignore for a second. 'Only, I'm kind of right in the middle of something here.'

Like booking a lunch table for five at The Ivy, thought Ruth, which seemed to have been the sign-off to the conversation she'd heard as the door opened. The woman seemed very calm, which was a surprise, but unless she was a world class actress and hiding something, all that was about to change. Most people reacted powerfully to bad news; maybe Elizabeth Chadwick was made of sterner stuff.

Ruth handed her a business card bearing her name and the number of the Cruxys switchboard, and watched while it was scrutinised front and back. She waited some more as Chadwick then gave her a careful once-over, from her no-nonsense shoes past the neutral business suit to the top of her cropped dark hair.

No visible reaction. She said, 'Cruxys Solutions. What is that?'

'We're private insurance and security company and—'

'You're *selling* something?' Chadwick looked annoyed, and stepped back ready to close the door. 'For heaven's sake—'

'Wait, please.' Ruth held up her hand, and for good measure placed her foot inside the door. 'It's about your husband.'

'James? What about him?' The words came out with a snap, which told Ruth a lot. She revised her opinion about how this was going to go. Some remembered hurts were lurking in there somewhere, which could mean a very short meeting.

She hesitated. The front door of the townhouse was at street level, and offered little privacy for what she was here to discuss. 'May I come in? It's a private matter.'

Something in her voice must have finally penetrated Chadwick's reserve, because after a moment she stepped back inside. 'All right.' She turned and led the way into a beautiful drawing room with large comfortable chairs, elegant paintings and an abundance of fresh flowers.

Dressed and decorated by an expert, Ruth thought, but not a place that felt lived in. More like a trophy pad for occasional visits. It had the cold feel of a hotel room, with all the necessary pieces but none of the personality of its owner. The only difference was, to live in this kind of place in this area, you had to have more than a hotel room's amount of money.

She took a seat on a long sofa and Mrs Chadwick sat nearby. 'My husband, you said?'

'That's correct.' Ruth took out her cell phone and brought up the briefing document she'd been sent earlier that morning by the response team at Cruxys. It described the kind of policy taken out by James Chadwick and gave a summary of his background and family details. 'A little over six weeks ago your husband approached us and took out a protection contract. It's like an insurance policy, but provides assistance and security for you and your family in case anything should happen to him while on business away from home.'

Elizabeth gave a small shake of her head. 'I don't know anything about that. And why should anything happen to him? He's a business consultant, for God's sake. The worst he could suffer would be a paper cut or a missed call. Are you sure you've got the right man? It sounds ridiculous.'

Ruth didn't bother arguing the point. Evidently all was not well in the Chadwick household. 'I'm absolutely sure. The contracts were originally created for people working in hazardous professions – the oil, gas and mining industries, for example. It's not just the jobs they're doing, but the places they work in can be very inhospitable, especially with the current terrorist threats. Other professions began taking out the protection as well, quite a few of them in apparently safe positions. For them it's peace-of-mind protection.' She hesitated. 'Your husband never mentioned it?'

'No. He didn't. But since he spends most of his time in hotels in London, Paris and New York, that's hardly surprising.' The sense of bitterness was suddenly vivid. 'And I can't think what hazards he'd be facing. What does this contract provide for, exactly? I mean, *has* anything happened to him?'

The instinctive response would have been *you mean you don't know?* But Ruth stopped herself in time. Instead she explained, 'Mrs Chadwick, these contracts contain a number of optional clauses. Most responses, as we call them, are activated by family members when they receive news of an accident or… or worse. We then put a programme into action. This can provide all manner of help depending on the specific contract, ranging from appropriate medical treatment through to financial assistance, repatriation if that's required, and looking after the family while their affairs are being resolved.'

'Repatriation. You mean of a body? Do you think James is dead?'

'We don't know anything at the moment, which is why we're pursuing various avenues of information. What we do know is that the contract he took out contains an extra, critical element;

it's referred to in-house as a Code Red clause. Simply stated, if our systems don't hear from the client every five days, usually by an automated code number sent in by text from his cell phone or email, then we are to assume something is wrong and we initiate the Code Red alert. That means contacting his family, friends, employers and known contacts, and beginning a search based on his last known location.'

'What?' Chadwick gave a brittle laugh. 'That sounds like something out of Hollywood. What if he simply forgot to dial in or lost his phone?'

'He couldn't forget as long as he had his phone on him. The code would be activated by the device recognising his thumbprint. Every time he picked it up, it would record him as mobile and active. No call means no phone use. If he'd lost his phone he could still call in by a landline or another cell and give the appropriate code. In our experience, clients who take out this level of the contract have never been known to forget – it's too important to them.' She checked her screen. 'It's now been six days since the last code call came in on schedule. I have to ask you, have you heard from him in that time and do you know where he might be? It could be something quite simple – that he's unwell in a hospital somewhere. But we have a duty to find out, for your sake as well as his.'

Elizabeth Chadwick blinked at the reminder, evidently finding it difficult to take in the details. Then she shook her head and said shortly, 'I don't know where James is – and frankly, I don't care.'

'I see.'

'That I doubt, Miss…' she consulted Ruth's card, '…Gonzales. The truth is, James and I are separated. I haven't seen him in several months and we only communicate by email or text. In fact, I've applied for a divorce.'

'I'm sorry. We didn't realise.'

'Why should you?' She stopped for a moment and dropped the cell phone with a clatter onto a small coffee table between them, before looking around in a distracted manner. 'Would you like tea? I think it's about time, don't you?'

Without waiting for a reply, she stood up and left the room.

-

Ruth listened to the distant sounds of a tap running, the rattle of crockery and a drawer being closed. Kitchen sounds, as intimate and everyday in most homes as the radio, even in this cold place. Her attention was drawn to the cell phone on the table. The screen had lit up, no doubt from the impact of the device landing on the table, and was open at the contacts page. She leaned closer. Most of the entries were women's names, from Davina to Fiona, Georgina, Gail and Ilsa. After a quick glance towards the door, Ruth reached out and touched the screen, scrolling down until she came to the 'J' section.

No James listed. Had she really blanked him out of her life to this degree?

She touched a clock symbol to one side and found herself in the history screen, showing calls made, received or missed. Again most seemed to be women, three of them today, all lasting several minutes. Elizabeth Chadwick might be troubled by a broken marriage, but she clearly wasn't short of girlfriends to console her. She scrolled down. The exception to the regular calls in and out over several days was somebody called Ben. A lover, perhaps? Or a lawyer tying up details for the divorce action? Then she recalled a name from the file: Benjamin. The Chadwicks' son. Currently at boarding school in Hertfordshire, just north of London.

She heard the chink of crockery and spun the phone away just in time. Elizabeth Chadwick entered the room carrying a tray of tea, milk and sugar.

'I'm sorry if I was rude,' she said, setting down the tray. 'But hearing his name can set me off.' She handed Ruth a cup and indicated milk and sugar. 'He was supposed to be in London this week to take Benjamin to an exhibition. Ben had got permission to be out of school because it's a subject he's studying for a technology module. He and his father used to build and fly model airplanes and gliders; it was the one regular point of contact between them and frankly, I used to encourage it. Better to have them off crashing their kit planes in fields than having no time together at all.'

'What happened about this exhibition?'

'James said he'd got it all planned, but when we didn't hear anything from him, Ben had to cancel the idea because the school wasn't happy for him to go by himself. He was very upset; he's always looked up to his father, in spite of our… difficulties. But this was unforgiveable, even for James.'

'So he hasn't done this kind of thing before?'

'No. He'll change visit dates sometimes to suit himself; business pressures, he always says. But not like this. It doesn't seem to bother Ben much because he knows his father will find a way of making up for it.' The muscles in her cheeks flexed and she shook her head. 'He's not going to find this one so easy to get over.'

Ruth didn't mention the obvious: that if anything bad had happened to James Chadwick, making up for a missed date with his son was going to be the last thing to happen. Instead she said, 'So as far as you know, he's still in the States.'

'Yes.'

'That's a start. Can you confirm the addresses we have for you and your husband?' She handed over her cell phone showing the details on file with Cruxys.

Elizabeth nodded at first, then scowled. 'Two are correct – this one here and the one in Annapolis. But I don't know anything about this one.' She stabbed an elegant fingernail onto the small screen. Ruth glanced at the detail. It showed an address in Newark, New Jersey.

'Could it be,' Ruth suggested carefully, 'a rental property he took on because of your marriage problems? We're having both addresses checked out, just to make sure.'

'I've no idea. It could be anything. Maybe he's moved on already, although I'd be surprised. His company office is in New Jersey so I've no idea why he'd have a place in Newark.'

'It's convenient for the airport… late arrivals, early departures. He travels a lot, you said.'

Elizabeth didn't appear convinced. 'If you say so.'

Ruth changed tack. 'What you just said – that he might have moved on. Is it possible? I'm not being nosy, but it could be something we have to consider.'

Elizabeth almost laughed. 'God, you mean James might be shacked up with another woman? You clearly don't know him… although it would be preferable to him just disappearing like this and not knowing – especially for Ben.'

Ruth hesitated, sensing there was an undercurrent of meaning to what Elizabeth had just said. 'What about you? Have you moved on?'

'You don't pull your punches, do you?' Elizabeth gave a faint smile. 'I almost have, as a matter of fact. Not that you should put that in any report, if you don't mind. To put it bluntly, I don't intend remaining single and bitter for the rest of my days. Is that shocking?'

'No. Of course not.'

'What do I tell Ben?' Her earlier hostility at the mention of her husband's name appeared to have diminished, replaced by concern for her son. 'He'll be crushed.'

'That depends on you. We can assign a counsellor if that would help. What we have to do is track James's last moves, see where he was six days ago. That shouldn't take too long. Our New York office is checking with his employers, so we'll work outwards from there.'

Elizabeth's eyes narrowed with cynicism. 'You mean Stone-Seal? Good luck with that.'

'Why do you say that? It's an economic consultancy, isn't it?'

'Is it? If so, they don't talk to anyone – even family. I called once, trying to get an urgent message to James. I'd tried his cell but he wasn't picking up, so I figured he was in a meeting. Ben wasn't well and I guess I overreacted – but that's what mothers do when their kids are unwell, isn't it? Anyway, the place is like a bubble; employees go in but families have to line up with the rest of humanity and take their chances. They refused to tell me where James was and said they'd get him to call me back. I tried appealing to the woman who took the call but she was adamant that she couldn't disturb him.'

'And did he call?'

She sighed grudgingly. 'Yes. Five minutes later, as it happened. He sounded annoyed, so I must have interrupted something important. Anyway, I don't know what they do there, but when it comes to confidentiality, they could teach the Pentagon a thing or two.'

3

Tommy-Lee Roddick checked his field of vision, taking his time to cover every available inch of landscape. There wasn't much else to do here, stuck in this God-awful box, save smoke, look out at the nothing scenery and check the prisoner didn't croak. He took a pack of cheap cigarettes and a lighter from his shirt pocket and lit one, drawing the smoke long and deep. The loose-packed tobacco burned fiercely, emitting a grey cloud, the bitter fumes sending a stab of pain through his chest. He cursed softly. Whatever shit they put in this it wasn't all tobacco, but it served a purpose.

It irritated him that he still didn't know where in hell this place was. He'd been driven here in the night, busy sleeping off too much drink to care or notice. And while he had a decent sense of direction, he needed some kind of visual aid to make even a guess at his surroundings. But outside this window all he got was rocks, grass and more rocks.

Could be anywhere in the world, except he knew it was somewhere in the US.

He dragged on the last of the smoke and dropped the butt into an old tobacco tin, watching as a strand of grey curled into the air, dancing like a spirit before clouding against the ceiling.

He checked his watch. It was getting late, past six. The top dog of the three men who'd brought him here had told him they'd be back at six. He hadn't said where they were going nor what they were doing, and Tommy-Lee knew enough not to ask. Most likely praying and getting orders from their mullah or imam or whoever the hell was leading them. Couldn't do nothing for themselves most of them, without going up the food chain and praying to Allah for guidance.

Iraq had taught him that much.

He levered himself off the bed and went over to the bucket and relieved himself. Then he splashed water on his face from a container by the door. It did little to make him feel better about being cooped up in this shitty little place miles from anywhere, but he figured the fifteen-thousand bucks he was being paid for the privilege would be worth it once he got the job done and was out of here and on his way to wherever the hell he felt like going – preferably another nowhere place but with a choice of good bars and bad women.

He wiped his hands on his pants and stared at his reflection in an old truck wing-mirror tacked to the wall. Saw grey, thinning hair, and skin like tanned leather, and eyes the colour of dried canvas staring right back. It wasn't a face to be proud of, but then he'd never been pretty, even as a kid.

He shook his head, wondering how he'd come to be doing a job of work for a bunch of Arabs after his time in Iraq. No way you could account for fate; it just picked you up and dropped you into something with no regard for irony. Not that he'd told them what he'd done in the military nor where he'd been; far as they knew, he was just a working stiff who could get a job done no questions asked. And if it meant agreeing to not showing his face outside while he was here, he could cope with that. Hell, compared with some of the places he'd been, this came close to exciting.

Probably wasn't much out there to see, anyway, if his guess was right.

He stepped to the chair and picked up a large hunting knife in a greasy leather scabbard. He'd stolen it from his pa as a kid forty years ago. The savage beating he'd taken as the only suspect had been worth it, especially as he'd never admitted to it at the time, claiming it must have been a vagrant seen in the neighbourhood. Lucky for him, old Lucy Beckett down the track said she'd seen the man, too. Not that it had gotten him an apology for the beating; toughening him up for life was how his old man would have called it. But getting one over on the old bastard at age fourteen had been his rite of passage, and not long after that he'd walked out and never gone back. Freedom.

He smiled at the memory, even after all these years. With the first money he'd made from robbing a grocery store three weeks later, he'd mailed his old man a photo of himself holding the knife and wearing a go-suck-on-that-you-evil-fuck grin stretching from ear to ear. With a bit of luck it had given the old bastard a seizure.

He slid the knife from the scabbard and caressed the bone handle. It was smooth in parts and chipped a little on the edges, but still good to hold. He positioned it so the light shone off the heavy curved blade, and touched the sharp edge with his thumb. Gentle as the touch was, a tiny line of blood spots welled up as the skin parted. He rubbed them off against his forefinger, enjoying the stinging sensation.

In the hands of his mean-drunk father, this blade had always scared him half to death. Now it was his. And as he'd done a few times, he could use it to scare others.

He turned his head and for the first time focussed on the other bed. The prisoner was lying on his side, watching him, eyes wide with fear over the strip of grey cargo tape across his mouth, snorting down his nose like a pig in mud. Dressed in a crumpled white shirt, dark pants and once-polished shoes, he looked like he might be a banker or a lawyer. Except this man's hands were cuffed to the bed frame, the same as his ankles, and he hadn't moved in over twelve hours.

4

Eighteen hours after talking to Elizabeth Chadwick, Ruth cleared immigration and customs at Newark Liberty International airport. A meeting with Richard Aston, her superior at Cruxys, had confirmed that the search for James Chadwick was moving across the Atlantic, his last known location, and that she was required to help out. As she walked out onto the crowded concourse at Terminal B, she saw her name on a square of cardboard being held aloft by a familiar slim figure.

'Welcome to America,' said Andy Vaslik with a grin. He dropped the name card onto a passing baggage cart and gestured towards the main exit. 'Out this way.' He didn't offer to take her bag.

'Please tell me this wasn't your idea, Slik,' Ruth muttered, 'bringing me all the way over here.'

'Not guilty.' He made no response to the nickname, which she'd given him at their first meeting. 'Aston figured we'd worked together so well last time, and since I was already here in New York on a visit, it made sense. If you don't agree I can always send you back.'

'Makes no difference to me. Why should it?' Ruth tried to work out if he was teasing her. They'd last teamed up in London a couple of months back, and after an initial frostiness – mostly on her part, she was ready to concede – had worked well together. It had been Vaslik's first job since being headhunted by Cruxys. A former New York City cop and then agent with the Department of Homeland Security (DHS), he'd proved himself able to adapt very quickly to different environments.

Richard Aston, the lanky former Parachute Regiment officer and now Operations Commander at Cruxys, had avoided telling her who she was going to be teamed with on this assignment, and she thought she knew why; he liked his teams to spark off each other and not become complacent or comfortable. Typical officer mind games, she decided. But it worked.

'It will be an investigator supplied by the New York office,' he'd said briskly, handing her an envelope containing briefing notes and flight details, tickets to be collected from the information desk at Heathrow.

'I didn't know we had one.'

'As of the end of last week. Greenville agreed funding. We've already got a senior person from the FBI to set up and run the office, and he's currently recruiting personnel with suitable backgrounds to staff the office and work in the field. It seems we're the good boys and girls of the Greenville group at the moment, thanks to your success with the Hardman assignment. They want to follow our operating model more closely.'

Greenville Inc, was a Dutch-US security and salvage conglomerate. Keen to get more market share in the private security business, they had bought a major share in Cruxys. Things had become complicated with one of Ruth's previous cases involving a child kidnap by rogue Israeli and American operatives working on an extraordinary rendition exercise against a terrorist banking fund. Thanks to recent American recruit Andy Vaslik and a former Diplomatic Protection Group officer named Gina Fraser, the kidnapped girl had been rescued and returned to her mother. But it had been a close call and for a while the Greenville investment in Cruxys had hung in the balance, the parent company wary of involvement in what had been a messy business with illegal ops implications and questions in Congress.

'So who's got first call on this?'

'This is a cross-company response because of the twin nationalities. We have primacy because Chadwick's contract is with us. But you might need to defer to the locals for their expertise and knowledge. I'll leave that to your judgement. Any problems, call me.'

There had been nothing more to say, and she had headed for the airport.

Now Vaslik was leading her to an anonymous rental car at the kerb, being watched over by a Port Authority officer. He helped her stow her case in the trunk, then shook hands with the cop, whom he evidently knew, while Ruth climbed into the passenger seat and waited for him to join her.

'Is this your new posting?' she asked. It would make sense, since Vaslik now had experience of working with the Cruxys model, and he knew New York like the back of his hand.

'Actually, no,' he replied, taking the car smoothly away from the kerb, 'I was due back in London after a few days here, and got the call from Aston to stay on for this assignment. When he told me you were on your way over, how could I refuse?'

'Funny man. So where are we going first?'

'Chadwick's apartment here in Newark. It's not far.'

'There's no trace of him, I take it?'

'No. He's dropped right off the map. I called his employers but they haven't heard from him, although they claim that's not unusual within their corporate structure. Like most of their consultants, Chadwick's pretty much his own man; as long as he completes ongoing projects and brings in regular business, they don't keep real close tabs on him.'

'That's not helpful.'

'I know. That's why we have a meeting with them later.'

Something in his tone of voice made her turn her head. 'That sounds significant.'

'I'm not sure. The woman I spoke to was guarded, as if she didn't want to say much. If I had an employee go missing, I'm pretty sure I'd want as much help as I could get. I figured it would be better to see them face to face.'

'Makes sense. What about his home addresses?'

'He doesn't seem to have been the world's greatest mixer; I checked both places but came up empty. His neighbours either don't really know him or haven't seen him in a while.'

'He was a busy man, according to his wife.' She gave him a summary of what Elizabeth Chadwick had said, and the state of their marriage.

'Is it possible he could be off somewhere having an extra-marital fling?'

'You mean revenge sex?' Ruth shook her head. 'He doesn't sound the type. Too intent on his job for any hanky-panky.'

He looked across at her and grinned. 'Do people actually say that – hanky-panky?'

'Well, I do. But I'm quaint like that. If you've already checked his apartment, why are we going again?'

'Because there's something I want you to see. I need your take on a situation.'

He refused to say anything else, and soon they were driving through a residential district of Newark, with apartment blocks either side. It looked a little run down in places, which possibly explained Elizabeth Chadwick's initial reaction on hearing the location. But the streets were wide and full of activity, and no worse than a lot of other cities Ruth had seen.

They passed a large hospital and Vaslik turned off the main road and pulled up in front of a neat, cream-clad apartment block with balconies on each floor. The street was quiet, lined with trees and the area looked prosperous and pleasant, another indication that James Chadwick wasn't short of money.

'Chadwick's apartment is on four. He's been here a little over six months, according to the super. Travels a lot, keeps to himself but seems pleasant enough.' He jumped out and led the way into the building. They took the elevator to the fourth floor and he led her along a short landing and stopped outside a door, where he produced a key.

'Is this legal?'

'I borrowed it from the super, so yes.'

He pushed the door open and Ruth followed him inside. They were in a small lobby area with wood-block flooring, a shoe rack, a row of coat hooks and a side table. Neat, unfussy. But the air smelled musty, as if the place hadn't been used in a while.

She waited for Vaslik to say something, give her a hint about what she should be looking for. But he merely gestured ahead towards the main living area. She stepped forward and stopped dead.

The place had been trashed.

A small tornado might have made less damage, but not by much. Cushions had been gutted, fabrics slashed to ribbons, a small television lay disembowelled and drawers had been emptied onto the floor. A large Afghan-style rug had been tossed aside and even a couple of the wooden floor blocks had been dug up and left where they lay.

She looked at Vaslik. 'Should we be in here?' To any civilised police force in the world this was now a crime scene and by standing here they were importing all manner of contamination from the outside.

He nodded. 'True enough. But I wanted you to see it with no preconceptions.' He took two pairs of disposable plastic overshoes from his coat pocket, and they slipped them on. 'I already gave it the once over,' he said. 'But I don't think a forensic search will show anything we can't figure out for ourselves. Carry on looking and tell me what you think.'

Ruth stepped through the debris into a small kitchen, an even smaller shower room and toilet and two single bedrooms. Whoever this had been designed for, it wasn't a family or anybody who liked a feeling of space.

The same scene of destruction had been visited on each room, and whoever had done this had taken their time and missed nothing. Broken lights, crockery and mirrors; books, magazines and DVDs; woodwork ripped apart, even the sink panels torn open and the waste pipes wrenched away from their mountings. The refrigerator was lying on its side, the carcass bearing signs of boot damage and a white patch where water had spilled out and dried. The door was open with the cooling system humming desperately, but there was nothing inside for it to cool down. In fact it looked unused, and she could only conclude that Chadwick didn't spend much time here.

Lucky for him.

She wondered if the neighbours were deaf; all this damage must have made a hell of a noise. She checked the flooring in each room and the walls. But there was no sign of the one thing that might have existed had James Chadwick actually been here at the time of the search – blood. No smears, no splatter, nothing to suggest a struggle might have taken place.

Bizarre.

She returned to the front lobby, where Vaslik was bending to pick up something lying in the corner behind the door. It was a slim address book.

'I didn't notice this before,' he said. 'They must have missed it, too.'

Ruth looked at it. Maybe it hadn't been considered important enough to trash, or they'd been interrupted and forced to leave in a hurry. She took it from him and opened it.

As she did so, three of the pages fell loose. She turned them over.

The first page was from the 'E' section. It held the entry for Elizabeth Chadwick, her cellphone number and the London address. It had been outlined several times in bright, vicious red, the paper torn where the pen nib had dug into the page. Ruth felt a tug of alarm and checked the second page. It was from the 'B' section and listed the phone number and address of Ben Chadwick's school. It was also outlined in red.

'They didn't miss it,' she concluded. 'This was deliberate.' She turned over the third slip of paper with a feeling of foreboding. It was a blank page for notes, and carried a chilling message:

Do as we say or lose them.

5

The prisoner had been sedated, one of the men who'd brought him here had told Tommy-Lee. It was the same man who'd got talking to him in a down-town Kansas City bar just a couple of days ago. He'd sounded American, talked football like he knew the game and drank nothing but Pepsi. A real all-American kind of guy. Tommy-Lee hadn't thought much about the non-drinking bit; he'd known a few guys who'd hit the wagon over the years. They'd always seemed fine, although he reckoned they sounded kinda sad, too, like they'd lost a bit of spark along the way and couldn't figure out why.

This guy – he'd introduced himself as Paul – had called himself an entrepreneur. Tommy-Lee didn't really know or care what that was, only that the guy was buying drinks which was fine by him. He could call himself Buddha if he wanted, long as he kept paying.

About an hour later, after more drinks and Tommy-Lee had mentioned he was looking for work, Paul had asked him if he wanted to earn some ready money, no questions asked.

As liquored as he was becoming, Tommy-Lee knew right away that it had to be something a little off-the-wall. Guys in bars – especially in Kansas City – didn't throw money around if they were into a legitimate line of work. Just didn't happen. And there was something about this Paul guy that gave off a vibe that was down deep and dark.

But Tommy-Lee was near broke and he'd said yes, right off. Fact was, he had no immediate prospects, so any money was fine by him as long it was legal tender. Didn't mean he had to like the man paying him, though.

'It'll be easy work,' Paul had explained, leading him over to a corner table where they could talk in private. 'You seem a pretty solid kind of guy, I can tell. Just had a run of bad luck, that's all. Can happen to anybody.' He leaned forward, his breath sweet. 'Fact is, I overheard you talking to a pal of yours in here a couple of days ago. See, I know you have no love for the military or Uncle Sam. Am I right?'

Tommy-Lee gave the man one of his looks. Normally that was enough to shut down an unwelcome line of conversation; but this Paul just seemed to absorb it and shrug it off without a flicker. He didn't much like knowing he'd been watched before now; that was definitely creepy. But since the guy was offering paid work, how much did it matter?

'I've had my run-ins, sure. Ain't ashamed to admit that. So what?'

'Nothing wrong with that at all.' Paul called for refills. 'Neither,' he added, 'would collecting a little payback for some of the hard times, if you get my meaning.'

Tommy-Lee frowned. With what he'd already drunk he was struggling to hold onto the line of conversation. 'How does that work? You saying you work for the government?'

'No. Not at all.' Paul smiled genially and clapped a friendly hand on his arm. 'Let's just say I have access to some rerouted funds… sort of liberated cash that nobody's going to miss and doesn't need to go back into the system. And you could have some of it. The beauty is, there are no taxes to pay. How does that sound?'

Tommy-Lee understood that bit, no problem at all, and any tiny suspicions he might have suffered disappeared in a flash. What the hell, money was money and he needed some real bad. 'It sounds sweet. Doing what?'

'I want you to look after somebody for me. Keep him quiet and secure for a few days. Think you can do that?'

Tommy-Lee had nearly laughed. Keeping people secure had once been his specialty, he'd said, although gut feel had cautioned him not to mention where or who they were. This Paul wasn't exactly dark-skinned, more Latino in colour. But you never knew how people would take the news that he'd once been a jailer and interrogator in Iraq. Especially if they'd ever done time themselves. Hell, step across the road to another bar with white-collar workers and he'd be a hero; right here, right now, though, it could just as easily go the other way.

'Looking after people is what I used to do,' he said, and mentioned doing guard duty at a correctional institute in Indiana. It wasn't quite true; in fact he'd been on the wrong side of the bars doing short time on the institute's farm as a security level 1 prisoner. But there was no way this guy would ever find that out.

Paul had seemed satisfied at that. 'I knew I'd chosen right.' He looked down and nudged a small leather briefcase at his feet. 'See this? I'll pay you as much money as I can get in this briefcase on completion of the job. Shouldn't take more than a week.'

'Yeah? How much are we talking about?' Tommy-Lee had ducked his head for a quick look. It was a pretty sizeable item with a heavy strap and a brass lock. How much cash could a briefcase like that hold, he wondered?

'Fifteen thousand US dollars,' Paul had murmured quietly. 'Small notes, well-used and easy to spend. You'd have nobody asking why you're breaking fifties or hundreds, and you'd always have money in your pocket, free to go wherever you like. But you have to come with me right now. This is kind of urgent and we have a drive ahead of us. You in?'

'Can I ask who this guy is?'

Paul hesitated, then said, 'Sure. I guess that's only fair – and I trust you. You don't need to know his name, but he's a former military officer.'

'What kind of officer? A general?'

'No, nothing that heavy. Lower scale but with his eyes on the top. He put a couple of friends of mine away… friends who got caught shipping a few mementoes back from Afghanistan.'

'Mementoes?'

'You know the kind of thing I mean… stuff they could have sold for a nice profit. It wasn't classified or top secret or anything like that. Nothing the government should have got worked up about. But this officer… well, he pushed it all the way because he wanted to make a name for himself. They were good men, too.'

'What happened?'

'They're serving a ten-year stretch, no remission.'

'That's harsh.' Tommy-Lee felt the jab of fellow-feeling for victims of the system. He knew how tough that was. There really hadn't been any more to it than that. He'd already overstayed his welcome with his pal, Dougie, who he guessed wouldn't miss him if he never went back and nor would his lady. What few items of clothing were at Dougie's place he could do without or replace later. Hell, with fifteen grand in his back pocket, he could buy a whole new wardrobe. He finished his drink and stood up, filled with bravado. 'Hell, I never did like officers much anyway. Let's go do this!'

Out in the parking lot they'd climbed into a pale blue Ford van and driven across the city, stopping at a small hotel to pick up two men Paul had said were work colleagues. He'd introduced them as Bill and Donny, which even Tommy-Lee in his drunken state figured were made-up names. Both were dark, with black, oily hair and deep eyes. Good men, Paul had told him; the best. But Bill and Donny? Come on.

Bill was big; over six foot tall with a weight-lifter's chest and shoulders, he was somewhere in his twenties and had a surly mouth. Donny was younger, skinny, with wild, wiry hair and looked like a geek fresh out of college.

Laurel and Hardy more like, Tommy-Lee thought, and shook their hands. Bill's grip was surprisingly fleshy and soft, while Donny barely touched fingers before sticking his hand back in his pocket. Tommy-Lee shrugged it off. He'd trade courtesies with these guys' dead mothers if it meant he got paid.

But no way were they fully paid-up citizens of the US. He'd swear on that, no matter what Paul had said about his pals in the military doing time.

6

Ruth took out her cellphone and hit speed dial.

'What are you doing?' asked Vaslik.

'I'm calling this in. Whoever did this knows where Elizabeth Chadwick lives and where Ben goes to school.' And God help them if we're already too late, she thought.

The call was answered instantly. It was to a direct number for insider use only, and the responder had the calm, controlled voice of a professional.

'Cruxys. Go ahead.'

'It's Gonzales,' she said briefly. 'Subject is James Chadwick, currently a Code Red. Confirm?'

A faint clicking of keys and the operator said, 'Correct. How can I help, Miss Gonzales?'

'His Newark address has been trashed and there are signs that whoever did it is now in possession of the UK address details of his wife and their son's boarding school.' She read out the message in the address book, knowing that the call was being recorded. 'I strongly recommend we send response teams to both addresses and that they move the Chadwicks to a secure location until we know what we're dealing with.'

'Will do. You believe there's a direct threat?'

'Absolutely. I'll send photo details in a second.'

'Very well. Teams are on their way.'

'One other thing. I need a full backgrounder on James Chadwick. From college through to now. What has he done, when and where? Anything that's out there. The details we have are too sketchy to be of much help.'

'On the way.'

Ruth cut the connection and took a photo of each piece of paper, and sent them off to Cruxys for the files. It would demonstrate the clarity of the threat made, although not the reasons behind it. She said to Vaslik, 'Something he did must have stuck to him. This kind of threat doesn't come out of the blue.'

'I was going to ask what you thought,' he said mildly. 'But that doesn't seem necessary now.'

'No.' She gestured at the ruined apartment. 'This wasn't a search; it was too calculated and deliberate. It was part of the message.'

'I agree.'

'Have you spoken to the neighbours?'

'Out at work, most of them. It's that kind of building. If they did hear anything, they're not saying. What they hear doesn't concern them and what they don't doesn't matter. But whoever did this was clever. They thought of that before they went to work.' He bent and picked up a plastic rectangle from the floor. It was a building contractor's site plate with the legend **GO-LINE CONSTRUCTION – *we build fast!*** followed by a telephone number. 'This was on the landing outside. If anybody heard anything, they'd have figured Chadwick was having some work done. It's pretty common.'

'When did it go up?'

'According to the super, a week ago. He had no reason to question it.'

'So just before Chadwick disappeared.'

'You got it. I called the phone number and the company claims they haven't got any crews in this area. And the signs get damaged or go missing all the time, mostly taken by college kids and drunks as trophies.'

'It would be nice if we knew the point of the message.'

'Beats me. But I've seen it before. It's scare tactics; you want someone to know you can reach out to them anytime, even within their own home, you do this. Smash their possessions, destroy their peace of mind… and most of all let them know you can come back any time you choose and do it all over again – or worse.'

Knowing a little of his background in the NYPD, Ruth said, 'That sounds like organised crime.'

'It is, mostly. And it works. A straight break-in is scary enough; a lot of home-owners never want to go back inside the place again. Throw in this kind of destruction and you really have got somebody on the run.'

'Isn't it counter-productive?'

'Not in the cases I saw. It made the victims freak out and crack under the pressure. They pretty much caved and gave in to the next demand. Adding other family locations, though – that's a twist.'

'Is that what Chadwick did, do you think – upset somebody?' Ruth was trying to picture any normal person's reaction to this scene of mini-devastation. According to his file and his wife, Chadwick was a business consultant, engrossed in his work to the exclusion of all else. Wouldn't he have reacted to this like any normal citizen and called the cops? Or was there a reason why he might have freaked out and gone into hiding, if that's what he'd done? It might explain his sudden vanishing act, but not his going completely off the radar to the possible detriment of his family.

She walked back through the rooms, trying to pick up a sense of something that would help. Some places were like that; you could almost feel a message in the atmosphere, the décor or the possessions left behind that gave a feel for what the victim might have been engaged in.

But not here. There was nothing. Just a chilling message that was clearly intended to mean something to James Chadwick.

Do as we say or lose them.

'I think we need to speak to his employers,' she said. 'Get whatever they can tell us about what he was working on.'

Vaslik nodded. 'Makes sense – although I'm not sure what kind of business consultant would attract this sort of attention.'

Ruth moved over to the bedroom window, the overshoes squishing in the silence, and looked out from the corner of the apartment block across an expanse of grass and plants no doubt cultivated solely for their lack of maintenance time. It spoke again of Chadwick having money, but instead of an ultra-fashionable and desirable location like the Chelsea pad in London, this one spoke of convenience, simplicity and practicality. A man's place.

Through the foliage on the trees and bushes dotted across the area, she could see where the street curved round to skirt the property, with another apartment block sitting with its back to this one. A small brick-built structure with a cement-block roof stood at one side of the building, and she could see two sports bikes and a small scooter chained up inside.

And a man, watching her.

-

She moved back out of instinct. He was of medium height, youngish, dressed in dark blue workman's overalls and a hardhat, like a hundred other building or utility workers you could see any day of the week.

Except that utility workers didn't normally use binoculars.

'Slik,' she called softly, and turned her head away, yawning deliberately but keeping her eyes on the man. She saw his hand move as he adjusted the focus and knew she hadn't imagined it. 'Slik, in here.'

Vaslik stepped into the room and she gestured for him to move round to come up behind her. 'The bike shed in the next block. Is he doing what I think he's doing?"

Vaslik moved closer, his breath touching her hair. 'Damn. He's a spotter.'

'What?'

'Posted to keep an eye on the place, to see who turns up.'

As they stared at each other, the man lowered the binoculars and revealed tanned skin and dark eyes, with a slim moustache over the 'O' of a mouth opened in surprise.

Then he was gone.

'Let's go.' Vaslik turned and ran for the door.

Ruth hit the front stairs, figuring she could get out faster that way than waiting for the elevator, while Vaslik disappeared through a fire exit towards the rear of the building. She could hear the twin echoes of her breath being bounced out of her and the slap of her shoes as she jumped three steps at a time, and hoped she didn't meet any little old ladies coming the other way. Otherwise one of them was going to cartwheel downwards – and it wasn't going to be her.

She cleared the last few steps and burst through the entrance door into the open and turned right, towards where she figured the watcher would be going. The street was empty, save for cars parked at the side. No people, no movement; just a few birds scattered across the grass, proof that he hadn't come out this way.

She turned back, breaking into a run past the apartment block back towards the main street where they'd turned off. He'd done a switch. The guy had clearly done his homework and scoped out the area to find a way out if he was spotted by a resident. Now he'd be looking for the cover of other people where he could blend in and disappear.

She picked up speed and emerged on the main street and took a left, using the apartment block as the swing point. If he was headed this way, he should pop up somewhere along here. She slowed to a walk, eyeing buildings and stores, lines of vehicles and a number of pedestrians going about their business.

She kept walking, sticking close to the buildings and checking against the odds for signs of blue overalls and a hardhat. Great as camouflage most of the time, they would be a dead giveaway for a fugitive if he hadn't dumped them.

She passed a real-estate agency and a flower shop. Still nothing. He must have moved faster than she thought and was probably several blocks away by now. She was about to turn back when she caught a flicker of movement at the corner of her eye and a figure burst out of a narrow alleyway between two buildings and slammed into her.

Ruth cried out and instinctively grabbed for something to hold onto as she was knocked sideways. A woman close by cried out in alarm, and Ruth became dimly aware as she rolled on the ground, of coarse dark blue fabric clutched in her fist and a man's breath, hot and sickly in her face.

He was lithe and strong, and surged back on to his feet. He tried to wrench himself free, but she had too strong a grip on the lapel of hisc overalls and used his momentum to pull herself upright. He hissed at her, a spray of saliva touching her skin, and his hardhat spun away, revealing coarse black hair, dark eyes and a face twisted in fury. Then he chopped viciously at her wrist, breaking her hold as a button popped loose from the coveralls and the fabric tore. He staggered back several paces but instead of turning to run, he moved towards her and brought one hand up.

He was holding a knife.

She had no choice; he was too close for her to outrun him and there was nowhere to go without endangering others. She stooped and took off her shoes, then moved forward towards him, gripping a shoe in each hand.

It wasn't what the man was expecting. She was supposed to have cowered in fear, frozen to a standstill at the sight of the blade, or turned to run. Not this. He hesitated, a frown of indecision crossing his face. Then he snarled and launched himself at her.

Ruth waited until the last moment, then stepped to one side. As the man was almost upon her, she swung her arm in up and round in an arc. Her fingers were curled inside the shoe, with the stubby heel to the fore. She felt the impact all the way to her shoulder as her shoe connected with the side of his face. His own weight did the rest, and he cried out and careered past her, colliding with the side of a delivery truck and dropping the knife.

Then he turned and ran.

Ruth dropped to her knees, her legs wobbly, and watched him go. A woman rushed across to help her, and a stocky man in jeans and a check shirt came round the side of the delivery truck and grabbed her other arm.

'Are you okay, honey?' said the woman, patting her shoulder. 'God, that was horrible. You should tell the police. I mean, in broad daylight? I can't believe it!'

'It's getting worse, I tell you,' the trucker muttered, and picked up her other shoe and handed it to her. 'But I ain't never seen a move like that before, lady. You wacked him good!'

Ruth smiled and said, 'I'm fine, really. Thank you both.'

Then Andy Vaslik was standing next to her with a quizzical expression on his face.

'Damn,' he muttered. 'I can't leave you alone for a second, can I?'

7

They'd headed on out towards the south-west, driving for several hours with one stop to buy supplies, although Tommy-Lee hadn't known much about that; he was sleeping off his drink in the back surrounded by half a dozen or so sealed cardboard boxes and a shrink-wrapped pallet of bottled water. The first he'd really known was when they'd pitched up in the middle of the night in this nowhere place, surrounded by a silence so intense it was almost painful on the ears.

Bill and the skinny geek had unloaded the supplies, which included some prepacked pants, underclothes and shirts for Tommy-Lee, along with the water and juice and a crate of canned food and some fresh fruit. The cardboard boxes, he noted, had remained on the outside. That done, they'd wandered off to check out the area, Paul explaining that they needed to make it secure. While they did that he'd shown Tommy-Lee the layout of a small building which from the smell of oil he'd figured had once been some kind of workshop.

It was tight on space inside, mostly because of two beds and not much else apart from the supplies. But the sight of the handcuffs on one of the beds had done a whole lot to sober him up, and he'd listened carefully to Paul's instructions. Shit, this was for real!

The prisoner, Paul had said, was coming in the following day. He would be dropped off and handcuffed to the bed, and under no circumstances was he to be allowed free except for when he wanted to use the latrine bucket or to wash himself – and even then with one ankle restraint in place. He'd leave a key, of course, once the man was delivered and secured. The sedative he'd been administered would keep him quiet for a good while, and other than dripping water into the man's mouth every hour or so to keep him hydrated, all Tommy-Lee had to do was leave him to come round when he was good and ready.

Then they would be back.

'I got it,' Tommy-Lee had muttered. 'Secure at all times. I know the procedure.'

'Good.' Paul had nodded. 'You are also to stay in here with him. No going outside, even under cover of darkness. There are farmers here, and occasional passing traffic, so you sleep, eat and drink inside.' He'd paused for a couple of beats and stared hard with eyes bright as a buzzard Tommy-Lee had once seen in a wildlife center. 'To make sure, I'm going to lock the door from the outside. But you'll be OK with that, right?'

'Sure.' Actually, it wasn't because even with his background he hated being locked up. Didn't matter that it was a wooden box he could probably bust out of if he had a mind. But no way was he going to say that to this guy.

'And I need your cell phone.'

'Say what?' Tommy-Lee didn't exactly have a busy address book of people he liked to touch base with, but the idea of handing over his cell came as a surprise.

'You'll get it back, I promise. It's just a precaution. In any case, out here there's no signal.'

Tommy-Lee shrugged, suddenly too tired to argue. 'Sure. Why not?' He handed it over. Battery was near dead, anyway. He'd left the charger at Dougie's place. He'd probably sold it on eBay by now.

'Good. Any questions?'

He shook his head. Truth was, he had a whole lot of them, mostly about who the prisoner really was and what was going to happen to him aside from being locked up in this shitty box. But with the look Paul was giving him he didn't figure it would be a good idea to ask. He also wanted to point out that there was a whole ton of laws about kidnapping and taking a person across state lines and probably even more about messing with military brown-nosers. But that, too, could wait.

'No. Everything's cool.'

Now the smell of fear and faeces was hanging off the man on the bed like a cloak. It was humiliation, the first part of a process Tommy-Lee had learned in Iraq a long time ago while interrogating insurgents. He'd been good at it, too. Had gotten himself a good rep for making prisoners talk, even when they didn't want to. Some had said he was the best there was. But that was before one of the inmates had gone and died on him and an investigations commission had brought the roof down on his head.

He spat on the floor and stepped over to the other bed, hunkering down so that his eyes were on the same level as the prisoner's. Time to earn his money. He was holding the hunting knife in front of him so the man on the bed could see it clearly, and smiled at the way his eyes went wide and wild like a cow about to be slaughtered. It was another part of the process: the threat of imminent punishment.

The man was making grunting noises and shaking his head, and Tommy-Lee watched, fascinated, as he tried to shrink his body away through the wall behind him. It was a reaction he'd seen and enjoyed countless times before; the response to absolute power over another human being. He reached for the bottle of water and dribbled some across the man's face, deliberately hitting his eyes and nose. More grunting noises, this time high-pitched like he was about to explode.

Not quite water-boarding, Tommy-Lee knew, but the threat was the same. Block up a man's nose and mouth and they can feel death sitting right there on their shoulder, waiting to take over.

He waited for the man to go still, then reached over and ripped the tape away, taking some skin and stubble with it. He held the knife right in front of the man's eyes so he could see it close up, see his own shit-scared reflection in the blade's shiny surface.

'Be still,' he cautioned, and was surprised at how good it felt to actually speak in this tiny airless space; how clear and commanding his voice sounded. 'I'll give you a drink, cross my heart. And I'll take off the cuffs so you can piss and wash yourself. But first you have to know something that might just save your life. You listening to me?'

Another part of the process: the offer of potential release. Didn't matter how tough a man thought he was, how committed or brain-washed by hate or politics or religion or arrogance; they all wanted to grab a hold on life. On freedom.

The man nodded and went still.

'First thing is, you should know that there's a bunch of ragheads out there who I think want to do bad things to you.'

The man's lips parted and a noise came out, but it was unintelligible, a croak through dry vocal chords and a gummy mouth.

Tommy-Lee held up a finger. 'Don't speak. Just listen. If we get along here, and you cooperate, everything will be just fine.' He dribbled more water over the man's lips and averted his head when he choked and coughed, spraying the liquid into the air. 'Easy, pal,' he said softly. 'You gotta calm down. Spit on me again and I'll leave you to go dry. Hear me?'

Another eager nod, this time with eyes fixed on the water bottle in Tommy-Lee's hand. The man's tongue flicked out, fissured with dehydration, and dragged itself across cracked lips.

'*Please*.' The word was squeezed out, the whisper no louder than a breath of air.

Tommy-Lee tilted the water bottle, slowly this time, so the man didn't convulse or choke. Last thing he needed was for the guy to die on him before Paul and his pals got back. A dead body would probably get him nothing but a whole lot of trouble he didn't want.

As the description entered his head, he wondered for the first time why his subconscious kept seeing those words. Then it hit him. On the way here from Kansas City, the men in front had barely spoken to each other. But just once, through the alcoholic haze that had taken him in and out of sleep, he'd heard some vaguely familiar words coming from the one called Bill, before Paul had choked him off and told to shut up, but in English.

Tommy-Lee had never learned much Arabic, other than a few brutal commands needed to get a prisoner's attention. But he knew enough from what Bill had said to have guessed which part of the world these three men really came from. And it blew any story about friends, and military jail and an over-eager officer right out of the water.

What surprised him more than anything was that he really didn't give a damn.

He had a job to do and he was going to do it.

8

The StoneSeal offices were located in a glittering, wedge-shaped tower of steel and tinted glass on an intersection close by some rail tracks in New Jersey. Surrounded by other buildings bearing the pallid air of new builds as yet untouched by the acid bite of city fumes, it gave Ruth the impression of a company hiding in plain sight; there but beyond the reach of ordinary mortals unless by invitation.

Vaslik led the way into a large reception atrium, where an attractive young woman was seated behind a long counter. Around her was an impressive bank of camera monitors and computer screens. Two uniformed security guards were seated close by, with another patrolling a mezzanine floor at the top of a whispering escalator. Other than the men in uniform, the atrium floor and mezzanine were empty.

'Ever had the feeling we're being watched?' Vaslik murmured.

'Don't remind me,' Ruth said. She was feeling self-conscious. She had a slight tear in her jacket sleeve where she'd been knocked over by the spotter, and a puffy area of redness under one eye. In spite of that she knew she'd been lucky to have got away unscathed. Vaslik had suggested calling it a day and getting her checked over by a doctor, but she'd refused. They had too much to do and wimping out wasn't her thing. After making sure the attacker's hardhat and knife were safely bagged up for examination later, she'd suggested they get to the StoneSeal offices.

'How can I help you?' The receptionist was polite and brisk. If she noticed the fight damage to Ruth she was too well-trained to show it.

Vaslik gave their names and added, 'We have an appointment with David MacInnes.'

'I'm sorry – he's been called out of the office.' The response was automatic and conveyed no discernible flicker of regret. 'Can I take a message?'

Vaslik checked his cell phone. 'In that case how about John DeGeorgio?' Ruth glanced past his shoulder. The screen showed the names of the three top individuals in the company; MacInnes was CEO, DeGeorgio was Operating Director and a woman named Karen Simanski was the Financial and Technical Director.

'Sorry, but he's unavailable. In fact there's a major client conference going on and they've asked not to be disturbed.'

'Miss Simanski?'

'Her too.' She stared up at Vaslik as if waiting for him to drop another name on her. One of the security guards got to his feet and edged closer as though a signal had been activated. He was large, with the bearing of an ex-cop, and wearing a holstered gun on his waist. He said nothing but stared at Vaslik and Ruth in turn. The other guard gave a flick of his hand and the man on the mezzanine began walking down the escalator towards them.

'I'll show you to the door, sir – madam.' The first guard said, and moved round from behind the desk to lead the way out.

Vaslik hesitated for a moment, then reached into his inside breast pocket and produced a small wallet. He flicked it open and Ruth saw an ID card with his photo, and the familiar logo of the Department of Homeland Security. 'That's not necessary,' Vaslik said. 'We won't be leaving just yet. You might like to get hold of your head of security or head of personnel – I don't care which. Or are they in the client conference, too?'

It stopped the guard in his tracks, and he threw a confused look at the receptionist as if he hadn't been prepared for this. His colleague made a hurried gesture and the man on the escalator stepped off and stayed where he was.

'I'm sorry,' the receptionist said, her face flushed. 'I didn't realise. I'll get Janna Conway, our Human Resources vice president.'

Five minutes later, Vaslik and Ruth were seated in a third-floor conference room. Across the table sat a woman in her forties, with a tinge of a Caribbean accent and a ready smile.

'My apologies for the misunderstanding downstairs,' she murmured warmly. 'But our front-of-house staff hadn't been made aware that the appointment with David MacInnes was made by a government agency.' She waited for a response, but there was none, so continued: 'And the client conference came up rather unexpectedly which meant our senior team was called away at short notice. How can I help?'

'James Chadwick,' said Vaslik shortly. 'We're trying to locate him.'

A flicker of an eyelid and Mrs Conway nodded. 'I see. I'm afraid all I can tell you is that he has taken an unexplained leave of absence.'

'So you know where he is?'

'No, I don't mean that. He didn't inform us of the details.'

'That's because he's gone missing.'

A momentary hesitation. 'That's not what I was told, Agent…' She looked for the security pass attached to his jacket. '…Vaslik.'

'I guess you were misinformed. The facts are that you don't know where he is, nor does his family. We have good reason to believe that he might be in some kind of trouble and we'd like to find him.'

'Then I'm not sure how I can help, Mr Vaslik. I can pull his staff file, but I know for a fact that it contains his home address and financial details as permitted by law, but no personal details that would indicate where he might be now.'

'Perhaps we can see his workplace, then,' he countered.

She hesitated and sat up straight. 'I'm not sure that's allowed. This is very irregular, you know. Are you aware that StoneSeal is on the approved contractors list to the federal government? We have important security issues here.'

'I'm sure you have, Mrs Conway. As do we. Which is why it would be unwise to be seen to stonewall an investigation into the disappearance of one of your employees. If he's in any kind of trouble, the least your company can do is allow us to start tracing his movements so that we can relay some information to his wife and son, don't you think?'

Ruth was impressed, and had to fight to maintain a blank expression. She wondered where Vaslik was going with this, and how far he'd get before somebody decided to check with the DHS and bring the ceiling down on them for impersonating US law enforcement officers. But since she was powerless to stop him now he'd gone this far, she was going to have to sit it out and wait to be locked up.

'I'm sorry – I didn't mean to give that impression at all, Agent Vaslik.' Mrs Conway's voice had lost some of its warmth, and now held a slight veneer of panic. 'I should have mentioned that our consultants don't spend much time here, and therefore don't have assigned workstations. They hot desk on an as-needed basis.' She stood up and smoothed her skirt. 'As a matter of fact there are a few of Mr Chadwick's personal possessions here. We thought it best to keep them in our secure room until we knew what to do with them. But I'm sure I can let you have a look through them if it would help?'

Vaslik smiled. 'That would be most kind. Thank you.'

Seconds later they were following Conway at a brisk pace down two flights of stairs and into a long corridor with doors either side. The décor was clinical and cold, and each door carried a key-pad and swipe mechanism. Ruth wondered how much hot desking was going on behind the doors. It certainly wasn't giving off the aura of a busy office building.

Conway stopped outside one of the doors and used a card on a metal chain around her neck to swipe the lock. The space inside was a storage room, with shelves around the walls holding a variety of office equipment, boxes and filing cabinets. She bustled over to a plain cardboard box on a shelf and lifted it onto a table in the centre of the room.

'This is all there was, I'm afraid. We don't really encourage our consultants to keep much here for security reasons.' She gave a brief smile, and when Vaslik showed no sign of looking into the box, she got the message and moved towards the door. 'Excuse me. I'll be right outside.'

As soon as she had closed the door behind her, they looked in the box. Conway had been telling the truth; there wasn't much inside. A small leather briefcase, which was empty, a calculator, several pens, three coloured markers, an envelope containing a mix of currencies, mostly in coin, a Bartholomew folding map of Central United States, and a conference brochure for an event in Denver, Colorado.

'He wasn't exactly the hoarder type, was he?' Vaslik murmured. He checked the briefcase again and dropped it back in the box. 'Darn. I was hoping for something like a desk diary at least.'

'He's a consultant,' Ruth reminded him. 'They do everything on tablets and smart phones. It goes with the image. This is interesting.' She picked up the brochure, which was a glossy folder for a conference on unmanned aircraft systems.

Vaslik looked over her shoulder and pulled a face. 'I used to fly model gliders as a kid. This stuff is way out of my league.'

'What, you playing with toy planes? Somehow I can't picture that.'

'Yeah, well, I'd send them up but they didn't always come home again. In the end I ran out of money and enthusiasm.'

'But this isn't about airplanes or gliders; it's about drones. Big boys' toys.' She opened the folder and checked the list of events, which included speaker panels, workshop sessions and demonstrations, all aimed at, among others, end-users, suppliers and service providers.

'So?'

'His wife told me he was supposed to be taking his son to a model aircraft exhibition this week in the UK, but failed to confirm. It's one of the reasons she started throwing a hissy-fit when I mentioned his name.' She flicked the brochure. 'Anyway, it couldn't have been this one – it's here in the US and this one's in three months.'

Vaslik took the brochure and thumbed through it. As he read, his face became more serious. 'These are pretty hard core. It mentions military and aerospace, along with academics and technical contractors. This isn't for beach flyers on a weekend away.'

Ruth was already unfolding the map. She laid it out on the table. It looked fairly new but showed signs of having been unfolded and refolded several times. The inch-wide margins around the edges contained some scribbled jottings, while the map itself had been marked with circles and question marks, but these seemed almost random with no specific connection, and were spread across the central states. She folded the map again. It would be interesting to take a closer look later.

'What are the chances,' she said quietly, 'of getting these things out of the building without the heavy mob and Miss Frosty Pants at the front desk throwing the furniture at us?'

Vaslik produced his wallet and DHS ID. 'They wouldn't dare.'

'Are you sure about using that? What if they check?'

He smiled. 'Did I forget to tell you – I'm on the reserve list for Homeland Security. Once in, never forgotten.' He put the brochure in his inside pocket and waited for Ruth to tuck the map inside her jacket, then turned towards the door. 'Come on – let's go.'

They stepped outside and found Mrs Conway waiting as promised. She pulled the door closed and checked it was locked, then turned to lead them back along the corridor.

'Stop right there!'

Three men were striding towards them, blocking the narrow space. The man in the lead wore an expensive suit and an air of outrage. He was accompanied by two armed security guards.

9

Tommy-Lee lifted his head off the pillow. He'd picked up the faint sound of a vehicle approaching. It was no more than a distant hum, but out here in these flat lands any man-made noise could travel for miles without hindrance. And this one was getting closer. Since noon he'd heard only three other vehicles, all beaten-up trucks or pickups that had gone by without stopping.

He dropped the battered copy of *Universal Hunter* magazine he'd found in the van on the way here and checked his watch. It had stopped. Must be the dirt-cheap battery he'd bought from a street trader a week ago. Thieving bastard. He wondered if it was Paul and his goons on the way in. He had no idea where they disappeared to every time, but it couldn't be far. They always seemed fed and watered, so he figured they must have a base not far away, probably in some cheap motel off the nearest highway.

He rolled off the bed. Went to the strip window where he could see a section of the road bordered by a line of buffalo grass about a quarter of a mile away, travelling arrow-straight from east to west. If a vehicle was going to pass by, he'd see it soon enough.

He heard a grunt from the man on the bed, and went over and gave him a trickle of water. It set off another bout of coughing, so he stopped pouring and slapped the man's shoulder a few times until it was over. It wasn't that he cared for the man's health one bit; he simply didn't want a corpse on his hands.

Earlier on he'd unlocked the cuffs and told the man to take off his soiled clothes and clean himself off. The smell had got pretty ripe and it was already bad enough in the enclosed and over-heated space without making it worse. He'd dropped the bag containing the change of cheap work pants, shirt and underclothes on the bed, then turned his back while the man got busy with a water bottle and a cloth in the corner.

He had an uneasy feeling about the three men; he didn't like the way they seemed to communicate with each other through shifty looks and slick movements of their hands. Even when they went into a huddle and he couldn't understand a word they said, but it was better than all the silent stuff.

He especially didn't like the butt of a semi-automatic he'd seen tucked into the waistband of the one called Paul or whatever the hell his real name might be. Truth was, he was beginning to realise that he'd been suckered into this situation by the promise of easy money and his own desperation. He'd taken the guy at face value, but hadn't given a thought to what the hell was going on or why he was being paid so much to do so little.

As for the other two, they never so much as looked him in the eye, much less talked to him. It was like he didn't exist and it was starting to get to him. Fricking ragheads – even Paul, who now he thought about it actually looked just like so many guys he'd seen in Iraq. They weren't all dark skinned, in fact some of the men and kids were almost white and he'd seen some with blue eyes, which was really freakish. Even the women, who he'd admired at a distance whenever he could. Cute, some of them, with flashing eyes that carried a world or promise… if you wanted to be gutted like a fish and dumped in some back-alley along with the trash.

Still, he was here now, so best get on with it. Maybe he could get out of here in one piece and be on his way, richer and happier than he'd ever been.

'You better get your shit together, you know?' he muttered, when the coughing had ceased and the prisoner indicated he wanted more water.

'What… what do you want with me?' The words were hoarse, squeezed out through a throat as dry as the sun-baked earth outside this hut. Tommy-Lee could tell the man was educated even without the expensive clothes and the soft hands, but he wasn't curious enough to want to know more. Curiosity, his old man had often said, was a short cut to trouble and pain.

'Ain't me that wants you, pal. It's the three camel jockeys who brought you here. I'm just playing warden, is all.'

'Why?' The man's eyes were filled with fear and lined with the salty crust of dried tears. His cheeks were sunken and he needed a bath and a shave, which Tommy-Lee figured were both about three days overdue.

'Why what?' The noise of the motor was closer now, bumping along the connecting track leading from the road, and he got ready to stand up and meet the three men. Might as well show willing even if he didn't like what they stood for.

Fact is, he didn't know what they stood for, only that it couldn't be for this guy's health and wellbeing. Maybe he'd pissed one of them off at some stage and this was payback time. Wouldn't be the first time a guy had upset the wrong person. But since they were paying him good money to follow instructions and mind his own, he figured he could put up with it.

'Why are you helping them? Ragheads, you called them.'

'Yeah. But don't let them hear you say that. I don't think they're the kind of folks with a sense of humour.'

'So why?'

'Money. Why else? Man's got to make a living, right? You do it your way, I do it mine. I bet you don't like all the people you work with. Same here, only my options are more limited.'

'Do you even know what they want from me?'

'No. And I don't want to. Ain't none of my business, neither.' He hesitated, then said, 'Are you saying you don't know?' He wondered if this guy was trying to play him. He'd figured that most people kidnapped and kept cuffed to a bed in the middle of nowhere would have trawled back through their life and worked out from what they'd done, who they owed money or who they'd hurt, stuff like that, and knew what the deal was. Maybe he was dressed nice but really just as dumb as nuts.

'No.'

He was lying. Tommy had an eye and an ear for lies, learned while interrogating insurgents in Iraq. You couldn't hide a lie completely, no matter who you were, what language you spoke. Once a lie was out there it was just waiting to be seen by anyone with the right skills.

'You sure about that?'

'Yes. Listen, you've got to help me.' The man tried to sit up and winced when he was brought up short by the handcuffs. He sank back, his eyes on Tommy-Lee. 'My name's James, by the way—'

'I don't give a shit what your name is, so stop right there!' He didn't want to know names, didn't care what the hell the guy was called. One thing he'd learned in Iraq was that knowing a prisoner's name was a short cut to being drawn in and suckered. Some of those detainees could sweet-talk information out of you without you knowing, all under the guise of being friendly. As far as he was concerned a prisoner was just a number and nothing else. Names just got in the way.

But the man on the bed wasn't hearing him. 'You're doing this for money – I understand that. But I could pay you more. Double… treble what they're offering. I have a wife and boy. Do this for me, for God's sa—'

Tommy-Lee slapped his hand over the prisoner's mouth. 'Enough, you idiot!' he hissed. 'Shut the fuck up or we'll both end up dead.'

The vehicle had stopped outside, right behind the workshop where it would be invisible from the road. Two doors opened and slammed shut again, angry and tinny. That would be Bill and Donny. A brief pause, then the engine was cut. He waited. The third door opened and closed with an almost gentle thump. Like someone who respected his ride.

Paul.

He was the thinker, Tommy-Lee knew; the quiet ones usually were. He always moved carefully, too, like he was in control. Not like the other two who seemed generally pissed at the world and stomped around like they wanted to break something or somebody. They'd be standing there now waiting for Paul's signal to move, while he studied the area around the old airfield. He did it every time they came here; Tommy-Lee had caught a glimpse through the window one time and was accustomed to the sounds of their movements even if he couldn't see them. The two goons just waited like they knew their place. It was like a ritual, as if their boss was sniffing the air, sensing trouble and getting ready to react.

When he was through doing that they'd go into a huddle before Paul would stick his head inside the box to make sure everything was okay. Then the other two would disappear off towards the large hangar. Tommy-Lee had seen them the last time they were here, and the geek, Donny, was carrying a toolbox.

He had no idea why they did that every time; it was only an old hangar, for God's sake. Maybe it had something to do with the sealed cardboard boxes he'd seen in the van coming down here that first night. He hadn't seen them since and he knew they hadn't contained food or water.

'Please help me.' The prisoner rolled closer with a pained grunt, breathing sour air into Tommy-Lee's face.

'Not a chance,' Tommy-Lee said firmly, with no hint of regret. This was his one opportunity to make some money and he wasn't going to screw it up. Not for this guy, not for anybody. He didn't trust Paul or his two pals any further than he could spit, but he figured if he played it right, he might just come out of this the right way up and be on his way.

Still, he did wonder what was so interesting about that hangar. And the boxes he guessed they'd taken over there.

10

'What's the meaning of this?' The man in the suit might once have been handsome, with sleek, swept-back hair and the tanned skin of a politician. Heavily-built, with an impressive chest and gut pushing at the buttons of his suit, he radiated the powerful aura of a man with total confidence in his authority and status. 'Mrs Conway, what are these people doing here?' He didn't wait for her answer but signalled to the two guards and said, 'Search them.'

One of the guards stepped towards Vaslik and signalled him to lift his hands away from his side. The other man approached Ruth and did the same.

But Vaslik had other ideas. He took his Homeland ID out of his pocket and flashed it at the guard. 'I don't think so,' he said softly.

The guard checked the ID and stopped, then looked at the man in the suit. 'He's Homeland Security, Mr MacInnes. What do we do?'

MacInnes held out his hand. 'Let me see that.'

Vaslik allowed him to take it and waited while MacInnes scanned the document before thrusting it back at him.

'This is outrageous,' he snapped. 'We're an approved contractor to the US Government with at least five ongoing contracts and several more bids at tender stage. We shouldn't have to put up with this level of discourtesy. Why are you here?'

'I made an appointment which you failed to keep,' Vaslik said easily, showing his lack of concern at the CEO's blustering attitude. 'We're looking into the disappearance of James Chadwick, one of your employees.' He nodded at Ruth. 'This is Miss Gonzales from the UK; she's an investigator here on behalf of Mr Chadwick's family.'

MacInnes turned his glare on Ruth. 'Investigator? You mean police?'

'I'm with a company called Cruxys,' said Ruth. 'Part of the Greenville Corporation.'

'Greenville? I've heard of them. Aren't they private military contractors? What the hell does Chadwick's disappearance have to do with a bunch of mercenaries?'

Ruth didn't bother arguing the difference between Greenville and Cruxys; she didn't think MacInnes would listen. 'There's no connection. Cruxys is an insurance company and I'm tasked with trying to find Chadwick and get him home to his family. That's all.'

MacInnes studied her for a couple of seconds, then huffed, 'I don't care who you are, you have no right being here. And Chadwick is a consultant, not an employee. As such he is free to come and go as he sees fit.' He looked at Mrs Conway. 'Did we not make that clear?'

'Don't blame her,' said Vaslik. 'She explained the position but I wanted to check any personal effects Mr Chadwick might have left behind.' He pointed a thumb at the storage room. 'There are a few items but of no help whatsoever. But we could have found that out if you'd seen us earlier.'

MacInnes grunted and signalled for the two guards to back away. 'I was busy, as I'm sure you were told.' He hesitated then moderated his tone as if unsure of his ground. 'All we know is that Chadwick hasn't reported in for a few days. It's not entirely unusual for consultants to change their timetables due to the pressures of work; we don't ask for daily routines because that's the way we structure our business methods.'

'And what is your business, exactly?' Vaslik asked.

'Classified, mostly. We undertake a lot of work for various branches of the government, but also for commercial and industrial clients. We have nearly two dozen consultants in specialised fields, and over a hundred employees here and in satellite offices.'

'And what is Mr Chadwick's specialised field?' When MacInnes hesitated, Vaslik added pointedly, 'I can always run his details through the contractors' system. But it would help us if you saved me the time.'

MacInnes said, 'He's what we call a general corporate advisor and financial consultant.' He waved a vague hand as if signalling the details were of little importance, and that Chadwick was fairly low down the tree.

'But he's successful at what he does, would you say?'

'Yes. Highly.' The confirmation came reluctantly, as if MacInnes sensed a trap he couldn't see coming. 'He operates in a specialised but highly lucrative market and is one of our highest grossing earners, if you must know. For that reason we allow him perhaps greater latitude in his movements than others.'

'Did he do much government work?'

'I can't comment on that. You'll have to get a court order for that level of information.'

Vaslik grunted. 'Come on, man, I'm not asking for details; he either did or he didn't. Yes or no?'

A brief hesitation, then, 'He didn't, no. I preferred him to stick to the corporate sector of our operations. We have many highly-qualified specialists on the government side of our business; James is better suited for corporate work.'

'So he was a valuable member of the company,' said Ruth. When MacInnes didn't respond, she said, 'Yet you don't sound very concerned about his absence. Are you saying this kind of disappearance is customary behaviour for James Chadwick?'

MacInnes blinked at being challenged. 'I'm not saying that at all. We value all our employees, direct or otherwise. James Chadwick is extremely conscientious and diligent, perhaps more than most. It's what accounts for his success. But I don't pretend to keep track of all our consultants. I was only alerted to his absence forty-eight hours ago.' He glanced at Conway for corroboration, and she nodded after a momentary hesitation.

'The facts are,' MacInnes continued heavily, 'A man has failed to report in, for reasons that are unclear. We don't treat our people like children, and if anyone doesn't want to be contacted for some reason, that's up to them. They may have to face certain consequences, as they would in any commercial enterprise.' His eyes challenged them both to deny the possibility. 'James has been working on a number of high-profile assignments just recently, so I think his absence, while regrettable, is understandable.'

'Doesn't that worry you?' Ruth asked. 'If he's been under some stress he might be unwell.'

MacInnes shrugged it off. 'Of course it concerns me. But he's a resilient man… a grown man, I'd add. I'm sure he's fine.'

Ruth blinked at the man's evasive attitude. She tried another tack. 'Does he have an internal itinerary – something you use for payroll purposes?'

MacInnes shook his head as if by instinct. His eyes were suddenly cool and blank, and they knew he was going to refuse.

'We do, but you really will need signed authorisation to get it. It's commercially sensitive. Now, if you'll excuse me, I have other things to deal with.'

'That may be the case,' Vaslik said. 'But the people he saw most recently and just prior to his disappearance might have information we can use. The last ones to see him might have information about why he hasn't called in. If he was stressed, they might have noticed.'

MacInnes shook his head as though the notion was absurd. 'That's not good enough. Get me signed paperwork first.' He nodded pointedly at the two guards. 'Show them out.' Then he walked away.

–

Vaslik drove to a small restaurant where the tables allowed them the freedom to talk easily without being overheard. They ordered steaks and fries, with lots of coffee. It was time to review where they were in the investigation, but the sight and smell of food reminded Ruth that she hadn't eaten a proper meal for at least fourteen hours and was feeling faint from hunger and jet-lag. It also seemed time to talk about mundane things for a few minutes.

'You know your way around here,' she said, after giving her order to the waiter. 'Like you know the place.'

'I should do; I spent several months attached to the local precinct running surveillance on a Vietnamese criminal gang.'

'What were they doing?'

'Mostly petty stuff: drugs, stolen property, illegal gaming and prostitution. But their main line of work was kidnapping to order.'

'There's a market for that?'

'There was. The gang would take on contracts to lift a member of a family or a corporation and hold them until the people who'd organised the kidnap got what they wanted. The victims and organisers were mostly within the Vietnamese and South-east Asian communities, which made it hard for us to keep tabs on them. I seemed to spend all my time eating and drinking in local restaurants and trying to be invisible.'

'Did it work?'

'Well, I survived, so I figure it did. The gang members weren't too shy of shooting a cop if they felt like it. They played the odds and worked on the basis that identifying any one of them was hard for us unless we got inside help. If that happened and they felt targeted, they'd disappear to one of the big cities until the heat died down. Mostly, though, the locals wouldn't help for fear of reprisals. In the end we got lucky.'

'What happened?'

'They made a mistake and kidnapped the niece of a local Triad boss.'

'Ouch.'

'Ouch is right. He got his men to bring him one of their leaders and began sending him back in pieces until his people got the message. Fortunately for us and the local community, the Triad boss didn't stop there; the moment he got his niece back he ordered the kidnap gang quietly wiped out to the last member.' He gave a dry smile. 'We were accused of allowing them to do it, but the truth was we never stood a chance of stopping them. If we'd tried, they'd have shipped in more and more soldiers we didn't know until the job got done.' He paused and changed the line of conversation. 'What have you been doing recently? How was the Australian trip?'

'Personal protection, paperwork and a nightmare – in that order.' Ruth knew what Vaslik was really asking: after they'd finished working together on the child kidnap case in London, she had gone to Australia to recover from a damaged shoulder and to try rescuing a dying, three-year relationship. Her partner, Lisa, had applied for an exchange program with the Sydney police and she wasn't sure if she would be coming back. The meeting had been fine, the shoulder healed well and she had topped up her sun tan, but the relationship was still in limbo.

'Sorry to hear that.' Vaslik sounded genuine. 'This job's hard on any kind of personal life.'

'Yeah. How about you?' Last time she'd heard Vaslik was single.

'Same thing. Worked some assignments, including one over here, got to see my family… and now this.'

They paused long enough to eat, after which Ruth pulled out her smart phone. It was time to get back to work. She showed Vaslik the summary notes on James Chadwick. It was deliberately short on detail and left lots of potential gaps, but clients of Cruxys were only obliged to provide certain essential facts relevant to their general work. If they chose to be economical with the truth, short of checking international databases for criminal activities, there wasn't much Cruxys could do but take the contract and pray the client wasn't involved in serious organised crime.

> James R. Chadwick – b. 1972. Son of a stockbroker in Chicago, married (Elizabeth) with a son (Benjamin Ian). Attended university (1991-1996) – maj. In economics, business and finance, recruited to NY investment firm and posted to London (1998-2003). After a successful few years and discovering he preferred working with people he joined the US Air Force (2005-2011). Left with a good record and joined StoneSeal (2012 -), a security and economic consultancy in New Jersey, offering advice and commercial vetting intelligence to start-up corporations and others.
>
> Travels extensively between US and Europe, lectures on economics and corporate security for small and medium-sized ventures and NGOs (non-governmental organisations).
>
> Hobbies: not known. Interests: not known.

Vaslik put the smart phone down on the table and shook his head. 'There's got to be more to him than this. If he cheated somebody on the stock market, it's been a long time coming back to bite him. And I can't believe it has anything to do with his college days. It doesn't feel right.'

'And why take out a Red Alert contract? There's nothing to suggest he was in any danger with his work.'

'Unless it was something to do with his military service in the USAF.'

'That's a stretch. What could he have done there?'

'If he was operational I guess he might have flown combat jets. But there's nothing to suggest he did that.' He took out his cell phone and excused himself. 'I'll be a second.'

He was gone a few minutes. When he returned he said, 'I've put out feelers. My contact promised an answer by morning. If there's anything there, he'll find it.'

'What about MacInnes? Are we going after the itinerary?'

'There's no point. I don't have the authority to make it happen, and it would take days to get a request for possession through the system any other way. They could just stonewall us on the grounds of confidentiality or secrecy.' He paused. 'Anyway, I'm not sure we'd find anything.'

'What makes you say that?'

'MacInnes is a bully. He's on top of his pile and likes everybody to know it. As he made it clear, he's a contractor with his fingers in lots of pies, and one freelance business consultant, good as he is, isn't going to lose him any sleep; he can replace him tomorrow. Besides, I reckon the company probably makes more money through government contracts than MacInnes was letting on. The business side would be small change in comparison.'

They paid the bill and Vaslik took Ruth to a small boutique hotel to rest up. It had been a long day and she felt ready to drop.

–

Vaslik was back by nine the following morning.

'What have you got?' Ruth asked as they walked to his car. She felt a little stiff in one arm where she'd been bruised, but other than that and the redness under her eye, she felt good to go.

'It's official: Chadwick wasn't a combat pilot. That leaves out any kind of retribution-revenge thing from air strikes or collateral damage. No obvious misdemeanours, reports of bad behaviour or disciplinary action, nothing like that. In fact he completed officer training top of his class and finished up a captain. Smart guy.'

'And that's it?'

He gave a dry smile. 'Well, not exactly. It's what my contact couldn't find that's interesting.'

'Couldn't?'

'Chadwick's service record got mysteriously pulled just over a month ago.'

'You're kidding.'

'It was marked 'Restricted Access', too, so whoever did it had some juice. There's no way of finding out who pulled it or why… but there were some bits they left behind.'

Ruth stood by the car and glared at him across the roof. 'Christ, Slik, are you going to get to the point or not?'

'Absolutely. My contact said there was an addendum to Chadwick's service history that had been left on a separate file, buried in among some assessment summaries. All it said was that on completion of officer training he was encouraged to apply for a transfer to another branch of the service. He has two other languages and great grades from university, and they must have liked the sound of him.'

'Who's 'they'?'

'Air Force Intelligence. It seems that back in the day, James Chadwick was a spook.'

11

Ruth climbed in and shut the door. 'Why does that revelation worry me just a bit?'

Vaslik smiled. 'You and me both. It doesn't mean he was into anything bad. And there's nothing left on his file to show he was operational or involved in anything left-field. Most people working in military intelligence are analysts, researchers and the like.'

'So he was a desk warrior.'

'Probably.' He started the car. 'Where to now? We've got two key pieces of evidence in the trunk, don't forget.' He was referring to the hardhat and the knife, which would both have fingerprints all over them. 'I can call some favours and get them evaluated to see what they show up.'

'They'll keep,' Ruth replied. 'I vote we go back to StoneSeal.'

'Really? That didn't go too well yesterday, remember.'

'I'd like another crack at Janna Conway. I think she might talk to me. I got the feeling she would have been more help if MacInnes and his armed goons hadn't come bowling along when they did.'

'What are you thinking of asking her? That's if you even get inside the building without getting your butt kicked.'

'Think positive, Slik. We girls have our ways. Yesterday we didn't get a chance to ask about friends or work colleagues. There must be someone he was friendly with. He might have been freelance but he couldn't have worked in a total vacuum.'

Vaslik thought it over and his expression showed it had given him an idea. 'It would help if we got a look at Chadwick's job application. It might fill in some of the gaps about him. And you're right – it would be good to find out what kind of social life he had outside of work.'

'Assuming he had one. It might show what made him take out the Cruxys contract.' They drove along in silence for a while, then Ruth asked, 'Do you think StoneSeal is on the level?'

'Why do you ask?'

'Elizabeth Chadwick didn't like them. She was bitter, I got that, but I also got a sense that she was talking from intuition. And did you pick up any kind of atmosphere about the place? I couldn't make it out. There was a lot of space but not much activity. And why all the weaponry?'

'I know what you mean. I asked my contact if he'd ever heard of them. He had but he wasn't sure what service sector they were in. But as an approved contractor to the federal government, they would have authority to employ a heavier level of security than most companies. Which throws up another possibility.'

'What?'

'Their staff would have undergone standard vetting procedure before being allowed anywhere near any government facilities or systems. StoneSeal should have kept a copy of that procedure, and that might throw up some leads.'

Ruth sat back and mulled it over. She knew enough about the world of military intelligence to know that it wasn't all James Bond, being mostly unglamorous work involving communications intelligence and analysis, cryptography, security, surveillance, counter intelligence and reconnaissance. But that was one side. On the other it was murky and in the shadows. If an officer had any kind of restriction on his military record, it meant he or the section he'd worked for had been involved in highly classified activities that would probably never see the light of day.

Yet somebody had possessed the clout to move Chadwick's file very recently. Was that for hiding even deeper or for another reason?

Vaslik pulled up round the block from the StoneSeal building. 'You go in alone. I'll wait here.'

Ruth walked into the building and was met by the same empty space, the same receptionist but two different guards.

'Good morning. How may I help you?' If the receptionist recognised her, she gave no indication.

'I'd like to talk with Janna Conway in Human Resources,' said Ruth, and gave her name.

She smiled as she spoke, but it drew no response, save a brief double look, no doubt because of her accent.

She and Vaslik had agreed that if Conway was like most HR people, she would know more about the company's employees than was on their files. If not, she would certainly have an ear for any rumour floating around. And changing the focus of the questions and the person making them might promote some useful answers.

'One moment, please.' The receptionist tapped some keys and spoke briefly, then made a signal to one of the security guards, who walked over and handed Ruth a visitor's pass. 'If you go with Germaine, he'll show you upstairs.'

She was escorted back to the third floor, but this time to an office on the sharp side of the wedge-shaped building, with a pleasant view both ways overlooking the road intersection outside. Mrs Conway was waiting for her in the doorway and invited her to sit. The room was pleasant, functional and the only personal item on show was a photo of a man and teenage girl, their smiles as alike as two peas in a pod.

'Your husband and daughter?' said Ruth, indicating the photo.

'Yes, that's right. Michael and Rainna.' She smiled, plainly proud of her family, then added, 'You're not American, Miss Gonzales.'

'Please call me Ruth. No, I'm British. I've been assigned to work with Mr Vaslik on this matter.'

'I see. In what way are the British involved?'

'I was tasked to liaise with James Chadwick's wife, Elizabeth about his disappearance. She's British and lives in London. Part of my remit is to ensure they have every assistance in finding out what happened to him. As you might imagine his son, Ben, is very upset. He's about the same age as your daughter and has taken it very hard. In view of his father's apparent disappearance while working over here, it was decided to extend the search to the US. I was asked to come over and help.' She added, 'I'm sorry for bursting in on you again like this, Mrs Conway, especially after yesterday. I hope we didn't get you into trouble.'

'No. It was fine. And please call me Janna. Mr MacInnes is very sensitive about the government side of our work, that's all. It's a tough business to be in at the moment and we're all aware that contracts are never guaranteed to last.' She hesitated, then added carefully, 'I mean he may have over-reacted to your visit.'

'Yet you're still willing to see me. I'm surprised I made it past the front desk.'

Janna gave a brief laugh. 'The security guards look tough, but they haven't shot anyone recently.' She sat back and waited.

'Well, I thought of some further questions you might be able to help with, if you're willing.'

'Of course.' Janna glanced at the photo of her husband and daughter and frowned in understanding. 'It must be awful for his family, not knowing what's happened. How can I help?'

'I understand that as a consultant or employee working for an approved government contractor, James would have undergone a fairly rigorous vetting procedure, is that correct?'

'Yes. We would have run our own vetting procedure, but his background would have been subject to a federal agency vetting, too, even if he wasn't necessarily engaged on government-related contracts.'

'Would it be possible to take a look at those records, please? I know it's asking a lot, but frankly, anything I can find about him might help locate his whereabouts.'

Janna frowned. 'I wish I could help you – and normally I would. But I'm afraid it's not possible. The files have been removed.'

'Who by?'

'I don't know. I was asked to send the complete employee record to Mr MacInnes. It would have included everything, his vetting summary, assessments, assignment details, personal data – everything. That was the last I saw of them.'

'When was this?'

Janna hesitated and her voice dropped slightly. 'Yesterday, not long after you left.'

'I see. And I don't suppose it would be worth asking him?'

'No. He will probably repeat what he said yesterday.' She shrugged. 'I'm so sorry about this, Ruth, really. I'm not sure what else I can tell you. But I'm sure Mr MacInnes will do all he can to help.'

'What about friends?' Ruth switched the focus and tone deliberately away from the negative. 'Did he have any that you know of?'

'I'm sorry?'

'Work colleagues socialise. James must have forged some relationships. Was there anyone in particular?'

'Well, he was a married man...'

'I'm not implying anything untoward. But he must have had some colleagues closer than others. Was there anybody he had drinks with or with whom he shared interests or activities? Anybody in his private life, for example?' Ruth hesitated. 'I'm sure you want to help, and your discretion is admirable. But we need to find him. Nobody vanishes so completely like this unless there's something very wrong.'

Janna hesitated and dropped her gaze for a moment. 'I don't know what to tell you.'

'Whatever you know… whatever you've heard,' Ruth persisted gently. 'Anything, however remote or unlikely, please tell me. If it gives me a lead it could be of enormous help to James and his family.'

There was a long pause, then Janna said, 'There was a rumour about Valerie. I didn't give it any credence, personally… but she and James seemed fairly close, I heard.'

'Who's Valerie? Do you have a surname?'

Janna blinked. 'You've already met her. Downstairs. Valerie DiPalma – our receptionist.'

'Could you ask her to come up here, please? I'd love to speak with her.'

'Of course.' She reached for the phone and asked for Valerie DiPalma. She listened for a moment, before replacing the phone and frowning. 'I don't understand.'

'What?' said Ruth.

'She's not there. The security guards said she felt unwell and went home. Right after you arrived.'

Ruth stood up. 'Can you give me an address?' She felt the press of urgency. It just seemed too coincidental, the receptionist leaving the building so suddenly.

Janna tapped her keyboard and scribbled down the details on a slip of paper, and held it out. 'She's listed online, so please don't tell her I gave you this information.'

'Of course.' Ruth took the piece of paper. It showed a Newark address. If DiPalma had been close to Chadwick, she was probably the only person who might have some idea about why he had gone off the radar and where he might be now. They could only find that out if they got to her before she, too, disappeared. 'Thank you, Janna. I appreciate your help.'

12

Tommy-Lee turned as the door opened and Paul stuck his head in. He didn't say anything but checked everything with a look, then signalled for Tommy-Lee to follow him outside.

The man on the bed watched them, unblinking and silent, then turned his back and huddled up close, like he knew something bad was about to happen.

The evening air hit Tommy-Lee like a sledgehammer. It was warm and sweet and tasted of dust stirred up by the arrival of the van. But it was still a million times better than the foetid air he'd been breathing inside the box. He winced at the brightness of the light after the gloom, and shielded his eyes. It would have been good to have his shades, but they were back in Dougie's place and he was hardly in a position to go back and get them.

He took a deep breath and feasted his eyes on the open spaces. Wherever they were, the scenery went on for ever. He turned and looked at his temporary home. He hadn't seen it in daylight before. It was an ancient shed, like a small workshop, with warped overlap wooden walls and a corrugated metal roof. A battered wooden door hid the inner door, and windows down the side showed the bare wood of the inner skin but nothing of the box inside.

Damn, he had to hand it to Paul and his goons; you'd have to come right up to this place to see that there was more to this old place than first appeared. He turned and looked round and saw the two goons scuttling away towards the hangar, kicking up spurts of dust as they went. It looked like they were in a hurry and he guessed they must have been told to shake it and get under cover before a car came along. Donny was hauling his toolbox as usual and struggling to keep up with Bill, who kept looking at him and waving at him to go faster.

Big, stupid dumbass, thought Tommy-Lee. Would have been quicker if he'd stuck Donny and the box under his arm and carried them both.

'What are they doing, re-wiring the old place?' he said with a grin, and immediately wished he hadn't. Paul fixed him with a stare that could freeze water and slapped a hand on his shoulder, making him turn back to face the door to the room.

'That's no concern of yours. However, this is.' He moved round in front and pushed a slim nylon zip bag against Tommy-Lee's chest. 'Open it.'

Tommy-Lee did and found he was holding an electronic device with a plastic case, about the size of a hardback book. He turned it over and saw a screen with several buttons down one side. It had a hole in one edge for a jack-plug and another for a charger.

'It's a DVD player,' he said. 'I stole a bunch of these off a truck once. Got three hundred bucks back in Kansas City. Man, I got ripped off that time, let me tell you.'

Paul ignored him. 'You know how to work it?'

'Sure. Enough, anyway. Had plenty of time to play with them before I unloaded the whole consignment. What's on it?'

Paul nodded towards the room. 'That's for him to see. I want you to show him.'

'What, just that? No message?'

Paul hesitated, then said, 'Show him first. Let him have time to understand what he's seeing. Then ask him if he knows what it represents. He should answer yes, because it's very clear. But he might pretend otherwise – that it's nothing to do with him. He might scream and shout and plead with you, but you must ignore him, no matter what he might say, what he might tell you… or what he might offer you. Make no mistake, Mr Roddick, no matter what he offers you, ignore it.' He leaned forward until their faces were inches apart, the smell of his cologne suddenly vivid and heavy in Tommy-Lee's nostrils. 'Do. Not. Listen. Everything he tells you will be lies. You understand me?'

'Yeah, sure. I got it. Ignore him. Then what?'

'Then we come to your special… talents, Mr Roddick.'

'Huh?' Tommy-Lee wasn't sure he'd heard right. What the hell was he talking about?

'Your interrogation techniques, of course. Don't all prison guards have them?'

'Well, I wouldn't exactly call that a talent – and we never actually interr—'

'No matter.' Paul cut him off mid-stream with a gesture of impatience. 'Your part is simple. You allow him to run out of steam, then you impress on him that the contents of this disc were filmed just yesterday… and that my men are still in position where those films were shot, close by.'

'Will he understand what that means?'

Paul smiled. It wasn't a pleasant sight and Tommy-Lee figured there was something real bad about this man. It was like a dark light deep down in his eyes, but you could see it if you knew what to look for. And Tommy-Lee knew sure enough. He'd seen the same light in the eyes of detainees in Iraq and a few other places, and it carried something rotten and twisted and dangerous.

Paul said, 'I'm sure he will understand perfectly. But just to make sure – and I don't care how you do it – see that he gets the point fully about what will happen if he doesn't agree to do what I've already asked him.'

'What will you do to him?' The moment the question was out Tommy-Lee wished he'd never asked. It breached an invisible line he instinctively knew he should not have crossed, taking him from being an impartial, paid observer to something else altogether.

It made him one of them.

If Paul shared the same thought, he didn't say so. Instead he murmured coolly, 'Just bear this in mind, Mr Roddick: you'd better convince him to comply.' He checked his watch. 'You have until this time tomorrow, when we come back. Not a moment longer. Because if he says no, it won't be a good outcome for either of you.'

13

Valerie DiPalma's address was east of Newark's Independence Park, in a street of neatly-painted clapboard properties and small businesses. Conveniently close, Ruth decided, to make James Chadwick's apartment easy to reach and keep any relationship – if that's what they had – nice and private.

'Looks nice,' she commented. 'Upmarket chic.'

'It is,' Vaslik agreed, and slid the car into a convenient space. 'There are worse places to live if you have to be close to New York.'

Through the side window they could see the park alongside. It was busy, with games of soccer and baseball, walkers circumnavigating the pathways and others merely sitting and enjoying the atmosphere.

Vaslik led the way, and they reached a small apartment building with a bank of six entry-phone buttons by the front door. Ruth pressed the button against DiPalma's name and signalled to Vaslik that she would take the lead.

'Yes?' The words were slightly distorted by electronics, but the receptionist's voice was clearly recognisable.

'Miss DiPalma, it's Ruth Gonzales. We spoke earlier at StoneSeal. May we speak with you, please?'

'Wha… why?' DiPalma sounded close to panic and her voice faded as if she had backed away from the speaker. 'I'm sorry… I'm not feeling very well. Can we do this another time?'

'Not really. It's very important that we find James. I'm sure you want that too, don't you?' There was no response and for a second Ruth thought she'd been cut off. Then she heard the woman breathing and added gently, 'We're not to here to make judgements, Valerie. We just want to find James.'

There was no answer, but the buzzer sounded and there was click as the door catches were released.

Valerie's apartment was on the second floor at the back, and looked out on a small yard. She was waiting for them. Dressed in jeans and a man's shirt she looked very different from her desk persona at StoneSeal, somehow less distant and cold, and more vulnerable. She stepped back inside and allowed them to enter. It was a small place, comfortable and light, enough for a single person or a couple who liked close proximity. Furnished in a modern, stylish collection of Scandinavian design, it suited its owner for colour and neatness.

Ruth smiled and handed the woman a card containing her cellphone number, but received only a muted response. She took the offered seat on a two-seater settee while Vaslik took a hard-backed chair by the door, signalling his detachment from the conversation.

'I don't know what you think I can tell you about Mr Chadwick,' Valerie said softly, fingering the card. 'There must have been some misunderstanding—'

'We're not interested in your relationship with him,' Ruth said flatly, cutting through her words and making her blink in surprise. 'A man's gone missing and our task is to find him. What your relationship with him might be or might have been is your business, not ours.' She leaned forward, fixing the young woman with a stare. 'Seriously, it's the twenty-first century, Valerie; people get together, become friends or closer – it happens. That's not what we're here for. And neither will we discuss what you tell us with anybody else. We simply need your help in finding out what happened to James and hopefully to bring him back.' She paused, allowing the woman time to think.

'I... we were friends,' Valerie said at last, her face going pink. 'At least, it started that way. He was always nice to me, very polite and correct. Not all men are. We bumped into each other locally a couple of times and we always seemed to laugh a lot, which was nice. I knew he was married, but I could tell he wasn't happy. We were friends at first but it changed…' She looked away, tears forming in her eyes and her voice breaking. 'I'm sorry. I don't know where he is – I promise. I wish I did. I'm worried sick about him.'

'Tell me how he was recently,' Ruth asked. 'You know his moods, his demeanour; how did he seem to you?'

'I'm not sure. He was always busy with work, but we really couldn't discuss what he was involved in. He was very correct about that.'

'Okay. Was he unusually stressed or secretive? Did he show any unusual changes of temperament? Anything.'

'He was under pressure, sure. But that wasn't unusual. But… about two weeks ago he told me he thought he was being followed.'

'Who by?'

'He wasn't sure. A man, that's all he said. I thought he was joking at first. We'd been talking about him being away for a few days on one of his assignments and he kept saying, 'That's classified, ma'am', in a dramatic voice, even when I asked him where we should eat later that evening.' She smiled at the memory and blushed, then looked stricken.

'What?' Ruth prompted her.

Valerie nodded towards a door at the side of the room. 'We were in there… in bed. He had something on his mind, I could tell. I asked him what was wrong and he told me he kept seeing the same man in the street.'

'Where?' said Vaslik.

'Twice near his apartment and outside the StoneSeal building. He said he was sure the man was following him. I said it could be work-related; the security agencies running a background check like they do occasionally. But he said he wasn't working on anything government-related and why would they need to do that?'

'Did he describe this man?' said Ruth.

'No. He just said a man.' She looked at them in turn, brushing away a tear rolling down one cheek. 'I promise you, I have no idea where James might be. This isn't some kind of thing to hide what was building between us; if we were going to get together permanently, we'd do it and be upfront about it.'

'Had you talked about that?'

'Talked around it, sure. Joked about it, too… in a kind of dreamy, wouldn't-it-be-nice way. But we hadn't made the final decision.' She reached into her pocket and pulled out a tissue. 'I'm sorry.'

Ruth allowed her to mop at her eyes, then said carefully, 'Valerie. I know what it's like between work colleagues who develop feelings for each other. It doesn't matter how careful they are, eventually they talk – first about each other and their feelings, then about work, other colleagues and anything else. It's normal. Stuff comes out because that's how things develop. It's natural.' She glanced at Vaslik but he nodded for her to continue. 'Did James confide in you about anything else? It might not have been work related, or about his marriage. But anything… his life generally.'

'You mean like the guy following him?'

'Yes.'

She thought it over, then said, 'There was something he told me about six weeks ago, I think it was, maybe a little more. He'd been to give a talk at a technology convention near Chicago some weeks before that. They'd asked him to participate in a demonstration, and he was excited to be doing something that wasn't about the usual subjects StoneSeal worked on, like economics or business. Anyway, he told me that he was on his way out of the convention center after finishing the demonstration, when he was stopped by a delegate who wanted his help with a business project he was putting together. He told the man he wasn't able to do that because of ongoing work commitments, but the guy wouldn't let it go. He said he was interested in getting a new project off the ground and needed some expert help, and would pay James well to help him. He mentioned twenty-thousand dollars as a fee.'

'That's a lot of help,' said Vaslik.

'That's what he said. He figured the guy was a fantasist just blowing off and wanting to come over as a big shot. But he eventually agreed to have a drink with him, as he figured it might be the best way to let him down lightly without causing offence. They went to a bar and the man chatted about nothing in particular, then asked about James's family. James thought that was getting intrusive, so he decided to leave. That's when the guy dropped a bombshell.' She stopped and dabbed at her eyes, gently shaking her head.

'What kind of bombshell?' Rush asked, and leaned forward. 'Valerie? What did this man say or do?'

'He... he suddenly got very angry, as if James had promised him something than let him down. He made it obvious that he knew a whole lot more about James than he'd first pretended; he knew where he worked, where he lived – even that James was something of an expert in the specific field he'd been talking about at the convention.' She shivered. 'James said it was creepy, how quickly he switched from being friendly to being very threatening, and how he seemed to know all about James's life going back years – as if he'd been studying him.'

'What did he do?'

'He told the man he couldn't help him and walked out. It was the only thing he could think of. I asked him why he hadn't called the police, but he said the guy was clearly a nut and he didn't want to make waves. But I know he was thinking about it for a while after and he said he might mention it to somebody. But I don't know if he ever did.'

'You said James was an expert in this field of technology. Did he talk to you about it or mention any specifics?'

'No. He'd once mentioned that he was planning to take his son, Ben to a model exhibition in England, and said he'd always been into that kind of stuff. But he… we didn't really talk about that side of his life much. I think he found it very difficult and I didn't want to intrude. To be honest, it was easier for us both to avoid the subject.'

'But the convention definitely wasn't work-related?'

'No. He told me it was all separate from work. I think it was his way of unwinding.' She gave a small shrug. 'I think he knew I wasn't really into it so he didn't discuss it.'

Vaslik said, 'Do you remember the name of the convention?'

She gave it some thought and said, 'It was something like Unmanned Aerial Expo or words like that. Sorry – I don't remember exactly. It was near Chicago airport, I know that, because he mentioned getting a shuttle bus that had been laid on for exhibitors and delegates.'

When Vaslik didn't say anything, Ruth glanced at him. He was sitting very still, his forehead creased in a frown as if he'd experienced a surprise.

Valerie noticed his expression, too, and took it to mean he'd misunderstood her. She added quickly, 'I'm sorry. James said it was all about unmanned systems for commercial and private use. He reckoned it was going to be all the rage very soon but he wasn't sure that it was a good thing. He certainly seemed to know a lot about it, and said there was a certain type of technology that had started out as a toy, but was now available in advanced versions with dangers that hadn't been fully considered.'

'What kind,' Ruth interjected, 'of unmanned systems was he talking about?'

'Quad-something or other, he said. I can't recall now. Radio-controlled flying machines, anyway.' She smiled. 'He's a bit of a geek on the quiet.'

'Quad-copters?' Vaslik sat up. 'Did he say quad-copters?'

'That's it. He showed me a picture on Google. It looked like something out of Star Wars.' She looked at Vaslik. 'Does that help?'

'Maybe. Maybe not.' Vaslik was looking serious. 'There are lots of different types and names. But most people call them drones.'

14

As soon as they were back in the car, Vaslik took out his phone. Ruth waited to see who he was calling, but realised he was using Google.

'Damn,' he said finally. 'This is hard core.'

'What is it?'

'The conference Chadwick attended; it was the Unmanned Aerial Systems Expo at the Allstate Arena near O'Hare International Airport. These things are commercial-level right up to military and law-enforcement grade. They're used for anything from traffic surveillance through to land surveys, forestry and locating missing persons. Chadwick must really be into this stuff.'

'He'd have to be good to be invited to take part, then.'

'I guess. I've seen these things fly; it isn't as simple as it looks and there are all sorts of rules and regulations about where you can use them. Still, it doesn't tell us why this mystery man was trying to get Chadwick to show him how to use them.'

'Maybe he was genuine and after some easy help.'

'What, twenty-thousand bucks' worth? That's a lot of money for a startup to throw around. I'm pretty sure there are Xbox generation kids out there who could do it for next to nothing.'

'How far are we from the Cruxys office?'

'About fifteen miles or forty minutes if the traffic's good, maybe longer. Why?'

'I need to make a couple of calls, one on a secure line.'

Vaslik started driving while Ruth dialled up the Cruxys office to warn them that they were coming in. The local bureau chief – and thus far, the only employee in situ – was named Walter Reiks, an FBI veteran, and he promised to be there to help them. They were soon in moderate to heavy traffic heading towards New York City. Ruth closed her eyes and tried to make sense of things while she had the chance. Everything told her that James Chadwick was in trouble. He had a good relationship with his son, a not-so-good one with his wife, and a burgeoning closeness to Valerie DiPalma that looked from one side as if it might go the distance. So why would he simply disappear without explanation? Work stress might have contributed, but from what they knew so far, he hadn't seemed on the edge of a breakdown.

Except there was the mystery man from Chicago and the watcher from Newark to account for. What the heck was that about?

They arrived at the office, which was in an unimposing twelve-story building on W 31st Street, and made their way up to the sixth floor. Vaslik was carrying a plastic bag containing the knife and the hardhat. A man with a buzzcut and the obvious look of a law-enforcement professional was there to greet them, standing by an empty reception desk.

'Good to meet you both,' he said briskly, shaking hands. 'Walter Reiks. We're still setting up here so please forgive the lack of decoration and formality. There's an office and a secure line you can use down this way and I've arranged coffee in five minutes. Let me know if you need anything else.'

'You've been briefed about the Chadwick Code Red?' Ruth asked him.

'I have. Any news so far?'

'A little,' said Ruth. 'But so far it's muddy and not looking great. We'll circulate a report later for all eyes.'

'I look forward to it. Come this way.' He led them to an office with two chairs and a desk, and left them to it.

Ruth called London and got through to Aston, and gave him a brief summary of what they had discovered so far. It sounded disappointingly little in the telling, but Aston was quick to acknowledge that it was early days. His voice on the speaker unit sounded calm and encouraging.

'What do you need?' he said when she finished speaking.

'The first thing is talk to Elizabeth Chadwick again, and if possible, her son Ben. There's something that doesn't quite gel about Chadwick's expertise with UAVs or drones. So far it's the only thing we've found that might offer an explanation about his disappearance. If he'd got an in-depth knowledge about drones, it might help to know where he got it.'

'Is there anything that stands out?'

'Two things. He's always had an interest in flying model airplanes. But radio-controlled kits are a long way from drones.'

'What else?'

'He used to be with Air Force Intelligence.'

'Really? That's something we didn't know about. I wonder why he didn't disclose it. But I think that might be your answer. The US has a highly advanced drone development programme and they're not all about warfare. There's a constant spill-over into commercial use with smaller machines. Can you follow up his record locally?'

'Andy Vaslik already tried. Chadwick's service record was on restricted access… and it got pulled a month ago.'

'It would be good to know why. He left the USAF what – four years ago?'

'That's right. But maybe they've got him on a string as a reservist.'

'Or somebody thinks he's gone rogue, in which case they'll be on his trail, too. I'll leave it to you to do some digging, but be careful. In the meantime I can patch you through to Elizabeth and Ben Chadwick; we've got them at a safe house. Hold one.'

Seconds later, she had Elizabeth on the line. She sounded stressed and irritable, rather than concerned. 'How long are we going to be kept here?' the woman demanded. 'I have a life to lead and Ben needs to be back at school. Have you found him yet – and why are we being forced to hide like fugitives?'

Ruth bit her tongue and said, 'Not yet. I'm sorry. We have some leads but I can assure you that James isn't doing this on purpose.' She was tempted to tell Elizabeth of their suspicions that her husband had been taken for unspecified reasons, but knew that would do more harm than good. Instead she said, 'We only moved you because we found information that led us to believe your address and Ben's school address had been taken during a break-in at James's Newark apartment. It could be entirely unconnected, but I'm sure you can see why, with James's disappearance, we didn't want to take any chances. Keeping you and Ben safe is our main concern. It's what James would have wanted.'

'I see. I'm sorry, I didn't mean—'

'Please, don't apologise. I'd be climbing the walls if it were me. The thing I have to ask is, you mentioned James had an interest in flying model airplanes. How involved was he and at what level?'

'What? How does that help find him?' Elizabeth replied. 'He flew models, that's all I know. He always had done since he was a boy, I think. Frankly, it never interested me and still doesn't.'

'In that case can I speak to Ben, please?'

'Why?'

'Because he might know more about James's interest in models. I know it sounds odd, but the more we know about James, the greater chance we have of finding him.'

'I see. Wait.'

There was a long silence than Ben Chadwick came on the line. He sounded very young and worried. 'Hello? Have you found my dad?'

'Not yet,' said Ruth. 'Ben, my name is Ruth Gonzales. You can call me Ruth. I'm in New York helping to search for him and it looks like we could do with your help.'

'Me? But how? I mean, I don't know anything.'

'You know about flying models, like your dad does.'

'Oh. Right. What kind of investigator are you?'

'I look for missing people.'

'Do you always find them?'

'Always. Nobody can stay hidden for ever, Ben. Everybody leaves a trace, and it's up to me and my partner, Andy Vaslik, to find those traces.'

'Are you a cop?'

'I was once. Andy, too. He's American and was with Homeland Security. You've heard of them? Like the FBI.'

'Of course. Man, that's cool.' There was a rumble of conversation and he said, 'Sorry – what do you want from me?'

'How good was your dad with flying machines?'

There was a short silence, then he said, 'He was fantastic. He knew all about them. Gliders, kit planes, model helicopters – all of them. He was going to take me to an exhibition this week but he wasn't able to make it.' His voice faltered on the last few words.

'Drones. Did he ever talk about drones?'

The boy's voice perked up again. 'Yes. He said drones had changed the nature of warfare. I saw some television programmes about them and I saw what he meant. Reapers and Predators, they're called, and they carry weapons.' He paused and his voice went low. 'They kill people.'

'What about small ones, Ben? Did he talk about small drones, like the kind they use to monitor traffic and take aerial surveys?' She was aware of Elizabeth in the background probably on the verge of freaking out at all this talk of weapons and killing and in danger of closing down the conversation just when it was getting interesting.

'Yes, a lot. He said they were as different from kit planes as Formula One cars are from family sedans. He called them sedans instead of saloons, but I knew what he meant. You know he's American, right?'

'I do, Ben.' She put a smile in her voice and hoped it was apparent at the other end. 'Your dad's a bit of a geek about drones, then?'

'Way more than a bit. I'm doing a science and tech project at school, and he's given me loads of stuff to use. I'm hoping to have a drone of my own one day and he'll teach me to fly it!'

It was her opening for the next question. 'So he knows how to fly them, too?'

'Of course. He's an expert. He told me once that he gets calls from all over asking him to talk about them. It's not his job but he does it for fun. He showed me a DVD once where he was racing other drones over a course using GPS coordinates. He won by a mile. You know what that is, GPS, don't you?'

'Yes, Ben, I know. Where was this race?'

'I don't know. Somewhere in the States on an air force base. He tells me this stuff all the time, but I don't always remember the details, because some of them are complicated.' He paused. 'I don't mean complicated.'

'Confidential?'

'Yes, that's right. But he doesn't tell me anything secret.'

There was more murmuring in the background and Ruth knew the conversation had run out of time.

'I've got to go,' said Ben hurriedly. 'It's been great talking to you, Miss Gonzales. Find my dad. Please.' Then he was gone and his mother was talking.

'Was all that really necessary?' she muttered angrily. 'You got him all excited talking about flying models. How does that help?'

Ruth counted to five, telling herself that beneath the anger and resentment, Elizabeth was worried, probably as much for her husband as her son's future. She wondered how she herself would be feeling if she was being kept in a safe house without any information about when she might be able to go home.

'I'm sorry, Elizabeth,' she said calmly. 'Ben's been a great help and I appreciate you letting me talk to him. He's being very brave.'

'Braver than me, you mean? I'm sorry. Call me when you have anything.'

The phone clicked and she was gone.

Ruth looked at Vaslik, who shrugged. They both turned as the door opened and Walter Reiks appeared. He looked worried.

'Sorry, folks,' he said quietly. 'I've got a couple of people out here waving badges. They say they're on official business.'

'What sort of business?' said Ruth.

'They want everything we've got on James Chadwick.'

15

Vaslik looked at him. 'Who are they?'

'One is FBI. Him I can deal with. The other says he's with the Pentagon Force Protection Agency.'

'What is that?' Ruth asked.

'They're a civilian agency set up after nine-eleven by the Department of Defence, with responsible for security in and around the Pentagon.' He looked between them. 'Seems like our Mr Chadwick has attracted some heavy-duty hitters.'

He turned and beckoned his visitors. Footsteps echoed along the corridor and two men entered the office.

Both men wore dark suits, were clean-shaven and in their early forties. But that's where any similarities ended. The first man brushed past Reiks without formality and stood looking at Ruth and Vaslik, feet apart as if ready for a fight. He was close to six feet tall, thin, with the look of a former military man and an unfriendly glint in his eye.

'I'm Special Agent Lars Bergstrom,' he announced shortly, 'Pentagon Force Protection. This is Special Agent Tom Brasher, FBI.' He gestured behind him at the other man, who was shorter and fleshier but looked a lot friendlier.

'Ma'am… sir,' Brasher said and nodded.

Reiks walked over to the desk and perched on the edge. He didn't offer the newcomers seats, but said, 'Maybe you could enlarge for Miss Gonzales and Mr Vaslik, here, on what it is you want from us – and why.' He spoke politely enough but it was clear that, new as he was to the Cruxys organisation, he wasn't about to give way to Bergstrom's heavy-handed tactics.

'It's simple enough.' Bergstrom ignored Ruth and fastened his grey eyes on Vaslik. 'We've been informed that you have an interest in James Chadwick, who appears to have dropped out of sight for no accountable reason. Correct?'

Vaslik nodded. 'That's right. But how would you know that?'

'We have our sources.' Bergstrom's eyes flickered sideways, inadvertently betraying the fact that his source was the FBI. 'My question is, why are you looking for him? And what the hell is Cruxys, anyway?'

Ruth cleared her throat to establish her presence. She didn't like Bergstrom or his manner, and suspected this was his usual method of approach; go in hard and tough and bully his way past objections to get quick answers. She also guessed that he knew precisely what Cruxys was because he would have researched it thoroughly before coming here. She didn't doubt that, hard-nosed as he was, Bergstrom was also professional enough to have checked his facts.

'We're an insurance and security company,' she said calmly, 'as I'm sure you already know.' She waited for him to interrupt, but he merely lifted his eyebrows and studied her with a blank expression. 'We became aware a few days ago that James Chadwick had broken his normal routines and disappeared. He has a security contract with our company – a form of insurance, if you like – and part of our remit is to help and support his family while we find out what has happened to him. That's what we're doing here.'

'Yes, I know all about Cruxys… and Greenville, Miss – Gonzales? Seems like a neat business model you have there. You're British, right?'

'Yes.'

'Okay. Tell me, how did you 'become aware', as you put it, that he'd gone off the radar? You must monitor all your clients' movements very closely.'

'Only those who ask us to.' She saw no reason to go into details unless he demanded it. 'We've spoken to his wife and employers, who have no idea where he is, and we're now trying to narrow down the search based on his last known movements and contacts. But it's a big country.'

'Any luck with that?' Brasher chipped in. He seemed a lot less aware of himself and spoke with studied calm.

'Not yet. But it's early days.'

'Indeed it is,' Bergstrom muttered. 'Perhaps you'd be good enough to show us what you do have.' It wasn't a polite request, more like an order, and Ruth wondered what his problem was.

'Show us ours and you'll show us yours, you mean?' she said. When he didn't reply she added, 'Why don't you go first.'

His eyes glinted and the muscles in his jaw tensed. He stared hard at Ruth as if suspecting that she was teasing him and shook his head. 'We don't work like that, Miss Gonzales. As a visitor to this country I'd like to remind you—'

'That's fine.' Brasher stepped forward and raised a hand. This time he had a harder edge to his voice. He threw Bergstrom a look which told the other man to pull in his head and said, 'I think we need to put our cards on the table. It's obvious we have a lead on information here, so maybe we can cut to the chase.' He smiled. 'I'm sure everybody here knows that what we discuss goes no further unless it has to.'

Somewhere in the background a door opened and closed. Reiks nodded. 'Good idea. Before we do, how about coffee? I believe supplies have arrived.' He winked at Ruth to show he was playing for time, then stood and walked out of the office and down the corridor. Moments later he was back carrying a vacuum container and a stack of cardboard mugs from a nearby coffee bar. He handed them out and dropped sachets of sugar and wooden stirrers on the desk and let everybody help themselves. Then he went out and dragged two chairs inside for the visitors and resumed his place against the edge of the desk.

'Go ahead, Special Agent Brasher,' he said. 'It's clear you know more than we do.'

Brasher stirred his coffee and took a sip, then sat down and waited pointedly for Bergstrom to do the same before saying, 'We'd like to know the current whereabouts of James Chadwick. He filed a report recently suggesting he'd been threatened and followed by persons unknown. Recent analysis and review of the details lead us to believe that there's a facet to his claim that was missed first time round. We think he might have become involved in something serious.'

'What kind of serious?'

'It's possible he's become engaged in a potential terrorist threat against the Pentagon and other federal government facilities.'

16

The atmosphere back inside the box tasted to Tommy-Lee like licking the soles of his boots. After the brief taste of fresh air outside, he could hardly breathe for the foul smell of body odour, the latrine bucket and the growing presence of flies.

He placed the DVD player on his bed and listened for the fading sounds of the van heading east along the road into the darkening sky. After delivering his orders and the DVD player, along with spare batteries for the storm lantern, Paul had allowed him to sit outside for a few minutes until Bill and Donny had returned from the hangar. It was, he figured, the only concession he was likely to get because Paul needed him to talk to the prisoner. Quite why he couldn't do it himself he hadn't yet figured out, but maybe he thought it was beneath him.

The moment the two goons were on board, Paul had motioned for him to get back in the room and locked the door behind him.

He opened the DVD player. It looked store-bought new and smelled of plastic. He wondered how much they'd paid for it. It seemed a pretty odd thing to do, having him play the contents to the prisoner. And he wondered why Paul hadn't yet spoken to the man himself. In fact he'd behaved pretty much as if he wasn't even there, shackled to the bed. Like he didn't exist.

Still, he'd come across officers in the military like that back in Iraq; they didn't like to acknowledge that they were part of what the detainees were going through, and came in and got out again like their asses were on fire. Unlike some of the spooks who came and went all the time; they were all hardcore and ready to do stuff if they had to. But most would walk in, tell Tommy-Lee what they wanted to know, then leave it to him to do what he had to because they'd been told he was good at it and didn't mind getting his hands dirty.

Pussies the lot of them. He wondered if that was Paul's problem.

He heard a grunt from across the room and looked up. The man was barely half-sitting, his body twisted at an angle because of the handcuffs. He was looking at Paul, and the DVD player as if he knew it was the next stage in what was happening to him. His next words confirmed it.

'Is that for me?' His voice was a croak but he didn't ask for water this time.

'I guess.' Tommy-Lee nodded and stood up. He opened a bottle of water and held it to the man's lips. It felt lukewarm but that was all they two of them were going to get.

When the man had had enough, he lifted his chin and lay back, letting the last of the water roll around the inside of his mouth a few times before swallowing.

Tommy dragged the chair across so the DVD player could sit right where the man could see it. Then he hit the PLAY button.

The first thing he saw was a street scene. It didn't look like any street he'd ever been in and he figured it had to be somewhere foreign; it had that look about it. Then the camera panned across a white street sign with red and black lettering. He couldn't make out the red letters because it was in some fancy script and the camera wasn't too steady. But the black letters were easy to read: SYDNEY STREET, and then in red again, only bigger, S.W.3.

The scene cut and shifted, this time to an elegant building set among huge trees, a mixture of conifers and evergreens, and sculpted gardens among expansive, rolling lawns. A group of teenage boys in smart blazers and grey pants were walking from a side building into the main entrance, with a man in a suit hurrying them along with impatient gestures. Something told Tommy-Lee this was out in the country somewhere; there was that look you get outside of a city, of light and open spaces. Something about the building reminded him of that British television series, *Downton Abbey*, which his pal's Dougie's girlfriend had a thing about. The time he'd had to sit through that crap because Dougie was too pussy-whipped to turn it over. Still, at least he was spared that for now.

The camera panned away and settled on a large sign at the entrance to a neat, gravelled driveway. The sign read: TIVENHALL PREPARATORY SCHOOL FOR BOYS.

The effect on the prisoner was electric, like nothing he'd seen or heard before. The howl began deep in the man's throat and made the hairs on the back of Tommy-Lee's neck stand on end.

'Hey, what the—?' He grabbed the man by the shoulder and shook him hard, but it didn't seem to register. Instead his body arched off the bed and only the handcuffs prevented the man from rolling to the floor.

Tommy-Lee didn't mind admitting to himself that right then he was frightened. He'd dealt with more than a few detainees in Iraq who'd gone batshit crazy in the end, enraged by their circumstances to the point of wanting to throw themselves straight at a gun if they could have done so. Some of the worst had been the little guys, the sort you could almost pick up with one hand, lean and mean and all sinew, muscle and hate. Suddenly, after months of seeing a near-docile individual who wouldn't say boo to a goose, you were dealing with a crazed human being with more strength than four people, who'd throw off a couple of guards trying to restrain him with no more effort than shrugging off a coat. They'd kick and spit and if you got in the their way, no matter how strong you were, they'd take you down as if you were a ten-year old.

He pushed the DVD player to one side and leaned on the man, pinning him by his shoulders until he started to go quiet.

It took a while, all the time with the guy staring up without seeing him, his mouth working and dragging in air as if it was his last.

'Easy,' Tommy-Lee muttered, and leaned over to put himself in the guy's line of sight. But it didn't do any good at first; whatever the prisoner was seeing, it was something, somebody or somewhere a long way from here.

After a while the tremors running through the man's body ceased and he turned on his side facing the wall and went quiet. His eyes were closed and his breathing gradually went back to normal. He was covered in sweat but that was normal in this shitty box. At least sweat showed he wasn't too dried out that he might die.

Tommy-Lee stood up, scooped up the DVD player and went back over to his own bed. There was probably a bit more film to come so he decided to watch it by himself.

He killed the sound, which had been all background hiss but no commentary, and took up watching from the point where he'd seen the school sign. There were more scenes of the houses in Sydney Street, with one in particular where the camera zoomed right up to a front door and hovered on a black, fancy iron door knocker with a horse's head. Then it cut away and showed a busy street full of shoppers, like a mall but narrow and crowded with stores.

He fast-forwarded the film after a while until a new scene came up. This showed a park through some chain fencing, with a bunch of kids playing baseball in the distance, and nearby, a couple of old people sitting on a bench and laughing at something they'd said. And right away Tommy-Lee knew this scene was in the US.

Then the camera began to pan round, making his eyes go funny, and suddenly he was looking at an apartment block on the other side of a street. It looked neat and brick-built, and the front entrance suddenly grew in the lens and showed a line of entry-phone buttons and a speaker box with a grill. He wondered what this was about when the camera began to move forward and he realised the guy holding it was walking across the street towards the apartment block, and the detail of the picture was changing as he changed the focus.

He must have stopped right close to the entry-phone because the next thing Tommy-Lee saw was a white card alongside one of the buttons and a name.

Valerie DiPalma.

Then the screen went dead.

He shook his head. Damned if that made any sense. He hadn't got a clue what the places were or where, but it obviously made sense to the guy on the other bed, otherwise why the howling wolf act just now?

He heard a noise and looked up. The prisoner had relaxed fully and had turned his head and was watching him. He was still sweating and red in the face with his exertions, but no longer breathing heavy.

'You want some water?' Tommy-Lee asked.

'No.' The croaky voice said otherwise but that was the man's choice; he wasn't going to force it on him. 'I want to see the rest.'

Tommy-Lee thought it over. He had to show him, there was no question, otherwise Paul and his buddies might take it seriously. 'Are you gonna go all lunatic on me again if I do? 'Cos I tell you, you do that again and I'll swat you like a fly.'

'No. I'm fine.' The prisoner tried to sit up, but fell back with a sigh.

Tommy-Lee moved over to the other bed and showed him the rest of the DVD.

17

There was a lengthy silence while they all digested what Brasher had said.

'Chadwick a terrorist threat?' Ruth said. 'How do you make that out – and how long have you known about any of this this?'

Brasher looked nonplussed, as if they were questions he hadn't been expecting or maybe didn't want asked. He took out a slim notebook from his coat pocket and flipped it open, checking the details before explaining, 'Three weeks ago James Chadwick made a late-night phone call to US Air Force Office of Special Investigations in Quantico, Virginia. He was described by the duty officer as sounding agitated and didn't seem to know who he should speak to. He expressed concerns about an individual who had approached him in Chicago some weeks prior to that date. He'd been attending a conference and exhibition on the use and development of small UAVs – that's unmanned aerial vehicles – for commercial use. This individual, who introduced himself only as Paul, said he was seeking expertise as he and his colleagues were looking to capitalise on the potential of drones in the commercial sector.'

'Them and Amazon,' Reiks commented dryly. 'Did he say why he called the Air Force and not the FBI or Homeland Security?'

Brasher nodded. 'Not specifically, but we know Chadwick served with USAF Intelligence several years ago and it seems reasonable to assume that as a former officer he decided to seek directions from them first. He told them of his concerns and how this person had offered to pay him a substantial sum of money to help him with a start-up venture involving UAVs, but needed someone with expertise to help train him and his colleagues to fly and demonstrate the machines. Chadwick described this as very un-businesslike and an unlikely scenario for a start-up. As you probably know, he's a financial and business consultant so I guess if anybody had an opinion on the matter, he would. Anyway, he said his concerns were heightened when he made it clear he was unable or unwilling to help and the gentleman became forceful and aggressive.'

'Sounds like a nut job,' Reiks ventured. 'What happened?'

'Because he had no specific threat to speak of, he was advised to call us at the FBI.'

'And did he?' said Vaslik.

'Yes, he did, only three days later.' He tilted his head sideways. 'My guess is he was unsure of what to do, so he may have been debating following through on his initial call. Anyway, he was put through to our Joint Terrorism Task Force and talked to a member of our investigative support team. He relayed the conversation he'd had with this Paul guy and also mentioned that he was thought he was being followed. He was particularly concerned because this Paul guy had made it clear that he knew a great deal about Chadwick's personal life and family details here and in London.'

He stopped and sat back, snapping the notebook shut.

'And just from that,' Ruth said, 'the FBI believes he's a terrorist threat? You're kidding. It sounds as if he was the one being threatened.'

'I didn't say it was justified, but we have to go with what we've got.' He seemed to lack a degree of conviction in what he'd said just moments before and Ruth wondered why.

'Don't tell me,' she said softly.

Reiks looked at her. 'What?'

'We screwed up.' The admission from Brasher came out hard and flat and he looked embarrassed, his face flushing.

'How?' Vaslik asked.

'The support specialist who took the call passed it on up the line for action, but it coincided with a flood of high-level alerts and reports of terrorist-related activity which had to be investigated as a matter of extreme urgency. Chadwick's call wasn't ignored in any way, but it was rated as of secondary importance to other parallel reports and threats at the time.' He rubbed a hand across his face at the shocked silence from the others in the room and added, 'By the time the team got back to it a day or so later, it was suggested that Chadwick might have been…' He stopped and waved a hand.

'A what?' said Ruth.

'A fantasist.' He sat forward and looked around at the faces with more than a degree of professional embarrassment. 'Some were of the opinion that he was nothing more than a former Air Force spook wanting to see this approach as more than it actually was. In their defence I have to say it's not uncommon for former law-enforcement or security agency personnel to have a heightened sense of perspective about these things. They relate it to their own experience and the state of threat today, and it builds up in their minds to something bigger. And because they often have access to more specific inside contacts than the general public, they find themselves pumping it up a little.'

'That doesn't explain,' Vaslik murmured, 'how he got slapped with the terrorist threat label.'

Brasher stuffed the notebook back in his pocket with a degree of defeat. 'It's a precaution, that's all. The report was reviewed by our intelligence analysts in the last couple of days, and their conclusion was that Chadwick must have been compromised in some way. And because of his Intel background, he would probably have access to information that would be of help to terrorists. I'm not excusing my colleagues in any way… I'm just saying how it is.'

Bergstrom had been silent throughout Brasher's words, merely sipping his coffee and staring into the cup. It was an indication that he probably already knew about the stuff-up and had said plenty on the subject already.

'What's your take on it, Agent Bergstrom?' Ruth asked him. 'Do you think he was fantasising?'

He took a moment to answer, and Ruth thought he was ignoring her altogether. Finally he said, 'I don't know, Miss Gonzales. Frankly, we shouldn't dismiss anybody who makes a report of this nature, no matter who they are. But Tom's right about one thing: there's been an unusually heavy flush of alerts, internet and phone chatter coming in for the past few weeks, all pointing towards something about to happen. When it reaches a certain pitch like that it takes a vast amount of work to weed out the crap from the real intelligence. The two things together – the chatter and Chadwick's report – served to cloud the issue. It shouldn't happen but it does. As we know to our cost.'

'What sort of chatter was it?'

'It's difficult to analyse clearly and I haven't seen all of it – only those bits that affect me and my colleagues. There have been many references to a high-value 'hit' on a government facility. None of them are specific and it's mostly wishful thinking. But there have been a couple of recent references to – and I quote – "The wounded beast, damaged but not brought down in the glorious holocaust." That last reference has been used by some jihadists to refer to nine-eleven, and in many views the wounded beast is the Pentagon.' He shrugged. 'It's as valid an explanation as any.'

There was a silence until Reiks said, 'So what's the current view? That commercial drones are the next jihadists' weapons of war?'

Brasher looked grim. 'God, I hope not. We'd never see them coming.'

'Is that even possible?' Ruth asked.

'It's worse than that – it's real. The machines Chadwick was talking about at the conference are extremely high-tech and capable of some amazing stuff. They can move at anything between forty and seventy miles per hour and the payload capabilities and flight distances are being stretched all the time.

There are strict regulations governing their use in certain areas, but they're being tested, too.'

Vaslik said, 'I suppose they're easily available?'

'Sure – if you have the money. My guess is they'd probably steal one to avoid paperwork or records. And I doubt they'd be signing up for any authorised training for the same reasons; it would leave too much of a trail.'

Ruth nodded. 'That explains why James Chadwick was approached.'

A silence descended on the room while they all considered the probability of anything like that happening. After the horrors of 911, it didn't take much for any of them to imagine anything so seemingly outlandish; in modern guerrilla or terrorist warfare, anything was possible if the technology was available.

Ruth decided to take a break and the others agreed. She excused herself while Reiks got busy arranging more coffee and some sandwiches. As she walked down the corridor towards the washroom her cell phone buzzed.

It was a withheld number. 'Gonzales.'

'Ruth? Hi. Thank God I caught you.' It was Valerie DiPalma. She sounded animated, the words pouring out of her in a rush. 'I've found something but I don't know if it's important or not. Can you come over to my place? I was clearing out the trunk of my car just now and I found an iPad hidden under a blanket. It belongs to James.'

18

'This sounds crazy, I know,' said Valerie on opening the door to Ruth. 'I'm not sure how long StoneSeal are going to put up with me being away, but I couldn't face going in there and answering questions so I decided to get busy to take my mind off things. When I found the iPad in the trunk of my car I had to talk to you.' She led the way inside the apartment and pointed to a table where the iPad was sitting. 'I recognised it the moment I saw it. Would you like a drink?'

'No, thank you,' Ruth replied. She opened the iPad and began running through the emails and document files. If James Chadwick had chosen to hide this in Valerie's car, he must have had a reason for it. It could have coincided with his apartment being trashed and he'd placed it in the only location he could think of at short notice.

It was quickly clear that James rarely used this iPad for direct business-related purposes. There were few emails, save for brief memo notes he'd sent to himself as reminders, and a few related to general commercial and finance matters that had caught his attention. But there was almost nothing heavily related to StoneSeal apart from general reading matter, notes for further research, lecture outlines and some family topics she didn't open. After a while she began to recognise the style and pattern and was able to rattle through them at speed.

But it was the saved photos and web pages that immediately grabbed her attention. For some reason Chadwick had saved a number of Google Earth maps, most of them focussing on the central US states, like the folding map from the storage room back at StoneSeal. The site searches told her nothing by themselves to account for why he'd been looking at them other than having all been saved recently. Whatever his reasons it showed a clear interest that seemed a lot more than casual. She moved on and found a collection of screen grabs showing what she instantly recognised as airfields, and links to a number of websites dedicated to looking at little-known, defunct, lost or abandoned bases. One site in particular listed abandoned airfields by state, and a quick click of the keys took her to aerial shots of old runways and roads, of taxiways and buildings, some encroached on by more modern building developments and facilities, others still clearly in use for other commercial purposes. More photos showed derelict hangars and support buildings, weed-strewn runways, rusting fuel storage tanks and rotting piles of brickwork and other rubbish. Then she found faded copies of original plans and black-and-white photos of buildings in their prime taken many years ago.

She sat back, puzzled. Abandoned airfields focussed on the states of Nebraska, Kansas and Oklahoma. But what was he looking for?

She checked his history of Google searches. A few took her to websites showing details of Unmanned Aerial Vehicles, or drones, with photos of a whole range of machines including spider-like multi-copters. She didn't know what to make of these; they could have been picked as part of Chadwick's general interest. But how could she tell?

Other searches referred to 'Freedom', with links to towns in the US with that name. Then she found a list of searches that all had striking similarities and felt her neck go cold. They included entries for USAF, USAF Intelligence, Office of Special Investigations, Quantico, Virginia.

Ruth was holding her breath. She was thinking back to what Special Agent Brasher had told them. James Chadwick had been looking for somebody to contact about his fears; about a man named Paul. He'd probably started with the USAF he'd once known and worked his way through a number of searches, trying to narrow down the focus to a specific area, a specific office. No doubt things had changed a lot since his days in the service.

She needed to show this to the others. Bergstrom probably not so much but definitely Vaslik, Reiks and Brasher. She debated keeping it to herself and Vaslik, but realised this had already gone too far; that whatever had happened to Chadwick must in some way be related to the man named Paul, to drones and to abandoned airfields.

She looked up to find Valerie watching her with an air of sombre anticipation. 'Did James ever mention a man named Paul?'

'No. I don't think so. Who is he?'

'Maybe nothing. Just a name that cropped up.'

'Is that it?' the young woman asked softly. She was clutching her hands tightly together and Ruth felt guilty at having inadvertently zoned her out.

'I'm sorry,' she said. 'I didn't mean to ignore you. To be honest I'm not sure what I've got here. But I think I'll have to take this away for a more detailed look.' More than anything she needed a quiet space to do it in and to even get some techies involved as well to do a little in-depth digging. Whatever Chadwick had been searching for lay in this device; the exact why and how they were all linked together was something else entirely; but either way, she had a gut feel that this might be their only chance of finding James Chadwick's current whereabouts.

Valerie nodded. 'Of course. If you think it will help.' Her face was drawn and she looked ready to drop. 'You'll tell me if you find anything, won't you? I didn't realise...' She looked up at the ceiling as a tear rolled down her cheek. '... I mean, I knew how I felt about James, but this... suddenly I know it's a lot more than I realised and it's driving me crazy. I daren't go anywhere in case he calls.' She brushed the tear away. 'I'm so sorry – I must seem a mess. But I just want him back safe.'

Ruth switched off the iPad and stood up. She could only guess how Valerie was feeling right now, but there was nothing she could say that would adequately allay the woman's fears. If James was out there they would find him. But it would be like searching for the proverbial needle in a haystack. 'We've had talks with the FBI,' she assured her, 'and they're helping out. That's a lot more manpower that we can use but until we get a lead to where he might have gone, we're only guessing. If you can, I suggest you go back to work; it would be better than sitting here waiting, I promise. You'd better give me a note of your cell phone and where you'll be staying.'

Valerie nodded and scribbled the details on a piece of paper. The address and phone number were for somewhere called Allentown. Ruth thanked her and walked down to her car. As she stepped out of the front entrance, a man staring at the list of entry phone buttons suddenly turned and walked quickly away. She watched him go, puzzled by the move but her mind on the contents of the iPad. The man was stocky, with a bald patch and short, heavy legs, dark hair and a moustache. He was dressed in a jacket and pants and carrying a small backpack slung over one shoulder.

She shrugged. He could have been a potential tenant checking out the place or a man in town looking for a friend. She had to be careful not to get paranoid about this and start seeing shadows where there were none. It was an easy habit to slip into in this business, where faces and people seemed to crowd into the same arena, while mostly having nothing to do with the case in hand other than of simply being there.

She walked to the car and jumped in, anxious to get back to W 31st Street to meet up with Vaslik and show him what she'd found.

19

On the way back she used the time to think about Chadwick's search for airfields. Why was he checking them out and why focussing on fields in remote areas? Then came a related thought: Ben Chadwick had mentioned his dad flying a drone in a competition on an air force base. Was that the connection? Lots of space, flat, even terrain and presumably no chance of overflying housing or built-up areas. It made sense, but only took her so far. Without a definite lead she could end up going round in circles.

She parked the car and hurried up to the sixth floor, where she was buzzed in by Walter Reiks.

'Bergstrom's gone,' he told her, 'but Tom Brasher's hanging on to see what you've got.'

They walked along the corridor and joined the two men, and Ruth placed the iPad on the desk and showed them what she had found.

'He was a busy man,' Brasher concluded, flicking expertly through the searched sites and opening photos and saved screen grabs in rapid succession. 'And definitely interested in drones… and airfields.' He checked the gallery which contained numerous photos of individual machines and their technical specifications, his son Ben, a good looking but serious kid in his early teens, and a smiling Valerie DiPalma in numerous shots against New York skylines. He seemed about to give up when he sat forward. 'Now, who's this?'

They all leaned over to see. He'd stopped on a thumbnail of a man walking along a quiet street. He opened it to a full-screen view. The photo had been taken from above and late in the day. The detail wasn't perfect, with what appeared to be a glossy film over the scene shown, and a glimpse of nearby tree foliage filtering the available light into fragments. But it was clear enough to show a man of medium height, well-built and with dark hair and a trace of stubble around the jawline.

He clicked on the next photo. It was the same man, but this time taken on a different street near a line of arched sandstone-coloured structures.

Reiks grunted and moved closer. 'Hey, I know that place: it's the East Orange Transit station on Main.'

'Are you sure?' said Brasher.

'I should be. I worked the area undercover when I was with the Bureau and spent more hours camped out around there than I care to remember.' Reiks pointed at the screen where they could make out a green-and-white street sign in the background. 'See, that's the sign for North Arlington Avenue. But what was Chadwick doing there?'

'He lives near East Orange General,' Vaslik said quietly. 'I know the area, too. He could have been walking from home to the station to take him into the city. It's not far.'

'Can you go back to the first photo?' Ruth suggested.

Brasher did as she asked. 'What about it?'

'That's outside his apartment. I recognised the street.' She didn't need Vaslik to corroborate the fact, but he nodded. She pointed at the plastic bag Vaslik had placed by the side of the desk, containing the hardhat and knife. 'The same place we got these.' She explained briefly where they had come from.

Brasher leaned over for a closer look, but didn't touch the bag. 'I can get them looked at.' He leaned back and flicked a finger under one eye, looking at Ruth with a smile. 'I was wondering what the story was, but I'm too polite to ask. I take it the man you tangled with isn't one of these faces.'

'No. He's a new one.'

He turned back to the photo of the man in the street. 'So where was Chadwick standing when he took this?'

'Inside the building.' Ruth pointed at the glossy area where the light seemed fuzzy. 'Probably through a window on the fourth floor; see where the light's reflected off the glass?'

'She's right,' said Vaslik. 'Can you go back to the station shot?'

Brasher did so and zoomed in on the man who looked as if he was turning away to go under one of the arches.

'Looks Latino,' said Reiks. 'Like a million others. Could be anybody. Are there any more?'

Brasher brought up another photo, but it lacked definition and was darker, as if the camera had been in the shade. Even so it showed the man was now in conversation with another individual, this one bigger, heavier and with the hunched shoulders of a bodybuilder.

'Can we run prints of these?' Brasher looked at Reiks.

'No problem.' He handed Brasher a business card. 'We haven't yet set up all our printers but if you send them to this email I'll run some off in the other office.'

A couple of minutes later they were all holding copies of the photos while Reiks excused himself to attend to a phone company rep.

'It confirms it,' Vaslik said softly, 'Chadwick was no fantasist. He was being followed.'

Ruth held her breath, but she wasn't thinking about this photo. Her mind was racing back to the man checking name cards outside Valerie's apartment block.

Vaslik noticed how still she'd gone. 'What's up?'

'How far is it,' she asked, 'from Chadwick's apartment to Independence Park?'

Vaslik thought about it. 'Not far. About four miles, give or take. Why?' Then he caught on. 'You saw something.'

'Yes. As I left Valerie DiPalma's apartment there was a man outside checking the name tags. Mid-thirties, heavy. Maybe middle-eastern. He looked... I don't know – shifty. But I didn't think more about it at the time.'

The atmosphere became electric.

'Damn,' said Vaslik. 'We should have thought of this. If they've been watching Chadwick, they'll have picked up on his relationship with DiPalma.'

Ruth dialled Valerie's number, her heart thudding.

No answer.

She shook her head. 'She told me she wasn't going anywhere.'

She headed for the door and Vaslik followed, throwing a look at Brasher. 'Can you ask the local precinct to send a patrol car by? This could be an attempt to lift her as well.'

'Will do,' said Brasher, picking up his phone.

20

This time Vaslik drove, pushing hard through the traffic with the expertise of long experience working undercover in this city. While he focussed on not killing anybody Ruth kept trying Valerie's number, quietly berating herself for not having reacted to the instinctive warning signals she'd picked up earlier about the man outside the apartment.

Twenty minutes into the journey they received a call from Reiks. He sounded upbeat. 'Brasher's had to split for a meeting, but he got a patrol car to drop by DiPalma's place. She's OK. She said she was asleep and didn't hear the phone. The responding officer believes she may have taken something like a sleeping pill, or it could be exhaustion. DiPalma's promised to keep the door locked until you get there.'

Ruth breathed a sigh of relief and disconnected. She relayed the news to Vaslik.

'We need to move her,' he said. 'If they're tracking her to put pressure on Chadwick, it won't be long before they make a move.'

'Put pressure on him to do what, though?'

'Well, if they want him but can't find him, it would be a simple way to get him to show himself.'

'And if they've already got him they'll use her as leverage to make him do whatever it is they're after.'

'Right.' He steered round a cab double-parked near a delivery truck. 'It would help if we knew what it was this mystery guy really wanted.'

Ruth said nothing. It was like looking down on a giant puzzle when they only had some of the outside pieces to work on. The rest was all supposition and guesswork.

–

They arrived at the apartment block to find a patrol car standing outside and a black female officer chatting with a woman and small child. The officer nodded goodbye to the woman and turned to face them as they approached the entrance.

'Sir, madam – you mind giving me your names and showing me some ID?' She had one hand resting on her hip and looked ready for anything. It was obvious that Brasher's call must have lit a spark under the local police precinct and they'd taken the call seriously.

Vaslik gave the officer their names and showed her his driver's licence. 'We know what this is – it's a potential kidnap intruder scare called in by Special Agent Brasher of the FBI.'

The officer nodded. 'No problem. I already checked with the tenant, a Miss DiPalma, and she's fine. She looks done in but I gather she's had some bad news and it's worn her down. I don't suppose either of you can see the guy in the area?' She gave a minute jerk of her head towards the street without looking round.

Ruth had already been scanning the street and the park across the way, but she couldn't see anybody resembling the man she'd seen earlier. But he could be using the trees or other people in the park as cover and only a thorough search of the area would prove that.

'No,' she said. 'I'm sorry for wasting your time.'

The officer smiled. 'Damn, I love that accent. And no need to apologise, ma'am – it's what we're here for. Have a good one.' She gave Vaslik a more lingering look before climbing back in her car and driving away.

'Christ, Slik,' Ruth muttered, almost laughing with relief. 'Pull it in. We're working here.'

They went up to Valerie's apartment and knocked on the door. She let them in with evident caution and looked at Ruth with puzzlement. 'What's going on?' she asked, stifling a yawn. 'I asked the patrol officer but she just said she'd been asked to check on the address after a nuisance call was made.'

Ruth explained about the man she had seen downstairs, and that they had found evidence that James had indeed been followed by persons unknown. 'I don't mean to alarm you, Valerie, but if anybody is trying to get to James, they might do so by using you. We think it would be a good idea if you could go away for a few days, somewhere nobody would know about. Can you do that?'

'I suppose. I could take a few days' vacation. But why? Have you found any trace of James? What about his iPad – has that helped?'

'The iPad was very useful,' Vaslik said calmly. 'You did the right thing calling us. We haven't finished looking through it yet but we're being helped by the FBI and they'll let us know the minute they find anything.'

'Whoever this is,' she said tentatively, 'whoever you think it is… there's a chance that they already have him, isn't there? Otherwise he'd have called me.'

'We don't know that,' Ruth told her. 'The first thing is to get you to safety; I'm sure James would want that.'

It seemed to act as the trigger they needed. They waited while she went through to her bedroom and packed a small case, then checked the apartment was secure before accompanying her downstairs to her car. While Ruth kept her talking for a moment, Vaslik ran a check on the vehicle to make sure it was clean.

'Keep your cell phone on you at all times,' Ruth warned her, 'and don't come back here until we tell you it's safe to do so. And if you hear from James… or anybody else, call us immediately.' She handed her one of Walter Reik's business cards. 'If you can't reach us, call this man and he'll do whatever's necessary.'

Valerie nodded and stowed the card away in her purse. 'Thank you,' she said, her eyes welling up. 'Thank you, both. I'll wait to hear from you.'

They drove back to the Cruxys office and found Brasher had returned. He pulled a wry face. 'The consensus is that this Chadwick business is serious. I've sent the photos of the guy on the iPad to our technical people to see if NGI can pick him out.' He paused to explain, 'Sorry – that's our current facial recognition system. It's called Next Generation Identification. If the face is anywhere on our database, there's a good chance it'll find him.'

'How long will it take?' Vaslik asked.

'Normally it shouldn't take more than twenty to thirty minutes. But with all the activity we're seeing at the moment, there's a rush of stuff being pushed through all marked top priority. I have to warn you, it's not infallible; but it's a whole lot easier and quicker than going through millions of mugshots.'

While they waited Ruth took over the iPad and looked again at Chadwick's searches for airfields. The discovery of the photos of the man had energised her, and she sensed that they had picked up their first solid lead. It proved that Chadwick hadn't been imagining things about being followed, although there was still a possibility the man named Paul could have been nothing more than an obsessive who'd latched onto him.

But obsessives sometimes became dangerous.

The photos of the airfields were bugging her. She couldn't put her finger on it and she was certain she hadn't seen any of these sites before. Yet a fragment of something was tugging at her memory, demanding attention.

She flicked through the various links; more of aerial shots of runways and taxiways, of fuel storage tanks, outbuildings and hangars, the latter mostly of wood and metal construction with rusting corrugated iron roofs and lots of windows. Many of the airfields appeared to be in partial use, some as museums, some as private flying clubs or small commercial bases. All the pictures carried the same air of melancholy she'd picked up seeing old WW2 airfields back in England, their structures slowly fading into the ground beneath them, remembered and praised by a shrinking few, remnants of a bygone age.

She pushed the iPad away, the links and pictures a clutter of confusion. She turned instead to the map she and Vaslik had found among Chadwick's personal effects at StoneSeal's offices.

She spread it out on the desk and studied the circles and notations she'd seen earlier. Most of the writing meant nothing, seemingly no more than a private code of abbreviations that presumably only Chadwick himself would be able to translate. There were numerous small question marks and asterisks dotted here and there, as if he'd been marking the locations for further investigation, but with no indication of what he might have been looking for. A couple of place names had even been underlined, presumably with a definite aim in mind to look at them in more detail later. But one thing still very apparent was that the circles on the map were all in the same three states she'd noticed before: of Nebraska, Kansas and Oklahoma.

She revised her thoughts on needles in haystacks. This could turn out to be more like grains of dust they were searching for.

While Ruth had been focussing on the maps, Brasher had been talking with Vaslik. He took out his cell phone and hit speed-dial. It was picked up immediately and he asked to speak to somebody called Janice. Moments later he said, 'Jan, I'm on the Chadwick thing at the Cruxys offices. Can you give me the description Chadwick gave of the man who he said was following him?' He waited, then listened for a few moments before saying thank you and disconnecting.

'Chadwick was asked for a description of the man who approached him, this Paul guy. He said he was mid-height, stocky but not fat, and could have been of Latino extraction but sounded pure American.' He tapped the screen of the iPad. 'It's not the guy you saw outside DiPalma's place, Ruth – there's no moustache. Could it have been muscles, here?'

'No. He wasn't that big or that young – and he walked upright. He looked very... ordinary.'

'Most of them do. So now we've got three guys, possibly connected, possibly not.'

'And the watcher I tangled with at Chadwick's apartment,' Ruth reminded him.

He nodded. 'Him, too. It's getting crowded.'

'I wonder why Chadwick didn't send in the photos when he called in his report,' Vaslik said. 'He must have known it would strengthen his claim.'

'Maybe he never got the chance,' Brasher replied quietly. 'If this Paul guy was watching him this close, he might have figured that sooner or later he'd talk to us and decided to cut to the chase and take him.' He stopped as his phone buzzed and excused himself to take the call. He listened for a few moments, making quick notes on his notepad, then told the person on the other end to pull up a file of the suspect, before turning to the others with a mixed look of triumph and uncertainty.

'We've got a hit.' He tapped the photo of the second man, the weightlifter figure seen under the arches at the Transit station. 'NGI says his name is Bilal Ammar. Aged 28, he's been here about fifteen years, came over from Egypt with his father, an IT consultant on a work visa and settled in Queens. When his father died of cancer he dropped out of school and became radicalised at a local mosque in Queens. He came to our attention mixing with a known pro-terror support group running a website calling for jihad against the West. Most of the group are hot-heads who like mixing with protest marches and starting fights. Ammar was picked up in connection with two serious assaults on anti-jihadist Muslims who were trying to calm things down at a couple of larger mosques in the city.'

'How come he's walking free?'

'The usual: they couldn't prove anything because the victims were unwilling to identify him. In the end they had to let him go, but it was enough to get his face added to NGI.' He lifted his hands. 'At least now we know he's acquainted with this guy Paul, whoever he is… and quite possibly the other guys as well. And if we get the prints off the knife and hardhat, that might give us another one.'

'Great,' Ruth murmured. 'So we've got a potential terrorist cell.'

21

After running the remainder of the DVD Tommy-Lee found sleep was hard to come by. It wasn't just the prisoner's first crazed reaction that had rattled him, though; he was thinking about the money he'd been promised and how if he wanted to enjoy it, he had to make sure he could get away from here with his skin intact. Because one thing was certain: the more he came to know Paul, the less likely he could see himself being allowed to walk off into the sunset with a hearty handshake and a briefcase full of cash if things didn't work out the way the man wanted. No way.

That meant he either had to cut and run now, before things went bad… or he worked to make himself indispensable to their plans. He had no illusions about what those plans might be, only that he valued the idea of the money more than he cared about the man on the other bed. Whatever James – the name was out there now and couldn't be unheard – whatever James had done to get himself to this situation, it surely wasn't anything to do with being in the army and turning in a couple of Paul's friends to the authorities. It had to be a lot heavier than that. But that was James's problem and he didn't want any part of it.

James had been awake most of the night, too, he knew that. And it didn't take a college degree to guess why. After watched the rest of the DVD in silence, he'd asked to be allowed to wash and use the bucket. After that he'd asked Tommy-Lee to run the DVD again, this time with the sound cranked right up in case there was a faint message, a background noise – anything he might be able to latch onto. But there was nothing.

Now it was daylight again and time to get down to business.

Paul had said they'd be back about six this evening, which was their normal schedule. He'd already worked out that they avoided coming here in full daylight because they didn't want to be seen. Evenings, however, were easier, and they could always duck out of sight if they had to. But as he was learning fast, that Paul was a tricky bastard and quite capable of pitching up early if he felt like it. And being caught out without having done his job as promised would be one serious mistake to make.

He stood up and washed his face, opened some tinned fruit and sliced meat and gave some to the prisoner. He'd already sworn that when he got out of here, he was never going to touch sliced peaches, segmented pears or apricots again. Ever.

They ate in silence, Tommy-Lee standing occasionally to watch as a car or a truck trundled by on the road. He hadn't actually asked Paul what would happen if anybody decided to stop here and take a look around. All he knew was, if anybody did stop, he'd be over to the prisoner and clamping a hand over his mouth to stop him shouting for help.

He needed that money too bad to let it go just like that.

When they were both done eating, he dragged the chair close to the other bed and sat down. This time he was holding the knife, what little light there was kicking off the polished blade.

He took no notice of the look on James's face, nor the way he shrank back against the restraints; this was business and he had a job to do.

'That DVD,' he said, talking casually, like he might with a friend. 'They told me I had to show it to you and make sure you understood what it meant. You got that, right?'

No reaction. The prisoner was too busy staring at him as if he'd grown horns. But that was good; it showed he'd thrown the guy off-balance, which was a chink in anybody's armour. On the other hand, Tommy-Lee was used to dumb silence, which most detainees figured was their best weapon against jailers.

Little did they realise until the shit hit the fan that silence was only temporary; that after a while and the right 'treatment', they'd be singing like birds. True, there was usually a strong element of bullshit to look out for, even downright lies. They'd say just about anything to make it stop, often with just the right element of fact to make it worth checking out and to stop the rough stuff. But in the end the truth always came out.

Just occasionally one of the detainees would surprise them all by finding some way, some deep-down reserve to help them end it completely. Even with strip-searching and cell checks, there was a way of accomplishing it if they were determined or desperate enough. In his opinion it was no big loss. It just meant a lot of paperwork and everybody scratching around to cover their asses and pretend it hadn't happened on their watch.

He reached back for the DVD player and switched it on.

'Sydney Street,' he said, eyes on the screen. 'Now, I figure you know where that is, am I right? Looks a nice place.'

Nothing. Eyes staring right through him like he didn't exist.

'Come on, does it look familiar to you? Huh? Yeah, I guess it does.' He forwarded on to the close-up of the door. In interrogation sessions it was important to demonstrate right off that you had absolute control over the situation, in this case to show the prisoner that he, Tommy-Lee Roddick, dictated what would be seen and when. 'See this house? That's your front door, right? Nice place. Looks safe. Comfortable. Like, once you're in there, ain't nothing can touch you.' He leaned forward into the prisoner's line of sight, dropping his voice to a whisper and playing with the man's imagination. 'Well, pal, not for much longer, if you don't stop dicking around with these guys.'

Nothing.

He shrugged and ran the film back to the school, where the boys were being shepherded into the big fancy building.

'Now, I *know* you recognised this place, because this is where you lost it big the last time. It's a school, I can see that – and a real fancy one, too. I have no idea what a preparatory school is, I admit, but I don't exactly give a whole lot of shit, either. But something tells me you got a boy there, am I right?'

This time there was something deep in the prisoner's eyes, a flicker of light that showed he hadn't entirely zoned out. He'd known detainees who could do that; they just shut down like robots losing power, as if they'd gone somewhere else and left the body behind, and nothing you did could reach them. At least nothing that didn't involve 'treatment'.

Then the lights would come back on sure enough.

He placed the DVD player to one side and picked up the knife. The prisoner's eyes followed the blade for a couple of seconds, then clamped tight, his lips trembling and sweat pouring down his face.

Tommy-Lee put the knife down again, and picked up the DVD player. Hard then soft, that was the way to do it; remind them of the threat then come right in with a switch in focus to throw them off-balance. He ran it forward, this time to the bit near the park showing the apartment building.

'Hey, I'm kidding,' he said, and slapped the man's shoulder until his eyes flickered open. 'I'm playin' with you. Look at this bit here.' He shoved the player right under the man's nose. 'It looks like New York or Chicago or wherever. Now *that*, I know you know. I saw your face and you recognised it right off. So where is it, huh? Tell me. And who is Valerie DiPalma? She your sister? A hooker? Your part-time squeeze?'

For the first time the prisoner showed a definite physical move: he shook his head. But Tommy-Lee recognised it as a sign of inward denial. He wasn't responding to the DVD or Tommy-Lee's questions, but to his own predicament, trying to shake the whole thing loose like a bad dream that wouldn't go away.

He put the DVD player down and placed one foot on the bed rail, easing the chair up onto its back legs like he had all the time in the world. The ancient wood creaked loudly in the room, making the prisoner blink. 'So. What are you thinking here, huh? You gonna do what they're asking which, fuck me I ain't kidding, I have no idea what that is? Or are you gonna wait for the head man to come in here later today and use that big semi-auto he keeps tucked in his pants to blow your stupid head off? And, by the way, it's a forty-five so it would do that easy, no problem. I just hope I'm not in the room when he pulls the trigger, know what I mean?'

This time there was a definite flicker of the eyes.

Yes. It was the sign Tommy-Lee had been waiting for. It showed he was getting through and that the man wasn't completely away with the birds. He pitched his weight forward, slamming the chair back onto its front legs and making the shed tremble so that a thin curtain of dust rained down from the ceiling. When he spoke, it was loud and angry and threatening and damned if it didn't make him feel good for the first time in years.

'Come on, get with the program, my friend!' he yelled. 'You know what he'll do? He'll make a call to his boys, the same ones who took the footage of the house *and* the school *and* the apartment where Miss DiPalma lives, and tell them to go on in and start cutting! You want that on your conscience? Huh? *Tell me, Goddammit!*'

With that he stood up, kicking the chair away and grabbing the knife, and stepped over to the window to stare though the glass at the nothing scenery outside. He was breathing hard through his nose, like a bull wanting a fight, and could feel the blood pounding in his veins. Man, he hadn't felt like this in a long time; knowing you were within an ace of getting a response from somebody who didn't want to talk but would do so eventually, anyway. It was almost better than sex. True, it might be a bullshit answer full of lies and distortion, but any response was an opening. Create that and you had a way in. Sooner or later, they'd crack.

'You really don't want them to do that, my friend.' This time his voice was low and soft, the voice of a friend. Which was bullshit, of course, but it worked more times than it didn't. 'You don't want to let them crazy ragheads loose on your nice little house and your cute little family, I'm telling you. Because they will, I know. I've seen 'em do it. Not these three who brought you here, but others just like them, in Iraq. They waste entire families to get what they want. Sometimes they do it just to show they can. Wives, daughters, sons… girlfriends – anybody and everybody.' He turned and lay down on his bed without looking at the prisoner, like he didn't care. It was time to let the message sink in.

'It's your choice, my friend. Your choice.'

–

'I know what they want from me.' The words were just loud enough for Tommy-Lee to hear and he lifted his head and checked his watch.

'Say what?' He'd had his head down for nearly an hour, drifting in an out of sleep. Fifty-eight minutes for the prisoner to decide to say something voluntarily rather than having it forced out of him. Not bad considering the circumstances.

'I know what they want. Can I have some water, please?'

'Sure.' Tommy-Lee swung his feet to the floor and grabbed a bottle of water from the diminishing supply against the wall. The food was getting low, too, he noted, and wondered if it was a sign that they hadn't got long to go before they could all be out of here.

He tipped the bottle so the prisoner could take it at comfortable pace, and lowered it when he began to cough. But it wasn't like before, when he looked as if he was about to croak. This time he seemed calm and in control, although his skin was the colour of uncooked dough and he looked clammy all over. Smelled bad, too.

'Come on, then. What do they want?'

'First your name.'

'What?'

'Tell me your name. You know I'm called James.'

The statement seemed to give the prisoner a tiny boost, and Tommy-Lee swore silently to himself. Shit, there it was again: he'd been suckered into entering the one circle you never went into with detainees – the one where you knew their names. Once you had that they became more than numbers or codes on a roster sheet or a cell door; they became people, with history and family and stuff.

'Tommy-Lee,' he said finally, and felt like it had been torn out of him. 'It's Tommy-Lee.'

James didn't say anything for a few moments, as if allowing the knowledge to sink in. Then he said, 'They're planning something. Something bad.'

'Like what?'

'I don't know exactly. But I'm pretty certain it involves UAVs.'

'What?'

'Unmanned aerial vehicles. Drones.'

Tommy-Lee looked closely at him, trying to figure out if the guy had lost the plot or was fooling with his head. 'What? You mean like Reapers and stuff?' It didn't sound likely, he knew that; the only people with that kind of weaponry in the US was the US military.

'Not those. Smaller, commercial grade models. Radio-controlled, fitted with cameras. They're used in land surveys and aerial photography, law-enforcement and checking out pipelines and fences. Have you heard of quad-copters?'

'No, can't say I have. But why would these guys be interested in drones? And what for? And why go to all this trouble?' He waved a hand to include the box, the beds and themselves. 'It don't make sense.'

'It doesn't have to make sense, Tommy-Lee. Not to them.' The prisoner turned and looked at him. 'They're terrorists. They're planning to kill people.'

22

'How long for those fingerprints to be run?' Ruth asked. She was on the phone to Brasher, who had been called away to a progress meeting on one of his other cases. She, Reiks and Vaslik had eaten snacks that they didn't really want, if only to keep up the sugar levels if something kicked off and they had to move fast. Now time was ticking by and they were all getting jumpy.

'Not long,' he said. 'They told me they've got plenty, on the hat and the knife, so if the prints are anywhere on the system, they'll shake out sooner or later.'

She went back to staring at the map while Vaslik ran through the iPad to see if anything stuck out. An alternate pair of eyes might throw up something others had missed.

In the end she sat back in frustration and spoke at the ceiling.

'Correct me if I'm wrong but we appear to have a former USAF spook with expertise in unmanned aerial vehicles who's gone missing, possibly taken by another man or men who allegedly want him to help them fly drones or quad-copters for an obviously bullshit reason. We have at least three men in the mix, one identified as a violent extremist with jihadist leanings. This man, Chadwick, seems to have been researching airfields or locations in remote places, which must be tied in in some way to drones, but we have no idea why.'

Vaslik nodded. 'That's all I've got, too.'

'Pardon me for saying so, Slik, but you don't seem that frustrated by the lack of information.'

'You reckon? Maybe I'm just better at hiding it.' His phone rang and he picked it up, pushing the iPad to one side. He listened for a couple of minutes and made some notes, then cut the connection and turned back to Ruth with a blank look.

'A thought occurred to me while you were out,' he announced. 'Where are the drones this man Paul was talking about? We don't know if he already has them or has yet to acquire them, where they are or anything like that.'

'True. So?'

'I did some research on the subject earlier. There's a ton of regulations you have to go through if you want a top-level drone that isn't just for flying around your kitchen or back yard and amusing the kids. If you're serious you have to get licences and do a training course and lots of other stuff. It takes time and money.'

'And leaves a trail.'

He nodded. 'Most of all, it leaves a trail. And if this Paul and his buddies are what we think they are, they wouldn't want to do that.'

'Which is why they may have kidnapped an expert in drone technology, thus avoiding licences, training and paying a pilot.'

'Right. That solves some of their problems, but not all. It still leaves the drones themselves.'

'Good point.' With everything else going on, Ruth hadn't given it much thought. 'Where would he get them – it? He'd have to steal one.'

Vaslik smiled again. 'That's another thing, if you were planning something, would you rely on a single machine… or would you have backups in case something went wrong?'

'I'd have backups. Even with somebody like Chadwick helping to teach them, they couldn't guarantee they wouldn't screw it up or the machine didn't malfunction. The same question holds, though: where would he get them?'

'That's what I asked Tom Brasher to find out.' He nodded at the phone. 'He just finished running that question through every database he can find, here, the UK, Interpol and a few others.'

Ruth refrained from throwing her chair at him. He had news and wanted to draw it out, that much was obvious. 'So?'

'Seven weeks ago a shipment of six quad-copters from EuroVol in France, bound for L.A., went missing while in transit through the FedEx Express Global cargo hub at Memphis International Airport.'

'An inside job?'

'Had to be. So far there's no trace of the shipment or a despatcher who worked in that section of the hub on the day it went missing.'

'What kind of machines are we talking about?'

He looked at his notebook. 'They're described as a batch of EVO Moskitos complete with video screens and cameras. Serious stuff by the sounds of it, used for aid relief in remote areas, according to Brasher.'

'So they'd have quite a range?'

'I guess. He's getting confirmation of what was included in the shipment so we know what we're dealing with. My guess is that if these were intended for LA, they were for the film industry. A few companies are already using drones for location surveys and test footage, so they'd be top of the range.'

'Anything else?'

'Yes. The despatcher's name was Borz Dortyev, described as a legal immigrant originally from Chechnya. Brasher's running a background search for more details. Dortyev had been with the company for six months before he skipped. Prior to that his employment record has him once living in Queens, New York.'

Ruth felt a glow in her stomach. Even without confirmation it was beginning to look as if there had been a plan all along. Dortyev would have been well-placed to keep an eye out for any shipments coming through the Memphis hub and sideline them out of there if they looked useful. But was he connected to the men surrounding James Chadwick, and if so, how closely?

'Brasher might do well to check whether Dortyev has any contacts in France.' When Vaslik looked puzzled, she explained, 'Air France's main cargo hub is called G1XL, at Paris-Charles de Gaulle. French shipments aimed for the US would begin there. It would be a good place to start.'

'You're right. I'll pass it on. But how the heck do you know about that?'

'I had to track a missing person through the airport a couple of months back and got an in-depth tour of the place from one of their security geeks.' She smiled to herself. The official, whose name was André, had been most effusive and even got a little too touchy-feely in one of the transit sheds until she'd pointed out not unkindly that he might have stood a better chance if his name had been spelled Andrée. 'It's a pretty impressive operation but like all airports, it has its weak points.'

'I'll do it now.' He turned and sent off a quick text message to Brasher. The FBI man had told them that it was the best way to contact him as he was on the move so much attending to a backlog of cases. But this was one he didn't want to let go of.

When Vaslik finished he looked back at Ruth, who was once again scanning the map they'd found among Chadwick's effects at StoneSeal. 'No ideas with that?'

She shook her head. 'It's just a map with a few scribbles but nothing leaps out at me. He could have been planning a hiking holiday for all I know.'

'Right. Suddenly James Chadwick, corporate and UAV nerd is a mad trail hiker? I don't see it.'

'Me neither.' She stood up and took the map over to him. It was about time for some fresh eyes on the damned thing. 'See what you can find,' she told him. 'It's there, I can feel it – it's just a matter of nailing it.'

Vaslik spread the map out and got to his feet. Ruth knew he'd taken a look at it before, but with focussing on other aspects of the case, such as the Newark/New Jersey locations and liaising with Brasher, he'd pretty much left this one to her.

She left him to it and went in search of some tea. Reiks directed her to a pharmacy nearby, where she found tea bags, which she took back and served up to Reiks and Vaslik before re-joining in the study of the map.

'Have you noticed,' Vaslik said after a few minutes, 'that the circles are located in the three states, of Nebraska, Oklahoma and Kansas?'

Ruth nodded. 'I saw that. The same three states he was Googling for airfields. But I have no idea why. There are no place names in the circles; in fact they look as if they're in the middle of nowhere.' She tapped the edge of the map. 'He also wrote some stuff down, most of it in pencil and too faded to read. But there's one word here which I can read.' She pointed at a single word on the border of the map. It had been underlined once, and unlike some of the other scribbles, was in ink. 'He also made Google searches for the same place.'

Freedom.

They stood and stared at it for a few moments, then Vaslik said dramatically, 'I think, Miss Gonzales, that we're going to need a bigger map.'

23

The hinges on the door had been fitted all wrong, Tommy-Lee could see that. He'd done enough construction work in his time to know you didn't use butt hinges on the outside of the frame and door, like they'd been done here, but recessed them for a neater finish and safety. He'd figured there was something off the first time he'd looked at them, but he hadn't given it much of a thought until now.

Now things were different. After what the prisoner had told him he needed to get outside and breathe some fresh air, then take a look-see at that hangar Bill and Donny spent so much time in. Sitting here on his butt was starting to freak him out.

He checked his watch. Nearly three in the afternoon. Jesus, where the hell had time gone? He had to get moving. He checked both ways for signs of movement and listened for the noise of an engine. Nothing. Quiet as a graveyard, only emptier. He took out his hunting knife and set to work. Lucky for him Paul hadn't thought to get him to empty his pockets. Also lucky was the fact that the construction crew had used big cross-thread screws but hadn't tightened them up all the way. They'd been in too much of a hurry, he figured, and had nobody checking their work.

It was the work of a few minutes to unscrew the hinges on the frame itself, and he eased the door clear just enough to squeeze through, leaving it propped with the lock still engaged. That way, if the three men came back early, he'd have time to replace a few of the screws and pretend everything was fine and dandy.

He glanced back at the prisoner. 'Don't you go anywhere, you hear? I won't be long.' Then he was through the gap and the outer door and in the open, breathing cool air and breathing in the aroma of wide open spaces. Man, that was so good. He was never going to spend so much time indoors ever again once he got out of here. It would be open air all the way.

He set off across the grass, eyes firmly fixed on the hangar. Now he was out here and not seeing just a slice of the picture, it looked huge. True it was pretty much a wreck, like it was a prop in a disaster movie, but still impressive. He made sure to keep a check on the approach road and didn't tread anywhere where he'd be likely to leave tracks. Wouldn't do to leave footprints and let anyone in on his secret excursion.

The closer he got to the hangar the bigger it looked. A lot bigger. It was like it suddenly expanded once he was in its shadow, dominating and aggressive in spite of its sorry state of disrepair. Then he was standing by the front corner, the wooden walls looming high overhead, silent save for the sound of the breeze hissing through the battered woodwork. All down one side was a line of windows, many of the panes broken, some slipped but hanging in there, all of them coated with years of wind-blown dust and so weather-beaten and scratched you could hardly see through them. This place must have been built for cargo planes, he figured, or maybe bombers. The sliding doors looked like they hadn't been used in years, with the metal tracks and runners wheels all gummed up with dirt and grit. He took one last look around to check nobody was coming, then stepped inside.

The silence and sense of space hit him right away. It took him all the way back to when he was a kid and going to church on a Sunday; there was the same interplay of light and gloom, and the feeling of openness above his head. Only instead of heavy wooden beams above the congregation, this place had a network of steel struts holding up the roof, with rusted pulleys and chains and light fittings hanging there like dead things. And instead of pews and chairs down at ground level, all he could see in front of him was a vast expanse of concrete floor, stained black and cracked to hell as if a giant mole had tunnelled underneath and ripped it up. Elsewhere weeds had taken over and stood three feet high in places, with lumps of concrete, cement and nameless pieces of ironwork poking up through them as if trying to reach the sunlight before they got swallowed up altogether.

A few small birds scattered out of the roof as he stepped forward, the sound of the wings echoing like ghosts. He shivered and continued walking, watching where he put his feet. There were holes in the floor where the ground beneath had subsided, and he skirted these with care. Other times he took the precaution of avoiding clumps of thick weeds in case they harboured snakes. Last thing he wanted was a bite from a pissed-off rattler or a cottonmouth; he'd be dead before the day was out.

He stopped and looked around. Most of the solid segments of walls were peppered with small holes where the fabric was beginning to come apart with age and neglect. Over to one side were some boards on the floor, which looked like they might cover an inspection pit. Overhead was a large pulley and chain affair, rusted to hell, and alongside the boards was a pair of huge steel H-beams which looked like they would have once been an inspection hoist.

Away on the other side of the hangar was a low structure along the wall which he guessed had once been an office. He decided to check that first. If the two goons had spent any time here, he was guessing it wouldn't have been in the main hangar space, where the air was drawn in through the vast open doors and pushed out through a smaller door at the rear of the building. Whatever else they were, he didn't have them down as stupid enough to stand around in the open where they could be seen by anybody passing by on the road.

He sniffed the air as he crossed the floor, picking up a gamey, mouldy aroma. It reminded him of rotting fruit in the garbage dump outside a supermarket. Probably food the men had thrown aside or maybe a kill brought in from outside by predators. But there was something else, too, much more alien to a place that hadn't had any use for at least thirty years.

Burned metal and plastic. It got stronger the closer he got to the office, hanging in the air like a screen as he passed through the door.

A trestle table stood in the middle of the room. On it was a moulded crate about two feet square, the kind he'd seen a film crew using one time. A smaller one stood alongside. The outside of each crate was ribbed and had carry-handles at each end with twin clasps on the front and a lock in the center. He counted ten more crates on the floor, five large, five smaller, with a pile of flattened cardboard boxes – the same ones, he guessed, that had made the journey down here with him – spread over the floor. He approached the table with care, checking he wasn't going to step in anything that would leave tracks.

He knuckled the side of the bigger crate. It sounded hollow and shifted on the table. He lifted the lid. It was empty save for some foam packing, moulded to take something fairly big and more or less rounded in shape. Whatever had been in this crate he figured must have been fragile or valuable or both. There were markings on the side and lid, but he couldn't figure out what they meant. The smaller crate was the same; empty save for moulded foam and bearing the same series of numbers and letters.

He went over to the other crates and hefted the nearest one to test the weight. It was heavier and didn't have that hollow empty feel of the one on the table, although the lock and clasps had been popped. The shipping numbers he noted, were consecutive.

He stepped over to the cardboard boxes. More labels and numbers, with the thick cardboard creased where plastic ties had cut into it. A bundle of these ties were now lying a few feet away. He'd worked in a transport warehouse for a while and knew these were freight packs. You didn't have to know what any of the markings stood for, only that they had to match a cargo manifest or delivery note. He nudged one of the boxes to one side and saw a familiar logo: FedEx Express. Next to it was a bar code and a number, and a roughened area where a label had been ripped away.

Over by the window was a pile of heavy fabric on wires, and he couldn't figure out their function until he spotted hooks in the wooden wall either side of the windows.

Curtains to block out the light.

He turned back to the unlocked crate on the floor. He hesitated only a moment, then lifted the lid. It gave a suck of air and he emitted a further fresh tang of plastic. He laid it back with care and studied the inside of the box.

A layer of thick, dark foam covered the contents and he lifted it gently, picking carefully at the edges of the foam until it came clear. Whatever was inside was coloured a white, in a plain plastic bag, and fitted snugly into its foam nest. It was a casing of some kind, sort of crab-shaped and slightly oval with four protruding arms and a cylinder about an inch wide attached to one side and sticking out of the top. He fed his fingers down the side of the casing, easing the object out of the foam bedding and lifting it clear. Then he placed it on the table.

For a moment he couldn't make out what the hell he was looking at. It could have been a fancy piece of household electrical equipment, maybe a dehumidifier or one of those automatic vacuum cleaner robots he'd seen once. Only he knew it wasn't. This was something special; it had to be with all the special packing and moulded foam and locks and stuff. And the sheen on the casing looked expensive and high-tech, like... carbon-fiber? Maybe that was it – like they used in race car bodies.

He bent close and peered through the plastic bag. There was some writing down one side; a name in fancy colored letters.

EuroVol~2. And the four arms were contoured and stubby, each with some kind of socket-and- nut assembly on the end facing up, with gaps where he could see a glint of copper wiring. And each of the wings had louvered air vents down each side.

He turned the object on its side. The bag was taped shut but he could make out two U-shaped objects inside with locating pins. On the underside of the main body were four holes with locking clips. It didn't take much to figure out what these were: they were legs, only like the landing skids you see on mountain-rescue helicopters.

So, James had been telling the truth. Now he remembered seeing really neat stuff like this on the Discovery Channel. What had James called it? A quad-something? Quad-copter, that was it.

He put the object back in the box, careful to place it just as he'd taken it out, and lifted the lid of the smaller crate alongside. He removed the foam and this time saw what looked like a game console. It was white, with a stubby aerial, two small joysticks, and lights and buttons he couldn't even guess at, and fitted with a small screen on a mount. He lifted the console out and found another layer of foam covering a neat array of plastic propellers, a pack of batteries, strips of electrical wiring, small wrenches and some other stuff he couldn't guess at, and a small aluminium-cased camera on a stalk.

Not a game console; this had to be the control unit. A control for the drone. A drone they could make fly and do whatever it was they wanted.

A faint buzz interrupted his train of thought and made him snap to. Wind? No, too regular. There shouldn't be any—

They were back early. Shit, it was time to boogie. He closed the cases and replaced them just the way he'd found them. No, wait: the bigger one on the table had shifted slightly, leaving a faint mark in the thin layer of dust. He nudged it back into place and checked the others, blowing dust around to cover any bare patches. They looked right but he couldn't tell for sure.

Fuck it. He'd have to trust to luck. It was time to bug out and get back to his box, pretend like he'd been doing nothing all day but sleeping and pouring water into the prisoner.

He skidded out of the hangar and took a moment to check the source of the noise. The association of ideas with the drones inside made him look up. Nothing in the air that he could see, so it could only be coming from the east or west at ground level, somewhere along the road. Definitely a vehicle engine, he decided, and turned his head a little. And coming from the east. It was some way off yet but he had that feeling in his bones: it had to be them. He monkey-ran, bending at the waist and touching a hand to the ground whenever he stumbled. After a dozen paces he felt pains building in his legs and stomach as the unexpected exertions pulled at little-used muscles. Avoiding clumps of grass and dodging areas of soft sandy soil where he'd leave a mark, he fetched up at the workshop door, gasping for breath and hearing a roaring sound inside his head.

He checked the road one last time. No sign yet, but the sound was definitely closer. He slid back inside, pulling the outer door shut, then slipped through the inner door and pushed it into place, making sure the lock was still engaged. He threw a quick glance at the prisoner, but he was facing the wall, breathing heavily and didn't seem to have noticed Tommy-Lee's return. He grabbed his knife and started replacing the screws. Most of them were in place when suddenly the van was pulling to a stop right outside, the brakes squeaking and the tyres hissing on the grass.

His fingers were trembling with the effort and he dropped a screw. Swore softly and fumbled around on the wooden floor. Saw the glint of silver where it had slipped down a crack between the floorboards. *Shit.* Paul would be bound to see that. He dug it out with the point of the knife, bringing up a sliver of wood in his haste. He covered the scar it left behind with yesterday's shirt and pushed the screw into place, turning the blade of the knife and catching his finger as it skidded free. A line of blood welled up and he felt the cut stinging as it filled with his sweat. He wrapped it in his handkerchief and jammed his hand in his pocket, and had just enough time to get over alongside the prisoner and grab a bottle of water before footsteps approached and he heard Paul issuing instructions outside.

Only then did he realise James was unconscious and barely breathing.

24

In addition to shopping for a more detailed map to give them a closer picture of the three states, Vaslik raised the question of food. They couldn't go on burning reserves all day without eating something solid and hope to remain effective.

'A burger,' said Ruth, her stomach reacting to the idea with approval. 'I'd love a good burger.'

'You got a red meat craving going on?' Vaslik grinned as they went down in the elevator. 'Must be the hunting instinct kicking in.'

'A bit. Isn't New York supposed to be the home of great burgers?'

'Actually, I think California has the edge. But that's only my opinion and don't repeat it outside this box or you'll get me lynched.' He screwed his face up in thought. 'Right. I know just the place. We'll get the map first, then eat.'

He led her to Penn Station where they found detailed maps of Nebraska, Oklahoma and Kansas, then through a maze of side streets until he stopped outside the front of a plain looking restaurant.

'It's not a burger bar,' Ruth pointed out.

'You're right, it's not. Which is why it's the best-kept burger secret in the city.'

Inside, they joined a short queue at a counter in the rear and Ruth left the ordering to Vaslik.

'Trust me,' he said, 'you won't regret it and you'll never forget it.'

'Well, I never had a man say that to me before,' she murmured.

The burger was every bit as good as Vaslik had promised, and Ruth felt a whole lot better.

'OK,' she said, wiping a speck of juice off her cheek, 'back to basics. I have a slight concern now that Brasher's gotten himself involved—'

He looked at her and raised a hand. 'Did you just say 'gotten'?'

'Yes, I did and may God and my old English teacher, Mrs Stubbs, forgive me. I've been infected. Anyway, Brasher's involved and I appreciate what he's doing, which is running down the fingerprints on the knife and hardhat, chasing up the drones and the despatcher *and* trying to ID the men we've picked up pictures of so far.'

'Yes. So?'

'Well, what about our job? We still have a responsibility to track down James Chadwick. I don't want us to lose sight of that in the FBI's big-picture view.'

He nodded. 'I agree. But having Brasher onside is a big step forward. All that stuff you just mentioned, we couldn't check it out because we don't have the resources. But Brasher's got the muscle to get things done and that gives us the freedom to concentrate on searching for Chadwick. And Brasher knows this looks like more than just a kidnap or a guy who's simply ducked out of sight for a while through pressure of work or a busted marriage. And he's already thrown up a name with extremist connections and the missing shipment of drones which my blood tells me is somehow connected. I don't know how yet, but it's a feeling.'

Ruth stared at him so hard he reached up and touched his face. 'Have I got grease on my chin?'

'No. What did you just say?'

'A lot. I was blabbing. Which part?'

'Something about Brasher having muscle and what it gives us.'

'I don't know… oh, yes – the freedom to search for Chadwick. What about it?'

She dropped the napkin she was holding and jumped to her feet. 'Come on – we need to get back and check the maps.' She suddenly felt a surge like electricity going through her, but it would need a careful study back in the office to make sense of it.

'Hey, come on,' Vaslik said, following her out into the street. 'Tell me what I said. If I had a moment of brilliance, at least allow me to enjoy it.'

'You said Freedom,' she told him, walking at a rapid pace back towards the office.

'So what? It happens to be one of the core principles of our constitution.'

'Not that kind of freedom. Freedom with a capital 'F'.' Chadwick had written that word in the margin of the map and underlined it. 'I think it's a place, not a concept.'

By the time they arrived back at the office Vaslik was punching the keys of his cell phone. As the elevator slowed to a stop on the sixth floor he said, 'Do you know how many places called Freedom are in the continental US?'

'No idea. Hit me.'

'Fifteen. Can you believe that?'

'Of course. It's a reflection of what early settlers felt on reaching the New World, with the promise of religious, political and social freedom. They were big issues back then. And then there was Hollywood, of course, but that came much later.'

'Funny,' he muttered dryly. 'So how come you're an expert on American history?'

'I hate to point it out,' she reminded him with a deliberately condescending smile, 'but it was our history before it was yours.'

They were in the office poring over the maps when Reiks stuck his head round the door. 'It's Brasher – and I think you'll want to hear this.' He nodded at the phone. 'Press the conference button.'

Vaslik did so and said, 'We're listening, Tom.'

'Hi. We have information on two issues,' said the FBI man. He sounded tense. 'The first is about Borz Dortyev, the FedEx despatcher in Memphis. His name came up when we fed it into the database search engines. We already knew from FedEx company employee records that he used to live in Queens; but now we have a docket on him. And guess who he's a known associate of?'

'No idea,' said Ruth. That wasn't strictly true because she knew there could only be a couple of possibilities. She could see by the expressions of Vaslik and Reiks that they had the same idea, but didn't want to puncture Brasher's balloon.

'One Bilal Ammar,' Brasher announced. 'The bodybuilder type. They attended the same mosque at the same times and Dortyev was picked up and processed on the same day as Ammar but at a different location where an anti-jihadist protest was being prepared. That's enough to make us think they were acting together with others in a group.'

'Nothing on the mystery man named Paul?' Ruth knew he must be the key to this; the other men might lead to him but if it followed the examples of most previous cases of extremist group structures, they would most likely prove to be minor players compared to him.

'We're still crunching the data on that.'

'OK. What's the other thing?'

'I'm not sure if this is as helpful, but we picked up some details about the company that manufactured the stolen drones. They're called EuroVol and based in Toulouse, which is an aviation and technology center in south-western France. Their CEO and technical whizz is named Patrick Paget, and he's in New York right now. I think you should talk to him.'

'What's he doing here?' asked Vaslik.

'Trying to save the business. It's a small but go-ahead company and the failed delivery could cost them dear. They're working round the clock to deliver a replacement batch and he came over to keep the customers happy. If he stays in business and the client's prepared to wait this could take his company up to the next level.'

'I agree we should talk,' Ruth put in. 'When and where?' She doubted Paget would be able to help much with finding the missing drones, but if he was the top technical man, he might shed some light on why his machines had been the focus of a heist. There were after all plenty of manufactures here in the US, so why steal from a French company?

'I've asked him to come by our office in Federal Plaza in forty minutes. He's on his way to the airport back to France, so he doesn't have much time. If you can make it down here I'll buzz you in.'

She looked at Vaslik, who nodded. The maps would have to wait. 'We're on our way.'

25

Ruth and Vaslik arrived at 26, Federal Plaza and were met on the 23rd floor by Tom Brasher, who cleared them through security and led them to a room along the corridor.

'Paget's not here yet,' he told them. 'We'll keep it as short as we can. I gather he's on a tight schedule and I don't want to make his visit here any worse than it has been.'

They sat down and waited. At one point Brasher asked, 'This contract thing you have going at Cruxys. You can't go on searching for ever. When does somebody decide to pull the plug on it and call it a day?'

Ruth looked at him. 'I don't know. I've never had to face that situation.'

He grunted. 'So you always find your man, huh?'

She didn't reply. It was an unwinnable argument.

Patric Paget proved to be what none of them had expected for a CEO and technical expert. He was tall, dark-haired, lean and tanned, with film star looks and somewhere in his late thirties. Dressed in tan pants, brogue shoes and a check sports coat, and carrying a leather overnight bag, he moved with the easy grace of an athlete, attracting glances from passing staff, yet seemingly unaware of any of them.

'I hate him already,' Vaslik muttered from the side of his mouth.

'Really?' said Ruth. 'I'm thinking of changing teams.'

Brasher made introductions and everybody took a seat at the table. 'Thank you for coming by, Mr Paget,' he said. 'We won't hold you up for long, but just in case, I've arranged a helicopter flight out from the Manhattan heliport on the èast river just a few minutes from here.'

'Thank you, Mr Brasher. I appreciate that.' He spoke excellent English with a discernible accent, and if he felt at all uncomfortable at being inside one of the major law-enforcement centers in the city, he hid it well. He sat back and crossed his legs, eyes flicking over the three of them. 'How can I help you?'

'These machines – the drones that went missing. Can you describe them for us? We're trying to figure out why anybody would steal them.' Brasher added with a smile, 'I don't mean to denigrate your products in any way, of course.'

Paget gave an easy shrug. 'Of course. You mean, why mine and not your own American-produced models?'

'Yes.'

'That puzzled me at first, too. There are certainly machines produced here of equal capabilities and value as those made by my company, I cannot deny that. Also much easier to get hold of, I think, than waiting for a shipment from France. But after visiting Los Angeles and talking with the client who ordered them, I believe that is where the answer lies.'

'How so?'

'First, let me show you what we are talking about.' Paget reached into the side pocket of his bag and produced a glossy brochure. The front cover showed a drone in mid-air. Shiny and white, with the company name stencilled down its side followed by a digit: **EuroVol~2**, it was sleek and beautiful, more like a household item than a system for taking aerial photos. Four rotors held the machine aloft and two skid-like structures beneath formed the landing gear. 'The current name for this model is the *Moskito*,' Paget went on to explain. 'but this particular batch was called the number two because it took the place of our first machine which is now no longer in development.' He gave a wry grin. 'I don't know if it will help, but these six that were stolen are the only ones with this number, so there is no confusion with others. It was an important order and for us something of a trial production.'

'In what way?' Ruth asked.

He looked directly at her for the first time, and she felt his gaze assessing her, but not in a critical way. 'The client is a film production company in Hollywood. They wanted a few refinements for technical reasons that only film studios think are important.' He flashed a smile. 'We have the same kind of people in France, believe me. They can be… difficult to work with, but we believe in rising to a challenge.'

'What did they want?'

'There were certain issues about stability in adverse wind or thermal conditions, dust- and water-proofing, payload concerns for cameras and a modification to the parachute system. As it happened, they were all dealt with very quickly as we had allowed for some modifications in our initial designs. Many of our earlier machines, and now of course, the *Moskito*, are used for disaster aid, capturing film footage of areas hit by floods and similar problems and even carrying small parcels such as vital medicines to places where aid convoys cannot go.'

Brasher lifted his eyebrows. 'Did you say a parachute?'

Paget shrugged. 'It's true that if a machine fails, which can happen if certain conditions overcome the ability of the controller to keep it in the air, then it makes sense to try and rescue the machine. Otherwise, *paff*.' He slapped both hands together. 'They are expensive. So, a parachute is a way to avoid losing one.'

'You say 'certain conditions' can bring them down. Like what?'

'Violent wind gusts, unusually heavy rain, radio interference or simply a loss of signal because they have been flown too far from the controller and do not have a 'Go home' system, as some do. Even simple mechanical failure can happen if they have not been prepared correctly. I discounted that because we sell ready-to-fly machines – that is to say, all a client has to do on receipt is to assemble the rotors and skids, check the flight controller and video screen are powered up and that the signal is clear, and away they go.'

'Excuse a dumb question,' said Ruth, 'but why the screen?'

'Not dumb, I assure you. It gives a drone's-eye view of where it is going, what it sees and, with the camera mounted on a gimbal, it gives the operator 360-degree vision.'

'And the parachute?' said Brasher.

'You simply press a button on the flight control unit,' Paget flicked over to a page showing a photo of the unit, 'which activates a small gas-pressure cartridge to expels the parachute. Gravity does the rest. But instead of a parachute, the client asked for a modification.'

'To do what?' Ruth asked.

'The original specification said that they wanted to use the machines for promotional purposes as well as for capturing camera footage. The modification required the facility to release colored smoke from the parachute canister. I told them smoke would not be possible, but our technicians came up with a solution which they liked even better. We suggested colored powder instead. The press of the button releases the canister lid and the powder is sucked out through vents in the side of the tube. Like smoke, only not.' He lifted his hands in a typically Gallic shrug. 'Crazy, *non*?'

'Could this be used to scatter anything else apart from powder?' said Ruth. 'Like liquid in the form of a spray?'

Paget gave it some thought. 'Yes, I suppose. It could be adapted to take a pressurised spray which would be released by the same mechanism, but it would depend on the weight. But who would do that, and why?'

If Paget was expecting an answer to that question, he was disappointed. Instead he was rewarded with a stunned silence as they all digested the implications of what he had described.

Brasher was the first to speak, and his voice sounded tense. 'You said the answer to why your machines got stolen in the first place lay with the client. Do you mean somebody there might be responsible in some way?'

'Not at all. I say that because it was discovered only yesterday that the studio has already sent out advance publicity showing our machines in an action movie they are producing. They created mock-up video trailers using our marketing footage of the *Moskito* in action, only instead of showing the drones taking camera footage, the studio had added computer generated imagery showing them dispersing smoke over a battlefield.'

'Who could have seen that?'

'Anybody who reads movie magazines or watches DVDs. Or they could have read the news on the studio's own website and in various magazines. They made no secret of it because they wanted to capture the – what do you call it – the kudos of getting there first.'

'And these stolen models – the *Moskitos*, Mr Paget – have they all got this modification to the parachute system?'

'Yes. All.'

'And they're – what did you call it – ready to fly?'

'RTF – yes.'

'And what's the possible payload?'

'Almost two and one half kilos, or five pounds.' He Paget glanced at his watch. 'I am sorry, lady and gentlemen, but my flight…'

They all stood up and thanked him for his time. Then Ruth said, 'One last question, M'sieur Paget. How difficult are they to fly for an amatuer?'

He pursed his lower lip. 'It needs practice, and a basic knowledge of aerodynamics if you wish to be precise. But the greatest requirement in my opinion is manual dexterity and speed of reflexes.' He bent and picked up his bag. 'The best pilots in my experience are *joueurs* – kids who play lots of games like *Playstation*. Or professional pilots.'

'How long would it take an expert to teach somebody?'

'That is simple. In my opinion, if you have an expert, why waste your time with a student?'

After Paget had gone, the three of them sat staring into space. It didn't take much imagination to see that they were on the brink of something potentially terrible… or nothing at all. The drones had either been stolen as a method of dispersing a gas, liquid or powdered substance in the air over a specific area, or had been acquired for sale on the black market by people who didn't care about observing any rules or regulations.

But if it was the latter, why involve Chadwick?

'Are we barking up a tree or what?' Brasher said to the ceiling. 'Does this sound like a dirty bomb threat to you?'

'No, we're not and yes, it does.' Ruth felt a knot growing in her gut. In her experience, when it came to terrorism, if you considered what was possible from all the evidence available, no matter how fantastic, you'd be a fool to ignore it. Because terrorists didn't allow second chances. They struck when they could and threw everything into the opportunity to make the maximum impact, even at risk to themselves.

Unlike ordinary activists, they didn't always care if it failed because they'd got their publicity, anyway. And if the worst happened and they didn't survive the event, they had their rewards in heaven awaiting them.

Brasher looked at her. 'Are you sure? Only, I can tell you, there are no records of extremists in the US using or acquiring chemical or biological weapons in the past decade or more. Not one.'

'There's always a first time.'

'Ruth's right.' Vaslik's voice was flat, and he looked at Brasher. 'Just because there's no record, doesn't mean they haven't tried.'

26

'Hey – wake up!' Tommy-Lee shook James's shoulder in case he was just playing for time. 'Come on, man,' he hissed. 'You don't want to fuck about with these guys, I tell you. They ain't fooling.'

No reaction. He bent to put his ear close to the man's face. He was breathing but it sounded too faint and whispery to be normal. His face was beaded with sweat and dark patches showed in the fabric of his shirt under his arms and across his chest. He touched his forehead. Jesus, the guy was burning up.

He splashed water from the bottle over James's face to see if that would help. It made him stir but not enough to make a difference.

Then the door opened and Paul was standing there, his nose twitching in disgust at the rank odour in the room.

'Problem, Mr Roddick?' he asked quietly. He was chewing on an apple and looked rested and refreshed, hair combed and his shirt laundered and ironed. He looked at Tommy-Lee then at the prisoner and lifted his eyebrows. For all his reaction, he might have been discussing a minor situation with the state of the room.

'He didn't wake up properly,' said Tommy-Lee, and gestured with the bottle. 'I've tried reviving him but he's running a temperature. I think it's this room. He needs water and air and light. I can give him water but not the other things.' Even to his own ears he sounded desperate, but all he could think about was the money he'd lose if the prisoner croaked. Because one thing was certain, if that happened, Paul would blame him for not looking after the man.

Paul appeared to be thinking it over. Finally he nodded slowly. 'Did you show him the DVD?'

'Yeah. Three times. He freaked out.'

'Of course he did.' Paul's expression was cold. 'Because he now knows what we'll do if he refuses to comply with my instructions.' He took a last bite of his apple before tossing the core through the door behind him. 'Take him out and walk him around. But stay out of sight. You have thirty minutes to get him wide awake and talking.' With that he turned and walked away, leaving the door open.

Tommy-Lee got the cuffs undone and lifted James off the bed. He wasn't too heavy, but neither was he helping much, his feet dragging and his head lolling back and forth like a town drunk. In the restricted space in the room he almost had to drag him out of the door, but as soon as he was in the open, he could hold him upright more easily. He shuffled six paces one way and six paces back, and felt James beginning to respond.

'Come on, man,' he muttered softly. 'We gotta get you mobile, you hear me?' He stopped shuffling and gently slapped James's face, making his head snap upright. 'That's better. Now breath deep... breath some of that nice fresh air. Taste it? It's sweet, right? Hold on – you need water, too.' He eased James down against the side of the shed and went back inside for the water bottle. Then he splashed some over his head and held the bottle to his lips so he could drink.

Twenty minutes later James was standing unaided, but looking punch-drunk. His colour was better and he'd stopped sweating, but he kept breaking into a shiver as if he was running a fever, so Tommy-Lee made him sit down again.

'You know they're going to want an answer, don't you?' Tommy-Lee told him, holding up the bottle to give him another drink. He knew all about dehydration from Iraq; you didn't take in enough liquids in extreme heat and your body would begin to shut down. Leave it too long and you were beyond help.

'Yes. I know.' James signalled that he'd had enough water and looked away, shaking his head. 'I don't know what to do.'

'Really? My advice is do what they say. Can't be too hard, right?'

James stared at him, and Tommy-Lee saw deep in his eyes what might have been a look of pity. 'Are you serious? They want me to teach them to fly *drones*. The man who calls himself Paul originally told me that he was in a start-up venture interested in drone technology and wanted me to put on a demonstration for investors and partners.' His face twisted in an expression of disgust. 'It's rubbish, of course. They want to use them… they want to *kill* people.'

'Whoa. Hold up there. You said that already. But how do you know that?'

'Because I used to be in Air Force Intelligence. I know about terrorists. I also know about drones and startup businesses and the kind of people running them. I also know that if they had any kind of a business, I'd be in their offices right now drinking coffee, not being kept prisoner in this sweat box.' He looked around as if noticing his surroundings for the very first time. 'Where the hell is this, anyway?'

'I don't know. Kansas, Oklahoma… somewhere like that. These drones, if you do what they want and teach them real quick, they'll let you go, right? Ain't no need for any of your family to get hurt if you do that.'

'Is that what they told you?'

'Hell, no. They didn't tell me nothing. I'm just doing a job.'

A flicker of contempt. 'Of course. You're being *paid* to hold me here.'

Tommy-Lee looked away, then turned back and nodded. Wasn't any way he was going to apologise for what he was doing. He had a right to earn a living same as anybody else. And just because this guy thought Paul and his buddies had the worst of intentions didn't make it so.

Just then Paul strode round the side of the shed and tossed a paper bag into his lap. 'Salt tablets, candy and Tylenol. He's dehydrated and needs glucose. Get those down him.' He looked at James to see if he was awake, then squatted in front of him and held a cell phone out so he could see the screen. 'We appear to have a problem, Mr Chadwick. A serious one, so I want your full concentration.'

James stirred but looked confused. 'What?'

'This woman and man – who are they?' He scrolled through a number of photos, then back again. There were half a dozen in all, taken in various locations. 'I should remind you that the answer you give could be important to your wellbeing, so don't try to lie to me.'

James shook his head. 'I don't know. I've never seen them before. Why are you asking me?'

'Because I think you have the answer. Take another look, Mr Chadwick.'

'I don't know – I promise,' James insisted, his expression conflicted. 'Where were they taken?'

'The woman was first seen visiting your wife in London.' Paul clicked on a photo showing a woman in a business suit with dark, cropped hair standing outside a house with a gleaming black front door.

'She's probably just a friend. My wife knows lots of people… I don't know who they all are – I've never met most of them.'

'Really?' Paul looked sceptical. 'It's possible, I suppose. But somehow my instincts tell me that this particular woman, with her smart but ordinary suit and with a very… shall we say, business-like manner, does not look the kind of person to indulge in a nice cup of tea and a chat. Or am I misreading one of your wife's friends?'

'I don't know. I guess not.'

'No matter. Now this one.' Paul clicked on another shot. 'The same woman was recorded calling on your apartment in Newark and,' another photo, 'entering this building where your employers are located. This time she was accompanied by this man.' The photo showed the woman with a tall, slim male in a suit. 'Do you know him?'

'No, I don't.'

A shrug. 'Maybe not. It could be a giant coincidence, I suppose. We live, after all, in a small world, don't we? But the same person turning up three times? I think not. She also visited the apartment building where Miss DiPalma lives.' Another photo, this time of the woman alone.

James said nothing for a long moment, eyes on the phone as if he were hypnotised. Then he breathed in defeat and said quietly, 'I'm only guessing… I can't be certain, but I think I know who they might be.'

'Good. Now we're getting somewhere.'

'There's a firm called Cruxys in London. They're like an insurance security company; they provide financial cover and assistance for clients working in hazardous occupations.'

'Cruxys? So these two people are… what, insurance workers?' Paul's eyes went cold. 'Are you trying to insult my intelligence?'

'It's true! They're… they're like investigators.'

'Investigators.' Paul leaned forward and forced James to look at him. 'Are you telling me these two people are actually looking for you, Mr Chadwick? Is that what they're doing?' He seemed surprised at the notion.

'Yes. It's part of the contract. If a person goes missing, they mount a search to locate them.'

'I see. But that raises a question: why would you have such a contract? Do you undertake hazardous duties in between advising businesses on their startup plans, Mr Chadwick? Is that what you're saying?'

'No, I… I took out the contract for my family's benefit. It was peace of mind, that's all.'

'How long?'

'Pardon?'

'How long ago did you take out the contract?' Paul's words were spaced out, slowly and with emphasis.

'It was… I started it several weeks ago… maybe more. I don't remember.'

'I see. After I first contacted you – is that what you're saying?'

'About then, yes.'

'These Cruxys investigators; what kind of people do they employ?'

'I'm not sure.'

'Really? A professional like you and you didn't check their credentials on such an important issue?'

James sighed again. 'Some are former police or other law-enforcement personnel.'

'Other? What kind of 'other'?'

'Security professionals… and ex-military.'

Paul said nothing for a long while, but stood up and walked away a few paces, head bent in thought. When he returned, he said quietly, 'In that case, Mr Chadwick, I think we have to make some decisions, which are easy for me, but not so easy for you.'

'What do you mean?'

'It appears that the game has changed, by the addition of these two… investigators. We now have a situation of some urgency. Unlike some of my friends, I never underestimate the ability of pursuers to stumble on the truth. So, let us understand each other. We now need to move quickly, so here is my proposal, with no room for negotiation. If you refuse to do what I have asked, I will make three simple phone calls; two to England and one to Newark. I assume you are intelligent enough to work out what those calls will involve, but let me make it absolutely clear, just in case. I promise you now, if you do not agree, we will wipe them all out; your wife, your son, Ben, and your slut. Would you like to see *that* on film? Do you think you could live with it, knowing you were responsible for their deaths and had done nothing to save them?'

He didn't wait for an answer but walked past them to the door of the shed and gestured abruptly for Tommy-Lee to get himself and the prisoner inside.

Tommy-Lee stood up and helped a stunned James to his feet, guiding him through the narrow door and sitting him down on his bed. When he turned away Paul was waiting by the door, his face bleak.

'You have tonight and tomorrow, Mr Roddick. When we come back I want him on his feet and ready to do exactly as I say. Otherwise they're all dead.' Then he stepped back and pulled the door shut and Tommy-Lee heard the key turn in the lock.

27

By the time darkness fell Tommy-Lee still hadn't heard the van leave and wondered what the men were up to. They must still be in the hangar with the drones; there was no other reason to keep them here.

James was asleep, his breathing now even and less frantic after an initial attack of near-hysteria following Paul's final words. The Tylenol and candy had helped, Tommy-Lee figured, along with exhaustion. He wet a piece of torn shirt and placed it over the man's forehead, which was still hot, then took out his knife and walked to the door.

Two minutes later he was outside and studying the hangar. For a while he couldn't see a thing except for a faint static glow on the side where the office lay. Then the glow changed and morphed into three flashlights moving around inside the building. He got ready to duck back into the room and pull the door shut, then realised they were moving towards the opposite side of the hangar door and the runway. He held his breath. They were all together, walking in a line that didn't vary in distance, like they were joined by a rope.

When they disappeared round the side of the building, he pulled the door to behind him, resting the hinge side against the frame, then set off across the grass after them. By the time he reached the corner where the lights had gone, he was breathing heavy, although not from his exertions; this was crazy and he knew it, but he had to know what they were doing.

The lights were about two hundred yards away at a guess, and heading away from the hangar down the old runway in a line. That made sense; if they were moving in the dark, even with flashlights to help them, staying on the concrete would be a lot easier than heading out into the uneven terrain of rock, brush and potholes waiting to trip them up.

But why were they spaced out that way?

The problem he faced was the lack of cover out here save for the dark. If one of them should turn back for any reason he'd be caught wrong-footed with nowhere to go.

He compromised by keeping to the edge of the runway, where the grass and brush were heavy enough to give him an even chance of staying out of sight if he had to hit the ground fast.

He counted his paces to give himself a feel for the distance he was covering, eyes fixed on the lights. They didn't seem to be getting any closer, which was good, and as long as he could see three still moving, that was all he had to worry about.

Then he realised they'd stopped moving. *Had they sensed his presence?*

He froze and lowered himself to the ground, moving slowly. Quick movement, even at night, gets spotted easily, he knew that from his military training. He could hear the murmur of the men's voices now, carrying on the night breeze with nothing out here to stop them. And they were closer, about a hundred yards he figured.

The lights were still in a cluster, but now much closer. He edged forward, treading carefully to avoid dry strands of brushwood and hoping he didn't step on a snake.

Eighty yards. Their voices were more than just a murmur now, and he could pick out Paul's quite easily over the other two. He sounded impatient and snappy, a man who liked giving orders and having no time for delay in others.

He sank to his knees and edged closer, pushing aside clumps of coarse grass with his hands.

Fifty yards.

He was close enough now to see that the three men were all wearing headlights and standing around four of the crates from the hangar; two large, two small. Maybe that explained the way they'd been moving: they'd been carrying the crates in a line. By the lights he could see that Donny was on his knees and holding one of the white drones, which now had its skids and propellers fitted. He placed the drone to one side, then lifted one of the control units with its video screen out of the smaller box next to it. After a few moments he stood up and said something to the other two, and all three men moved back several feet and spread out.

Donny hunched over the controls and there was a frantic buzzing noise and a flick of light, and the drone seemed to shake itself before lifting off the ground and into the sky, the white casing a ghostly blur reflecting the glow of the men's headlights. When the buzzing began to fade, Paul said something sharp. Donny replied and seconds later the buzzing grew again and the drone appeared in the lights, moving about fifteen feet off the ground. It flitted back and forth unevenly, then shot away again and over their heads.

It was now heading directly towards the position where Tommy-Lee was hiding.

He burrowed backwards, keeping low, then turned and scurried away on his elbows and knees as fast as he could, toes digging into the ground to give him purchase. Seconds later the drone passed right over his head and he hugged the earth and froze, then turned back towards the men. He watched it go but didn't dare move; he was still in their direct line of sight and all it would take was for one of them to take their eyes off the drone and they might spot him. As soon as it flitted away to one side, drawing the headlights with it, he started moving again to give himself some distance in case it came back.

Suddenly the buzzing took on a higher, more frantic pitch and Tommy-Lee turned round to look. There was a flash as the drone was caught in one of the men's headlights for a split second, then it dipped suddenly and hit the ground with a dull crunch.

He heard Bill laugh. But Paul said something ugly, cutting the big man off in mid-stream. Then Donny stood up where he'd been kneeling on the ground and walked away like he'd lost his pet dog.

Paul hadn't moved; he stood like a statue, watching Donny. Then he lifted his head and said something sharp to the big man, who turned and began walking in a wide circle, head swinging left and right like a guard dog, the light playing on the ground wherever he looked. When he turned his way, Tommy-Lee ground his face into the dirt and didn't move a muscle. He was pretty sure the big lug wouldn't see him this low down, but he held his breath all the same, breathing in the aroma of sun-baked soil, jackrabbit shit or whatever the hell else was lying around here.

After a couple of seconds Bill's headlight swung away and he resumed his patrol. Tommy-Lee relaxed. That Paul must have the instincts of a jackrabbit; yet he was sure he hadn't made a wrong move and given away his presence. So what had spooked him like that?

Then he recalled the camera he'd seen in the bottom of the smaller case, and the screen attached to the control unit. Damn, he'd been careless; the thought that they might have been able to see him watching them made his blood run cold.

Even as he thought it, he saw something. It was a flicker of movement beyond where the men were standing. It was too quick to identify, but something low to the ground. He figured it might be a fox or a dog, come to see what was going on, and Paul had seen the same movement.

He breathed more easily and moments later saw Donny rejoin Paul. The bigger man was giving the geek a hard time, the words snapping out like a whip in the dark. Donny didn't say a thing, just stood there and took it, head down like a beaten child. After a while Paul seemed to run out of steam and the geek went back to kneeling on the ground again, only this time working on the other two crates.

Ten minutes later another shape took off, dipping sharply towards the ground before recovering and disappearing into the dark just like the last one. This one had a small red light on it, showing its position about fifteen feet above the ground and moving to one side some fifty yards away.

Tommy-Lee figured it was some kind of locator light so they could follow its progress in the dark. Maybe the last one hadn't been working properly. The light didn't stay on for long. After several manoeuvres that took it closer and closer to the ground, it suddenly flew high in the air like it had been fitted with a booster rocket, the buzzing frantic and high-pitched. He heard Paul shout a warning and saw Bill running off to one side to get out of the way. But it was too late. The red light dipped and went down to the ground way faster than it had gone up.

There was another crash followed by a howl of frustration from Paul. This time Bill was silent. Paul strode across to Donny and swung his arm in a roundhouse punch. There was the sound of a fist on flesh and Donny gave a shrill cry and fell to the ground, his head-light flying off to one side.

Tommy-Lee had seen enough. The morons had as much chance of keeping those things in the air as they did of flying to the moon. Whatever they thought they were going to do, they weren't going to accomplish anything except make holes in the ground and smash up their toys.

All he wanted was his money and he could be out of here.

As for Chadwick, he'd have to take his chances.

He was turning to go when he heard a phone ringing, followed by Paul's voice. He sounded angry.

'I told you who they work for. All you have to do is track the movements of any personnel from London. Use the brotherhood to enter the company's systems. There are only two of them and one is a woman; it should be simple enough. Do *not* let them get in my way. I don't care how you do it, but find them, follow them and stop them! End it now!'

28

Donny Bashir was feeling sick to his stomach. Which he thought was pretty odd, considering he hadn't eaten properly for days now. As his mother would have surely told him, he was hardly big enough to sustain a diet in the first place; drinking only water and nibbling at biscuits was no way to stay healthy.

The fact was, the very idea of eating had begun to desert him in earnest the moment he'd heard Asim – or Paul, as he liked to be known outside their group – finally outline the precise details of his plan to strike a blow at the Americans and send a clear message around the world to demonstrate that nothing and nobody was beyond the reach of the truly committed.

Jihad, he had announced with ringing drama, was inevitable and just, and freedom was fast becoming a reality for all who were oppressed.

Freedom and the oppressed. Words he'd heard uttered often and with great passion back at the mosque in Queens, and during other meetings with like-minded individuals. And Asim seemed to use them as a daily mantra for driving himself and others on in what he saw as their holy duty. But was it really a possibility? And what would real freedom be like, anyway? In the last few weeks he had felt less freedom in the company of Asim and Bilal than he'd ever experienced growing up, as a student at NYU or in his job with Apple. With these two men he'd been watched every second, his day laid out before him with no time off, little or no opportunity to relax and absolutely no contact with outsiders under pain of retribution.

Was this what freedom would always be like?

He lifted his head from the pillow of the cheap motel bed and looked across at where Bilal lay sleeping on the other side of the room. The man mountain was snoring as usual, his feet poking off the end of his bed and his muscular shoulders at rest like slabs of meat. He slept like a baby every night and Donny wondered if anything made much impact on him, even the idea of killing many people if the plan they were engaged in came to fruition.

He checked the window. It was still light outside. His watch said four pm. An occasional vehicle rumbled by, but this back-road motel was in its dying days and didn't seem the kind of place to receive much commercial or leisure traffic. In fact it pretty much reflected the pattern of low-level, roach-ridden dives they'd been confined to for the past few weeks since getting together under Asim's directions; deliberately choosing cheap motels on county roads and moving every two or three nights so as not to attract attention.

Travelling under the guise of a university film crew working on a documentary about rural society in the states of Oklahoma and Kansas, they had elicited few questions, as Asim had predicted. After all, who would care about students and their strange comings and goings and late sleep-ins? In addition, they had the right props in the form of cameras and recording equipment in case anybody did ask. In fact Asim had even thought of that, making Donny shoot some footage of barns, roads and countryside, and record some commentary in case they were stopped and questioned.

It was forward planning, as Asim had explained, and it seemed to work. While Donny and Bilal were hardly of obvious white American stock, Asim looked and sounded like a university professor and was able to talk his way out of trouble with a few jokes and a genial manner.

Donny tried covering his ears to blot out Bilal's snores, but without success. The truth was he was too wired to sleep and felt like screaming with frustration… and not just a little naked fear. He'd given up everything in the name of jihad to join Asim and Bilal. Swayed by the words of visiting preachers at his mosque in New York, and a growing yet inexplicable feeling of discontent, he had allowed himself to be talked into the promise of achieving something glorious that would make his name live for evermore.

True, he had achieved much already, from his studies in IT and engineering at NYU Polytechnic, followed by his internship at Apple. But success had somehow failed to ignite the fire he'd been expecting and which everybody had told him would surely come his way if he applied himself to his studies.

It had been hearing Asim explain how a man could use his successes to build into greater success and glory that had finally captured Donny's attention. He had no idea how Asim had chosen him, only that within minutes of being introduced, he had found somebody who seemed to know and understand him like no other person had ever done.

He rolled over and felt a sharp jab of pain slice through his jaw where a tooth had become dislodged. It was a reminder that Asim's understanding was a double-edged sword, and of his ability to turn from light to dark in a flash. The beating last night had brought with it the painful realisation that his belief in Asim had slowly been slipping away over the past few days, especially after the two drones had remained in the air for no longer than a few minutes before crashing to the ground with disastrous results. Bilal hadn't helped; the big man, whom he knew was secretly taking steroids to maintain his grotesque appearance, which was surely contrary to Islam, was as openly contemptuous of Donny's skinny frame and bushy hair as he was his education, and took every opportunity he could find of calling him 'geek' and putting him down, even occasionally swatting him across the head like a misbehaving child.

He closed his eyes tight, seeing once again the awful mental reel of the second drone crashing to the earth, its tiny red light a taunting beacon to its imminent destruction and his failure to control it, followed shortly afterwards by a furious punch to the face from Asim and a snigger from Bilal as he fell down.

He couldn't understand it; he had aced the many games in circulation at school and college, no matter how complex and demanding, and understood the inner working of the drones in a way neither of the other two ever would, including making modifications to the parachute system capsule requested by Asim. Yet mastery of their flight somehow continued to elude him in spite of his efforts to relax and 'feel' at one with the machines in the way he knew he should.

He knew why it was, though; it was Asim's presence that was affecting him. The man's brooding aura and the way he carried his gun, and his sudden bursts of fury when something didn't go well or there was a delay he could not control, radiated out like waves of energy, making Donny feel sick and terrified.

Especially after events at the airfield, and the construction crew. God, he'd been so stupid, so blind.

Bilal's snores were getting louder. For a crazy moment Donny speculated on the best way of silencing the noise for ever, along with the pumped-up moron's open contempt for him. Maybe if he could summon enough strength to bring the wooden chair down across his throat or substitute his steroids tablets with something more lethal.

He rolled off the bed and stood up. It was no good; the moron would swat him across the room with no more effort than he would toss a pillow. Besides, thoughts like these were getting him nowhere and he was certain Asim had a way of sensing what was running through his mind. He needed to get out, if only for a short while. If he didn't, he'd go mad.

He picked up his shoes and stepped over to the door, easing it open and taking the key with him. As usual Asim had gone out to yet another meeting, telling them that they should wait inside for him to come and pick them up. Wherever the meetings were, they seemed to be almost daily and never at the same place in which they were staying. In fact, thinking about it, he'd never once been aware of Asim staying in the same motel, claiming he had people to see and plans to refine. Donny wondered who these mystery people were. He'd found the courage to ask that very question a couple of days ago, but had been told sharply to mind his business since the less he knew the less he could betray if anything happened and he got taken by the police or the FBI.

If he'd needed a reminder of his place in the pecking order, that had been it.

He pulled the door closed and slipped his shoes on, then walked across the parking lot to the road. The motel sat on the outskirts of a small town, with a deserted and abandoned gas station a hundred yards away which seemed to be sinking into the scrubby lot surrounding it as if going back to nature. He turned right and headed along the grass verge towards a cluster of buildings a quarter of a mile away. He hadn't been paying much attention when they'd driven through the town to the motel, but a sour comment by Bilal about a garish bar fronting the street had embedded itself in his mind.

A beer. That's what he needed. A Bud if they did it, maybe a Coors. He'd have to eat something to take the taste away, otherwise Bilal would smell it on his breath and tell Asim.

He walked quickly, hoping for two simple things above all else: one, that Asim would not come driving along the road right now, and two, that Bilal would continue snoring like the pig he was.

The bar was called Jokers, and seemed busy. Several cars stood outside, and three trucks. He took a deep breath and stepped inside.

Nobody even looked at him.

He let the door swing shut. Fifteen people inside, thirteen men and two women plus the bartender. He always did that on entering a building; he had no idea why, it was a habit he'd picked up as a kid. See the room and know instantly how many were there.

'C'n I do for you?' The bartended smiled and stood aside to let him see what was on offer.

Donny asked for a bottle of Bud and the bartender had it out of the chiller cabinet and on the counter inside three seconds. Donny paid up and drank it down almost in one, then asked for another.

Man, that was so good. He hadn't had a beer in a long time and felt himself starting to unwind immediately, a pleasant warmth spreading through his belly and right up his neck to his head. He'd show Asim and Bilal – and the 'expert' Asim had kept talking about; the man who would teach him to fly the drones. Damn, he didn't need teaching; he was a graduate of NYU and wasn't about to be shown up by any so-called expert. And Bilal could go swallow a bucket of steroids; brains beat muscles any day.

He glugged down the next beer almost as quick, this time watched by the bartender.

'A rough day, huh?' the man said automatically, and wiped a few stray spots of beer off the bar top. If he was curious about where Donny was from, he clearly wasn't about to come right out and ask.

'You could say that,' Donny replied, and signalled for another bottle.

This one came with a friendly warning. 'You want to slow down there, son. You look like you haven't eaten in a while, and that stuff can go to your head.'

Donny slurped back a mouthful and wondered why everybody he met these days seemed to be happy giving him advice and orders. Deep down he knew the man was right, and he'd come in here intending to eat as well. But the booze had washed away any caution he might have been feeling when he stepped through the door. Who the hell did these people think they were? First the college staff, then the Apple staff, now Asim and Bilal. Everybody assuming a right to tell him how to live his life. Even the two men standing at the bar a couple of feet away had turned and were giving him the eye, like he'd just landed from Mars.

'You sure you ain't serving 'em a little young today, Chuck?' one of the men said to the bartender. He was dressed in jeans and a check shirt like a gazillion other Americans, and sporting the same buzz-cut as many other men in their forties, clean-shaven and confident.

God how he hated their air of superiority and condescension. He should have seen the danger signs, but he was already too far gone.

'None of your business,' Donny muttered, and found his tongue beginning to stick to the roof of his mouth. Damn, that beer *was* strong. Or maybe he really should have eaten something first.

'Say what?' The other man had turned now, and was staring at Donny with a look of amusement.

'I'm twenty-four and it's none of your damned business if I drink,' Donny said. He'd spoken calmly enough, although for some reason it came out as a shout, accompanied by a spray of spare beer that he hadn't got round to swallowing.

'OK, that's enough,' The bartender leaned across the counter and tapped him on the shoulder. 'I'll have to ask you to leave. Now.'

'Why do you say that?' Donny hugged the half-empty bottle to his chest and pulled away. 'I'm not drunk!'

'I said, you're leaving.' The bartender stepped along the bar and through a flap to back up his request. The other two men stepped back to give him room.

'Fuck you!' Donny shouted, feeling what he was sure was an adrenalin rush, although he suspected it might be the beer and a rising sense of injustice.

The room went quiet and the man in the check shirt said, 'I think we can handle this, Chuck.' He put down his drink and stepped towards Donny. 'Excuse me, sir, but this is where you put down the bottle and leave. Nice and quiet.'

'Shit on you!' Donny squeaked, and backed up fast. 'You filthy American *kuffars* have got a lesson coming very soon… and you'd better watch out!'

The man raised an eyebrow. 'Say what?'

A few comments from the rest of the room began working their way into Donny's fogged brain. They sounded angry and aggressive, but he was past listening.

'Hear me now,' he continued, beginning to sway. 'We will strike at your heart, our insects delivering the sting of death from the sky… your own toys of death spraying our message of destruction on the head of your leader and ending his tyranny.' He threw out his arm in a dramatic gesture, launching a spray of beer from the bottle in his hand over a wide area, including the man's check shirt. '*Allah be praised!*'

'Like hell he will.' This voice came from right behind Donny, and he vaguely recalled seeing a big man in the corner when he'd come in. Sadly his mobile responses were working at quarter-speed, and he only had time to sense a movement before a heavy fist slammed into the side of his head and knocked him to the floor.

-

The man in the check shirt brushed the beer droplets from his shirt before bending to check Donny was still alive. Then he waved away the big man who'd hit him and took out a cell phone to make a call. When he finished speaking he squatted next to the dazed Donny and said quietly, 'This is your lucky day, son. I'm Lieutenant Coley of the Oklahoma State Police Special Operations Troop. My colleague is Trooper Turner and we're taking you out of here before you get yourself lynched. Maybe once we're in the car, you can tell me whether you're drunk, stupid or downright dangerous.' With that, he and Turner grabbed Donny by the arms and dragged him out of the door.

29

The following afternoon Tommy-Lee woke to the sound of an engine being driven hard. He recognised the sound and rolled off his bed, checking his watch. Damn, they were early. What the hell had lit their fuses?

He stepped over to the slit window. Nothing to see yet but the noise was getting closer. Whatever it was, it couldn't be good news. He checked on James, who was moaning in his sleep, and shook him awake.

'You'd better get yourself ready, pal,' he said, handing him a bottle of water. 'They're coming back and it sounds like they mean business.'

'What makes you say that?' James lifted his head enough to swallow some water, before flopping back on the pillow with a sigh. 'What time is it?'

'They're driving like they're being chased by the devil. And that means it's time for you to get serious, if you know what's good for you.'

James stared at him, eyes red-rimmed and bloodshot with lack of sleep. 'Good for me... or good for you?' He tried a wry smile, but it didn't come off, and only made him wince as his lips cracked. 'You do realise, don't you, that if these men are what I think they are, there's no way they'll let you go free when this is all over?'

Tommy-Lee shook his head. He could parlay his way out of most any kind of trouble, unlike this guy. 'You're wrong. I've been hired to do a job and that's what I'm going to do. They trust me. Fact is, though, these three don't know shit about what they're doing, and they're getting desperate. They've been playing with some drones out there and they've already smashed two that I know of, maybe more. Now they've got three, maybe four left and no more in the cookie jar. That means they'll do anything – and I mean *anything* – to get what they want. Now, I won't hide it from you, that might have got me a little worried, because I get the feeling these are three of the craziest motherfuckers I've ever met. And I've known more than a few. But I can handle myself in a corner. Thing is, can you?'

James was staring at him. 'How do you know that – that they've lost the drones?' He struggled against the cuffs to sit up. 'You've been out there, haven't you? You watched them.'

'Doesn't matter what I've done – I just think you should know what you're up against. There's Paul, the bossman, and a hunk of no-brain muscle named Bill who doesn't say much, and a skinny geek named Donny who looks like he just stepped out of high school. I reckon he's the guy you've got to teach to fly those drones.'

'No.' James shook his head. 'I won't do it.'

Tommy-Lee reached under his pillow for the knife. It was time to scare some real sense into this fool. If James stuck to this line of thinking, it meant all bets were off; there wouldn't be any fifteen thousand bucks and he knew that neither of them would get out of this place alive. But before he could do anything the van drew up outside in a rush and the doors were thrown open and slammed shut. No control this time, he noted, just a few terse words from Paul. The men made no move to come to the door of the room, however, instead moving away towards the hangar, their footsteps fading.

He jumped up and went to the window in time to catch a brief glimpse of Paul and Bill walking across the grass before they disappeared from sight. No sign of Donny, unless he was off to one side taking a piss.

He sat on the bed and waited, his head in a spin. Something felt wrong, but he couldn't figure out what. Then he jumped up again and washed his face and took a leek. Anything was better than sitting there waiting for the hammer to fall.

The movement seemed to stir the air in the room, and the smell of their unwashed bodies and the near-full latrine bucket along with some rotting fruit in one of the boxes nearly made him throw up. He'd somehow managed to zone all that out for the past few days, as if it was all in his imagination; but suddenly it had all become real again.

He threw down the filthy T-shirt he'd been using as a washrag and took a turn around the room; two paces one way, two the other. All the time he could feel James's eye on him. He felt like a caged bull he'd seen at a rodeo down south one time, the animal locked in a pen too small for its hunched muscle and sinew, and ready to break out in a burst of fury.

Then there was the rattle of the key in the lock and the door was thrown open.

It was Paul. He had one hell of a face on him and was carrying the semi-automatic Tommy-Lee had seen before. Only now it was out in the open. He didn't look as if he'd had much sleep and was about ready to cap somebody out of sheer spite.

Tommy-Lee stood and waited. He didn't know what had happened, but it wasn't good, he could tell that much. And as he'd learned over a lifetime in some dangerous places, a man who takes to waving a gun around when he doesn't have to is quite likely to use it on the first person he sees who gives him good cause.

'The situation has changed,' Paul announced, looking at James. 'I don't need you to teach anybody how to fly the drones.'

'So what are you going to do – shoot me?'

'No. I mean you're going to fly them for me.'

'What?' James looked as if he didn't care. 'You're crazy. Why should I help you?'

In response, Paul lifted the gun towards Tommy-Lee and pulled the trigger.

The shot was deafening in the confined space, and Tommy-Lee was spun round by the force of the bullet snatching at his ribs. It was like being hit with a baseball bat. He fell over onto the bed and screamed as a jolt of pain went through him, and saw the wall behind him was now ghosted with a red mist, with a hole drilled in the center.

'*Jesus! What the hell was that for?*' He clutched his side, then gagged as his hand brushed the open edges of the wound. His fingers came away sticky with his blood and he felt sick and nearly passed out.

'That's because I can, Mr Roddick,' Paul said calmly. 'And to demonstrate what I will do if I have to. Frankly, I don't care if you never leave this place alive. It's all the same to me.' He turned to James. 'But I think you've clearly underestimated what I will do, so take that demonstration as a reminder. Also,'- he reached over and picked up the DVD player from the chair, 'perhaps I need to remind you about a few things, just to focus your mind.' He turned on the player and dropped it on the bed.

'What have you done?' James cried, lunging against the cuffs, his eyes on the small screen. 'If you've touched my family I'll never do anything—'

'So far,' Paul interrupted him, 'I haven't done anything to them. But let me remind you of what we're seeing here. The first footage is outside your home in London, where your charming wife, Elizabeth, is currently staying. Chelsea, I believe the district is called; very expensive, very... safe. But not for much longer. I have a man not a hundred yards from her front door right now. At a phone call from me, he will go in and kill her. But not before using her as he would any common whore.'

'Wait!' James choked on his anger and tried to sit up.

'Next,' Paul continued as if he hadn't noticed, 'we come to the charming British public school where your son, Ben, is being educated. See the boys walking across the yard? They do that several times a day, going from their dorms to the classrooms and back, and to the dining room. I have two men nearby this time, both skilled at entering premises without alerting anybody. A call from me and they will enter the building and track down your son. There they will kill him in the most appropriate way they can think of. I've left that decision to them, but the most silent way will be, I believe, with a knife. Of course, if they should make a noise and be disturbed, then I cannot say who else will die. Probably quite a few of Ben's friends.'

'You bastard!'

'And lastly, we come to the apartment where Miss Valerie DiPalma lives. A lovely young woman, I can see why you have become… attached to her. But also vulnerable if I make one phone call to the man currently outside the apartment block and awaiting my orders.' He paused while James looked on aghast as the picture of the apartment block entrance rolled by. 'Unknown to Miss DiPalma, he has been following her whenever she leaves, and waiting nearby when she stays inside. He has also gained possession of a key to the rear door and emergency stairs. I have to admit that this man is perhaps the least attractive of those who will do what I tell them. He's an animal and likes to inflict pain, especially on lovely young women. But he also likes to take pleasure in them first. Now, Mr Chadwick,' he picked up the DVD player and threw it across the room, where it smashed against the wall, 'what is your answer? I'll give you ten minutes to think it over. After that you and your family will cease to exist. Your choice.'

With that he stood up and walked out, locking the door behind him.

30

Ruth and Vaslik were back in the Cruxys office poring over the maps, while Walter Reiks was explaining to an agency temp her duties which included answering the phone, taking messages and holding the fort until a full-time administrator was appointed.

Chadwick's original was the main focus and was pinned onto a cork-board on the wall. Ruth had put sticky notes close to the areas Chadwick had circled, and another alongside the word *freedom*, which had been underlined.

'This has to mean something,' she murmured, tapping the map with a pen. 'Why would he write it down and underline it? That's pretty specific.'

Vaslik went over to computer on the desk and punched a few keys. 'If we concentrate on those three states, I've got Freedom in Nebraska, described as an unincorporated community in Frontier County.'

'What does that mean – unincorporated?'

'It means it doesn't have its own governing municipality, but is run by a local township or county.' He punched another key. 'There's a map but not much in the way of a town. If you want to mark it, it's in the bottom left of Nebraska, close to the county line with Kansas.'

Ruth put a cross where he said and asked, 'Is Nebraska flat?'

'You could say that. Why?'

'Airfields. Chadwick was looking for abandoned airfields.'

'Doesn't mean the area has to be flat; just big enough to put in a runway, same as roads.'

'True. What else do you have?'

'There are two Freedoms in Kansas; one in Bourbon County, population at the last census, five-hundred and five. The other is in Ellis County, population one-hundred and twenty-five.' He punched more keys and said, 'Wait. It says there are more communities named Freedom in Kansas. This could take a while.'

'What about Oklahoma?'

'There's one in Woods County, population two-hundred and eighty-nine.' He sat back and puffed his cheeks. 'Checking out these places could take forever; it's a lot of territory to cover and we could be chasing shadows.' He stood up and walked over to the map and studied it. 'There must be dozens of abandoned airfields out there. We can't get round them all and Google Maps can only show us so much. And why would Chadwick be looking for an abandoned one, anyway?'

'It probably wasn't down to him. If it was this Paul guy, and he's planning what we think he's planning and wants Chadwick to teach him how to fly drones, he'd want somewhere quiet where he wouldn't have officials or cops breathing down his neck.' She shrugged. 'Other than that, who the hell can read the intentions of terrorists?'

Vaslik nodded. 'That's true enough. But why this remote? I mean, Kansas, Nebraska and Oklahoma are all a long way out from the main centres like New York, Washington or Chicago.'

'You're assuming they plan to hit a big city. What if they have somewhere else in mind?'

'OK, like what? Sporting events, conference venues, government facilities, military bases… the list is endless.' He raised a hand. 'Sorry – I don't mean to be negative, but this is huge. There's got to be a clue somewhere to narrow it down or we could be going round in circles forever.'

Ruth nodded. He was right. Without a specific target even the FBI, with all the data crunching facilities at their disposal, would have a hard time convincing anybody that any kind of threat was actually out there. She considered another approach. If you were looking for a target to aim at, did it have to be a fixed one? 'What would be the biggest propaganda target a terrorist attack could hit in this area? Forget the remoteness or the distance from the big cities.'

He pursed his lips. 'I'd go for one of the military bases.'

'Why? Why not a university or college campus, shopping mall or a sports arena? That would get headlines.'

'It would. But they're soft targets. Hitting them would be nothing like making a successful strike at the US military.' He went back to the keyboard. 'And there are... five military bases in Oklahoma alone, one of them an ammunition plant.'

'Ouch. And the others?'

'Let's see... there are three in Kansas; one of which is Fort Riley with over twenty-five thousand personnel. Nebraska has just one.' He looked up. 'Take your pick – they're all sitting there, all roughly in the same area.'

She shook her head. Vaslik wasn't passing off responsibility to her to come up with an answer; he was bouncing it off her to get them both thinking, the way any good team should. Logic told her that a stationery target was just that – a target. But would that really attract the attention of extremists hellbent on creating world-wide headlines? Most military bases were huge, some like cities. But they didn't usually give out maps to the public showing where the specific locations of personnel or top-level facilities were gathered, which is what most terrorist planners would be looking for. And a strike – even if successful – on a bunch of warehouses or near-deserted training areas would do nothing to gain them the news value they desired, yet the risk involved would be the same.

She studied Chadwick's map again. Trying to decrypt the scribbles in the margins had been a major tease from the moment she'd first seen them. Logic again told her that a man like Chadwick was accustomed to dealing in numbers and letters and specific details, a man who had passed through Wall

Street and London, then through the US Air Force Intelligence apparatus. All were environments where clear and concise thinking was paramount, and she was willing to bet that Chadwick would not have made these notes without some purpose. Maybe he'd heard them mentioned before he disappeared. They must have meant something at the time, something that had made the analytical side of his brain seek to retain them for consideration later.

She had an idea. She took the map down and carried it through to a photocopier in the outer office. She made three copies of the margins where the scribbled notes had been made and took them to Reiks and Vaslik.

'Photocopies sometimes make handwritten text clearer,' she told them. 'See what you can make from these just by looking at the scribbled notes.'

They sat and stared at the words, or portions of words. For several minutes there was just the distant sound of traffic in the street below, and a phone ringing in an adjacent part of the building. Reiks stood up and walked round the office a couple of times, then muttered something indistinguishable before going over to the corkboard where he pinned a sheet of plain paper. He wrote down several words, then stood back. 'That's what I see. How about you two?'

Ruth and Vaslik started at what he'd written. Alt… Van… FtSill… McA… Tin.

'Nothing,' said Ruth. 'Sorry. Slik?' She turned and found Vaslik was grinning. 'What?'

'I'll leave it to Walter,' he said.

'Military bases,' said Reiks. 'They're all military bases in Oklahoma.' He nodded at Vaslik who tapped the keyboard and waited, then nodded.

'He's right. Oklahoma has five facilities: Altus, Vance and Tinker are all USAF; Fort Sill is army and McAlester is an army ammunitions base.'

Ruth studied the map again. They were right. It defied logic in one sense, but there could be only one reason why Chadwick had noted down five military facilities in the state of Oklahoma.

'It's a list of targets,' she said softly.

Seconds later Vaslik had Tom Brasher on the phone with the conference button open.

'What's happening at any of the military bases in Oklahoma in the next two or three weeks?' he asked.

'Huh? Why? I'm in the middle of something here.'

'Humour us.'

'Military, you say?'

'Yes.'

'I have no idea. Hold on a second.' He put the phone and they heard him speaking in the background. When he came back, his voice sounded constricted as if he'd chocked on something indigestible.

'Which base are you talking about?'

'Any of them.' Vaslik named them all.

'Jesus, I hope you're not serious about this. Where did this list come from?'

Vaslik explained about the map and the scribbles. 'Chadwick was researching some issues to do with abandoned airfields, but he also made notes of these places, although we have no idea why.'

'Well, I hope to hell he wasn't serious,' Brasher muttered, 'because the day after tomorrow, Air Force One will be landing at Altus Air Force base where the president is due to give an inspection and talk to the personnel.'

For several seconds nobody spoke; the implications were frightening. Finally Brasher broke the silence, 'Perhaps you'd better tell me what it is you think you've discovered.'

Vaslik looked at Ruth and nodded. She said, 'We think Paul and his friends are planning a strike of some kind on the base using the drones stolen from Memphis.'

'Drones? How?'

'We don't know… but if you recall what Patric Paget told us about the modifications his techs made to the *Moskitos* for dispersing smoke, it won't be explosives.'

There was a further stunned silence while Brasher digested the idea. Then another voice joined in somewhere in the background and Brasher muttered an obscenity. 'Are you at Cruxys?'

'Yes.'

'Well, stay fucking put – I'm coming over.'

Somewhere in the building a phone rang, then stopped. Walter Reiks went off to check on the agency worker. When he came back he was looking puzzled and irritated.

'What's up?' said Ruth.

'I'm not sure. Did you leave word with anybody about your movements?'

'No. The office in London, but that was all. Why?'

Walter stuck a thumb over his shoulder. 'The agency temp just took a call from the London office asking if you'd arrived yet. She told them yes, but the caller rang off without leaving a message.'

Ruth exchanged a look with Vaslik, then picked up the phone and called London with a simple question.

'No, Miss Gonzales,' was the answer. 'Nobody called from here.'

31

Brasher walked in thirty minutes later with another man in tow. Neither of them looked happy, albeit for different reasons.

'This is SAC John Kraski,' said Brasher, nodding at his companion. 'He's been tasked with overseeing and providing analysis on all current warnings and alerts relating to potential terrorist activities and liaising with the Secret Service. You'll need to run your latest findings on the Chadwick situation past him.' His face was a complete blank but none of them needed telling that Brasher wasn't happy with being coat-tailed by a senior colleague.

Kraski looked as if he might enjoy chewing six-inch nails for fun. He studied each of the three Cruxys investigators as if they were lab rats, dwelling longest on Walter Reiks, who gave him a sour look in return. Tall and crisp as a window-mannequin, with pale skin and neatly-parted grey hair, Kraski exuded self-importance and an air of impatience.

'I think you've already heard pretty much everything we have,' said Reiks, 'but why don't we sit and talk?' Without waiting for anyone to answer, he walked along the corridor into a meeting room that smelled of fresh paint. There was a table and eight chairs, but nothing else. 'I'm sorry for the lack of facilities,' he said, gesturing for them to sit down, 'but we're just getting set up.'

'Who's in charge here?' Kraski asked bluntly.

'I am.' Reiks nodded at Ruth and Vaslik. 'My two colleagues, Ruth Gonzales and Andy Vaslik, are over from the London office conducting a search for a missing client, James Chadwick.'

Kraski didn't offer to shake hands, but gave a curt nod and sat down. 'OK, so where are you on this Chadwick business?'

'We have reason to believe that James Chadwick has been kidnapped by at least two men with extremist links – that is to say, extremist Islamic links – who appear to be connected to the theft of six drones from the FedEx hub at Memphis International. These drones are very high-spec machines which have been modified in such a way that they could be used as weapons.'

'On what?'

'We're working on that.'

'Really.' Kraski looked at them in turn, his expression sceptical. 'It's a bit thin, isn't it?'

'We don't think so, Mr Kraski,' Ruth said carefully. 'The evidence we've gathered suggests Chadwick could be coerced into fly the drones.' She placed Chadwick's map on the table. 'We know Chadwick was researching airfield sites in remote areas of the States just before he disappeared, and—'

'Why?'

'We're not sure, but bearing in mind his prior service in USAF Intelligence, we can only assume that he was given enough information to prompt him to look into the background of this plan. He's an expert in drone technology so it's safe to assume he knew they would want to do the training somewhere remote and free of observation by the authorities. He was probably only part-way through his research when he disappeared.'

'That's a lot of supposition.'

'You're right, it is.' Ruth met his scepticism without flinching. 'In addition, we know he singled out five military bases in Oklahoma, one or more of which we think may be the eventual target for an attack.'

'And you believe that target might be Altus, am I right?' Kraski glanced at Brasher, although apparently not to get confirmation; the look wasn't that friendly.

'It's not unreasonable. Your president is going to be there the day after tomorrow. We think the people planning this would view it as a prime piece of propaganda if they could carry out a two-pronged attack in the same place; one on a military facility, the other on the person of the US president.'

Kraski grunted. 'Right. So let me get these details straight.' He stared up at the ceiling with a puzzled frown. 'You claim to have a group of terrorists who may or may not have stolen a consignment of small commercial drones; these same men have tried to coerce or may now have kidnapped a business consultant who allegedly has some experience in flying model aircraft or UAVs, to assist in what you believe is an attack on the president; this same consultant, from what you're saying, has left a number of clues which point towards this attack taking place in Oklahoma. Is that it?'

Ruth didn't answer; a portion of her mind was focussed on who might have called for her earlier, and what it might mean. The fact that the call had purportedly come from the London office could mean only one thing: somebody had made a connection to the very recently setup New York office, and that person now knew where she was. The big questions were, who had called and why?

She pushed it to one side and focussed once more on Agent Kraski. His tone of hostility was abundantly clear, but she couldn't think what was causing it save for a huge dose of self-importance.

'Look at the map,' suggested Vaslik. 'It's all there.'

But Kraski ignored him. 'May I ask what is your background for this, Miss Gonzales? Have you worked in counter-terrorism before this?'

'I was in the British army for a number of years and then in the Ministry of Defence Police,' Ruth said. 'So yes, there's been a strong element of counter-terrorism work in what I've done. Is that a problem?'

'Not for you, I don't suppose.' Kraski's voice was casual, almost dismissive. 'But for me it certainly is. Do you know how many crazy, off-the-wall threats we hear about and investigate every week? Can you imagine how many man hours we would have to rack up if we took every apparent threat to its ultimate conclusion? So far you haven't told me how these toys will be used. I'm no expert but even I know they don't have much range or payload. Yet you say they'll be flown at this target and somehow used as a weapon?'

'Two-point-five kilos,' said Vaslik. 'And they're not toys.'

'What?'

'Two and a half kilos. The payload of the stolen drones. That's over five pounds. And they have a range of nearly twenty miles and can fly at anything up to seventy miles per hour.'

Kraski looked as if he had swallowed a bug. 'So?'

'Have you any idea what five pounds of C4 going off twenty feet above your head would do?'

The silence was intense, and Kraski looked embarrassed. As he and everybody else in the room knew, the concussive effects alone would be enormous, killing the closest and causing irreparable trauma to ears, eyes and brain to many more.

'You're forgetting something, SAC Kraski,' said Walter Reiks with a polite bite. 'While a Special Agent in several field offices with the Bureau, I handled a great many terrorist and serious organised crime threats. Based on the evidence I've seen so far, I consider this one to be real and imminent. This man Chadwick *has* disappeared, he *was* under surveillance by at least one individual with known extremist views and the drones *were* stolen with the help of another man with the same extremist connections. Furthermore, Miss Gonzales, Mr Vaslik and your own colleague here, Special Agent Brasher, were assured by the manufacturer that the drones are capable of dispersing powder, or can be further modified to disperse a spray.' He prodded the air with his words. 'A spray. That's really not something I'd care to ignore.'

Kraski flushed, although whether at the former FBI man's quiet tone of reproof or his reminder that he had been a field agent of long standing wasn't clear.

'That's as may be, Mr Reiks, but I've seen stronger evidence of other threats than this which have turned out to be just as unimpressive. You and your colleagues are asking us to believe that this man Chadwick is embroiled in a threat against the president's life. Well, on what you've just said and what Special Agent Brasher has told me, I can't see it.'

'But will you at least issue a warning to the president's security detail?' Ruth asked. 'Or better still, call off his visit?'

'I most certainly will not. In these troubled times there is always a threat level on the president's life, we're aware of that. But if what you're suggesting is that this inspection and talk should be cancelled, you can forget it. The president does not cancel his plans for anybody.' He stood up and threw a look at Brasher. 'I'll see you back at the office.'

After Kraski had gone, Brasher lifted his hands in apology. 'Look, I'm sorry. But we're being run ragged at the moment and everybody's trying to second-guess the next 'event'. Kraski's been sent to us to help analyse the threat levels and likely seriousness of something being carried out, and he's juggling balls just like everyone else.'

'Balls is right,' said Ruth. 'He couldn't have dismissed it more openly if he'd tried.'

Brasher nodded. 'Look, I can't openly help you if Kraski kicks this into the long grass, and I've already been assigned to a specialist task force which is going to take me out of the game. But there's no way I can let it go, either. What's your next plan?'

'It's still the old plan,' Ruth replied. 'We have to find James Chadwick.'

'If he's still alive.'

'He is, I'm sure of it. If this thing is real, they need him. I can't see them killing off the one person they think can help them carry out their attack.'

'But would he do it?' said Reiks. 'From what little I've read and heard, Chadwick strikes me as a straight-up guy. Helping with a terrorist attack would repel him, wouldn't it?'

'It depends how they colour it,' said Vaslik. 'They either hide what they're really planning behind some fancy corporate showpiece and get him to train their guy… or they go straight for the throat and threaten his family and friends.'

'You mean the DiPalma woman.' Brasher looked conflicted. 'That would certainly be an incentive. But she and the family are beyond reach, aren't they?'

Ruth nodded. 'They won't get to them – but Chadwick won't know that. If they're holding him, which is what it looks like, as far as he's concerned it's a very real threat.'

'OK. Let's assume this plan is real and they will do it – and the president is the target. I can advise the Secret Service that a threat is there, and that they should take all necessary precautions regarding this visit. But I can't do much more myself because Kraski will be watching me.'

'He's an asshole,' Walter Reiks muttered. 'Always has been.'

'Then we'll have to do it.' Ruth felt annoyed and helpless, but she wasn't about to give up. There was too much riding on it. 'We'll have to find them.'

Brasher looked startled. 'How? You don't know where they are.'

'We can't find Chadwick, that's true. But we might be able to find where their launch site is.'

'Jesus, how?'

Vaslik was nodding. 'If the drones have a range of about twenty miles, that's got to be the perimeter around Altus. We need to look for the outer edge and work our way in. Wherever he is, it will be close enough to the base to see what happens, but somewhere quiet where nobody will think of looking.'

Brasher nodded. 'Trouble is, that's a lot of open territory. However, I might be able to help you there. I know a guy out in Oklahoma City. He's a former Agency pilot with his own helicopter and he's dying of boredom. That will save you a lot of driving time.'

'Fine.'

He stood up and leaned over the map. 'But why did Chadwick write 'Freedom' on the map? If this guy is as focussed as you say, that must mean something. Is there a place called Freedom down there?'

'There is,' said Vaslik. 'It's up by the county line with Kansas.'

Brasher stabbed the map with his finger. 'That must be over a hundred-and-fifty miles from Freedom to Altus. There's no way these drones would cover that distance, even if the signals were good enough.'

'Maybe that's where they've been practising. It means we have to keep looking.'

Brasher nodded. 'Darned thing is, I can see Kraski's viewpoint. From a purely evidential angle, it sounds crazy. I mean, how do they think they'll accomplish anything with these drones? All we need to do is get the base to hold a turkey shoot and simply blow them out of the sky as they go over.'

'There are two problems with that, one of which you said yourself,' Ruth reminded him.

'Yeah? What's that?'

'One, they'll be lucky if they even see them coming. A single drone has little more radar signature than a few birds. And they'll be moving very fast.'

'Great. And the other?'

'We don't know for sure what the weapon is, but would you really want a canister of toxic gas being blown out of the sky right over the base?'

32

The moment the door closed behind Paul, Tommy-Lee rounded on James, forcing out the words in a hiss against the jagged pain in his side and the muzziness in his head. 'Are you stupid fucking *crazy*? Can you see now what I've been saying? You've got to do what he asks, can't you see that?'

'Really?' James looked calm, but his eyes were flicking between Tommy-Lee's wound and the spray of blood on the wall. 'He's going to kill us whatever I do.'

'So, you play for time, for Chrissake. Tell him you'll do as he says, and maybe we can work on a way of getting out of here before anything takes off. The guy's nuts, you can see that. Do you really want him to make any one of those phone calls?'

'How can we get away? He's got a gun. You think you can take him on with that knife you keep under the pillow? And you with a hole in you?'

Tommy-Lee shook his head, which didn't make him feel any less dizzy. He was desperate for an idea and knew that his options had suddenly got a lot smaller. With Donny somehow out of the picture, probably run off and miles away by now if he had any sense after last night, Paul and the muscle man would now be even more careful around him. 'I don't know yet. I'll think of something, don't worry. Maybe I can take him as he comes back through the door. If not, all I need is for you to play cute and go along with what he says. It's our only chance.'

James didn't say anything, but stared at the wall and sighed.

The ten minutes went by far too quickly. A click of the key turning in the door and Paul was standing there again, with Bill towering in the background. Only this time the big man was holding an assault rifle over his shoulder. In his hands it looked like a toy, but Tommy-Lee recognised it as anything but. It was a Bushmaster AR-15 fitted with a long magazine, with a rate of fire that could turn the two of them into pulp and the room into matchwood.

He became aware that James was staring at him, eyes flicking pointedly at the pillow covering his knife. It was obvious what he was thinking.

Tommy-Lee stayed where he was. His guts had turned to water and he felt a sense of deep shame wash over him as he realised that even without the appearance of the assault rifle, he couldn't do it. And it wasn't just the pain from his side that was holding him back.

He was plain scared.

'Well?' Paul's nose wrinkled in disgust at the smell – or maybe it was at the realisation that fear had rendered Tommy-Lee incapable of moving.

'Yes.' James's voice was low, but carried clearly across the room. 'I'll do it. But you must promise me that your men won't harm my family… or Miss DiPalma.'

'You have my word.' Paul smiled, then gestured at Bill to hand him the assault rifle and unlock the cuffs. 'You have made a wise decision.'

Moments later they were walking across the airfield towards the hangar. Tommy-Lee stumbled, as much from the brightness of the sun as the shock of his wound and the lowering of his defences, and wondered how he was going to talk his way out of this. Maybe the guy would see sense and let him go. Tough luck on Chadwick, though; he'd committed himself to helping them go through with whatever the crazy plan had to be.

'Aren't you worried we might be seen?' James queried, looking back at the road.

'Even if we are,' Paul replied, 'I don't intend being here very long. A further incentive for you not to make any mistakes.'

With Paul still carrying the Bushmaster, Bill lumbered ahead and went into the room where Tommy-Lee had seen the boxes and crates. He emerged with one small and one larger crate, carrying them with ease, and they all walked out of the main door and across to the runway. The sun was bright and hot, bouncing off the concrete and sending up heat shimmers in the distance, and a bird sang high above them.

It should have been a fine day to be alive but Tommy-Lee simply wanted to be sick.

Two hundred yards down the runway, Paul motioned them to stop and Bilal opened the two crates and lifted out the contents, setting them down with great care.

'You know these machines?' Paul said to James.

James looked down at them, then shrugged. 'I've heard of them but I've never seen one before. How did you get hold of them?'

'That does not concern you. Can you fly them?'

'I'm not sure I can. This is new technology... I'm not sure I could handle it.'

Paul's face went cold. 'Well, I'm sure you haven't *handled* a haulage truck before. But I imagine you could if you had to... unless you want me to put another hole in Mr Roddick, here?'

James nodded. 'There's no need for that. I'll try.'

'Good. Then do so. But whatever you do, do not break it. Any silly accidents, and I will simply shoot Mr Roddick. Then I will get my colleague to bring another machine. Break that one and you will die. But only after I make those phone calls to my men in England and New York.'

James looked stricken by defeat. He knelt down alongside the drone and began to check it over. It was soon evident by his manner that he knew what he was dealing with and being extremely careful to check every aspect of the machine, from the small propellers and video screen read-out to the buttons and toggles on the control unit. Eventually he stood up and nodded. 'It's fine as far as I can see. But I don't understand something.'

'What is that?'

'This drone is fitted with a parachute ejector, but there's no chute. It's got a secondary canister inside instead. What's that for?'

'You ask too many questions.' Paul tilted the rifle towards Tommy-Lee. 'Don't make the mistake of thinking I won't use this out here, Mr Chadwick. There's nobody around to hear it save for a few birds and some rabbits. And I doubt they care one way or another what happens to you.'

'You made that clear already. What manoeuvre do you want me to make with it?'

Paul looked down the runway. 'See that rock off to the left of the runway about three-hundred yards away? Fly the drone down as far as that, turn around it and hover overhead for a moment, then bring it back.' He added, 'No tricks, Mr Chadwick, and no crashes. Stick to about fifty feet going down and twenty feet coming back.'

James picked up the handset and motioned them all to stand well back. His hands moved on the controls and the drone sprang into life, the rotors buzzing furiously. With barely a shimmer, the drone lifted off and went high in the air, settling at about fifty feet. Seconds later, it turned and flew away down the runway, keeping a steady course all the way. When it reached the rock Paul had indicated, it slowed and began to turn, then hovered, like a giant dragonfly, the sun shining off the white casing. All the time James was focussed on the control unit and screen, only glancing up at the drone to check its position and flight path relevant to the ground.

Then Paul stepped forward. 'Release the parachute.'

James stared at him. 'I can't – it hasn't got one.'

'Do as I say. Press the release.' The tip of the rifle barrel lifted to emphasise the order.

James shrugged and pressed a button on the control set. As they watched, a spray of bright red blossomed out behind the drone and fell to the ground in slow motion, coating the rock and the area around it the colour of blood.

When the drone returned at twenty feet and settled on the ground with the lightest of touches, Paul nodded with satisfaction. 'See how simple that was? That is all I want you to do.' He turned to Bill, who was scanning the area around the airfield, and said, 'Pack it up with the others and load the van. We move out in thirty minutes.'

'Where are we going?' said James.

'That is something you will find out in due course. Now move.' He looked at Tommy-Lee and said, 'You help him carry the smaller case. And whatever you do, do not drop it.'

-

Twenty minutes later, Bill had driven the van to just inside the hangar doors and loaded the remaining crates into the back. He shut the doors and walked across to join Paul, who was standing by the inspection pit with James and Tommy-Lee.

'It's done.'

Paul nodded. 'Good. You know what to do now.' He watched as Bill hurried away and took two large plastic containers from the back of the van. He removed the caps and began sprinkling the contents all around the walls of the hanger. Within moments the heady smell of gasoline began to fill the air around them.

'A final reminder for you, Mr Chadwick,' said Paul. 'In case you are thinking of doing anything stupid once the drones are in the air, forget it. If I get even a hint of that, you know what I will do.'

'Them?' James looked puzzled. 'How can I fly more than one… unless…' He stopped. 'They're fitted with GPS, aren't they?'

'Correct. They are linked to a master control. Once airborne they will each fly on a pre-set course. All you have to do is get them up and make sure they stay there.'

'A set course. To the same target?'

Paul ignored the question save for a pinched smile. He turned to Tommy-Lee. 'Now, what was I saying about a reminder? Ah, yes. You were not entirely honest with me about your background, Mr Roddick. I am not entirely happy with that deception.'

Tommy-Lee looked at him, eyes dulled with fear and pain. 'I don't know what you mean. I told you the truth.' He swallowed hard and added lamely, 'I was in Indiana like I said.'

'I don't mean your prison record, which was also a deception. I'm talking about your two years of military service in Iraq starting in two-thousand and three. You were with the National Guard and assigned as a prison worker to Abu Ghraib and Camp Bucca. Correct?'

'No! You've got that wrong.' Tommy-Lee looked around desperately as if he might see a way out. 'That's bullshit… I was never at Abu Ghraib – you must have made a mistake.'

'There is no mistake. You were jailer and quickly became a lead interrogator.' Paul's voice was insistent. 'I've seen the military records and the reports into the activities of you and some of your colleagues. You tortured prisoners and made them suffer unspeakable indignities such as water-boarding and sensory deprivation. As a result of those things and the laxity shown by your commanding officer, you were relieved of your post and shipped back to the US in disgrace.'

'No, wait!' Tommy-Lee held up his good hand. 'OK, I admit I was out there, in Iraq. But I didn't do the kind of stuff you're thinking about; that was down to a few CIA spooks and some low-life detention center guards. Man, they weren't even properly trained, not like me. They were brought in by the CIA 'cos they knew what to do and didn't give a shit about procedure or human rights or none of that stuff, as long as they got results. They were animals. You gotta believe me.'

'I don't *gotta* do anything,' Paul said tauntingly. 'Except this.' He handed the assault rifle to Bill, then reached round behind his back and brought out a semi-automatic pistol. He flicked the barrel sideways for Tommy-Lee to move to the edge of the pit, and said, 'Kick the boards away.'

'What? No, wait! I—'

'Do it!'

Tommy-Lee shuffled over to do as he was told. Tears were now running down his face and his chest and stomach were jumping with fear and frustration. 'Man, this ain't right. I did what you wanted… I looked after Chadwick like you asked and I persuaded him to help you, even though he didn't want to. I did exactly what you said – I even refused to take the knife to you when he asked me earlier, so we could escape. That's gotta count for something, right?' He scrubbed at his face with his good hand and gave a shivering sigh.

'Really?' Paul glanced at James Chadwick. 'Is that correct? Well, I'm impressed. He, at least, has some courage. Now kick the damned boards away!'

Tommy-Lee did as he was told. The boards were thin and dried out by time and the elements, and one of them shattered and split, revealing the hole beneath. A strong stench of decay rose up like a vapour, and with it thousands of flies, filling the air around his head. Tommy-Lee tried to fend off the insects crowding against his face, filling his mouth, nose and eyes, and staggered away, but was pushed back by Paul. He stopped on the lip of the pit, then looked down and screamed in horror.

33

'Welcome to Oklahoma City.' The man waiting to greet Ruth and Vaslik in the main terminal at the city's Will Rogers World Airport was wiry and tanned and carried the healthy glow of an outdoor type. He wore jeans and a cotton shirt, with aviator glasses tucked into the top pocket, and seemed genuinely pleased to see them. 'Dave Proust.'

Ruth shook his hand. He had a crisp, dry grip and she guessed was in his mid-sixties but moved like a much younger man.

'Please, call me Dave.' He shook hands with Vaslik and gestured over his shoulder. 'You want to get coffee or something to eat before we set out? It ain't bad here – I've tried pretty much everything and I'm still standing.'

'Coffee would be good,' Ruth said. 'And we can show you where we'd like to go, if that's all right?'

He grinned enthusiastically. 'I can vouch for the coffee, and you show me a map and I'll tell you what's possible. Tom Brasher gave me a briefing on what you're looking for, so I have a good idea already.'

He set off at a brisk pace and led them to a small coffee bar where they ordered drinks before finding a table out of earshot of other passengers. Ruth relaxed; for the first time she began to feel that they might be getting somewhere instead of treading water. The decision to fly out here and use Oklahoma as their first jumping-off point had come as a relief, especially with Tom Brasher's suggestion to engage Dave Proust as their guide and pilot. But the journey here had not shaken off the suspicion that her movements were possibly being followed. She had studied the other passengers on the way here but none had looked remotely suspicious or had seemed even slightly interested in her or Vaslik.

Once coffee was served and stirred, Andy Vaslik laid out the map and gave Dave a summary of the situation.

The former FBI man studied the map for a while, then said, 'I know of only one Freedom; it's up on the Cimarron River – and it does have an airfield. I've landed there a couple of times, but I can tell you now it's nothing more than a runway, just south of town. You think these guys have been flying drones there?'

'It's the only lead we have,' Ruth told him. 'Chadwick wrote the name on the map and the circle he made is right on the spot where it should be. He doesn't seem the kind of man to make a note like that unless it meant something.'

'Well, he could be right, I guess. There are several airfields all over the state, many of them abandoned, some in the middle of nowhere and mostly to the south of here. They're not all government built, but those that were products of a time when they figured it was worth having standby airfields in out-of-the-way places, some with runways long enough to take tactical aircraft. The one near Freedom, though, that's pretty small and close to some homesteads. If these guys did their flying there, somebody would have seen or heard them.'

Ruth nodded. 'It's a long shot, I know. But we have to start somewhere.'

Dave folded the map and smiled. 'That's good enough for me, young lady. If I'd ignored every long shot during my time with the Bureau, I would have missed some golden opportunities. If this doesn't pan out, I know of a couple of other fields not far away, although none of them has the name of Freedom. What say we get on board and start flying?'

They finished their coffees and Dave led them out to a pickup parked near the front entrance. He drove them away from the main terminal to a line of hangars on the west side of the airport. He parked the pickup and led them through a security checkpoint and out to the apron where they saw a number of aircraft dotted around, some fixed wing, some helicopters. Pointing at one helicopter in a white livery he said, 'That's my baby. In case you're interested it's an Enstrom Shark. She's done some miles but she's sweet as a bee and loves to fly, same as me.'

They climbed aboard and stowed their bags while Dave went through the pre-flight procedure and spoke to the tower. Ten minutes later, headsets in place, they were airborne and heading in a north-westerly direction away from the airport.

'It'll take under an hour to get there,' Dave told them. 'So sit back and enjoy the ride.'

Vaslik put his head back and dozed, while Ruth stared down at the ground and realised what they had taken on. The countryside below looked vast, much of it seemingly given over to grassland, although from up here it was hard to tell. But it was already an indication of the kind of search they were setting out on.

-

She must have dozed off too because what seemed only minutes later she woke to a running commentary from Dave and felt the craft descending on a curving course towards a clutch of buildings far below.

'This is Freedom,' Dave was saying. 'As you can see, it's pretty small and isolated, with the airfield over there to your left. I'll take you around the outside of the town first so you can get a feeling for the layout.'

He did so, giving them a view of single-storey houses in separate lots, a handful of warehouse buildings and grain silos, mostly grouped around a single road. The airfield came into view as they reached the south-eastern outskirts. As Dave had told them, there wasn't much to it, just a single runway.

He set the helicopter down, watched by a couple of kids throwing a baseball. Ruth and Vaslik jumped out and ducked away from the spinning blades while Dave cut the engine and went across to talk to the boys. He came back shortly after with a smile on his face.

'We're in luck, but this isn't the place. The kids said there's been nothing here, otherwise they'd have heard it and come looking. One of them lives real close. But they say there's been talk of some UFOs about fifteen miles from here north of the US Six-Four.'

'UFOs?' Ruth echoed.

Dave grinned. 'It wouldn't be the first time; any kind of unexplained lights in the sky, it's got to be UFOs or a government black operation of some kind. But the kids say one of their school friends who lives over that way was out looking for rabbits a couple of nights ago and claims he found some busted-up machinery which he saw come down from outer space. They asked to see it but he's holding out for some money from the local county newspaper and told them to get lost. Putting it politely, they say the kid, whose name is Clay, is short a few balls of twine and talks crap most of the time, so there's probably nothing to see.'

'What do you think?'

'Well, we've got a name and it's close enough, so I figure it's worth going up there and having a chat, don't you?'

The flight took only a few minutes, and they landed alongside a small ranch-style farm with a couple of barns surrounded by open grass fields. As the three of them climbed out, the front door of the house opened and a woman stepped out followed by two teenagers, a boy and a girl wearing battered jeans and sneakers.

'Ma'am,' said Dave politely. 'Sorry to bust in on your day like this, but we're looking for some information and we hope you can help us.' He pointed at Ruth and Vaslik. 'This is Ruth Gonzales from London and Andy Vaslik from New York. They're a couple of investigators.'

The woman smiled at the courtesy. She was thin and tanned with a freckled face and wiry auburn hair, and looked tired. 'Well, you're not busting in on anything that can't be ignored. My name's Janice Bernhauer and these two are Clay and Judy.' She looked at Ruth. 'All the way from London? You must be dry as dust. You want a cold drink?' She didn't wait for a reply, but turned back inside, shooing the children in front of her.

The main room was neat and comfortable, with a long sofa, two armchairs, an air-conditioning fan blowing in one corner, a vast television in the other and a stack of books and magazines on shelves and side tables.

'You folks do a lot of reading,' Dave said, picking up a copy of a magazine with a garish looking front cover sporting a shot of outer space with a disc-shaped object in the middle.

'That and television, DVDs,' the woman said, coming back with a tray and four glasses of lemonade, which she handed out. 'There's nothing much else to do out here, so we keep ourselves entertained.' She sat down on the sofa and the children sat either side of her. 'Now, how can I help?'

Dave looked at Ruth, who picked up the baton. 'We're trying to find a man who's gone missing, Janice. We have reason to believe he might have come out this way.'

Janice shook her head. 'Well, we don't see many folks around here, but those we do, we notice. A man, you say?'

'Yes. In his forties, tall, dark-haired. A business type.'

Janice looked at the two children. 'Have you two seen any people you don't know?' She looked at Ruth again. 'They get out more than I do, so if anybody came by, they'd probably see them. How about it, you guys?'

Then girl, Judy, shook her head, eyes fastened on Vaslik as if he'd jumped out of the pages of a movie magazine. Vaslik pretended not to notice and looked at Clay, who wasn't saying or doing anything but looking slightly uncomfortable.

'Clay?' His mother noticed and scowled at him. 'Speak up, boy. I know you're holding something in, there.'

'He told everybody he found a UFO,' Judy burst out, and threw a needle-sharp look at her brother. 'An unidentified flying object. It was all bust up, too.'

'Clay?' Janice stared hard at her son, who had gone deep red and was giving his sister the evil eye. 'You found *what*? Tell me you're lying.'

Clay shook his head. 'It's true,' he burst out. 'It was up by the old riverbed. I knew there had to be something because I'd heard noises a couple of times before. And this time there was this light…' He stopped speaking and looked at his mother.

'Say what, Clay?' Janice's voice was calm and soft, but full of parental threat. 'If you saw lights, it must have been night – am I right? What have I told you about going out at night? What if you fell into a gully and broke your leg? And there are snakes out there!'

Clay looked terrified but stubborn. Vaslik leaned forward. 'You can tell us, Clay. It might be important in finding this missing man. What did you find, when and where?'

'Is there a reward?' Clay was pale with guilt, but clearly not above profiting from what he knew.

'If your mother says it's OK, then maybe. It depends what you tell us.'

Janice hesitated, then nodded. 'OK – but don't think you've got away with this, young man. You know what being grounded means? Well, in case you've forgotten, you're about to be reminded big-time – and that mountain bike along with you. Now tell the gentleman or I'll double it and add ten.'

Clay scowled but said, 'It's about four miles from here, in a dried-out riverbed close by an old airfield. It's a good place to find rabbits and stuff. I took my bike up there three nights ago, to watch some burrows. There was a good moon and I heard this noise up in the sky, a sort of buzzing sound like a hornet. It freaked me out at first because…' he hesitated and looked embarrassed, '…I thought it was a UFO. But then I figured it must be a small plane. Then I realised it was real close, but still not loud.'

'Good. What else?'

'The noise got closer, but it was too dark to see anything at first. Then I saw a red light, and it was moving real quick but in a crazy way like it was out of control, going one way then the other. After a while it went away, although not far, so I followed. I saw it go up in the air, then it went down again and…' He made a noise with his mouth as if he was clearing his throat, and threw his hands in the air.

'Sounds like it crashed, huh?'

'It sure did. One second it was in the air, the next it hit the ground and all I heard was a crunch, and somebody yelling. He sounded real mad so I kept my head down.'

Vaslik nodded. 'Sounds like it might have been a model plane of some kind, wouldn't you say, Clay?'

'I guess.' The boy looked at his mother but got a stony look in return. 'Except…'

'Except?'

'It wasn't.'

'How do you know that? Did you see it?'

Clay nodded. 'Some of it. I waited a real long time, 'til I was sure the men had gone away. Then I took a closer look at the place where it had come down.'

'What did you find?'

'Bits and pieces. Plastic mostly, and some metal… and some glass bits like a camera lens.'

There was a short silence. 'So this man took whatever it was away with him?'

Clay shook his head. 'No, sir. They left it where it was.'

'They? There was more than one man?'

'There were three. Well, actually four, only I don't think the fourth guy wanted to be seen.'

'What makes you say that?'

'Because he was lying on the ground about fifty yards away and watching them. I saw him because he didn't know squat about moving at night. I don't know what he looked like, though – he was just a shadow in the dark. But as soon as the plane hit the ground, he checked out of there without the others seeing him and went off towards the old airfield.'

Another silence. Then Dave said softly, 'Which old airfield's that, son?'

34

'It's an old place built in the fifties,' Janice put in. 'Something to do with the Cold War that never came to anything, thank the Lord. They built it along with a hangar and runway and stuff, but it was never listed and never went – what do you call it – operational. My father said it was a big secret that got forgotten. Nobody uses it for anything now. Leastways, nothing good, anyway, if my sense of smell tells me anything.'

'What do you mean?'

'Well, last night the wind was coming from over there and I swear I could smell smoke. You get kids or young people finding a place like that and they like to think it doesn't belong to anybody so they start fooling around. Could be nothing, of course, but something was burning.'

'Do you know if the fire department came out?'

'I doubt that, frankly. Our local department's had some serious budget cutbacks and they don't go anywhere they don't have to unless there's a threat to life or livestock. And I doubt an abandoned airfield meets either of those, if you know what I mean. All told, the place was a huge waste of money and it's better if they let it burn down if you ask me.' She gave Clay a fierce look that made him shrink in his seat. 'I told my kids to stay right away from there – the place is already falling-down dangerous. You don't know what else they built down there; there could be underground chambers and shafts or silos and the Good Lord knows what. It didn't need a fire to make it any less dangerous.'

'Mom, I never went inside—' Clay protested, but her look silenced him.

'I think we should take a look at this place,' said Ruth, and looked at Janice. 'Would you mind Clay showing us where he saw the men?'

Clay's eyes went big at the prospect, but Janice's went bigger. 'Will it be safe over there?'

'Safe as houses,' Dave assured her. 'We'll take a look overhead first, just to make sure. Then we'll go in on the ground.' He looked at Clay. 'You OK with flying, son?'

He might as well have handed Clay the keys to Disney; Clay nodded with enthusiasm and jumped to his feet.

'I've got stuff to show you first,' he said. 'I brought back some pieces of the machine. They're in the barn.'

Ruth caught the surprised look from Janice and forestalled another lecture. 'That was clever thinking, Clay. Let's have a look, shall we?'

They all trooped outside and into the barn, which smelled of warm hay and horses. A few chickens were pecking at the ground and shafts of sunlight coming through gaps in the wooden planking lent the interior of the building a comfortable atmosphere.

Clay went over to one corner and pulled aside a tarpaulin, then stood aside so they could see what he'd found. It looked like so much junk plastic that had been hit with a large hammer, but Dave Proust squatted down and immediately plucked one object out from the pile and held it in the air.

'Far as I know,' he said, 'UFOs don't have propellers.'

Ruth and Vaslik inspected it. It was small, no more than a few inches, but made of a durable plastic.

'I'd say this was a quad-copter,' Dave continued. 'I've seen them before. Most are small – like the kind kids would play with, even indoors. But I'd say this model was quite a bit bigger.' He sorted through the pile and picked up a section of gleaming white plastic with stylised letters emblazoned across it. Euro.

A jagged edge had cut off any further lettering but Ruth and Vaslik could see what it was immediately.

'EuroVol,' Ruth murmured. 'It's one of their stolen drones.'

With Janice's agreement, they went back to the helicopter and climbed aboard. It was a squeeze, but they were only going a short distance. Following an ecstatic Clay's directions, they took off and flew for about two miles until they saw an unnaturally straight line in the ground below. It was a runway.

Then they saw the smoke.

It was hanging in the atmosphere over the field and barely moving, a long pall of dark smoke spread out in a long tail where the turgid movement of air had gathered it up and pushed it slowly away from its source, which was a large square of blackened and crumpled steelwork that had once been a hangar. Beyond it was another shape, this one much smaller, but also smoking, although still standing.

Dave took them in on a curving course around the area and away from the smoke. There were no signs of vehicles or life, nothing to indicate what might have happened here. The airfield appeared to have been substantial in size, but if there had been any real intent about its development during the Cold War era, it would have possibly been for remote operations to be sited here in the event that known military fields were put out of action.

'Let's go see the place where you found the crashed drone first,' said Dave, and followed the boy's directions to the edge of a gulley nearby, where there was a safe spot of flat ground to land.

Once the engine stopped turning, they climbed out and Clay led them to a jumble of rocks and bushes, and pointed to a collection of plastic, electronics and wiring scattered on the ground.

'See? Right here.'

Closer inspection of the remains and the rest of some lettering on the side confirmed that the drone – or quad-copter – was a EuroVol machine. The casing had shattered on impact, revealing the interior with its wiring and circuits, and underneath, between broken skids, was a battered camera with a broken lens. There was also a tubular section of clear plastic with wiring soldered to one end, and mounts which had clearly been ripped away from the body of the drone on impact.

'We'd better take this in,' Ruth suggested quietly, so that Clay wouldn't hear. 'This was obviously a practice run that didn't end well. But if they stole six machines in all, they've got spares enough to play with.'

'But will it be enough to convince Kraski that it's serious?' said Vaslik.

'Kraski?' Dave looked up from a section of motherboard. '*John* Kraski?'

'You know him?'

'Yes, I do.' His expression could have curdled milk. 'I thought he'd have been retired by now. We crossed swords a couple of times before he moved into the Internal Investigations Section, which would've suited him like a second skin. Sounds like he's found himself another new home, though.'

'Can he really block any reports made through Tom Brasher?'

'I doubt that. He probably thinks he can because he's a self-important asshole. But if Tom Brasher's as convinced about this stuff as you two, he'll make sure it doesn't get stamped on. The one thing nobody's going to take a chance on is the president's life.'

Using a bag from the helicopter's stowage rack, they collected as many of the pieces of the drone that they could find, then scouted the rest of the area in a widening circle to make sure they had missed nothing.

It was Clay who found something, but without realising what until Ruth saw his fingers and the soles of his trainers. They carried traces of something bright red, and she thought he'd cut himself scrabbling about in the rocks.

'It won't come off,' he said after trying to wipe the colour away. 'Jeez – Mom's going to ground me forever!'

'Don't worry about that,' Ruth told him. 'Show us where you've just been.'

Clay led them over to the edge of the runway about eighty yards away, and a large rock. Both the rock and the ground around it were stained red.

Vaslik inspected the colour without touching it. 'It looks to me like a powdered dye,' he said quietly. 'But we should get Brasher's people to test it, just in case. Isn't that what Paget said the drones had been ordered and modified to carry?'

Ruth nodded. 'He did. Maybe they were using powdered dye to make their test runs.'

'Could be. Let's just hope that's all it was.'

Dave flew them all back to Clay's home. On the way, he gave the boy a stern warning.

'Now we know you've been telling your pals at school that you've got a UFO tucked away, and that you hope to sell the idea to a newspaper. Am I right?'

Clay looked horrified. 'Shit – how do you know that?'

Dave put his finger alongside his nose. 'Trust me, son. We know a lot of shit. And don't swear – it ain't nice.'

Clay didn't say anything, but stared out of the window. As they dropped towards the house they could see a pickup in the yard and a man talking to Janice. 'That's my dad,' Clay murmured. 'Am I in trouble?'

Dave shook his head. 'No, son. We'll square everything away with him and tell him how helpful you've been. But hear me out: no kidding anybody about UFOs, understand? Tell them what you saw was part of a weather balloon. We don't want good decent folks like your mom getting scared about aliens, do we?'

Clay nodded. 'OK. Do I get a reward?'

'Well, I'm not sure we can give you any money, but how about a note of thanks from the FBI? Of course, we'll have to run it past your parents first.'

–

Twenty minutes later they took off again and headed back to the airfield, leaving a proud boy with his parents and a promise that Special Agent Tom Brasher would be sending him a letter of thanks.

As the rotors came to a stop and they sat looking at the remains of what had once been an enormous hangar, Ruth's phone buzzed. It was Tom Brasher. She turned on the loudspeaker so they could all hear what he had to say.

'We just got a call from the Oklahoma State Police,' he announced. 'They picked up a kid not far from Alva, Oklahoma. He got stupid drunk in a bar and started mouthing off about – and I quote loosely – "*kuffars* and insects delivering the sting of death from the sky… your own toys of death spraying our message of destruction on the head of your leader and ending his tyranny. Allah be praised." And more stuff like that. He was lucky that two of the guys he was screaming at were state troopers. They hauled him out of there before he got himself lynched. It took a while for us to hear about it until his name got through the system and they checked into his background. Then they called it in.'

'Is he for real?' said Vaslik.

'Sounds like it to me, even without looking at his personal details. That stuff about spraying destruction and toys of death… that sounds like he was talking drones to me. When we ran his name it lit up a few lights. It turns out he's called Donny Bashir, and he's a known associate of Bilal Ammar, the bodybuilder who was seen talking to Chadwick's mystery man in Newark. They even attended the same mosque.'

'That figures.'

'Yeah. We also have him listed as being present during the Boston marathon bombing. A cop saw him laughing with a bunch of others and pulled him in for questioning. There was no proof he was involved, although he couldn't come up with a half-valid reason for being there, so they had to let him go. He was posted as a name to watch but then he dropped out of sight.'

'So what makes him a likely extremist?'

'Because of knowing Ammar – and being a tech graduate from NYU where he studied engineering, IT and – get this – chemistry.'

'Ouch. Was Ammar with him at the bar?'

'No. The local cops checked out a nearby motel and found the room they'd been using, but Ammar had gone. The owner gave a good description of him, muscles and all, but he couldn't recall the vehicle they'd used and they don't have CCTV.'

'Well, at least that's one person off the board,' Vaslik muttered.

'We're not close enough yet to get this put on the front burner, but we'll be working on him. In the meantime there are other threats coming in from New York, San Francisco, Washington and Chicago, all concerning imminent and convincing bombing campaigns. They're currently being investigated. We figure some if not most are simply phone and internet chatter tied in in some way to cause maximum disruption, but they're taking a lot of time and effort to check out thoroughly.'

'Could it be part of a wider campaign?' Ruth asked.

'My opinion? Yes. If they throw up enough noise and get our attention focussed on what seems like genuine threats in other cities, it disguises their real intentions. We're hoping to break this Bashir guy down to see if he's got the ability to make a dirty bomb, or if he's just mouthing off to distract us further, but the Staties aren't having much luck. They didn't know what to do with him so I persuaded them to hold him in the Woods County jail in Alva until I get down there. What we need is some hard evidence that makes it a real and genuine danger. Have you guys found anything?'

Ruth gave him a summary of their findings, but she could tell by his muted reaction that bits of a machine by themselves weren't sufficient to provide the kind of hard evidence he and his superiors wanted.

Then Dave Proust stepped in. 'Tom, we're about to go look at the airfield buildings to see if we can pick up any useful details. But it looks to me like somebody torched the place on purpose. If you want my gut instinct, this is for real. Nobody would dump a busted-up machine in the remote kind of place we found it in the hopes that somebody might stumble across it and tell the authorities. And the kid saw it flying at night, miles from anywhere. These guys, whoever they were, are for real, too.'

'I hear you, Tom. Give me a call as soon as you get back, OK? Oh, and don't go in cold.'

'Will do. Speak later.' He nodded at Ruth to cut the connection.

35

'Is it me or is this place creepy?' said Ruth. They were standing outside the helicopter and studying their surroundings. The air smelled thick with smoke, burned rubber and metal, and down here it was like looking through a thin veil that shifted violently with every final turn of the rotors.

It was clearly an airfield – or had been – but apart from the obvious runway and the two buildings in the distance, it looked long-abandoned, strewn with weeds and coarse grassy clumps sprouting out of the concrete like bristles on an old man's chin. The only thing to Ruth's mind that was missing was a ball of tumbleweed rolling across the landscape and some Morricone music in the background.

'It certainly has an atmosphere.' Vaslik was looking down at the ground alongside the helicopter. Dave had landed on a patch of stubby grass, but a couple of feet away the ground was dusty where a bowl of wind-blown soil had built up over time. 'But we're not the first to come here.'

The other two followed the direction of his glance to where a set of twin tyre tracks had cut the corner.

Vaslik knelt and ran a finger across the tread marks. 'These look pretty fresh. A commercial vehicle or a pickup.'

'Could be campers or hunters,' suggested Dave. 'Or kids fooling around.'

'What, out here?'

'Sure, why not? Clay did. But I'm thinking older kids – the kind who play with matches.'

'Humour me, Cochise,' Ruth said to Vaslik. 'How can you tell these are fresh?'

He grinned. 'God, you city folk just crease me up.' He cast around and pointed to where another tyre print further over was full of wind-blown dust. 'These are several days old. This one hasn't been dusted in yet.' He glanced up and nodded towards the two buildings in the distance. 'Shall we go look?'

Ruth shielded her eyes and studied the two structures. The hangar was nothing but a blackened skeleton of concrete, with the roof structure partly in place but hanging down on one side like a giant bird with a broken wing. Puffs of dark smoke drifted up in one corner, but most of the fire looked to have burned itself out. Even in this defeated and ruined condition, it wore the sad demeanour of a place long forgotten and left to decay. Like ancient barns and cowsheds back home in England, it was now just a footprint in history.

She looked up as a flutter of movement caught her eye. A flock of birds swooped by, twisting and turning in formation against the pale sky, changing places in bursts of bewildering speed, yet always tight together as if joined by hidden wires.

'Starlings,' she said aloud, caught for a moment by their air of total liberation. 'The hooligans of the bird world.'

Vaslik looked at her. 'I never figured on you as a bird watcher. Do you have any other nasty habits you haven't mentioned?'

'No. We get them in England. My dad's always complaining about the mess they make of his car.' She reflected on how odd it seemed, seeing the birds here in numbers, dancing to their own tune as if everything was quite normal and not threatening to go to hell at any moment. And about as different to the other flying objects they were searching for as it was possible to get. 'What did Brasher mean,' she asked, 'when he said don't go in cold?'

Dave hesitated, his face set. 'Let me show you.' He went to the helicopter and reached into the back. He took out a small, flat alloy briefcase and flipped the catches.

Inside were twin Sig Sauer 229 semi-automatic pistols. He handed one to Ruth and added a spare magazine, then did the same to Vaslik. Ruth checked the mechanism and load, set the safety and put the pistol and spare mag in her coat pocket. It felt intrusive and cumbersome, and she hoped she wouldn't have cause to use it. But better safe than dead.

Vaslik did the same with his while Dave handed Ruth an envelope. It contained some folded papers and a permit for a weapon, already showing her photo and thumbprint.

'What's this?'

'It's for show in case we get stopped. Andy doesn't need one – his licence to carry is still valid. If anything happens leave all the talking to me. The papers are indemnity forms in case you shoot anyone – especially me – and a non-disclosure agreement for any and all branches of law enforcement we might connect with.' He smiled. 'The government likes to think you won't go off and make a million by spilling the beans about federal or state agencies and their methods of operation.'

'So now I'm working for the US Government? How is that legal?'

'It's open to interpretation, I admit. But if we run into some bad guys I'd rather have you alive to argue the point afterwards than to have to ship you back in a box because we didn't take the precaution of giving you the option to defend yourself.'

'Fair point. And the photo and thumbprint? How did you get them?'

'Tom Brasher said he fixed it once he figured which way things were going. Some guy named Aston sent them over from your London office. He figured you might need them. He said there was a possibility you two were being followed and it might be connected with this business. It's better than nothing and only to be used in extremis.'

She signed the permit and papers and put them away in her coat pocket. 'Let's hope we don't need them.'

'Amen to that. But anything's possible. If Chadwick was lifted and is being held against his will to do this thing, I doubt the people holding him will let him go without a fight. I'd rather be ready for that.' He flicked open his windcheater and they saw the button of a semi-automatic against his side.

'This isn't your fight,' Vaslik pointed out. 'And we might be chasing shadows.'

'Go suck on it,' Dave retorted good-naturedly. 'If Tom thinks this is for real, then it's for real, and I haven't had fun like this is ages. Now, are we doing this or standing around wasting time?'

Ruth and Vaslik set out along the access road, keeping several feet of space between them, while Dave hung back and off to one side, ready to support them. The likelihood of there being a threat was slim to zero, but none of them was ready to take that chance.

The hangar was set back about a hundred yards from the runway, and still bore the remains of an ancient hoarding that must have once carried a name. Other than the faint outline of letters that might have spelled *field*, the wood had been scorched by the fire and was unreadable. The remains of the main doors stood open on their tracks, and as they approached they could see right through the building to a small rear door in a cinder-block wall surround standing open in one corner. A line of windows showed down one side of the hangar, the glass cracked and clouded with soot.

They stopped thirty yards back, listening and tuning into the atmosphere. Other than the distant sound of a bird singing, the only other noises were the faint hum of a breeze through the open roof and a clack-clack of a loose strip of wood hanging down by the main doors.

Ruth wondered if they were being watched from beyond the airfield boundary, but quickly dismissed it. She didn't feel that itch that came from imminent danger. If ever a place seemed dead, this was it, especially now that fire had come to seal its fate for good.

'I'll take the back,' she said, and fingered the Sig in her coat pocket. 'You want to do the front?'

Vaslik nodded. 'I'll give you time to get round there. Watch the windows down the side.' He turned and signalled their intentions to Dave with hand movements, and got a nod in return.

Ruth set off down the side of the building, walking steadily and relying on her peripheral vision to spot any movements. As she entered a patch of shadow cast by a section of cinder-block wall that still standing, she suppressed a shiver. It was just an old building, she knew that; but places like this carried their own aura, gathered by all the years of their existence and the people who had passed through it and left a trace of their time here. She didn't feel in any danger, exactly, but the sheer size of the place now she was walking in its shadow, as damaged as it was, seemed to tower menacingly over her, dwarfing everything around it.

She reached the first of the side windows and peered through a hole in one of the panes. She saw a room about fifty feet by twenty that might once have been an office or work area. The frame of a metal chair and trestle table stood in the centre, with a blackened, smouldering pile of what looked like sheets of board further along. But no people. Then she was past and heading for the rear of the building, skirting clumps of grass littered with abandoned sheet metal, concrete, tubing, wiring and other unnameable detritus, along with pieces of the roof and wall fabric that had fallen in the fire.

The access door was still in one piece, held open by a wedge-shaped lump of metal Ruth recognised as a wheel block. It was rusted and pitted with age, and had probably been there since the last plane took off and vanished over the horizon. She peered round the edge of the door and saw Vaslik standing at the front of the building. He looked tiny in comparison to the size of the opening. He gave her the go-ahead and she stepped through the door, heading for the office.

The flutter of birds darting about overhead made her stop and look up. It reminded her of some of the counter-terrorism training facilities she had been through in the Ministry of Defence Police. Abandoned warehouses and factories, most of them, used to simulate and perfect siege techniques, this wore the same air of desolation and decay, only with the added confusion of nature's own decorations. Melted snakes of electrical wiring and lengths of chain that had once held strip lighting were hanging from the roof struts like jungle lianas, while an abundance of weeds and grasses below, now crinkled and discoloured with the heat of the fire, had once been growing up to meet them. What little remained of the solid lower walls bore a network of cracks and fissures, with daylight showing through where the mortar had burned out and the cinder blocks had split open.

A thin mist hung above the floor where underlying pockets of moisture had been overheated by the flames, and the soot layer was spotted with the tiny craters where the incoming breeze was turning it back to droplets. Over on the far side of the hangar was a layer of wooden boards, and above it a rusted chain and pulley device. An inspection pit, she guessed. Her nose twitched at a different smell and she saw a small furry animal carcass lying in among the weeds, bloodied and ripped open, but showing no signs of fire damage. The predator must have been disturbed by their arrival and slunk away into the surrounding brush to await their departure. The carcass was now being feasted on by an army of flies that moaned and moved as they sensed her presence.

She swallowed hard and kept moving. A carpet of grit underfoot crackled as she walked, echoing off the walls like tiny firecrackers. She stopped and pulled out the Sig, checking the open space above the office area. If anybody was waiting, that's where they would be.

A whistle from Vaslik. He was halfway down the hangar, standing on an oil drum. He was checking out the same area, his gun held in both hands. He shook his head to give the all-clear and jumped down.

Ruth stepped up to the office door and nudged it open with her foot. It swung back with a groan then stopped. She peered through the gap at the hinges; no bad person waiting to ambush her. Just a thin veil of smoke, trapped in the confined space.

She moved inside.

The room had been burned back to concrete and metal by the fire, with its ceiling gaping open and still smoking. A few of the windows had survived, along with some of the original braided electric wires hanging from the wall where plug sockets had once been fitted. The room was empty of furniture save for the framework of the chair and trestle table, and beyond it she could now see what were not sheets of board but flattened cardboard boxes. Close by the window was a dark bundle of blankets and wires, oddly untouched by the fire. Stepping forward, she checked the table, which had a heavy-duty iron frame and the remains of a battered and oil-stained Formica top. She touched the surface gingerly with her finger, expecting to pick up years of wind-blown grit beneath the soot, but coming away with just the faintest trace of blackness.

She felt her breathing quicken. This was the place, she just knew it. A dust-free table, burned cardboard boxes – and the blankets that must have been used as blackouts. Whoever these men were, they had set fire to it but the damage hadn't been anywhere near complete.

She heard Vaslik enter the room behind her. Stepping past to the pile of burned cardboard, she nudged the sheets aside and saw the familiar label where the flames hadn't reached. FedEx Express. She took out her cell phone and took photos of the shipping numbers; it was probably unnecessary but it would give Brasher more evidence that what they were following was real and not some figment of their imagination.

'The table's been used recently,' she said, 'and those blankets didn't grow here out of nothing. They look like military surplus.'

He nodded and turned away. 'You're right. There's a mess of footprints out on the main floor, too.' He sniffed the air. 'Can you smell something?'

'It's a dead animal. A rabbit, I think.' She was about to suggest going to look at the other building when her phone buzzed.

It was Dave Proust. 'Folks, I'm inside the old workshop. You really need to come see this.'

36

The cooked smell of fruit and food was the first thing to hit them, followed by the underlying sourness of unwashed bodies. But it was the result of heat, not direct fire. If the intention had been to burn this place down, it had failed. Where the outside skin of the workshop had been badly damaged, the inside stud walls were mostly untouched, although the ceiling was hanging down in places and the air inside the room was choking and still.

After the vast space inside the hangar, it was quite a contrast. Dave Proust kicked the door wide open to disturb the air and let in more light, and handed them each a pair of rubber gloves.

'Looks to me like a prison cell,' Ruth said, and indicated handcuffs attached to the bed.

Dave nodded. 'I guess we know who was being held here. But the really interesting bit is over there.' He was pointing to the other bed, and an area of browned blood splatter on the pale wall behind it, with a hole in the centre. 'Somebody stopped a bullet.' He indicated the blankets, which showed a scattering of brown spots of blood. 'From the area of residue and the location of that hole, I'd say he was standing in front of the bed when he got hit. It was probably a slight wound; there's no sign of heavy bleeding that I can see, even on the floor to the door, unless they wrapped him up in something first.'

Ruth and Vaslik agreed. He was right. Unless the shooter had taken unusual care to staunch the flow of bleeding, the victim must have walked out of the shed under his own steam. Otherwise why bother if they were going to burn it down?

Ruth turned back to the bed with the handcuffs and lifted the mattress and pillow. Both were stained and filthy, but there was nothing to see. Whoever had been cuffed to the bed – and she figured Dave was right and that it had been James Chadwick – he had not been in a position to conceal anything that might help them find him.

Vaslik checked out the other bed and lifted the pillow. It revealed a large hunting knife in a scabbard, the leather stained by years of sweat and dirt. Using part of the sheet to prevent his fingerprints contaminating it, he pulled the scabbard away; the knife looked old but the blade itself was clean and shiny, and razor sharp. Whoever had owned this had looked after it.

He looked at the bed. 'No cuffs on this one, and he had a weapon. So he wasn't a prisoner.' He frowned. 'Yet he got shot? That doesn't make sense.'

'Unless it was Chadwick,' Dave reasoned. 'Although I'm betting it was a low-level member of the crew posted to look after him. If Brasher gets prints and DNA off this we'll soon know the answer.'

Vaslik nodded at the boxes of water bottles and canned food in the corner. 'It looks like they had provisions for a while.' He stepped closer and pulled out a box containing bananas and apples, mostly blackened and rotting, the juices oozing through a hole in the cardboard. Some of the cans were bulging and looked ready to explode, and he left them alone. He turned back to the bed with the bloodstains, then inspected the lock on the door. 'Why would they make somebody share this dump with a prisoner? He wasn't going anywhere.'

'Maybe it was someone with no choice.'

'I guess.' Vaslik toured the walls and stopped, looking down in the corner. He stooped and came up with a DVD player. The casing showed some impact damage and was missing some bits but the screen was intact. He pushed the casing together and pressed the PLAY button.

Surprisingly, it worked.

The three of them stood in absolute silence as the footage rolled by. The pictures on the screen were made all the more threatening by the complete absence of commentary.

Within the first few seconds Ruth recognised what she was seeing. She felt the hairs stir on the back of her neck. 'That's where I met Elizabeth Chadwick. It's in Chelsea.'

The footage of Ben's school spoke for itself, and nobody spoke until the DVD clicked off. The implications of the threat held over James Chadwick's head were all-too clear: those closest to him had been under surveillance for a while, including the apartment block where Valerie DiPalma lived. It didn't take much to image how vulnerable and powerless he must have felt being presented with this footage.

'The team will bag this up,' Dave concluded. 'We'd better step out and leave the rest as it is. I'll call it in.'

Ruth felt relieved to be back on the outside and breathing in deep gasps of fresh air. It must have been bad enough for the guard in there, but intolerable on a shocking scale for James Chadwick, knowing all the time that there were men out in the world within reach of his son, wife and Valerie DiPalma, and there wasn't a single thing he could do about it. The sense of desperation must have been tearing at his insides.

She shook her head. There was something bugging her and she couldn't put her finger on it. But now she was out in the open, it was beginning to come to her. Whatever it was had been scratching away at the back of her mind ever since first stepping through the rear door of the hangar.

Then she had it: the smell she and Vaslik had both noticed. It had been too strong to be from a small dead animal, especially in that vast space. She'd subconsciously dismissed it because the aroma was followed closely by seeing the carcass. Yet it had lingered on the air more than she would have thought normal.

She said to Dave, 'Wait. Before you do that there's something I want to check. Give me a couple of minutes.'

She jogged over to the hangar and walked through the main doors to the side where she had seen the boards over the inspection pit. It was probably nothing but since she was here, she might as well check.

She ducked past the chain hanging from the overhead pulley and nudged one of the boards aside with her foot. Was that a heavy layer of soot?

The board moved with surprising ease. As it did so, what she'd thought was soot seemed to lift off and rise into the air. Then she realised what it was as a dense cloud of flies swirled around her head like a mini-storm, buzzing furiously. Her stomach heaved with revulsion as she felt hundreds of tiny bodies bouncing against her cheeks and getting tangled in her hair in their desperation to escape. But she was too stunned to react immediately by the sheer scale of what she glimpsed lying in the hole.

'My God. *Slik! Dave!*'

The two men came running and stopped dead when they saw what she was looking at.

'Now we definitely call it in,' Dave Proust said abruptly, and clamped a handkerchief over his face. 'This place is a major crime scene. He'll need to advise Homeland Security, too. No way is some pencil-head going to ignore this.'

'I'll do it.' Vaslik paused to flick some of the flies out of Ruth's hair, then took out his phone and called Brasher's number. He was patched through immediately to Brasher's cell phone, as he was on his way to Alva to interview Donny.

He took a couple of minutes to describe what they had found at the airfield, then came to what lay in the inspection pit. 'At least four males, possibly five, it hard to tell until they're pulled out of there. They look to me like Latinos, and some are wearing working clothes as far as we can see, including boots and gloves. Like construction workers.'

'Out there? Constructing what?'

'I'm coming to that.'

'Can you tell how they died?'

'They were shot at close range with an automatic weapon. There are dozens of shell casings in the pit around them, as if the men were ordered down there, then hosed down.'

'How long ago do you estimate?'

'Could be a couple of days to a week or more. With the temperature down there and the fire and flies… I'm only guessing. The bodies are a mess.'

'Christ, this is all we need,' Brasher breathed heavily down the phone. 'I'll arrange for the Oklahoma State Police and a forensics team, and some of our own people from the local bureau to get on the way immediately and lock the place down. What the hell were they doing out there?'

'It looks like they were a construction crew shipped in to build the inside of the workshop where Chadwick and one other, like a guard, were held. There was food and water and one of the beds had been fitted with handcuffs. Once the crew was done, it looks as if they'd served their purpose.' He looked across at Ruth, who waved her cell phone. 'Ruth's sending you photos of the scene and shipping labels on some cardboard boxes we think must have been used to bring the drones over. It should be easy to verify with Memphis FedEx by the codes on the boxes, but we've seen pieces of one of the missing EuroVol drones, anyway, so that's pretty much a formality.'

'Got that. Good work. Before I go, I have some intel about the guy who attacked Ruth.'

'That's good to hear. Let me put you on loudspeaker.' He pressed the button and Brasher's voice echoed around the hangar.

'Ruth, we've come up with a name to match the prints found on the knife and hardhat from that guy who attacked you in Newark. His name is Yusuf Kalil, of no fixed address but appears to be known in Newark and New Jersey as a local hoodlum. He has no known extremist links, but he's done time for robbery, aggravated violence and a sexual assault on a female minor.'

'Sweet guy,' Ruth muttered. 'Have you got him yet?'

'Not yet but we soon will. He arrived here on a student visa from Syria twelve years ago. Our guess is he might be a jihadi sympathiser but more likely he's a cheap muscle for hire.'

'Did you come up with anything on the man named Paul?'

'Funny you should ask.' Brasher's voice sounded upbeat. 'I issued the photos to all agencies, some with ID- and data-matching resources they don't like sharing on a general basis. You can guess who I mean.'

'Like Langley?' said Vaslik.

'In that general area, yes. Anyway, one of them came back with a positive ID. His name is listed as Paul Malick, aka Asim Malak, precise origins unknown.'

'So he's an illegal.'

'That's correct. We have nothing on him in the US so far, but from what little we do have he must have been living here under false papers for at least seven years, possibly longer. Our guess is he came in via Mexico or further south, and acquired papers that allowed him to travel in an out of the country on several occasions, mostly to Germany or Turkey, both gateways to the Middle East. The latest intel is that he's currently wanted in Egypt and Jordan for murder, bombing and organising crimes against the state, and is suspected of membership of organisations like al-Qaeda and specifically being allied to Abu Musab al-Zarqawi. If that's true the guy has some serious history. Either way they say he's considered highly dangerous and he's definitely linked to Bilal Ammar and others with known extremist and jihadist agendas.'

Ruth and Vaslik looked at each other. If they needed proof of something serious being planned, then the links were now coming together, pointing towards a disparate group of extremists who had got together in the name of jihad.

But that didn't tell them where this Paul, aka Asim Malak, had now gone, or where he had taken James Chadwick.

'So now will you call off this visit by the president?' said Vaslik. 'This is looking more and more like a serious, planned assassination attempt.'

'I already suggested that as soon as we got word on Malak, but got voted down. The president won't bow to terrorist threats on home soil because of the message that would send to Americans: that the person in the White House can no longer go wherever he likes – even a US military base – because of a threat? No chance.'

37

Woods County Jail was a low-slung building set in a quiet, spacious section of Alva, surrounded by stores, dealerships and government buildings. Ruth and Vaslik walked in through the front entrance and found Tom Brasher and a woman waiting for them.

'Glad you could make it,' Brasher said, shaking hands. He introduced his companion. 'This is Special Agent Karina Wright. She's been assigned to work with me on this case.'

'Hi.' Wright nodded briskly. 'Good to meet you both.' She was small and slim, with neat, dark auburn hair and the clear skin tone of a woman with a serious health regime. Ruth was surprised; anything less like Brasher was hard to imagine, but she figured Wright had to be more than just a pretty face to have been assigned to this job.

'I can't let you folks into the interview suite with us,' Brasher continued, 'but you can observe from the room next door. We don't have much time before due process begins. At the moment he's being held on charges relating primarily to drunkenness, disorder and threatening behaviour, but we hope to upgrade those in a few minutes. Let's get to it.' He nodded to a uniformed guard standing nearby who checked in their weapons and cell phones, then led them through security to an interview suite down the corridor. Ruth and Vaslik were shown into a room with a video monitor on one wall, showing another anonymous room with a table and two chairs. Seconds later, Brasher and Agent Wright appeared on the screen and sat at the table.

Donny Bashir appeared accompanied by two large guards. He looked shrivelled and terrified. With a mop of unruly black hair and a thin growth of beard around his chin descending to a prominent Adam's apple, he looked every inch the campus geek rather than a man engaged in acts of terrorism.

The guards made him sit then left the room, and Donny looked around him, shifting nervously in his seat and blinking, but avoided looking directly at the two agents.

Tom Brasher ran through the preliminaries, introducing himself and Special Agent Wright and confirming why Donny was being held. Donny said nothing, merely waiting, eyes fixed on the table.

Then Brasher changed tack and nodded at Karina Wright, who said, 'Mr Bashir, would you tell us how you met Bilal Ammar?'

Donny blinked hard several times, his head jerking up, but without speaking. In fact he seemed more stunned by Wright's soft voice than the question she had put to him. He looked away in confusion.

Wright repeated the question. 'We know you are friends with Bilal; what we'd like you to tell us is how and where you met him.'

Donny shook his head.

'You don't know him – is that what you're telling us?'

'No.' He said the word too loud, then hesitated and repeated it softly. 'I mean, no. He's not my friend.' He had a slight accent and his words were precise, as if carefully thought out.

'A colleague, then? You attended the same mosque in Queens, New York, isn't that correct?'

Donny nodded. 'Yes. Correct.'

'So now you remember him.'

He nodded.

'You're a long way from there now, aren't you? Are you down here on vacation?'

He looked troubled by the question and stared around as if suspecting a trick. 'I don't know what you mean.'

'Very well, I'll be more direct. What were you doing in the bar – Jokers, I believe it's called – when you were arrested?'

'I can't remember.'

'Can't remember what you were doing here or can't remember the bar?' Wright's voice, although soft, was relentless and probing, and Ruth and Vaslik could see why Brasher had allowed her to take the lead. Another reason was evident in Donny's reaction to her, which was nervous and almost embarrassed, as if he had little understanding or experience of attractive women. 'I hear you really tied one on down there, is that correct?' Her voice had taken on a light tone, and he responded with the faintest of smiles in acknowledgement.

'I guess.'

'And where was Mr Ammar when you were in the bar? He wasn't there with you, was he?'

'No. He was asleep. He sleeps heavily.'

'At the motel down the road.'

'Yes.'

'So, not the best of company?'

'I guess.'

'So you decided you needed some fun and went to Jokers, is that right? I mean, that's what vacations are for, right – having fun?'

'It wasn't.'

'Wasn't what – fun? Hey, I'm not surprised; you did get yourself arrested. Although I'm pretty sure your friends in NYU might call it fun, wouldn't they? Sort of rights of passage and that kind of stuff.'

'I guess.' He frowned, clearly thrown by the sudden shift in the tone of questions. 'Why are you holding me here? I want a l—'

'Actually,' Wright interrupted him and raised her hand, which made him flinch and stop speaking instantly, 'we're just trying to figure out why an intelligent NYU graduate like you, Donny, is hanging around with a thug like Bilal Ammar. He is a thug, isn't he?'

He nodded. 'I guess.'

'Of course he is. I bet you have more brains in your little finger than he does in his whole body. And what about Paul Malak? Is he a thug, too?'

Donny looked up, his face going pale. 'What? I don't understand… why are you asking about him? I never mentioned anyone called Malick, I—' He stopped speaking abruptly as if a switch had been thrown.

'Malick. I'm sorry, I should have said Malick, which is what he likes to be called. Although his real name is Asim Malak, isn't it?' She bent to catch his eye and said gently, 'You can tell me, Donny. Nobody else will hear you. It's just a name.'

Donny nodded and said softly, 'Yes. Asim Malak.'

'Good. That's great, Donny. And where is Asim Malak now, do you think? And Bilal Ammar, of course. Incidentally, we know they've left the airfield. And they've taken the drones and James Chadwick with them. So, where are they going?'

Donny stared at her, eyes wide, and swallowed hard, his Adam's apple bobbing furiously.

'I don't know.'

'But that was nothing to do with you, was it, what they did inside the hangar? Was it Malak or Ammar, Donny? Somehow I can't see Ammar being bright enough to be the boss, or Malak wanting to get his hands dirty with the other stuff.'

'Stuff?' Donny voice was almost a whisper, as if the question had slipped out unawares.

'You know what I mean.' Her voice was silky smooth now, almost gentle in its probing. 'The conversion of the workshop to a prison cell; the kidnap of James Chadwick; the theft of the drones. And the killing of the construction workers. All that.' She sat back. 'Frankly, I can't see a man like you being part of that. Not really. You seem a nice guy to me. You must have got taken along for your technical skills, isn't that correct?'

Donny said nothing, simply staring at her like a mouse confronted by a predator. And blinked once.

Then a tear rolled down his face.

'Interesting technique,' Vaslik murmured. But he was frowning.

Ruth wasn't impressed, but said nothing. She hoped Wright wasn't finished yet and that there was more to come. It had been a masterclass in interrogation up to a point, without a voice raised in anger, real or simulated. But the technique was oddly neutralised by Wright's underlying expression, which came across as slightly cruel, even casual. The smiles were there, along with the soft voice, but so was more than a hint of contempt and condescension.

They listened as Donny described the process of his introduction to Malak and his subsequent recruitment; a process that had led from a good job in Apple to the cell here in Woods County Jail. It poured out like a flood released, with no pauses for deliberate thought or fabrication. And at the end they had everything they needed to connect Malak and Ammar to multiple murder and a plan to bring terrorism to the United States.

What they didn't have was so much as a hint to the current whereabouts of the two men, James Chadwick or the drones. In that, it seemed Asim Malak had been ultra-cautious, keeping his plans very close to his chest and trusting nobody with the essential details – not even the location of the target itself.

While they allowed Donny a breather and a coke, Brasher had a hurried conversation with Wright in the corridor outside. When they resumed the interview, she focussed on one question.

'From what you've told us, Donny,' she said softly, 'and what we already know, Malak was planning a hit against an American target, yes?'

'Yes.' He finished his coke and sat back, looking drained.

'Did he ever mention the following locations? Just nod if you've heard of them. The places are: Vance. Fort Sill. Altus. McAlester.' She repeated them and watched his reactions.

Nothing.

'That's very good, Donny,' Wright told him. 'You've been a great help and that will be taken into consideration later.' She glanced at Brasher, and at a nod from him stood up and walked out of the room.

'What's going to happen to me?' Donny asked softly.

'Nothing bad,' Brasher said, 'as long as you continue to help us.'

'How?'

'We'll discuss that later. But it will mean you can go home to Queens again. You would like that, I suppose?'

Donny blinked and nodded. 'You want me to tell you about others like Malak, don't you?'

'Like that, yes. But you don't have to decide right now.'

Ruth and Vaslik turned away from the window and stared at each other in consternation.

'Is that it?' Ruth demanded. She was appalled at the lack of depth to the interrogation and the absence of hard information gained. 'We'd already figured out most of that – but we still don't know anything about where Malak is or what he's thinking!'

Vaslik opened his mouth to reply but was interrupted by Wright walking into the room.

She seemed unaffected by the interrogation session and was picking at a nail, ignoring them both. It seemed as if she had already dismissed the visit here as a job done.

'I think we should talk to him,' Ruth suggested. 'There are a couple of questions I'd like to ask.'

Wright didn't even look up. 'Well, you can forget that because it won't happen. You're British, right?'

Ruth bristled at her spiky tone. 'What does that have to do with anything?'

'Because we work differently here – and last time I looked this was our turf. That little prick is a nobody, a gofer who knows nothing. Frankly, I think this was a waste of my time.'

-

As Donny's interrogation came to an end, a white van with tinted windows and a Perspex roof vent pulled up outside the Woods County jail and slid into a space between an old Camry and a Mitsubishi pickup. The two men in the front sat watching the main entrance, while a third man in the back squatted by the side door, releasing the latch and sliding the door open an inch in readiness. The rush of cool air was a welcome relief and he licked his lips, suddenly wishing he could have a long drink to quench his dry mouth.

'This town is asleep,' said the driver, looking around at the quiet streets and buildings. He had a strong middle-eastern accent and spoke in English for the benefit of the man in the passenger seat, whose family was Libyan by origin but who had been born and educated in the US. 'We could walk up and down here and nobody would even notice.' He sniggered. 'These American don't know what's going to hit them.' He reached down to the floor and patted the stock of an M4 Colt carbine fitted with a 30-round magazine, one of three in the van. Then he picked up three pairs of orange ear-defenders and passed a pair each to the other two, and they got ready to slip them on.

Because any second now the noise in the van was going to be insane.

'Don't underestimate them,' the man in the back warned them. His name was Salem and he was a thirty-year-old former soldier originally from Yemen. He had been recruited for this job because of his military skills and experience, and spoke with certain knowledge. 'The American police have great forces available to them and will not hesitate to use them. You heard what your leader Malak said: if we fail, they will be all over us.'

'If *we* fail?' The passenger muttered sourly. He had made no secret of his disdain for the man in the back, brought into the assignment as if he and the driver were incapable of completing this simple task. 'You mean you, don't you? Isn't that why you were brought along – to show us how it was done?' He tapped a photograph of a woman taped to the front fascia. 'Just in case you have forgotten, it's the woman you have to look for, nobody else. The others are just – what do the Americans call it – damage?'

The man in the back remained silent. He had seen and done this kind of thing before. And unlike these two idiots he knew the risks involved and the potential outcomes. He was accustomed to following orders, but not from the likes of them, especially the driver who seemed much too excitable for this to end well. As for the passenger, who thought too highly of himself, he reserved a professional man's contempt for him and his tiresome show of bravado.

He thought about the man ultimately giving the orders and wondered at the hell he was planning on unleashing some distance from this place. He knew of him only as Malak, and wondered about the almost personal thing he had going with the woman in the photograph, for which he was risking them all to eliminate her.

He dismissed those thoughts and checked the tube he was holding, ensuring it was ready and that the second tube was close by. No more than three feet long and as thick as a man's arm, the tubes were olive green in colour, fitted with a foresight, rear sight and a trigger mechanism, with a webbing carry strap, although he wasn't going to need that since he wasn't going anywhere. They were LAW66 M72A3s – Light Anti-Tank Weapons – or rocket launchers, acquired, he'd been advised, through the same supplier who had provided the M4 carbines through a series of cut-outs in exchange for cash. Not that their provenance concerned him at all. As long as they worked and didn't blow up in his face, he didn't care who had done what to get them into his hands.

'Collateral damage,' he corrected the man without thinking. 'They call it collateral damage. You should remember those words because there will be plenty of it. If this thing works and you two also do your job there won't be anybody else standing, doesn't matter who they are.'

'What about the brother inside the jail?' said the driver. Like the others, he'd been given the barest of details about the job: find where the prisoner was being held, go in and hit them hard and get out fast. Nothing had been said about releasing the prisoner, even if he was one of them.

'What about him?' The front seat passenger cleared his throat and spat through the window. 'By his actions he betrayed us all. Let him rot in hell.'

38

'I want to talk to Donny.' Ruth faced Brasher the moment he entered the room. She was having a hard time holding in her anger at Wright's attitude, and how she appeared to have dismissed the possibility of Donny providing them with any useful information.

'What?' He looked surprised and waved a hand, frowning at the idea. 'Sorry – that's not possible.'

'I already told her that,' Wright snapped, stepping in close enough for Ruth to smell her cologne. Her mouth was set in a line and she looked ready for a fight. 'You're not authorised. This is our responsibility.'

'Why – because I'm British?' Ruth turned away and focussed on Brasher, who was looking nonplussed at the crackly atmosphere between the two women. 'There are several unanswered questions remaining, Tom. Donny probably has an idea where the others have gone even if he doesn't realise it. Men like Donny and Paul don't travel around together for several days on end without something slipping out, even by accident. And Donny's no idiot; he's probably managed to join the dots without even thinking about it.'

'That may be true, but Agent Wright is correct. Can you imagine what a good lawyer would do if he found out we'd allowed you to interrogate a suspect? They'd tear us apart and poor innocent Donny would become a YouTube sensation.'

'Really? I happen to know the FBI sits in on British interrogations in the UK whenever it wants if there's a US connection; why doesn't the reverse work for you?' She held his gaze, as much irritated by Wright's condescending and bullying manner as Brasher's instinctive default response to play it safe. 'Chadwick's wife is British, don't forget. That's what brought us this far and unveiled a real and genuine threat. I think you owe us that at least.'

'His wife is not my concern. Let me remind you this is an FBI matter.'

'Which we alerted you about in the first place and we came up with the evidence that brought you two out here. If you still have doubts about that, talk to Dave Proust.'

'I know what Dave thinks.'

'His name's Arnold Keegan, if you want to call him,' said Vaslik.

'What?' Brasher threw a scowl at him.

'The FBI bureau chief in London. Arnold Keegan. I know him quite well. You want me to call him? I'm pretty sure he'd back up what Ruth said.'

Brasher looked annoyed at being cornered, but after a few moments he nodded in defeat. 'OK. I guess it can't do any harm at this stage.'

'I disagree!' Wright snapped, face flushing. 'This is against all the rules.'

'To hell with the rules,' Brasher replied. 'They're right – we have a real and imminent threat against the president and we don't have time to stick to the niceties. Or maybe you'd like to call in and report me?' When Wright bit her lip and said nothing, he turned to Ruth. 'What do you want to ask him?'

'We know from the phone call to the office in New York that I'm being followed. How closely we don't know. But I'm willing to bet Donny knows about it because Malak is the controller behind this whole thing and would have mentioned it in case we showed up. Let me start with that – it might just throw him off.'

'Go ahead.'

Moments later Ruth stepped into the interview room, leaving Vaslik, Brasher and a fuming Special Agent Wright next door. Donny didn't look up, his shoulders slumped in defeat and exhaustion. She walked slowly around the room, her footsteps measured, passing close enough behind him to note the greasiness of his hair and skin and the smell of his nervousness in the air. She came to a stop in front of him.

'Hello, Donny.'

At the sound of her voice, Donny looked up. For a couple of seconds, he didn't react; then he jerked back, his mouth dropping open before he shut it again and swallowed, his Adam's apple jumping furiously. Now he was looking seriously nervous and said, 'Where is the other woman? I want to talk to the other woman!'

Ruth smiled. He'd recognised her, which he could only have done if he'd seen a picture of her. Now all she had to do was find out what else Donny's leader had let slip.

'You recognised me, right, Donny?' she said briskly. 'My name's Ruth, by the way. How did you know me?'

'I... I saw a photograph. You aren't American. Are you British?'

'It doesn't matter what I am. Tell me about the photo.'

'It was sent to Malak by his people in London and New York. Also the picture of a man with you, but in New Jersey, I think it was.'

'I see. So he has others working for him.'

'Yes. Several others. But I don't know their names.'

'That's fine. We don't need those yet. But one of these men knew how to find me in central New York, Donny. They contacted an office where I was working – a new place only just set up. Tell me how they were able to do that.'

He shrugged. 'Simple. Malak showed your photo to Chadwick; he didn't recognise you personally, but he guessed you were from the company in London that sent you here. Malak got one of the brotherhood to track you down and they found you had an office in New York.'

'You mean the Muslim Brotherhood?'

'No. Not them. This brotherhood… it's not an official name. They're just… people who are willing to help, that's all.'

'Help and weapons.'

'Some. Not all.' He scowled. 'Many are ordinary people, but they know others who can do these things.'

'So it's a loose network, is that what you're saying?'

'Maybe. Why do you people always assume any group of people is an organised terror cell?'

Ruth raised her eyebrows at this sudden show of spirit. 'Maybe,' she said heavily, 'because if they supply or use guns and violence, that's what they are.'

Donny shrank in his seat, refusing to meet her eye.

'Fine,' she said softly. 'Let's call them sympathisers, but not necessarily extremists. What else do they provide?'

'One is a computer expert who was with Egyptian Intelligence. I think that's who found you. When Malak heard you were so close, he was pretty angry. He said he would get you tracked down and…' He hesitated and looked away.

'And what?' Ruth rapped on the table with her knuckles to grab back his attention. 'And killed? Is that what he said?'

'Eliminated.'

'Do you know who's coming after me?'

He shook his head. 'No. I don't know. They're from outside. Malak said they are expert trackers and have already dealt with many traitors who have turned against the cause, wherever they try to hide.'

Ruth felt chilled at the idea of a mobile hit squad travelling the world to do the bidding of whoever could call on their services. 'Freelancers?'

'Yes. Wherever they have to go, they go. The brotherhood is all over the world.'

'You mentioned the cause. What cause is that?'

'Islam. Jihad.' He shrugged as if it was obvious. Or of little importance. Ruth concluded that right now, in Donny's eyes, it was probably more of the latter and he was wishing fervently that he'd had nothing to do with it.

'Is Malak part of a terror group, Donny? al-Qaeda? Al-shabab? Islamic State? Or is he a lone wolf?'

Another shake of the head. 'I don't know. He doesn't say anything about others. But I know he has contacts because I've heard him talking, although I don't know what he says.'

'But he can't be a loner, can he? I mean, all this planning, stealing the drones, kidnapping James Chadwick, setting up the airfield where he kept him prisoner and where you flew the drones. That takes time and money to organise. So who is he working for? Who's behind him? You must have an idea… bits and pieces you've picked up, fragments you've overheard. You're not stupid, we know that. So what's your guess?'

'I don't know, I told you. Yes, I heard bits, but not enough to form an opinion. I wasn't part of it; he deliberately kept me out of it. All he wanted from me was to prepare and fly the drones once Chadwick had taught me how.'

'Prepare? What does that mean?' This was something Agent Wright hadn't covered in her line of questions.

For a long moment Donny said nothing while his eyes went walkabout and his fingers became knotted together on the table top.

'Donny. Focus.' Ruth rapped the table again. 'What did you do to the drones?'

Donny's eyes filled with tears, and he swallowed hard, then said, 'Malak made me adapt the parachute tube fitted on the drones to take a cylinder.'

'A cylinder? But I thought they'd already been adapted to take powder. Isn't that what was used at the airfield – a red dye? We saw the rocks.'

'It was. But he got me to change them back. It was a simple process because it worked on the same principal. A radio signal would activate the parachute by releasing the cap on the tube, and the powder would be drawn out through the passage of air over the top in a gradual stream. It worked well in trials.'

'The red dye.'

'Yes.'

'But he got you to change them again. Did he say why?'

'He said the dye was not part of his original plan and he needed me to make some alterations.' He looked suddenly drawn and hollow, as if the full realisation of what he had been a part of was just now hitting him.

'To do what?'

'He asked me to fit sensors to enable something else fitted inside the parachute tubes to be activated, allowing…'

Ruth had to force herself to breath. 'Allowing what, Donny? Tell me.'

'He didn't say what was inside the tube, only that it would bring…' He banged his hands down on the table with a crash and shouted 'I can't say it!'

Ruth lifted her hand to stop any of the guards rushing in. They couldn't stop now; it was too crucial and they were right on the brink of a discovery, she was certain.

'What, Donny? *Tell me!*'

Then it came to her: she knew precisely what he'd been about to say. 'Bring what, Donny? *The sting of death from the sky… your own toys of death spraying our message of destruction on the head of your leader and ending his tyranny.* Was that what Malak said?'

Donny stared at her in dismay, and whispered, 'Yes.'

39

The tears were now streaming down Donny's cheeks and he was staring at her in disbelief. 'How did you…?'

'We know lots, Donny. What we don't know is what the sting of death refers to. Perhaps you can tell me.'

'No. I promise you, I can't, even if I wanted to – I don't *know*!' He clutched his face in his hands and bent his head to touch the table. 'This is all crazy!'

'But you're a chemist, aren't you? Wasn't that part of your training at NYU, among other things?' She leaned forward and got him to lift his head, staring him in the face, deliberately piling on the pressure. She had no reason to believe Donny was anything other than a techie originally brought in by Malak to fly the drones. But squeezing him on the question of the weapon involved might be enough to make him crack. 'Isn't that one of the reasons you were recruited at the mosque in Queens – to produce a chemical agent?'

He stared at her in confusion. 'What? *Me?* How can you think that? I did some chemistry at NYU, sure – that was part of the course. But I'm not a chemist! I don't know anything about that kind of stuff!'

Ruth sat back, giving him the time and space to calm down. His voice carried a worrying ring of truth, and she decided that if Donny was playing them as Wright had claimed, he was a world-class actor.

'All right,' she said. 'Tell me about Freedom. What does that refer to?' She deliberately didn't tell him where she'd seen the word; she was hoping that if he knew it he'd work it out for himself.

He frowned and scrubbed at his cheeks. 'Freedom? I don't know. Malak never said exactly. He used the word all the time but in different ways, like it was some kind of mantra. But he said lots of things without going into detail… as if was talking to himself. I think there were times when… it was like he wasn't even aware of me.'

'Because he didn't think you were important enough?'

'I guess. I never thought about it before.' He looked miserable and refused to meet her eye, and Ruth figured Donny was trying to come to grips with the knowledge that he'd only ever been a small cog in the machine, unimportant and no doubt easily expendable.

'OK. Let's assume he wasn't talking about freedom as a concept, like freedom from repression, freedom of speech or stuff like that. Did he use the word like… I don't know – a place or a code, for example?'

'Field. Freedom Field.' He looked up and blinked, like a small light had gone on. 'He said that the day before I… left. I asked him where we were going and he said Freedom Field. It's the only thing I can think of.'

'So it's a place. Where?'

'I don't *know*. He said the name… only not to me or Bilal; it was just something he mentioned sometimes.'

'What was the context?'

'Huh?'

'What else was he saying at the time? Did he say, 'We must go to Freedom Field', or 'How do we get to Freedom Field'? Words like that. The context.'

'Oh, right.' He bit his lip and said, 'I recall at the time he was like angry, but it wasn't at me any more for crashing the drones.'

'*Like* angry?'

'Intense. He did that occasionally, going into some other place as if he was reminding himself about what he had to do.'

Donny snapped his fingers a couple of times, then said, 'I've got it: he said Freedom Field, then something I can't remember and "...the fools would regret honouring the fallen because it was going to come back and bite them." That was it – I don't remember the rest.'

Ruth thought it over. Honouring the fallen? That sounded like a garden of remembrance. But there were hundreds, thousands of those scattered across the country, with one in most towns and cities. 'Fine. One last point, Donny, then you can get something to eat. Would you like that?'

'Yes, please. I think I've told you everything I know.'

'Maybe. Maybe not. My point is, this entire plan is bigger than it seems. Bigger than one man's idea for inflicting a blow on the United States; bigger than merely leaving a car bomb in a crowded place timed to explode, which is much easier. This is about chemicals – a dirty bomb. And a unique form of delivery. You don't exactly pick up dangerous chemicals or drones at B&Q, do you?'

'Huh?' He looked puzzled and Ruth realised he'd never heard of the British DIY chain.

'Like Home Depot.'

'Oh.'

'Instead, Malak would have needed finance and resources and manpower to get it going. And that's a lot more than a single man could do. You agree?'

'Yes. I guess. But I never saw anybody else except for him and Bilal.'

'Ah, yes. Bilal Ammar. We know he's no organiser. He's a lump of muscle.'

Donny scowled. 'He's a pig. I hate him!'

'I'm not surprised. He's hardly in the same league as you, is he?' She decided to throw in a change of direction. 'Was it Bilal who killed the construction crew?'

His mouth dropped open again and he went pale. 'I had nothing to do with that... it was all them, I promise you.'

'Tell me about it.'

'It was before Chadwick arrived. I was sent out to the far end of the runway because Malak wanted me to test one of the drones, to see that it worked and to try out a few simple manoeuvres. I did as he ordered and made sure it was assembled and functioning properly, then made some very simple manoeuvres.' He hesitated and looked away. 'I went even further than he told me because I didn't want him to see me if I made a mistake. While I was running the motors I thought I heard some noises, but I was concentrating on not crashing the drone, so I never gave it a thought.'

'What sort of noises?'

'Popping noises… very fast, but not loud.'

'You mean gunshots.'

'Yes – but I didn't know that at the time, I swear!'

'Go on.'

'When I got back Bilal was walking around outside the hangar waving an assault rifle. He was grinning like he always did and I could see and smell the gun-smoke in the air. He was also excited, which made me feel sick.' When Ruth looked blank he explained, 'He was clutching his groin and showing off his arousal to me as if I'd be impressed!'

'What had he done?'

'He showed me the hole in the floor… where the dead men were lying. I couldn't believe it. He said Malak had ordered him to kill them all because they had demanded more money for finishing early. Malak had refused and one of the men had threatened to tell the police. Malak ordered them into the pit and… Bilal shot them.' He shook his head. 'You have to believe me – I had nothing to do with it.'

Ruth breathed out slowly. It was most likely that Malak had never intended letting the men go in the first place. Once paid off, all it would have taken was for one of them to talk about what they'd been told to do, and his whole plan would have been thrown into disarray. 'Very well. Let's get back to Malak.

Where does he get his money? How does he have a call on the men he needed to watch Chadwick and his family in England and here in the States; to watch me... even to follow me halfway across America?'

There was a long pause while Donny digested and processed the question. Then he said, 'He talks to people all the time – pretty much every day.'

'By phone?'

'Yes. He has many. He keeps them in a box. He uses them once and throws them away.'

'So how do these people contact him in return?'

'They don't. He calls them – although sometimes he allows them to text him, but only once. Then he disposes of the cell. He says it's a fool-proof system so the CIA and NSA can't find him.'

'Do you know who these people are?'

He lifted his shoulders. 'No idea. And I never heard what he said to them. I've never seen him with anybody, but he kept disappearing during the day while Bilal and I slept, and never seemed to stay in the same motel as us. I assumed he was meeting up with people to discuss his plan. But about a week ago I saw him checking his laptop and he was furious about the lack of a signal because he couldn't contact anybody. He said a meeting would have to be postponed and the bid would fail.'

'A bid for what?'

'I don't know. A bid – that's all I heard.'

Ruth's phone rang. She glanced at the screen. It was Brasher. She was tempted to ignore it, but figured it must be important. She excused herself and said, 'Yes?'

'I think I know what he means by that,' Brasher murmured softly. 'Get out here. We need to talk.'

'I have one more question,' she insisted. 'The main one. It's critical.'

Brasher didn't reply immediately, but she heard Special Agent Wright talking angrily in the background. Eventually Brasher said, 'Go ahead but make it quick.'

Ruth disconnected and turned back to Donny. 'Let's go back to the plan. Malak's going to use the drone to spray a chemical agent over the target, right?'

'Yes.'

'But you don't know what that is. Presumably it will be a toxic substance.'

'Yes. He says he had another chemist put it together. But I don't know what it is.'

'How does he plan to do that – to release it, I mean?'

'There are set coordinates fed into the flight controls. Once there, a signal will activate the trigger and… and the spray begins to operate.'

'Tell me about the delivery system. How will the drone get to the target? Is that what Chadwick is there for, now you're no longer around?'

'I suppose. I think he decided to use Chadwick in the end anyway, because of the complexity of flying the drones. I wasn't able to keep even one in the air, let alone four.'

Ruth felt a chill down her back. After knowing what had happened to the construction crew it was easy to guess what Chadwick's fate would be once the deed was done. Then something else hit her. 'Four? What do you mean?'

Donny shrugged. 'Malak had me show him how to feed the numbers into the controller for all four drones. Thirty-four degrees seventy north,' he recited automatically, 'ninety-nine-twenty-five west.'

She didn't need to ask what the numbers referred to; instinct told her they were the map coordinates for the Altus Air Force base.

'Four drones.'

'Yes. It should have been six but I crashed two and that really made him pissed.' He flushed. 'Sorry.'

'That's OK.'

'They start off in different places but they'll converge as they get closer to the target area. That way Malak said there will be a chance of at least one of them getting through. He said it was for a military target, not civilian.'

'And you believed him?'

He shrugged. 'That's all I know.'

Ruth didn't want to ask, but had to. She knew from what Vaslik had said earlier when looking at the possible target bases that Altus had anything from upwards of four thousand personnel there at any one time. And that wasn't counting families, visitors and the surrounding population. Her lips were dry, but she didn't dare lick them. 'And then what?'

'Death. He said many people would die. Hundreds, possibly more.'

40

Ruth left Donny in the care of a guard and stepped out into the corridor. She found the atmosphere electric, with Special Agent Wright stalking away towards the front of the building and Tom Brasher calling her back.

Wright ignored him and slammed through the door, her shoulders stiff with anger.

Vaslik was standing inside the adjacent room looking nonplussed. Ruth said to him, 'What's going on?'

'She's going over Brasher's head to her supervisor to get him to alert Homeland Security and the Department of Defence. She heard what you got out of Donny and told Brasher he had to call it in now and launch a general alert and a major search of the area. Brasher said not yet and she flipped.'

'What set it off?'

He winced. 'Brasher told her they were the questions she should have been asking.'

'He's right; she totally missed the point. And we'd be crazy to sound a general alert – we have to find these people first. If the authorities flood the area with personnel, they'll go underground and try again somewhere else.'

'I agree.'

Brasher turned back towards them and sighed in resignation. 'I'll have to let her go. I can't stop her without locking her in a cell. She might come to her senses once she calms down. I guess I could have handled it better.'

Ruth wasn't so certain. Under the clean-cut exterior, Karina Wright struck her as one angry and ambitious lady who had already made up her mind and wasn't about to back down. Maybe being the first to break the news was her way of enhancing a career agenda.

'What was it you wanted to tell me about bids?' she reminded him.

'Well, first off, that was a classy approach in there; you were right on point and got him talking about what he thought he didn't know. I guess I have to own up to missing that, too.' He composed his thoughts for a moment, then continued, 'About six month ago the National Security Agency picked up some chatter about planned operations against Coalition force members. The sources were in the Middle East, but some of the servers being used were in the US and Europe. Some of it was the usual high-minded guff about hitting us where it hurt and teaching us a lesson, but there were some other exchanges that sounded different – kind of off the wall. For that reason they were noted but set to one side because the subject matter made no real sense.'

'Like what?'

'The exchanges were talking about bids, just like Donny said. The difference was, they talked about bidding for 'strikes'. It was thought they were using code words but we couldn't figure out what they meant. The word 'strikes' is clear enough in plain language, but we were thrown by 'bids'. It didn't fit, no matter which way we threw it in the air.'

'Couldn't they have been groups bidding to take on a job?' Vaslik suggested.

'That was our initial thought. There's certainly no shortage of them out there wanting to do something radical. It's long been known that most of the extremist groups are in competition with each other to hit the headlines and gain a name for themselves. But they appear to be subservient to some of the more powerful groups if something high-concept is being planned, and they back off fast when told to avoid conflicting operations. What threw us – and still does – was that the so-called bids had financial figures attached to them.'

'So where do we go from here?'

'Well, I think Donny just gave us a possible answer. What if the words he overheard alluded to the fact that this Asim Malak has come up with a uniquely modern method of funding his operation?'

'Go on.'

'He sets up the idea to make a major hit on the US, to the point where it looks viable. Then he hawks it around to a number of the wealthier extremist groups and their backers to see who wants a share of the action – in exchange for finance.'

'Like crowd-funding,' said Vaslik.

'Exactly.'

They stood and considered the idea. It sounded crazy and unlikely... yet in the modern world, almost to be expected. If, like Malak, a group lacked the funds to complete an operation, why not go out and sell shares to interested bidders? That way everybody was happy; the attacking group and any others with parallel interests.

'It's not so stupid,' Ruth said into the silence. 'The highest bidder gets to claim the credit for the strike while Malak and his men do the work and remain unknown. It's insane... but clever.'

'Of course it is,' Brasher agreed. 'It's a win-win for the bidders, too; they don't have to risk their own people carrying out the operation, but if Malak needs some expendable muscle, they can send in anybody they choose at minimum cost.'

Vaslik nodded. 'It makes sense to—' He stopped as a popping sound came from the front of the building, followed by a lot of shouting and the sound of breaking glass.

'Jesus, that's gunfire!' Brasher cried, and turned towards the door just as a whooshing noise came closer, over-riding the sound of the gunshots.

A split second later the whole building shook with the force of an explosion, and ceiling tiles rained down on their heads.

All the lights went out, and a loud groaning sound came from the walls around them as part of the structure began to give way.

In the distance, somebody began screaming.

41

'*Open fire!*' Salem screamed, and tossed the used rocket launcher out through the open side door. They were once-only use weapons, and he was going to need the other one if they stayed here much longer. The scene not eighty yards away was now one of carnage, with a gaping hole in the front of the jail where the entrance had been, and part of the roof structure was caving in with the groaning sounds of a dying animal.

He had waited until the passenger had slapped the fascia and shouted, '*It's her!*' before throwing back the sliding side doors on both sides to reduce pressure damage inside the van and bringing the launcher up to his shoulder. He caught a glimpse through the sights of a woman with dark hair standing just inside the front entrance of the building with a cell phone clamped to her ear. He had just enough time to think how angry she looked, and actually not that much like her photo, before he calmly squeezed the trigger.

The woman had disappeared in the explosion.

He coughed and spat out the taste of propellant which now filled the van, and reached for the second launcher. On the face of it he'd used one rocket to take out one person, but he was experienced enough to know that there would be other casualties inside the structure. Those that had survived would be stunned and blinded by concussion and dust, and mounting any kind of pursuit would take a long time.

Especially if he fired the second rocket in through the hole.

As he took hold of the launcher, something bounced off the inside of the roof and struck him on the cheek. It was an ejected carbine case. The front seat passenger was spraying the area around the jail through his side window, screaming unintelligibly over the clatter of casings hitting the metalwork and windows like maddened insects, their bright brassy colour flickering in the light.

The driver went to push past the passenger to join him in hosing down the crippled building, but the Salem saw him and shouted, 'What, are you crazy? Get us out of here *now*, you idiot!' He reached up and slapped the back of the driver's head to gain his attention, then spun round as the bodywork close by his head blew apart under the impact of a heavy bullet. He swore and turned. An officer in police uniform was kneeling off to one side aiming shots at the van with a sidearm. He had blood on his face and his shirt was torn and covered in brick dust, but he was standing steady and the soldier knew he was the main target and had only seconds left before the gun zeroed in on him.

He grabbed the carbine instead and fired three shots in quick succession. But his timing was thrown off as the driver took the van forward away from the kerb just as he pulled the trigger. The shots went wide, one clipping the officer's shoulder and spinning him round. He dropped his gun but scooped it up with his other hand and resumed firing, letting off four shots that slammed into the rear door panels as the van tore away up the street.

They raced out of town heading east on the US 64, leaving behind the noise of fire alarms and a pall of smoke as part of the jail began to burn. There were no signs of pursuit and Salem wondered how long that would last. By now phone calls and radio alerts would be going out all over the State, and armed response teams would be converging on the area and setting up road blocks.

'Five miles from here,' he said to the driver, 'you will see a cross-section with three trees on the right. You can let me off there.'

'You're a fool, you know that?' the driver said, fighting to get the maximum possible speed out of the van. 'They will catch you before you have gone ten miles. Stay with us and we stand a better chance of getting away on the major highways. Once we get to Oklahoma City we can lose ourselves and the brotherhood will provide sanctuary.'

Salem ignored him. It was an argument he'd heard before when he'd first met up with these two men for the trip to Alva. He'd brought his own vehicle, an old pickup he'd acquired in a cheap car lot just outside Oklahoma City. It blended into this area like sand on a rock, and he'd left it parked in a turn-off along the US 64 where nobody would notice it. He planned on taking the network of back roads all the way south, and for the bales of straw he'd picked up along the way to be his cover. He had documents that would stand any scrutiny, and after months of attending night classes at the American School in Sana'a, in Yemen, he could talk American English with sufficient ease to convince any cop in a hurry that he was an innocent seasonal farm worker doing his job.

These two, however, seemed to think that this van carried some kind of magic cloak that would take them all the way to Oklahoma City and beyond without being noticed. More fools them.

He checked the rear windows. Nothing yet. But it wouldn't be long in coming. The one thing the Americans had going for them was organisation and response.

'Slow down,' he said to the driver, as the nearside front wheel slammed into a small pothole in the blacktop. 'You're driving too fast for this part of the country; you'll end up getting us noticed or killing us.'

'Screw you,' the driver muttered, and pushed his foot down even harder. 'My job is to get us out of here. Yours is to sit there and shut up!'

Salem waited. The driver was too pepped up on adrenalin to register what he was doing, but he wouldn't have to stay in this death trap much longer. He peered through the windscreen at the road ahead. The turning was coming up fast. Too fast – and the driver showed no signs of slowing down.

'Here!' Salem said. 'This is where you drop me.'

'We don't have time,' the driver replied, and swept a hand off the wheel to gesture at the road behind. 'For all we know they could be marshalling their forces to hunt us down. You'll have to sit there and watch our backs.'

Salem sighed and put the tip of the Colt's barrel against the driver's neck. 'Actually, you stupid pig, I don't have to do anything. But I will blow your idiot head off if you don't stop right *now*!'

The driver yelled in alarm and slammed on the brakes, sending the van into a snaking skid across the road before wrestling it back under control. Seconds later he was bumping along the grass verge and pulling to a stop at an intersection. The road left was little more than a track, but the one to the right was metal all the way. A clutch of trees stood nearby, just as Salem had said.

Salem jumped out, still holding the Colt carbine pointed at the driver's head. The passenger was staying very still, eyes glued to the front, but he didn't trust either of them to try and stop him the moment he turned his back. But he wasn't going to allow them the pleasure.

'Drive,' he commanded them. 'And don't stop until you are far away from here.'

The driver swore, then stamped on the gas and swung the wheel hard. But instead of continuing along the highway, he turned right and took the back road Salem had planned on using.

There was little he could do about it now, and on reflection it could play to his advantage. The van would be far more obvious out in the open country while he could lose himself pottering along at a steady pace, minding his own business.

He watched as it disappeared in the distance, dragging with it a plume of dust that rose in the air and hung there like a giant flag. Once the police got helicopters in the air that dust trail would stand out for miles.

He ran towards the trees and jumped into the pickup, and started the engine. He would take the 64 instead, then work his way south further along. After all, what cop would suspect a farm hand in a fifteen-year-old, rusting pickup carrying a load of straw and time on his hands to be part of an attack on a county jail?

He was just sorry this junker didn't have a radio. He'd always had a liking for country and western music.

42

The scene back at the jail was pandemonium. The front of the building crumpled, preventing access for rescue workers, but it was clear that the explosion had taken out the reception and security area and everybody in it. The bodies of three guards and civilian workers were evident among the rubble, along with the bodies of another guard and Karina Wright outside. The policeman who had opened fire on the van was sitting in a state of shock, still clutching his weapon, with blood oozing from the wound in his arm.

People were flooding in from surrounding businesses, stores and local administration buildings, and a harassed officer was shouting orders to get props under the sagging ceiling structure to reach people trapped under the fallen beams and brickwork.

Tom Brasher grabbed Ruth and pushed her towards the rear of the building while Vaslik made his way to the front to see if he could help. He passed two guards carrying an injured woman and saw two men lying unconscious against a wall, covered in dust. The air out here was thick with smoke, and he grabbed a fire extinguisher and sprayed a lick of flame coming from a demolished section of wall leading to the front lobby.

Amazingly one of the security guards who'd checked them in was standing in a corner where a section of wall had left him completely untouched. He was blinking in shock and looked at Vaslik as if he'd seen a ghost.

'You OK?' Vaslik said, and shook his arm.

The guard nodded. 'I think… I guess so. What happened?'

‘I don’t know. I think it was a rocket launcher. My colleague and I checked in our weapons and phones when we arrived. Where are they?’

‘Over here.’ The guard stumbled to a bank of secure lockers and opened one, and let Vaslik help himself. He stared uncomprehendingly at Vaslik and said, ‘What the hell do we do now?’

‘Make sure the building’s secure and help your buddies.’

He left the man and ran down a corridor where he found a fire door standing open and ran outside, heading towards the front entrance. The sound of gunfire had stopped so he didn’t expect to find anybody. In any case he figured that with all the confusion, there would be few armed officers or guards out here to do anything if the attackers launched another assault.

He skidded to a stop among the ruins of the entrance. It was as if a giant tin-opener had torn open the building, exposing the inner structure along with electrical wiring, water pipes gushing fluid and workers trying to clear rubble to reach the injured.

He recognised Karina Wright’s body, but she was beyond help, so he ran over to an officer with blood on his arm who was being tended to by a civilian on the front grass.

‘Where did they go?’ he asked.

The officer pointed, his eyes dulled by shock. ‘They headed south, then turned east… a white van with side doors… and one of those plastic windows on the roof.’ He sucked in air at a sudden movement of his injured arm. ‘Christ, man, it came out of nowhere. They had a rocket launcher and fully automatic weapons… and they just… they just hosed us down!’

‘How many men?’

‘I saw two but there had to be a driver, too. The launcher was in the back.’ He pointed to a tube lying in the street. ‘That’s it there. I returned fire and scored some hits but it didn’t slow them down any. They didn’t give a damn about who they hit… are you going after them?’

‘I might just do that.’ Vaslik punched in Dave Proust’s number and the former FBI man answered immediately.

'What's going on there?' Dave demanded.

'The jail's been hit,' Vaslik told him. 'Three guys in a white van. There's no way the locals can get a response in the air in time, so we'll have to do it. Can you get here and pick me up? I'm right outside the jail. Look for the smoke – there's enough space to land on the intersection nearby.'

'On my way. Three minutes.'

Moments later Tom Brasher and Ruth arrived and Vaslik gave them a summary of the situation.

'What are you going to do?' said Brasher.

'Stop them if we can. Dave's on his way in and the attackers are heading east. It shouldn't take long to catch up with them.' He checked his gun and handed Ruth her weapon and cell phone.

They soon heard the throb of rotors, and turned to see Dave's helicopter appear over the rooftops. It hovered for a few seconds to clear the intersection beneath, flattening the trees and scattering dust and smoke further over the surrounding buildings, before settling on the asphalt.

'I'll clear it with the local force and state police,' Brasher said, 'Just don't go getting yourselves killed. I'd come with you but I need to talk to a few people in Washington before this gets out of hand. We can't afford to have law enforcement all over the Altus area, but the White House needs to know what the situation is. Call it in when you find them.' He nodded at Vaslik and clapped Ruth on the arm, then ducked back towards the building.

Ruth and Vaslik ran across to the helicopter and jumped on board.

'Those guys must be suicide jockeys,' Dave shouted as they belted themselves in and the machine rose in the air, over the noise of the rotors. 'They have nowhere to go but open country. That means they could be looking for hostages. If we're quick maybe we can stop that happening. You guys ready for this?'

They both nodded.

'Armed and ready,' said Vaslik.

43

'I can't see them.' Dave was looking down on the US 64, flying at five-hundred feet and studying the traffic heading directly east. With his experience of flying, he'd told them he would be able to discount anything but white vans in an instant. Other than the highway, they could see only a thin network of narrow roads sprouting away north and south into open countryside with few buildings and even fewer moving vehicles.

Earlier, as they were heading out from Alva and leaving behind a growing pall of smoke from the burning front section of the jail, he had described the road layout in the area and where the attackers might be headed. 'If they keep going east on the six-four, they'll clip the Salt Plains Wildlife Refuge and State Park. Then it's a long road to nothing.'

'Is the park big enough to hide in?' Ruth asked.

'For a while, I guess. But it's pretty open and there's a lot of water and trees to navigate. In a van, I wouldn't rate their chances on staying there for ever or not coming to grief with a busted axle or a burst tyre.'

'Where else could they go from here?'

'I guess a city would be their main aim. If they keep heading east until they hit the US Three-five, they could turn south towards Oklahoma City or Wichita in the north.'

'Unless they plan on joining up with Malak at Altus.'

He nodded. 'There is that. But that must be close on two-hundred miles. That's a lot of driving on open roads and they must know they'll be on every local and state cop's radar by now. Frankly, I'm not sure these guys figured things out too well. They're either crazy or dumb. Attacking a county jail in this territory, they were putting themselves way out on a limb.'

'Maybe that's what Malak wanted,' said Ruth. 'I got the impression from what Donny said that he's a one-man show and doesn't care much for the people he uses. They were a useful diversion while he disappeared.'

'Wouldn't be the first time that's happened,' said Dave. 'But if you ask me, wild as it seemed, it still took some planning. He had to get the men and the weapons together, and I doubt he'd have gone to the trouble unless he had something to gain by it.'

'What do you mean?'

Dave turned his head and looked at her. Suddenly she gained an insight to the FBI agent and man hunter he had once been, focussing instinctively on understanding and interpreting the situation that had unfolded. 'Think about the timing: he can't have been interested solely in busting Donny out of the jail because he wouldn't have had time to get this team together. If we were in the middle of a big city, sure – he'd have had men on tap and ready to go. But out here?' He shook his head. 'It's too big and open. They were already on their way when Donny got arrested.'

'So why, then?' Ruth asked the question but deep in her heart knew the answer already.

'I think he was after you. This guy's a thinker, we know that. He knew you were out there and that you must have come all the way from London to find Chadwick. That probably shook him; it showed personal commitment. So he must have figured that you'd hear about Donny being captured and that you'd want to talk to him. Wherever he was taken would be the best place to stop you.'

'Killing two birds with one stone,' Vaslik agreed. 'Getting Ruth was one; shutting Donny up would be a bonus.'

'That's about the size of it.'

Ruth stared down at the distant fields and roads below, and felt a shiver of apprehension. It was hard to imagine any one man being so committed that he would go after a single person this way who wasn't his primary target. But then, Malak was just that; he was committed to striking a blow against the United States and a man with that level of self-belief and determination would have seen any threat to his plans as one worth dealing with, even at the risk to the men sent to do the job.

She looked up to find Vaslik watching her. He fluttered his eyebrows at her and smiled.

'What?' she said.

'Sounds like he'd got the hots for you.' He smirked and looked away, and Ruth dug him in the ribs with her elbow. She knew he was only trying to lighten the atmosphere, and appreciated it. But the thought that she had become a specific target was unsettling.

'There,' Dave said. 'One o'clock heading south – a dust cloud. Hold tight.'

He took the helicopter down, aiming at a distant plume of white visible along a narrow road through a patchwork of vast fields. It quickly became obvious that the vehicle creating the dust was larger than a car but smaller than a truck and travelling very fast. Seconds later they had more detail: it was a white van.

'It's them – see the roof vent?' said Vaslik.

Dave nodded. 'Got it. What do you want me to do – track them while we call backup?'

'No way.' Ruth didn't hesitate. 'We have to stop them before they find hostages.'

'Attagirl.' He grinned and took the machine to within a couple of hundred feet of the van. At that height they could see that the rear doors had been peppered with holes and one of the glass panels was missing. As they watched, a head appeared briefly out of the passenger side window and looked up at them in obvious shock before ducking back out of sight. The van wobbled in response before the driver brought it back on track, narrowly missing a line of potholes along the verge.

'Well, now they know we're here,' Dave commented, 'we'd better get ready to duck. This could get heavy.'

As he spoke, the rear doors of the van flew open and the same man appeared. He stared up at them for a few seconds, then turned and brought something out from the interior of the van.

'Assault rifle!' Dave shouted, and took the helicopter away to the left and up, the engine howling in response. Ruth and Vaslik held on tight as behind them they heard the brief stutter of shots being fired, but none came anywhere near them.

Dave levelled out and stayed a quarter-mile out to one side, where the gunmen couldn't reach them with any accuracy unless they stopped to take careful aim. 'We need to get in front of them,' he said, and increased speed, leaving the van behind.

After a few minutes he brought the helicopter round on a long curving course until they were facing back along the road towards the speeding van, now nearly a mile away but closing fast.

Ruth caught a flicker of movement to one side. Instinct told her there should have been none, and when she glanced over she felt her gut go tight. A track was bisecting the road the van was on, and driving along it towards the junction was a pickup truck.

A pickup with three children in the back, waving at them.

'Dave!' She pointed. If the pickup continued at its present speed, it would meet the men in the van. And that could only have one outcome.

Hostages.

But Dave had seen them. He nodded and took the machine down fast. The airframe rattled as the wind battered the fuselage, and it seemed to Ruth that the helicopter was standing on its nose with the ground below coming up much too quickly. Then he levelled off and the tail dipped before the skids touched the ground with a thump alongside the junction.

The van was now closing in, a billowing trail of dust testament to the speed it was travelling.

Vaslik was out first, gun in hand and running to meet the oncoming pick-up. He was waving his arms at them to stop, but it didn't seem to be making any impression on the driver.

Ruth jumped out and watched the van. For a moment it seemed to be holding its course along the road.

Then without warning the van turned and tore across the verge, bursting through a thin line of wire and rough grass. Once clear, it began to speed up, bouncing over the uneven ground and trailing an even greater dust cloud like a pillar of smoke in its wake.

This put the men in the van on an intercept course with the approaching pickup, and it was clear what their intentions were.

Ruth turned and stared at Dave, who had joined her, the rotors of the helicopter still spinning slowly. 'We have to do something.'

He took in the scene unfolding, with Vaslik still running but too far away from the pickup to be able to help. And Ruth saw by Dave's face that getting back in the air would take too long; by the time he did that, the terrorists would have stopped the pickup and be in command of the situation.

Dave shook his head and turned away, reaching into the baggage compartment. When he came back he said, 'Are you any good with these? If not, say so and I'll do it. But I'm better with a handgun.'

He was holding an M4 carbine.

Ruth nodded. 'I think so.' It had been a while since she'd used a rifle, but she'd always prided herself on being reasonably accurate. The problem right now was, there was no time for error or hesitation because one glance told her the van was closing in fast on the pickup which was now slowing, the driver undoubtedly confused by what he or she was seeing.

'You've got about twenty seconds,' Dave said calmly as Ruth took the weapon. 'Don't waste time on the tyres – it won't stop them. Aim for the driver's door; these rounds'll punch right on through.' Then he knelt by her side and slapped his shoulder before clamping both hands over his ears.

She realised what he wanted her to do. She knelt alongside him, instinctively checking that the safety was off and the rate of fire selector was turned to a three-round burst. The weapon smelled oily and new, and she wondered if this was another Tom Brasher decision, just in case. If it was, the man had been amazingly perceptive.

'Two hundred yards.' Dave's voice was steady, counting off the distance between the van and the pickup.

Taking a deep breath she zoned out everything else around her; the pickup drawing to a stop, the children in the back jumping out and staring towards the charging van with open mouths, the dying whine of the helicopter engine. Vaslik was still running, holding his gun in the air to draw the terrorists' attention and make them slow down. But they weren't stopping. In fact the side door was now open and the barrel of a rifle was visible where the gunman inside was trying to draw a bead on Vaslik.

Nothing else mattered, Ruth told herself. Just stop the men in the van. She breathed easily, nestling the butt of the rifle into her shoulder and bending her head to the optical sight. She felt the warm mass of Dave's shoulder beneath her supporting arm, and the brief movement of his head as he watched the van. The view through the rubber eye-piece blurred for a moment, then cleared and steadied as she adjusted her stance against Dave and achieved a clear and steady line of sight. The van suddenly blossomed in the viewfinder, the face of the man in the side doorway bright and clear, struggling to line up his rifle on Vaslik while shouting something at the driver.

Ruth took another breath and let it out slowly.

'A hundred yards.' Dave again. 'Do it.'

Ruth squeezed the trigger.

44

For a long moment nothing seemed to happen. Yet Ruth knew the burst of three shots had drilled right through the center of the driver's door, leaving vivid holes in the thin white metal.

Then the vehicle's nose dipped momentarily before it began to slow and wander off-course, finally turning away and coming to a halt.

The moment it stopped one of the side doors opened and a man jumped out. He dodged away to put the van's body between himself and any incoming fire before Ruth could react. Seconds later the driver's door opened and another figure appeared. But this one wasn't moving easily. He dropped to the ground and rolled under the van, dragging a rifle behind him and tucking himself in behind the front wheel.

'I see two,' said Ruth. 'Two only.'

'Got it,' Dave muttered.

Ruth checked Vaslik's position. He was now running in towards the pickup and waving at the children to stay back. They finally seemed to understand that this wasn't a game, and turned and began running back along the track, followed closely by a man in a check shirt, coveralls and work boots.

'Firing,' Ruth warned Dave, and squeezed off another three-round burst, this time aiming at the man under the van, who she could see was bringing his rifle round to focus on them. The shots tore into the vehicle's lower bodywork, one bursting the tyre next to the gunman, and she followed them with another burst, this time seeing the ground beneath the van being chopped up by the high-velocity rounds and raising clouds of dust.

The gunman stopped moving.

-

Andy Vaslik was feeling a sharp pain in his side. He hadn't run this far in months, and knew any ability he might have had to use a handgun with accuracy was diminishing with every stride as his body began to shake with the effort and the rush of adrenalin. But he drove himself on, anxious to put himself between the gunmen and the children. He heard Ruth firing again and saw the effect as the bullets tore into the ground, and loosed off two hasty shots himself at the now stationary van to keep the gunmen's heads down.

He glimpsed movement behind the van, and saw a figure kneeling down with a rifle to his shoulder. And it was aimed directly at him.

He swerved to put the gunman off, but the man wasn't aiming for precision. Instead he let loose a burst of fire in Vaslik's direction before ducking back. But one round was enough; Vaslik felt as if he'd been punched in the arm. He stumbled as he was thrown off-balance and felt his feet skate from under him like a party drunk.

It was the suddenness of that move that probably saved his life.

He heard a snap as another shot tore through the air where his head had been, and continued rolling, trying to ignore the pain blossoming in his bicep and to focus on not giving the gunman an easy target. He came to rest and adjusted his stance, pushing his gun hand forward and firing three times. In the same instant he saw the van's side windows disintegrating as a volley of fire poured into them, and above the sound of a rifle, recognised the snap of a semi-automatic pistol as Dave Proust joined Ruth in firing at the remaining man, who threw himself down flat under the pounding gunfire.

Vaslik rolled twice more to change his position, then waited to see if the gunman moved again. When he did the man came up into a kneeling position and fired two rapid shots – but aimed at where Vaslik had been lying, not his new position.

Fighting a wave of nausea Vaslik put everything into the next few seconds. Recalling the endless live firing practice sessions in the police and with Homeland Security, he squeezed off three shots at the distant figure, then three more.

There was a long silence and the gunman didn't move.

Vaslik stood up and changed to his spare clip of ammunition, then waved a cautionary signal at Ruth and Dave as they moved closer. But the danger was over. As he approached the gunman he saw why: the gunman had been struck in the head by a single bullet, although from which gun was impossible to tell.

He flicked the rifle away as a precaution, then checked the man under the van. He was alive, still, but only just. His chest was a mess.

Vaslik waved the other two in and went to the rear doors to check the interior. Nothing but a launcher on the floor, along with bottles of water and two sports bags. He checked them out but they contained only extra clothing and wash things.

'One dead, the driver wounded,' he reported, when Ruth arrived, with Dave following behind, talking on his cell phone. 'Number three's missing.'

'I called it in,' said Dave. 'The local cops should be here soon with emergency services. I called Tom Brasher, too; there are going to be questions about our involvement here, but I figure he can act as a firewall if things get heavy.' He looked past the van to where the man and children from the pickup had now stopped running and were watching them. 'I'll go talk to these people and make sure they're all right.' He nodded down at the wounded man under the van. He was staring back at them, but his eyes were becoming unfocussed and full of pain. 'My suggestion: you might want to talk to him before he gets swallowed up in the system.'

'Good idea.' Vaslik hunkered down next to the man. Up close he could hear his laboured breathing, and a whistling sound from his lower chest. From that and the amount of blood it was easy to see he was in a bad way. But Dave's suggestion was a good one and he wasn't about to waste the opportunity. Once the emergency services got here, along with various law enforcement people from all over the state, the man would be rushed away and wouldn't be doing any talking.

'You speak English?' Vaslik asked.

For a moment the man didn't respond. Then he nodded twice.

'Good. What was your job here today?'

'Driv… driving.' The man blinked slowly, his voice raspy and his accent heavy. 'What—?' He looked around and Vaslik guessed he was asking about his colleagues.

'Your friend is dead,' he told him. 'Along with a lot of other people. Where's the other one who was with you?'

'Gone.'

'Who sent you here?'

'Broth…brother.' The man coughed, and a fine spray of blood appeared on his lips and ran down his chin.

'The brotherhood – I get that. But who asked for your help? Was it Malak?' He felt no compunction about questioning him; had they arrived a few minutes later, this man and his colleague would now be holding children as hostages.

The man shook his head. His eyes were becoming dulled by shock and his chin was dipping, but he clearly had enough determination left to remain silent about who he was working for.

'Do you know where Malak has gone?'

No response.

'Or Bilal?'

Nothing.

'How about the drones? Do you know about them?'

This time there was a flicker; it was momentary, hardly there at all, but it told him that the man at least knew what was going to happen. He wasn't surprised; the magnitude of what Malak had planned had probably seeped out among those committed to the same cause, and the unusual approach of using drones would have been seen as a clever use of America's own technology against them.

'That's fine,' Vaslik told him. 'You've heard of Freedom? Freedom Field? We know that's where it's going to happen. Pity for Malak is, there's nobody there. They've shut the area down. In fact, the only person there will be Malak himself. He's going to be a lonely man. Then he'll be a dead one.'

The distant sound of sirens drifted across the open fields, and the man's head lifted. He frowned at first, then nodded with difficulty and gave a faint smile, as if knowing he had a secret he wasn't going to divulge.

Vaslik felt a chill and looked past the man as Ruth appeared. She had heard the sirens, too, and was rolling a finger through the air in a signal for him to continue. There wasn't much time left. This was brutal, but they had to find out where Malak and his toys had gone.

'So where is it, this Freedom Field?' he said. 'It's going to be a big strike, right? An attack on the US military and the US president. You must know where it is.'

But the man said nothing more. Moments later he gave a deep sigh and his body seemed to collapse in on itself, and he was gone.

45

By the time the first of an extended convoy of vehicles arrived from the local and state police and emergency services, followed quickly by a police helicopter, Ruth was tending to Vaslik's wound, which was slight, and Dave Proust was explaining the situation to the father of the three children.

None of them could hide their disappointment at having been unable to find out more about Malak's whereabouts, although Vaslik was more pragmatic. He watched as Ruth used a bandage from Dave's first aid box to bind his upper arm, where the bullet had scored a shallow path without hitting anything vital.

'We know where he'll be,' he told her. 'We just don't know where *exactly*. But we will.'

'You're optimistic,' she murmured. 'Are you sure you're not in shock?'

'It's a scratch, nothing more.' He smiled but looked a little pale, and nodded at the incoming chopper. 'Bet that's Tom Brasher come to see how we kicked their asses.'

'Don't change the subject. And we both know he's not going to be pleased at the body count.'

He shrugged with his good shoulder and looked serious 'It's not him I'm worried about. It's the cops. This is their turf and they won't like the FBI muscling in. They're going to be even more pissed when they find out civilians just wound up shooting dead two terrorists.'

They weren't long in finding out just how bad that was going to be.

The first man out of the helicopter was of medium height and lean with the rank of a police captain, and had a face filled with thunder. He was accompanied by a civilian gofer scurrying along behind him and shouting details of what had been so far reported. The captain stopped to take a quick look at the crippled van and the bodies of the two dead men, then headed towards Ruth and Vaslik at a furious clip, scattering officers and emergency workers with an imperious flick of his hand.

'I'm Captain Hubert Danes of the Oklahoma Highway Patrol Special Operations Section,' the man declared loudly, coming to a halt. 'What in holy fuck do you people think you've done here? This is not some private game park where you can carry on your own little wars and take the law into your own hands. In fact who the hell are you? Tell me that!'

'They're with me,' Tom Brasher said, decanting fast from a police cruiser that had just bumped off the road. He held up his FBI badge. 'Tom Brasher, FBI. They're on approved business.'

'Approved by who? Not by me, that's for damned sure!' Danes stuck out his jaw and glared at Brasher. 'This is an unauthorised action and these three are now under my jurisdiction, so the Bureau can go suck eggs. They'll be arrested and charged with causing the deaths of those men and I'll see they appear before a judge tomorrow.' He turned and studied Ruth, Vaslik and Dave Proust in turn. 'I want your weapons handed over right now and you three had better not plan on going home anytime soon, because you won't – that's a promise.'

'What would you have preferred we did, captain?' Ruth replied quietly. She was reigning in an overdose of anger tinged with the aftermath rush of adrenalin after the shooting. 'Stood here and watched a group of children get taken into a hostage situation? Watched them and their father being killed like those people back at the county jail? Or is that how you treat your citizens out here when threatened with danger?'

'I would have preferred it, lady,' Danes snapped, 'if you people had stayed out of my state and out of my way. We have a procedure here in the state of Oklahoma, and we're the ones who dictate the course of action, not outsiders like you and your friends.' He blinked. 'And what the hell is that accent, anyway?'

'It's British.'

'Wait up!' Tom Brasher pushed forward, looking ready for a fight. He glared at the captain and said, 'Listen to me and listen good. These are extreme circumstances here; you've just had a county jail damn near destroyed by rocket fire, and officers killed along with support workers. I lost a young female colleague in the blast. The terrorists involved, which we know are part of an organisation called the brotherhood, were a direct and imminent threat to the lives of four innocent people, including small children. They've made threats against the lives of hundreds of military personnel and the president himself, and one of them is still on the loose. So let's stop the pissing contest and remember what might have happened if these three *civilians*, all of whom have law-enforcement backgrounds including the FBI and Homeland Security, hadn't intervened.'

'I don't give a damn who or what they are,' Danes retorted, now aware of a growing audience of his own officers, listening to the exchange with more than a hint of interest.

'Well, seems to me you should give a damn, Hubert.' A figure stepped forward into the argument. It was the father of the three children, a tall man with a quiet voice and weathered skin, who eased his way through the crowd until he was standing alongside the captain and towering over him. 'I've known you a long time – like I've known most of you fellas, on and off.' He looked round at the other officers before switching his eyes back to Danes. 'It sounds to me like you're forgetting yourself and who you serve.'

Danes snapped, 'Stay out of this, Harry – this is a police matter. I know you've had a bit of scare but it'll be best if you just leave this to me and run along home to be with your kids.'

'Aw, shut the fuck up, Hubert,' the man said softly, unfazed by the captain's bullying manner. He ducked his head at Ruth.

'Excuse the language, ma'am, only I guess I'm a little stressed right now.' He looked back at Danes. 'Fact is, the young lady here told it right; if they'd waited for you and your men to come along, my kids would all be dead or held hostage by those crazy bastards. Then what would you have done – quoted the law and tried to reason with them? Set up a *dialogue*, like they teach you in officer training?' He held up a large, calloused hand as Danes tried to say something. 'No, let me finish. Look at those men, Hubert – they were armed with M4 Colt carbines with 30-round magazines, for Christ's sake. In case you forgot, I'm ex-military and I know what that stuff can do. You think they were playing games? And you might not have given a damn, but one of these *outsiders* here was shot and wounded while putting himself between my kids and the gunmen, so I have more than a peck of interest in raising hell with the governor if you don't pull your darned neck in and see sense.'

Danes said nothing for a long moment. Then his red face turned slowly back to a normal colour as he calmed down. He grunted reluctantly, then turned to Brasher. 'You prepared to take responsibility for these people, Agent Brasher?'

'Absolutely. But I'm not taking anything away from you or your people, captain. This is your investigation. We'll all give statements whenever you want them. That do you?'

Danes nodded, then turned to issue orders to his team.

–

Brasher beckoned to Ruth and led her, Vaslik and Dave Proust away out of earshot of the crowd. 'Listen, I've got to sort out a few things here and call in the details of Agent Wright's death. This place is going to be swamped soon by news teams flying in from all over, so I think it might be best if you three disappear. You can give your statements later – I'll make sure Danes stays off your backs.'

Ruth nodded. 'Suits me. We'll have to get moving to Altus very soon, anyway.'

'I get that. But where are you going to start your search?'

'I've been thinking about that. If we work on the basis that the drones have an approximate range of twenty miles, that's the circle we draw around the base at Altus.'

'That's a pretty big circle,' said Dave.

'But it's a start,' Vaslik pointed out. 'They probably won't risk getting too close to the base itself because of security sweeps. That narrows down the corridor we have to check. Can we still rely on your help?'

Dave grunted. 'Just try keeping me out of it.' He frowned. 'Hang on, I just had a thought. Most military bases and some bigger civilian airports have geo-fencing in place to warn off unauthorised users entering their airspace. If these drones have GPS systems fitted, they might include a turn-back or disabling device on board.'

Brasher took out his cell phone and stepped away to make a call. When he came back he looked unsure. 'I just spoke to a colleague in Washington. He says most geo-fencing is user-related. That is, in normal circumstances, if these drones cross the geo-fencing perimeter around Altus, an SMS message would be triggered to alert the operator.'

'I can't see this Malak giving a damn about that,' said Dave.

'True. I've told my guy to call the Woods County Jail and ask Donny if the machines have a disabling device fitted. He'll call back as soon as he finds out, but I'm willing to bet that they don't; Malak would have thought of that.'

Dave gestured up at the sky, where the light was beginning to fade. 'I suggest we get refuelled then find a hotel. It'll be too dark to do anything if we set off now and I doubt Malak will be standing out in the open waiting for us. Better if we get there early in the morning and get down to it once we know he's there.'

Ruth said to Brasher, 'Has there been any more news about the bidding chatter the NSA picked up?'

He grunted. 'It's like eBay for crazies out there. The bids are going up all the time, some from names we've never even heard of before.'

'So it's working.'

'Damned right. This Malak is some piece of work, I'll give him that. But he's playing a high-stakes game. The big-money bids are coming from some of the most dangerous people on the planet. If he takes the cash and fails to go through with what he's promised, it's not us he has to worry about; his paymasters will have every asset they've got looking for him, and given that, I'd put his chances of survival at zero.'

'At least that would save us a job,' said Dave.

'Sure. For now.' Brasher looked round at them. 'But let's not forget: the genie's out of the bottle. How long before another bunch of crazies or an individual with a grudge decides to go down the same route and get paid for carrying out their nut-bag schemes?'

It was a sobering thought.

'Another thing,' Brasher continued. 'The dead men you found at the airfield were all Latinos except for one. They got a face and print match; he's a former army jailer who got kicked out after the Abu Ghraib abuses in Iraq. He's done some prison time since then on minor felonies. Now it looks like he got hired to carry on his old job looking after Chadwick.'

'Would he knowingly work for terrorists?' Ruth asked.

Brasher shrugged. 'Depends how desperate he was. Either way, he's paid the price.'

46

'Are you going to kill me like you did Tommy-Lee?' James Chadwick was seated in the rear of the blue van, his wrists cuffed to the bench seat. Malak was sitting across from him, occasionally checking one of his cell phones for text messages while Bilal was driving. Every now and then Malak smiled and nodded with satisfaction as he read the screen, then texted a rapid reply. When he was finished he stamped on the phone before tossing it out of the window and picking another from a box by his feet.

'Not if I don't have to.' Malak lifted his eyes long enough to give James a cold look. It was like being studied by a predatory fish, he thought. So very different to the man who had first approached him after the conference outside Chicago. Back then he had come across as genial, even excited, the typical wannabe thrusting businessman with his ambitions out there for everybody to see and smelling success if only he could get the kick-start funding and advice he needed.

He had even referred to his plan by name: Freedom. As if it were already real and in place. And when James had asked, to be polite, where his company was located, he had used the same name. Freedom.

It had turned out to be entirely false, of course, the real intent soon visible when James had turned down his request for help and the over-the-top offer of money. Yet even then Malak had seemed somehow different; hopeful, maybe, while quick and lively in his look and manner – what some in business referred to as a comer. Later, when James had tried every search engine he could think of to track the man or his company, he had come up with nothing.

Now, though, something in Malak had changed; he had a permanent dullness to his eyes and his nerves seemed stretched to breaking point. It was a look James had seen in too many entrepreneurial types who had gambled everything on a single idea with no backup plan and too few resources to dig themselves out of a hole. Poised on a precipice of their own making, they had become almost dangerous in their desperation to succeed.

But Malak was dangerous for entirely different reasons, and James had to admit to being terrified at the coming few hours.

'Where are we going?'

'You'll find out soon enough.'

It was the same answer each time. All he knew from the restricted view inside the van was that it was getting dark and they had been following a meandering route for the past couple of days, always on the move and using back roads. They had stopped only at remote motels, sometimes overnight and for a few hours during the day when Malak needed an internet connection. Another stop was coming up.

He adjusted his buttocks on the bench seat and leaned against one of the boxes containing a drone. That was another question to which he'd received a shrug and no comment: what hideous concoction lay inside the glass tube packed in foam that he'd seen Malak handling back at the airfield after the man named Donny had disappeared? He could only speculate, but the obvious conclusion was the stuff of nightmares.

But that wasn't the only danger inside the van; not two feet from where he was sitting were several small packs of what he was certain was some form of explosive. If it was C4, as he suspected, there was enough there to completely vaporise this van and everything else around it for a considerable distance. He'd tried figuring out what possible use Malak might have for the stuff. Was he going to load some on the drones and use them as flying bombs? If so he would need some form of detonator – maybe one of the mobile phones in the box. It would work, but the combined weight would stretch the carrying capacity and speed of the drones and make them more difficult to control if there was any turbulence.

So what was the plan? The only thought that came to mind was a suicide run; if all else failed Malak might choose a spectacular ending. But was that really his style? The more the man talked, the more James was beginning to read him and understand the character behind the cold mask. And something about his personality, as guarded as he was, spoke of a man who would not choose suicide unless all else was lost – an option of last resort.

Logic also told him that Malak wouldn't risk his own life unnecessarily when he clearly had a mission to accomplish. But what if fate intervened and they ran into a police or army patrol? It was clear that the one named Bilal was a violent thug with a love of guns, and thought himself invincible. But a volley of bullets would go through this van without stopping and one only had to strike the launcher or the C4 and…

He pushed the thoughts away, focussing instead on Ben and Valerie. Occasionally his thoughts dwelled on Elizabeth, but hardly to the same degree; that boat had sailed a long time ago, for which he blamed himself. He made a resolve, however, that if ever he got out of this jam in one piece, he would go see her and try to make some peace between them, if only for Ben's sake.

Malak sniggered and held out his cell phone so that James could read the screen. It was a breaking news report of a rocket attack on the county jail in Alva, Oklahoma, followed by the pursuit and shooting dead of the attackers by local law enforcement officers. The death toll in the attack on the jail stood at five, with two injured jail workers in a critical condition. One of those killed inside the jail, the report continued, had been a newly-arrested man named Donny Bashir, who was said to have had proven terrorist connections and was being interviewed by the FBI at the time of the assault. Police and FBI sources were speculating that the attack had been to gain Bashir's release.

'They're running around in circles. Like headless chickens,' Malak said softly, taking the phone back and snapping it off. More and more, Chadwick noticed as time went on, Malak the apparent American was given to using a more staccato form of speaking which made him seem both more foreign than he had first sounded, and increasingly more intense, as if he were now the person he had always aspired to be. It made him seem both tragically comic and frighteningly dangerous.

'They were your men,' said James. 'Don't you feel for them?' He no longer felt wary of asking such questions; whatever Malak had prepared for him in the coming hours was hardly going to be made worse by anything he said at this stage.

'They weren't mine. They were tools, like Bashir.' He gave a self-satisfied smile, and the intensity of his gaze so close was deeply unsettling. 'And there are others. They, too, will perform a task or die in the attempt. It is how things are done.'

'That's cold.' James nodded at the phone in Malak's hand. 'At this rate you're going to start running out of tools.'

'Never.' Malak leaned forward until James could smell his breath, and spoke so softly that it had to be so that Bilal up front wouldn't hear, 'There are always those willing to die for a good cause. Always. Have you not already realised that from everything you've seen over the past twenty-five years?' He grinned and sat back as if enjoying himself. 'Of course you haven't. You think it's a filthy Arab habit, so nothing to concern yourselves with. So what if a few dozen ragheads blow themselves to pieces? Let them do it… as long as they keep it to the Middle East where you westerners don't have to watch it! Well, your time has come and you had better get used to a new era in conflict!'

James said nothing. An inner light was glowing in Malak's eyes, and he realised there was more than a glimmer of the idealist in there. Yet somehow, as loaded with passion as it should have sounded, the words had come across as somehow a little too rehearsed, as if he were talking to like-minded individuals like the muscle-man up front, voicing words that were part of a common mantra they expected to hear.

'Another thing,' Malak continued, this time in a calmer tone. 'You Americans think you created the joint idea of enterprise and war, of big business making profits from conflict by manufacturing arms and munitions. But what of waging war itself – as a business? Huh? You ignore history at your peril. There have been armies since the dawn of time making profit from fighting, but in modern-era America, that has been seen as too disgusting to consider – until recently.'

'You mean mercenaries?' James decided to interrupt the flow, if only to show he wasn't intimidated by this man's passion. 'That's hardly an American invention.'

'True enough. But it's the United States that has taken the idea of paid armies to a whole new level, with its PMCs – its private military contractors; thousands of private soldiers and so-called black ops 'specialists' fighting on behalf of the state and doing its dirty work under cover, unaccountable and untouchable. Well, you're not the only ones who can play by those rules. You had better be ready for the reality of what you've unleashed because now there's a new game in town.'

'You're a mercenary? Is that what you're saying? Am I supposed to be impressed?'

Malak smiled. 'I don't care whether you're impressed or not. But you had better be concerned.' He held up a finger. 'As a business consultant I'm sure you'll appreciate that it's a very simple principle. Take one organised and patient man with an idea and lots of financial backers. Team him with others who care nothing for money or reward, but who share a deep, abiding hatred of a common superpower and a lasting faith in the hereafter. Now what do you have?'

James was horrified. There was no answer he could think of.

'I'll tell you what you have, Mr Chadwick: you have what you fancy business consultants might call a first-class business model: the ultimate weapon of mass destruction. And the best thing of all? It's constantly renewable, generation by generation, feeding on itself and gaining ground. In the end it will be everywhere and unstoppable.' He grinned and waggled his fingers in a ghastly parody of a comedian. 'Now that, my friend, is an idea you can take all the way to the bank!'

47

Ruth sat up with a jerk, eyes wide open, mouth gummy with the taste of last night's easily forgettable meal. She experienced a momentary confusion due to sleep deprivation and the events of the past few days, before tuning in to her surroundings and why she was here.

She was in bed in some nameless motel near Oklahoma City's Will Rogers airport; the luminous readout on the bedside radio clock told her it was 03.00am. She couldn't recall much about getting here or falling into bed the moment she'd eaten, only that Andy Vaslik and Dave Proust had waved goodnight, Vaslik to hit the hay and Dave to see about refuelling his helicopter for the flight to Altus in the morning.

Exhausted or not, sleep had not come easily. Her brain had kicked in within minutes of lying down, churning with thoughts of how they were going to find Malak and Chadwick and the lethal drones in such a vast landscape. So far she'd been unable to settle on a specific plan of action.

In an attempt to draw her mind away onto other things and to allow thoughts of mundane matters to deflect the problems that lay ahead, she had switched on the room's television. But it had offered only a partial success. The news programmes had been full of the president's visit to Altus Air Force base the following day, which had sent her spirits plummeting at the idea of what might happen if they failed to stop Malak's planned attack. Logic told her to stop looking, but she had been unable to turn off the repeated bulletins and live-action shots of the base and surrounding area, with elegantly-manicured reporters with huge microphones and logo plaques announcing their stations of origin, hopeful that something in there would trigger an idea, no matter how limited.

The main focus of their excitement appeared to be in the base itself, and a planned demonstration parachute jump by trainees from a C-17 Globemaster III cargo aircraft. There were other items mentioned, but the flickering screen and its attendant electronic buzz had soon dulled Ruth's attention and she had zoned out, turning on the laptop instead and trawling for possible leads to the location Malak was planning on using.

The word Freedom had danced across her consciousness in all its permutations, from concepts, place names, films, songs and snippets of writing and speeches of the great and the good. But none had led to anything useful. She had finally fallen into a restless half-sleep, her mind full of the mixed images and sounds of their confrontation with the men in the van and of skies filled with deadly drones like swarms of flies.

Now she was back to some semblance of full alertness, she jumped out of bed and splashed her face with water, then drank from a bottle in the room's refrigerator. She knew she was going to regret rising so ridiculously early later on, when tiredness would catch up with her, but she was being pushed forward by some tiny fragment of information, a miniscule sound bite perhaps, that had finally penetrated her brain and wouldn't let go.

But what the hell was it?

The television was still on, but with the sound down low, showing a slew of commercials for auto sales, dietary supplements and the benefits of home gym equipment being demonstrated by stick insects in makeup. She clicked through a few channels until she found a local news reporter running through the agenda for the coming event at the Altus base.

Within seconds, she had the answer that had been eluding her.

> 'The White House has confirmed that following an inspection and meeting with officers, staff and their families at USAF Altus, the president will attend a parachute demonstration by approximately thirty trainees exiting a giant Globemaster Three cargo aircraft. He will then go to an area of land outside the base perimeter which has been donated by local land-owner and farmer, Philip J. Duncan. This land is to be converted into a remembrance garden in honour of the fallen who passed through Altus over the years, having given their lives in the service of their country in Iraq, Afghanistan and other theatres of conflict in the name of freedom. Groundwork on the field, which is yet to be formally named but is now widely expected to include the word Freedom, will begin in the next few weeks, and…'

Freedom. Field.

Ruth felt a jolt of energy go through her and picked up her phone. First she called Vaslik and got him to turn on his television, then called Brasher and prayed he was awake.

He was. 'What've you got?' he asked. His voice sounded dulled by lack of sleep but he was alert enough to know she wasn't calling just to say hi.

'I know where the target area is,' she said. 'It's a parcel of land outside the base to be used as a remembrance site. I don't know where – and I doubt the base office will tell me now with the president going there to show his support. But I think that's where Malak might make his strike.'

'Don't worry, I'll make some calls and get back to you. How did you hear about this? It was supposed to be unofficial until the last moment.'

'It was in a local news bulletin. The land's been donated by a local farmer to be used as a remembrance garden. It hasn't been formally named yet but the clincher is in the name. There's talk of the title incorporating the word freedom.'

Brasher swore softly. 'That's close enough. You were right all along, Ruth. Christ, I should have listened harder.'

'No need to beat yourself up. Until now it would have been guesswork, anyway, because if Malak had sensed too much interest he'd have simply changed his plans and we'd have lost him for good. Right now we need to get combing within a few miles of this Freedom place. I'm guessing Malak and Chadwick will be somewhere away from the base itself, but that's still quite a lot of ground to cover and we don't want to risk alerting him.'

'I agree. Incidentally, my guy got an answer from Donny about geo-fencing. Malak knew all about it and had him disable the devices. It means they can fly anywhere he chooses.'

Malak had indeed thought of everything, Ruth reflected. Not that it made much difference now; it was possible that the area to be known as Freedom Field lay outside the geo-fenced perimeter, anyway.

'There's something else,' Brasher continued. 'Word has just come in about two men seen acting suspiciously outside Fort Sill army base yesterday evening. They were in army combat uniforms but the person who reported it in was the wife of a serving officer and said they didn't move or look anything like serving personnel."

'Fort Sill? I remember seeing that name.' Ruth had a momentary surge of alarm at the idea that Malak had changed his plans after Donny's arrest and was going to launch an attack somewhere else instead.

'Right. It's a combat training and field artillery school about fifty miles east of Altus. The men were approached by military police and pulled automatic weapons. They killed one MP and wounded another before they were taken down and arrested by a backup patrol.'

'Not Malak or Bilal?'

'No. They turned out to be two unknown Middle Eastern males with false IDs and very little English. But one was carrying a sandwich wrapping from Chicago O'Hare International with a display date from two days ago. Our initial assessment is that they were probably flown in as a distraction attack. If so, it means that whatever network Malak's connected to is well organised.'

And the rest, Ruth thought. She didn't think she had to add to Brasher's worries by pointing out that the men had somehow managed to fly in, get equipped very quickly with false papers, a vehicle and automatic weapons, then find their way to Fort Sill without being spotted. That pointed to resources and good organisation.

'So what happens now? Are we still going in?'

'Just about. After your talk with Donny and the attack on Woods County jail, I reported up the chain of command about Karina's death and what we'd learned so far. Washington received only a partial call from her just before she died, but it was enough to get an internal investigation going into the circumstances leading up to her death and why she'd been going over my head.'

'I'm sorry to hear that. What are they going to do?'

'There were some calls from the most senior levels for a full-scale alert. I managed to resist that on the grounds that Malak would simply disappear along with the drones and whatever poison he's planning on using. They and the Secret Service agreed but as of now it's no longer in my hands.'

'Do tell.'

'There will be two Globemasters overflying the base, not one. The first will drop the genuine demonstration team at eleven hundred hours. But we got the landing target moved slightly away from the base center on the grounds of security to the president. The drop will be close enough to be seen and draw attention away from the second plane which will carry a team of our own Enhanced SWAT personnel. I hope we can get those men dropped right on the nail.'

'Assuming we can tell you where that nail is.'

'That's correct. Anybody suspicious is going to find a fully armed body of men dropping on their heads, hopefully before they can get those drones in the air.'

'What about Chadwick? He's an innocent in the middle of this. Will they know what he looks like?'

There was a brief hesitation, then Brasher said, 'They've been briefed and issued with photos, yes. But this could be a messy intervention. I wish I could guarantee his safety but I can't. He'll have to take his chances. I'll get back to you about the location of the target.'

Ruth said goodbye and cut the connection. She felt conflicted. Part of her wanted to isolate Malak as quietly as possible and deal with him without using outside forces. She could understand the FBI response, which was to protect the president's safety and the safety of the Altus personnel and their families. However, the hard truth was that however carefully an operation was planned and executed, there was always aa risk of it ending messily, leading to innocent casualties along the way. She just hoped that Chadwick wasn't one of them.

She got dressed and walked along to Vaslik's room. The door was open and he was gingerly slipping on his jacket.

'How is it?' she asked, helping him with the sleeve.

'It's a scratch.'

'Of course it is. And you're such a brave boy.' She grinned briefly, then told him what Brasher had arranged with the SWAT team.

He winced. 'I don't like the idea of being too close to that. Identifying the crowd will be easy enough, but if they see us on our own in the target area from a thousand feet in the air we could have ourselves a problem.'

'What else can we do? We can't stay away and leave them to it. By the time they get on the ground it could be too late.'

He nodded. 'In that case we'd better get to Malak and neutralise him first so we can wave a white flag.' He slipped his gun into his jacket and grinned. 'You ready, Gonzo?'

'I'm ready. And if you call me that again, Slik, there will be blood.'

48

Chadwick felt a shock deep in his gut. Was this what it had all been about? Had Malak just indicated in those few mocking, cynical words that this crazy scheme had as much if not more to do with money than extremism? That his entire organisation was a willingly gullible force, expendable and ready to die, with himself sitting at its head, unseen and untouched?

'Why is your hatred of America so deep?' he said. 'I take it you're the organised and patient man and the others are the cannon-fodder?'

Malak grunted. 'My parents and two sisters were killed by a missile strike when I was five years old. It was an American missile and they were in a school at the time.' His mouth twisted. 'So much for precision and reliable intelligence. Isn't that what the Pentagon is always claiming? Twelve other children and five teachers also died in that incident and countless others were maimed for life.'

James swallowed hard. The pain in the man's voice carried the ring of conviction. 'Where did this happen?'

'Where doesn't matter. I was taken away from the place two days later and never went back. But I never forgot.'

James thought about the timing and Malak's approximate age. It had to have been during the first Gulf War, in the early nineties. An accident of war, perhaps, of bad coordinates or intelligence, or simply a lack of care in designating a target. None of it mattered now, except that whatever the cause, it had created a monster.

Up front, Bilal said something and the van began to slow.

A man was standing by the side of the road.

'Turn in the gate here,' said Malak, and put his cell phone away. He looked at James and spoke carefully, the passion gone. 'We're going to change vehicles. Don't make the mistake of thinking you can use the opportunity to run. We're a long way from anywhere and I still have the phone numbers of the men watching your family. I will call them if I have to.'

James shook his head and remained silent. He was still stunned by the scenario Malak had unveiled, of a generation of future terrorist attacks driven by a man willing to use others to die in his desire for vengeance. The horrifying aspect was, it was an idea that he could see replicated by others with the same twisted zeal. If Malak succeeded in his ghastly plan, the idea would spread and, even if he disappeared, others would soon take his place.

Bilal stopped the van and turned off the engine. The silence after hours of being in the noisy echo of the vehicle was intense, and James struggled to catch the sound of Malak's voice. The terrorist had jumped out of the rear doors to greet the man waiting for them, and began issuing rapid orders.

Bilal came round the side and undid the cuffs, then dragged James roughly from the back and made him squat down by pressing his shoulder in an iron grip. James looked around and saw the man, a slim, dark-skinned individual in his forties, handing Malak a pile of clothing and boots. For a second he couldn't identify the items in the gloom, but then the familiar pattern of the fabric became clear; they were combat uniforms.

James looked past the two men and his mind raced ahead to what was about to happen, collating facts and stitching them together.

He was looking at a light army patrol vehicle complete with ID plates and numbers. With the uniforms, it was obvious what Malak was about to do. He was planning on going right into the area near the Altus air base! He wondered at the sheer crazy effrontery of the man, before cool reason took over and he saw the simple brilliance behind the move.

After all, who would question another military patrol among so many? With security so tight and every spare man and vehicle called into use, they'd be all but invisible.

His suspicions were confirmed when the newcomer patted the hood of the vehicle and said with only a faint trace of an accent, 'Fresh out of the repair shop an hour ago. It hasn't been signed out yet, so nobody will miss it for at least forty-eight hours. Those uniforms are all genuine, but don't go talking to other patrols. Everybody is on edge and ready to go operational. It's best if you stay on the move – and don't forget to salute if you see an officer.'

'Good work,' said Malak. He turned to Bilal and told him to get James on board and for both of them to change into the uniforms and boots. Then he said to the other man, 'You're coming, too.'

'What?' The man looked startled. 'No, you don't understand. Now I stole the patrol vehicle I have to leave – they'll know it was me.' He held out his hand. 'Give me the keys to the van and I'll be gone. I'm already getting too much flak because of where I came from and I can't stand it anymore. I said I'd help with this and the stuff for the men at Fort Sill, but that's it. I have a family to protect.'

Malak reached behind him and produced his pistol. 'I think it's you who doesn't understand. Now, you either stop your whining and get in the vehicle with the others… or I leave you here with a bullet in your cowardly skull.'

The man swallowed, then did as he was told.

49

From a few miles out it was evident in the clear, early morning sunlight that the area encompassing the city and base of Altus was considerable. Though it was level, with little natural cover such as woodland or dead ground, making a search in the short time they had available was going to be tough.

Dave Proust had brought Ruth and Vaslik in from the north-east, pointing out the Wichita Mountains on one side and Quartz Mountain on the other. 'They're the only hills we'll see from here on,' he told them. 'The rest is chequerboard flat.'

'That's not good,' Ruth commented, eyeing the distant air base and surrounding terrain. Flat was both good and bad, in that it helped them see further from the sky, but it gave Malak plenty of time to see them coming and take evasive action. Either way, they had a commanding view of the problem they faced if Brasher wasn't able to narrow down the location and scope of the area known as Freedom Field very soon.

'I can't go in too close.' Dave's voice floated into their earphones. 'Brasher got me special clearance but we won't be able to overfly the base. We'll have to turn soon and follow the perimeter at a distance and hope we see something.'

Just then Brasher's voice sounded in their ears.

'Okay, I got it. Freedom Field is a designated area of two acres situated a mile and a half to the north-east of Altus Air Base. That's where the president will be going, so we estimate your search area will be somewhere outside that location.' He read out the coordinates and Dave made a note before beginning to turn on a course that would bring them round in a wide approach to begin their sweep. 'You should be aware that the SWAT jump team is ready to go and there's now another team on the ground awaiting instructions. We're relying on you guys to give us a heads-up on Malak's position, but I've had instructions that if you don't respond with solid information by ten minutes before the designated jump time, both teams will go in. That being the case, I suggest you prepare to leave the area and give them a clear run.'

'Got that.' Dave turned his head towards Ruth and Vaslik with a faint look of puzzlement. 'Care to tell us why there's a ground team as well?'

'We got word from the MPs at Fort Sill. They found the car the two gunmen had used. It contained a thousand rounds of ammunition and packaging from three sets of army combat uniform and boots that didn't fit either of the detainees. Another thing: a local store owner had his car stolen during the night not half a mile away from where the car was found. A neighbour saw it being driven west out of town with three men inside.'

There was a silence, eventually broken by Vaslik. 'Three more. We have to assume they're armed.'

'I think we can bet on it. I just wish I knew what with. If they've gotten rocket launchers like the men in Alva, it'll be bad. My bet is they're in the Altus area already. It's only fifty miles on a straight road and they had several hours to get here.'

Brasher disconnected and Dave waved a hand towards an area in front of them and slightly to their left. 'On my map there's a small lake out there somewhere. That's where the coordinates will take us. If Malak's in position, he'll be where he can watch the action.'

'And upwind, presumably,' said Ruth. 'He won't want to get caught in his own spray. Can you check the current wind direction?'

'Good point – and yes, I can.' He busied himself on the radio and spoke to the control tower at Altus, and was given the latest report for the area. He thanked the person on the other end with a shake of his head and disconnected. 'It's blowing southwest towards the base but changeable. Ain't that convenient? The tower also said I should leave the area immediately or be forced to land. He didn't sound as if he was messing; authorisation overruled. I'd better pull out before they send an armed ship to investigate.'

'Does that mean the president's already in the area?' Ruth asked.

'If not, he's real close.' He checked his watch. It was 10.30am. 'They must have brought the programme forward. We don't have long. I'll tune to the local police network for a heads-up.'

He pressed a pre-set button and their headphones were filled with bursts of static and a relay of voices, contracted sentences and, to the outsider, the unintelligible and mostly unexciting terminology of law enforcement professionals.

Dave took the helicopter on a wider curve away from the base, but keeping the general area around the lake within sight. Not that there was much to see. The terrain looked devoid of landmarks save for a few scattered shrubs and trees, and the rigid line of a road running from north to south. The road itself looked almost empty, with little signs of moving traffic and only a heavy haulage truck being loaded at a barn to one side. Ruth concluded that if Malak was hiding out here, he'd found a good point of concealment.

'This whole area would have been checked by security, wouldn't it?'

'Sure would. They'd have had a Secret Service advance team here for about a week, with more flown in once word came in about Malak's threat. They'd have checked and re-checked buildings and trees for at least a couple of miles out in case of a sniper attack, even without a direct threat. With Malak, they'd have doubled the precautions. Like those guys.' He was pointing down at two military patrol vehicles at the side of a small farm, with several men in uniform moving around the buildings.

Ruth looked at Vaslik, who was shaking his head. The magnitude of the task they faced was suddenly right there in front of them. They could comb this open countryside for hours without seeing Malak and Chadwick, and be none the wiser until the drones were in the air and heading for the base.

'I don't get it,' she said. 'Why would Malak choose to attack a small area with only a few people present? To make an impact he'd surely go for the main event – the base with the personnel, the parachute display team and the president all in one area?'

Vaslik nodded. 'You're right. We could spend all day checking the countryside out beyond the base and all the time he's right inside our search perimeter.'

Ruth said, 'He must be close to Freedom Field itself. The last place anybody would look.'

'Except the Secret Service detail.'

'But what's to see?' She nodded out at the flat fields below. 'He's somewhere under cover – he must be.' Her stomach tightened at the thought that right now Malak could already be close to where the president would be standing very shortly. And if the reports from Fort Sill were correct, he now had three extra men to help him. 'He's playing safe,' she said. 'If he misses with the drones over the base, he and his men will be right up close where nobody expects it, to make an armed assault on Freedom Field itself.'

Then a voice burst through on the radio, shrill with panic. '*I've got reports of automatic gunfire between the base and the city of Altus! Two people down, possibly more. I say, automatic gunfire! We need assistance! This is not a drill. I repeat, not a drill!*'

50

Vaslik said calmly, 'It's a diversion.'

Ruth looked at him. 'To do what?'

'They're drawing forces away from this side of the base. Malak wouldn't risk pulling security in on himself – that would be suicidal and accomplish nothing. He's counting on reducing the opposition to give him a clear run at the presidential party. It means he's out here somewhere.'

'But where?' Dave muttered, and brought the machine lower until they were skimming the ground, all looking for anywhere three men might be in hiding. On the road below, the two military patrols they'd seen were racing away from the farm back towards Altus, leaving a dust cloud behind them. Barrelling down the center of the road they were flashing their lights to push the occasional other vehicle out of their way. Further over, the dark shape of an army helicopter rose sharply from dead ground and beat a path in the same direction, a crewman sitting in the fuselage door and scanning the ground below. 'That's a Black Hawk,' Dave said automatically. 'Most likely fully crewed and armed. They're not taking chances.'

The exchange of background voices on the radio continued unabated, a volley of instructions, reports and transmissions cut short as more responders joined the call for assistance and other demanded information on the location and number of the attackers.

'*Two... no, three*,' came the reply. '*Three males, armed with automatic rifles and one carrying a launch tube. All described as of middle-eastern appearance, dressed in jeans and T-shirts, one wearing a black head-cloth with white writing and… Jesus, it's the IS flag! I repeat, Islamic State!'*

An AS-350 helicopter in the bright colours of a national TV channel appeared briefly on their port side before banking away towards the city to join the chase for news, the pale oval of a face appearing in the window and studying them carefully before turning away.

'Wait.' Ruth turned to Vaslik. 'They're not in US combat uniforms?'

'That's what he said—.' His eyes widened in surprise at the information. 'Whoa. That's not right.'

'I know. If they have uniforms, why aren't they wearing them? They've ditched their only chance to blend in.'

'Maybe,' Dave ventured sourly, 'because getting themselves killed in US uniforms is against their religion.'

'Maybe. But I don't think so.' She was looking through the side window at another military patrol vehicle stationed close to a line of trees a hundred yards off the road. A soldier was standing nearby, scanning the area towards Altus and the base through binoculars.

Ruth followed the man's line of sight. A glint of light reflected off the small lake Dave had mentioned earlier, where the president would shortly be standing to give his nod of approval to the remembrance project. A number of figures were already moving around the area, with several vehicles arriving and parking nearby and police and army vehicles blocking off the approach road. More vehicles were arriving as the time drew close for the presidential visit, including a number of black cars with tinted windows, which stopped to form a protective cordon between the other vehicles and an area marked out by a line of posts with a rope barrier.

Ruth looked back at the army vehicle. The man with the binoculars had disappeared. But the vehicle still wasn't moving.

She took a pair of binoculars from an equipment pouch. There was no sign of the soldier and she thought she saw movement in the trees. 'Go back! He's there!'

'What?' Dave looked startled and glanced across at her.

She pointed at the vehicle and passed the binoculars to Vaslik. 'Why didn't that patrol move when the others did? A soldier was standing there and now he's gone.'

'Could be he's under orders not to move.'

'Unless that's where the three uniforms from Fort Sill went. Malak's passing himself, Bilal and Chadwick off as soldiers.'

Vaslik checked out the vehicle and the surrounding area, then nodded. 'You're right. A genuine patrol would have moved in closer just in case. And this is no time for comfort breaks.' He hesitated then said, 'Damn.'

'What?'

'There's a body on the ground behind the vehicle.'

Dave began to turn back towards the area. Suddenly Brasher's voice came over the air. '*Okay, people – time to get out of there. The SWAT team will be overhead and ready to go in five minutes. All aircraft are being warned away to give them clear air and you should do the same.*'

'That's a little difficult, Tom,' Dave replied. 'You'll have to cover us. We have a problem here with a vehicle and what looks like a body.' He gave directions so that a team could be sent to investigate. 'They'd better hurry, too – I can see the presidential convoy approaching already.'

He was right. A line of black cars was moving at speed down the road from Altus, with motorcycle out-riders front and rear.

Ruth felt her heart thumping. In spite of the tension and urgency and the pace at which events were moving, something was wrong with this whole setup.

'Tom, is your man still with Donny?'

'He is. Why?'

'I don't think he's told us the whole truth. He talked of a possible chemical agent being sprayed from the drones, but he's planning on dropping them all on a small area like this Freedom Field? It doesn't make sense – and it's too random. What if the tubes don't deploy or the wind blows the spray the wrong way?'

'What's your point, Ruth? It's getting a little tight here.'

'Malak's a planner – we know that. He's got organisation and he's selling this proposed strike on Altus and the president like crude oil futures. Why would he risk it all going wrong on a change of the wind? You've got to ask Donny what else he's using.'

A brief silence, then, 'I hear you. I'll be back in two.'

'I hope he's quicker than that,' said Dave. He was throwing glances at the sky, where the shape of a huge cargo aircraft could be seen approaching in the distance. 'We're running shy of time here.'

Seconds later Brasher was back. He sounded both mad and desperate enough to forget formal communications. '*The little shit was playing us, all right. He says there's only one – repeat, one – tube of chemical, because that's all Malak could get his hands on.*'

'What about the other drones?' Rush asked. As Brasher was speaking she was watching the Globemaster lumber in closer, and was sure the rear cargo ramp was already open ready for the SWAT team to make their exit.

'Explosives. He says the plan was for each of the remaining three to be fitted with a pack of C4, to be triggered automatically when the drone reaches the map coordinates. Coming in at twenty feet, anybody caught underneath will be wiped out. They're also carrying red powdered dye, although I have no idea why.'

'I do. It's for effect. With all the television crews around, he'll want to give his financial backers a show they'll remember. It'll go round the world in minutes.'

'So which ones will he use where?'

Vaslik supplied the answer. 'Didn't Donny say Malak knows how to change the coordinates? My guess is he'll use the spray over the base for maximum damage and reserve the explosives for Freedom Field where all the broadcast media will be focussing.'

Brasher started to say something, then came a shout in the background and his voice changed. '*You're out of time! The SWAT team's away... you'd better land now! Out.*'

He was right. One look showed the Globemaster banking away from the drop zone away, leaving behind a line of specks falling through the sky. They seemed to be dropping much too fast and too low, but it was clear they were going for a freefall deployment and a low-altitude opening to get on the ground as quickly as possible.

One by one, when it seemed far too late, the parachutes began to blossom like flowers and separate from each other in a mesmerising display of skill.

'Hold tight.' Dave took the machine down as fast as he dared, virtually standing it on its nose and hovering just above the ground a couple of hundred yards away from the army patrol vehicle. There were no signs of movement, but they could see the shape of a body on the ground nearby.

'He must be in the trees,' said Vaslik, and pulled his handgun, checking the load.

'Can you manage?' Ruth asked, and pointed at his wounded arm.

He grinned tightly and said, 'I've got another one. Let's go!'

51

James Chadwick watched from the interior of the patrol vehicle as the Globemaster droned overhead then banked away, leaving behind its human cargo hanging like a music score in the sky. Malak was nearby and Bilal was out of sight among the trees behind them, watching for security patrols, his assault rifle like a kid's toy in his hand.

Malak had made them put on combat uniform, boots and helmets. None would stand up to close inspection by genuine military personnel, but with the vehicle they were in, they had so far survived the passing of two other patrols and a police officer, all of whom had slowed on seeing them. Each time, Malak had jumped out and stood by the hood, using binoculars as cover in a pretence of scanning the ground. He had returned a wave from one patrol, a convincing imitation of a man focussing on his job and not open to interruption, but the tactic had worked; each of the patrols had driven on by without stopping and left them alone, intent only on spotting non-military or police vehicles.

James glanced towards the open rear door and felt his stomach rebel. He could just see the legs of the man who had brought Malak the patrol vehicle and uniforms; he was now lying dead with a bullet in his stomach. When Malak had handed him a rifle and told him to take his place alongside Bilal on the outside and get ready to help, he had protested that he was a mechanic, not a fighter, and did not belong here.

Malak's response had been swift and brutal. Waiting for a passing news helicopter to go by, he'd pushed the man out of the vehicle, then jabbed the barrel of his pistol into his stomach and pulled the trigger. The report, muffled against his body, had still sounded deafening to James, but the noise had gone unnoticed, drowned out by the clatter of the rotors overhead.

It was yet another sign of just how unpredictable this man was, and how unhinged his actions and attitude were fast becoming as his stress levels began to mount.

Malak climbed back inside as if nothing had happened and focussed on the parachute team, counting the jumpers out loud. He was toying nervously with a cell phone from the box by his side, and kept checking it was powered up. James guessed that at the critical moment he would use it to give word to whoever he was working with that the strike was about to take place.

He looked down at the box and saw that it now contained only two phones. There had been at least half a dozen yesterday, along with some strips of wire, the purpose of which had escaped him. So where had the others gone? And the packs of C4?

Then he saw noticed something that made his gut recoil. One of the phones was wrapped in packaging tape, and attached to it was a dark pack of C4. The tape had a number written on it in ink.

'What are they doing?' Malak's voice jerked his attention away from the box. The terrorist had stopped counting at twenty, and was scowling. 'Is that all? The news reports said there would be at least double that number.' He shook his head and pulled a face in disgust. 'Maybe that's all this warmongering president deserves; twenty fools who will also die with him.'

James said nothing; he was too busy wondering what other surprises the man had prepared for today. In any case, Malak wasn't interested in his views, only those tumbling around in his own twisted mind. Moments later he saw something that Malak had missed: another Globemaster was lumbering into view, this one higher and further back, on a parallel course but closer to the base. He felt a sense of excitement, even hope. He had no way of knowing for certain, but if the plane spilled another team, it could only mean that the first twenty currently dropping to earth were not trainees but… something else altogether!

Malak grunted and moved restlessly in his seat. His instincts must have been telling him something wasn't right. A sound like a moan came from deep in his chest, followed by slapping James's knee with the back of his hand.

'Get them in the air,' he said softly. 'Do it now. *Now!*' To reinforce the point, he took out his semi-automatic and held it in his lap. 'Remember – no mistakes and no tricks.'

James picked up the control unit and took a deep breath, adjusting the video screen so that Malak couldn't see it, pretending he was tilting it against the light. 'They're all set on the coordinates you entered,' he reminded Malak, and winced; his voice had come out a little too loud in the cramped interior. He pretended to flick on the power switch and wait for the screen display to light up, whereas it was already showing a full array of data. His heart was thudding and his mouth felt as dry as the dusty soil outside, whereas his hands were slippery with sweat on the plastic casing.

It had all come down to this.

He'd taken advantage of the few minutes while Malak had been standing outside playing security man to affect the outcome of the next few minutes. In spite of his earlier claim, using the screen's icons had been second nature to him. But it had been a close call; Malak had nearly caught him with the control unit in his hands and he hadn't had time to switch off the screen. All it would take was for Malak to spot that it was active and he would know for sure that it had been accessed.

He toggled the control stick and watched as the read-out showed data coming in from each of the drones where they had been placed during the night under cover of running a security patrol, each one about a mile out and a quarter of a mile from its neighbour. Malak had made him feed in homing coordinates into each one, and selected concealment locations which were invisible in dead ground away from any of the roads criss-crossing the area. Even a careful study of the area through binoculars would not reveal them unless a security patrol went off-road and actually stumbled over them. And he knew that wasn't going to happen.

Moskito One. In the air.

Two. Lifting off.

Three. A momentary flicker of the figures, then moving up.

Four. Nothing. He waited, then tapped the side of the handset and grunted. It was pure pantomime entirely for Malak's benefit and he hoped it was convincing.

'What is it?' Malak slid forward in his seat until he could see the read-outs. 'Number four – why is there no signal? What have you done?' His voice was frantic and his face became suffused with blood. 'Get me the feed for number four and the visual!' He was referring to the camera on each drone, which would show their progress on the video screen as they lifted off, and their flight path ahead.

'I can't.' James moved the control but with no reaction from number four. 'It's not responding. Isn't that the one Bilal placed closest to the base? It could be there's a signal blocker in operation. Maybe he hid it too well.'

Malak stared at him and James felt the full power of his gaze; the same power that the dead man outside must have experienced before being shot. He found himself counting, as if that would somehow provide a barrier against him suffering the same fate.

Instead of pulling the trigger, Malak grabbed the control unit and tried to get a reaction, but without success. He thrust it back into James's hands and pushed the pistol barrel hard against his forehead, grinding it into the skin.

'You have one chance only,' he hissed, his breath hot and sour. 'You will make sure the three other drones come in on target, or I will kill you. Then I will order the elimination of your wife, your son and your filthy whore. That is my promise.' To emphasise the point, he took out his cell phone and held it in the air.

James felt the sweat trickling down his forehead, and for the first time in his life experienced complete and utter helplessness. There would be only one outcome for himself, he was certain of that; the dead man outside was the clearest indicator. But he couldn't even countenance the same fate for Elizabeth, Ben or Valerie. He wasn't sure even now if he would have the courage to do the right thing if the situation arose. Disarming drone number four had been simple, but doing something physical was altogether different, as Malak was watching him far too closely.

'Asim! They come!' It was Bilal. He was pointing towards the area where the presidential party was gathering ready for the visit. Cars were arriving and parking under the directions of military police personnel, and a sizeable crowd had accumulated along with media vans and reporting crews around the wooden podium that had been placed there earlier. 'They are here!'

Malak looked surprised and swore softly. 'They are early. But no matter – the result will be the same.'

James looked too, and breathed a sigh of relief as the focus turned away from himself. Sure enough the presidential convoy was drawing up at the freedom field site, a line of black cars gleaming in the sun.

'Get the drones here – now!' Malak ordered him. 'How long will it take?'

'Two minutes.' James felt sick. 'No more than that.' He wondered if the security cordon around the president would spot the drones, and if so, what they would do.

'Who are they?' It was Bilal again, now standing by the open rear door and pointing off to one side. 'Is it a news team?'

Malak looked through the side window, and swore. One of the small civilian helicopters they'd seen overflying the area earlier was coming in to land not far away. Its descent was steep, and at the last second, just as it appeared about to smash into the ground, it flared level and hovered, the skids barely touching the coarse grass.

If Malak was expecting a news reporter or camera team to exit the craft, it was not to be. A man and a woman leapt out either side of the helicopter and ran in opposite directions, while the aircraft rose sharply back in the air. But instead of moving away, it held station at a hundred feet or so, a cloud of dust and foliage billowing from the downdraft of the rotors.

'What is it doing?' Bilal asked, his mouth open. 'Asim?'

But Malak's eyes were glued on the two people who had landed from the helicopter, his face expressing utter astonishment. James looked, too, and felt a jolt of hope. They were carrying weapons! And Malak had clearly recognised them.

And they were now heading in this direction.

'Get them!' Malak screamed, and reached out and slapped Bilal's shoulder to jolt him into action. 'Stop them now!'

For a second Bilal seemed rooted to the spot. Then he shook himself and lumbered out from behind the patrol vehicle and dropped to one knee, ready to open fire.

James felt powerless, his gut churning with fear. He had to do something – but what? He turned back to the video screen as the first of the drones headed towards the designated target area, the ground flashing by in a blur. He thought about simply making the drones dump into the ground, but knew he'd never get past downing the first one before Malak would shoot him dead.

He looked up through the front window towards the gathered crowd in the distance, and thought he saw a familiar figure stepping up to the podium and the assembled press microphones and cameras, amid a volley of flash-bulbs.

The US president.

52

Running away from the helicopter as fast as she could pump her legs, Ruth felt as if she had jumped into a giant vacuum cleaner full of grit. She ploughed on through the swirling haze of dust and debris being blasted up by the downdraft of the rotors, and felt the stinging sensation on her skin as millions of fragments of dirt lashed into her from all directions.

She caught a glimpse of movement straight ahead of her, and recognised the bulky figure of Bilal dropping to one knee, an assault rifle held to his shoulder. She threw herself to one side, thinking she'd heard a shot, but in the roaring pandemonium of the helicopter engine, couldn't be sure. All she knew was that she was still alive.

She fired twice at Bilal, but the dust was working as much in his favour as hers and he didn't seem affected. Behind him the trees were beginning to bend away and foliage was being ripped off the branches like confetti, and even the heavy patrol vehicle Malak was using was being rocked on its suspension.

She turned to look back and was stunned to see what was causing it. Dave Proust had turned the helicopter almost side-on and was focussing his rotors like a giant fan, creating a downdraft to stir up a shield and to put Bilal off his aim. The gunman, unable to focus on Ruth or Vaslik, turned his rifle and began firing at the helicopter as it moved past in a slow curve.

Ruth was dimly aware of Vaslik running forward and shooting, and opened fire herself as Bilal stood braced against the howling dust storm. He was holding the rifle in one hand like a pistol and shouting unintelligibly as he pulled the trigger.

Then she saw the helicopter move away and guessed that some of the rounds had struck the cabin.

With the abrupt cessation of wind and dust came an awesome silence. But Bilal recovered quickly and aimed his weapon into the sky and began firing wildly. But he was no longer aiming at the helicopter; the reason quickly became evident as a shadow passed through Ruth's field of vision.

'*Down! Down!*' a voice shouted, and she threw herself flat just as one of the SWAT team members passed over her head and hit the ground running. Without stopping to release his chute he lifted his Heckler & Koch machine pistol and sent a hail of bullets at the screaming Bilal, knocking him off his feet.

Ruth didn't wait. She jumped to her feet and ran towards the patrol vehicle, and saw Vaslik doing the same. Before they could reach it she heard a shot and saw Malak sliding behind the wheel. As the vehicle surged forward, a figure in combat uniform tumbled from the rear door and hit the ground.

James Chadwick.

Ruth dodged to avoid the charging nose of the vehicle, and saw Malak's frenzied face snarling at her from behind the wheel. She wondered how he thought he could possibly get away. A glance through the duststorm showed a frantic buzz of activity around the president as his secret service detail closed in around him and hustled him away from the podium towards the armoured vehicle he'd arrived in. She also knew what would be happening elsewhere: the outer ring of security would be turning to look for possible sources of attack, while the communications team travelling with the president would be calling up the standby medical team and alerting Air Force One to be ready for departure.

Just as she reached Chadwick, she felt the shockwave of an explosion.

She spun round in horror, half expecting to see Dave Proust's helicopter in flames. But instead saw a vast cloud of red dust hanging in the air some three hundred yards away, and tiny fragments of hard material spinning away and showering down on the SWAT team landing nearby and the fleeing patrol vehicle, which rocked and dipped savagely under the blast but continued going.

Seconds later another explosion came from further away, with another red dust cloud drifting on the breeze. Then a third.

Ruth turned to find Chadwick sitting up, his face in shock and clutching his ribs, where a splash of blood showed on his combat jacket. He tried speaking but couldn't get the words out, and she wondered how seriously he was hurt. She turned to the SWAT team member who had discarded his parachute and was standing over them with his weapon raised and said, 'This is Chadwick. We need to get him to hospital right away.'

Just then Vaslik arrived and kept James from trying to stand up, while the FBI man radioed for an emergency evacuation.

'What the hell happened?' she asked James, as he slumped against Vaslik's arm. 'Where's the fourth drone?'

He shook his head and tried taking a gulp of air, his head hanging low. 'Dis...disabled,' he murmured. 'Find... find it with GPS.' He looked up and stretched out a hand. 'Need a... a phone. Please. Need it now before I... before I forget. *Quick!*'

'Forget what?' Ruth looked at Vaslik, who shrugged and handed James his cell phone.

Crouched over the device and waving away their offers of help, James slowly tapped out a number, blood dripping from the sleeve of his jacket. When he finished dialling he struggled to sit upright, wincing at the pain and supported by Vaslik. Ruth noticed that he was watching the patrol vehicle in the distance and holding the phone out as if it were a television remote.

'What are you doing?' she queried. 'Let me help you.'

James shook his head. 'No. I'll do it. It's... my right.' He waited with his thumb poised over the SEND button. 'Promise me something?'

'Of course. What?'

'Don't let them have this... this phone. You'll see...why.'

In that moment Ruth knew what he was going to do as surely as if he'd told her in detail. She opened her mouth to say something, but the words stuck in her throat.

'Malak's going for the president!' Vaslik shouted.

He was right. The patrol vehicle had begun to turn towards the remembrance site and the watching crowd, and was putting on speed, the engine howling in protest as the wheels left the ground.

'No,' James said calmly. 'He's not.' He pressed the button.

It seemed to take forever for anything to happen, but in reality was only a heartbeat. Malak's vehicle, bouncing over the rough terrain in a mad dash, seemed to hesitate and lift for a fraction of a second, and hung in the air as if suspended on a wire. Then came a vivid flash of light and a clap of thunder as an explosion ripped the bodywork apart and the shattered remains began tumbling over in a lazy cartwheel of fire and flame, scattering burning debris over a wide area.

When Ruth looked at James, he had passed out.

She picked up the phone and passed it to Vaslik, who stripped out the Sim card and dropped the phone to the ground and stood on it, grinding it into the dirt.

-

It took Tom Brasher twenty minutes to fight his way through the cordon of Secret Service, military police and local police that had been thrown up around the area, and to confirm that James Chadwick was pronounced still alive and rushed away for treatment.

'Did Chadwick cause that explosion?' Brasher asked. He stared hard at Ruth and Vaslik, who exchanged a look but said nothing. Without needing to talk about it, they had agreed not to dump James into the frame. Brasher huffed impatiently. 'I'm just asking, that's all. Between us. I'm not looking to bust his balls.'

Ruth trusted Brasher completely, but she knew that nothing stayed completely secret among government organisations for long; especially with a scoop-hungry press already on the scene and demanding answers. Was it a suicide bomb that had gone wrong, or had somebody else intervened in some way to prevent an assassination on the president? She could see the headlines already, leading the world's media straight to the Chadwicks' door in search of a hero.

No, if Chadwick wanted word to get out about what he'd done, it had to be his choice, not theirs. He and his family had gone through enough already without adding media intrusion to their problems.

'According to James,' she said cautiously, 'Malak had rigged a spare cell phone with a pack of C4, for reasons we can't even guess. He didn't seem the sort to consider suicide, but who knows, if he saw no other way out?' She looked at Vaslik to see if he had anything to offer, but he gave a brief nod for her to continue.

'So Malak blew himself up?'

'In trying to get away and take the bomb to the president, he must have triggered it himself. You agree, Slik?'

Vaslik nodded. 'Couldn't have put it better myself. But what about the fourth drone?'

The change of subject made Brasher blink. 'What? Oh, yes. A military biohazard team is tracking it down right now. If Donny was telling the truth about that, it's likely to be carrying the chemical tube. Was that Chadwick's doing, too, keeping it grounded?'

'It must have been.' Vaslik spoke firmly. 'Nobody else knows how to programme those things. It would be a pity if that action got neutralised by anybody thinking he'd done something wrong, don't you think? You know what the press will do when they get hold of the story: they'll look for victims and heroes.' And even manage turn the heroes into victims, she thought cynically, if they saw a story in it.

Vaslik returned Brasher's look with one of complete innocence, then shook dust from his jacket and added casually, 'I need a drink. Anybody care to join me?'

'Count me in,' said Ruth, and waited for Brasher to signal his agreement. She knew they would soon be overwhelmed by investigators from every conceivable agency under the sun, and their every action would be taken apart and analysed minutely for flaws, gaps and inconsistencies. But for now she was trusting in the FBI agent to get them some breathing space.

He sighed. 'Yeah, I get the message. But don't go far, you hear? I'd hate to have to send the SWAT team looking for you.'

Ruth turned as Dave Proust joined them, a broad grin on his face at seeing they were all in good shape. 'Dave, do you know any local bars?'

He nodded. 'Sure do. I can even get you there in style.' He winked at Brasher and smiled. 'Who's buying?'